the
Gauntlet
and the
Fist Beneath

IAN GREEN is a writer from Northern
Scotland with a PhD in epigenetics.
His fiction has been widely broadcast
and performed, including winning the
BBC Radio 4 Opening Lines competition
and the Futurebook Future Fiction prize.
His short fiction has been published
by *Londnr*, Almond Press, *Open Pen*,
Meanjin, Transportation Press,
The Pigeonhole, No Alibis Press,
Minor Literature[s] and more.

the Gauntlet and the Fist Beneath

IAN GREEN

HEAD
ZEUS

An Ad Astra Book

First published in the UK in 2021 by Head of Zeus Ltd
This paperback edition first published in the UK in 2022 by Head of Zeus Ltd,
part of Bloomsbury Publishing Plc

9 7 5 3 1 2 4 6 8

A catalogue record for this book is available from
the British Library.

ISBN (PB): 9781800244160
ISBN (E): 9781800244078

Typeset by Divaddict Publishing Solutions Ltd

Runes and border on map © Shutterstock

Printed and bound in Great Britain by
CPI Group (UK) Ltd, Croydon CR0 4YY

Head of Zeus Ltd
5–8 Hardwick Street
London EC1R 4RG

WWW.HEADOFZEUS.COM

For Abigail

*Map of the Undal Protectorate, year 312 from Ferron's Fall
(1123 Isken), Private collection, Commander Salem Starbeck*

PROLOGUE

IN THE SHADOW OF THE GOD-WOLF

Floré and Janos crouched in the shadow of the dead god and watched the demons. The whipping winds of the rotstorm pulled at their armour and tunics, and the mists burned at their eyes and soaked the scarves around their mouths. Above, the bones of the god-wolf Lothal loomed, black ribs thicker than tree trunks curving out of the ground; a skull the size of a barn half buried in the peat. The ground was wet, stumps and hillocks of dark earth cut through by rivulets of ferrous water, all of it entwined and enmeshed by carnivorous rotvine. The rotvine creepers probed and sought sinuously for life they could feed on. Sporadic lightning cutting through roiling cloud cast light over the skeleton, and the mire below.

Floré pressed her gauntleted hand down onto a rotvine creeper that was snaking for the back of Janos's leg, and it crunched and squished between her armoured fingers. The remnant of the vine hastily withdrew into darkness as she wiped the residue onto some limp grass and glanced upward again. The bones drew her eye, again and again, and she remembered children's tales of a great wolf at the head of an army bearing chains and woe.

'I didn't think it was real,' Janos said, his voice struggling against the wind. 'Not truly.'

Floré pushed his shoulder and raised a hand to her mouth, hidden as it was by her scarf. Janos nodded and fell silent, and they continued to watch the demons.

There were three of them, lanky men or women whose legs and arms had too many joints, taller than the tallest human by a head at least, robed in black and hooded against the burning winds. High above them the rotstorm surged, clouds of jet black infused with streaks of gleaming purple lightning that cast a pulsing glow over the rolling landscape. It was enough light that Floré could see her prey silhouetted against the night beyond.

Crow-men: once human, corrupted by the deep rotstorm to monsters with arcane power and horrifying appetites. Aberrations in the skein. The three hooded demons were floating four feet from the ground, circling around a chunk of amethyst crystal hovering between them that gleamed with black and violet light. On the ground past them, perhaps a dozen squat goblins with rough grey skin and black orb eyes were arguing in a guttural tongue, fighting over scraps of what might have been meat, with stone knives and wooden spears in their hands, chittering and growling in turn. They had no sentries. Most of the goblins were pawing over the meat, but a few were arguing over scraps of metal they had salvaged from a skeletal soldier nearby, hissing past row after row of serrated teeth as they tugged dull bronze back and forth between them.

The ground under Lothal's bones was scattered with dead soldiers three centuries old, most gone to dust but some preserved by the waters, the peat, or some aura emanating from the dark architecture of the dead god. Floré wasn't sure which.

Past the demons and the goblins, a rottroll twice the size of a bullock snored as it slept, half submerged in a deeper stream of rust-red water, grey pebbled skin cast over an immensity of muscle and bone. Past that again, a single human sentry with a guttering torch, her body bundled against the acid mist as she gazed into the night. Behind the sentry there were maybe twenty or so more rust-folk hunkered into crude animal-skin tents. Floré took all of this in and breathed out through her nose, rolled her shoulders. Twenty rust-folk, a dozen goblins, a rottroll, three crow-men... The rest of her squad would even then be snaking their way through swamp and hell, led by Benazir, heading back towards the safety of the Stormcastle, mission abandoned. Floré rested her hand on Benazir's silver dagger, tucked in her belt, and bit her lip. All she could rely on was the mage, that he was truly as powerful as he believed. Floré pointed at Janos and then the rottroll, and the rust-folk beyond, and then pointed at herself and the crow-men hovering around the amethyst, and the goblins.

Janos took one gauntleted hand and grabbed her by the shoulder and leaned in close to her ear.

'Keep the crow-men away from me, and the rest I can handle. If we die,' he said, his breath hot against her skin even through his mask, 'I owe you a drink.'

Floré turned her gaze to his and looked long into

his eyes, dark in the strange light of the rotstorm, and overhead thunder rolled and then rain began in earnest. She pulled her scarf down and turned her face upward: a scarf wouldn't do any good against the downpour, and the rain might even wash some of the residue of the acrid mists from her skin. She felt the rain's icy tendrils cover her in moments, through cropped-short curls of ashen hair to her scalp, through the stained red cotton of her tunic and her armour, down to her core. The rain beat down and the furthest of Lothal's ribs was already lost to sight. She turned back to Janos and licked her lips. The rain tasted like copper.

'How about we kill everyone,' she said, feeling her mouth twitching with the shadow of a smile, feeling the thrill of it all filling her every nerve, her heart a war drum in her chest, 'and then we do some jokes.'

Floré didn't wait for a reply, rising smoothly to her feet and taking a few halting steps in the mire before breaking into a loping jog even as Janos behind her started to laugh and pulled off his own scarf. *He has a good laugh,* she thought, *deep and honest.* Another roll of thunder above as she headed down the final hillock towards the demons, *crow-men,* and her leather boots splashed through the bog and peat and dragging vines as from her belt she pulled Benazir's dagger. She was only twenty yards away when there was a shout from a goblin, and the crow-men stopped circling the amethyst shard and turned outward, still floating eerily above the ground, unconcerned by the pulling wind, the driving rain.

The dagger spun fast, the heavy blade coated in silver and etched in runes, the handle of worn antler with a weighted core of lead lending weight to the blow. A flash of intricate fractal lightning split across the sky, purple and red light pouring over the scene as the dagger sank into the chest of the first demon and it flew back and crumpled to the wet floor of the swamp below. Floré stopped running and unsheathed her sword, even as the rune in the dagger caught on flesh and started to burn and the demon on the ground wailed as it turned to a pyre, orange and red tongues of flame casting light over the goblins and the rottroll. The rottroll grunted something, rolling as it tried to pull itself to its feet, and the goblins chittered and shrieked. The other two crow-men circled closer around the amethyst, wailing or screaming orders. Floré could not tell. Flexing her knuckles, she raised her sword to her shoulder, throwing herself forward even as the goblins raced to meet her. She did not look at the rust-folk, the twenty seasoned warriors who would surely kill them both if Janos lost his nerve.

There was a cacophonous crack and the world went white for a moment as lightning shot not from the sky, but from the hands of Janos. The bolt of pure white had no branches, no tendrils seeking outward for a path of least resistance. It was a spear of white light and heat, passing over the heads of the charging goblins and into the chest of the rottroll that had just reared up to its full height. A feral grin pulled at Floré's mouth and as the goblins wailed and clawed at their eyes she remembered their positions and took three more steps and with two hands swung her heavy grey blade in sweeping arcs, planting her feet strong, feeling the resistance as goblin after goblin was cleft or thrown aside.

She blinked thrice and when she could see again the rottroll was collapsed in the bog, only so much charnel. As she dispatched another goblin with a cleaving strike of her sword, one of the crow-men flew at her, gouts of roiling fire rushing from its crooked hands in a sputtering cone of black and red. Floré rolled, and when she came up crunched a goblin's skull with the hilt of her sword and elbowed another trying to get at her ribs. Back on her feet she kept moving, and saw Janos standing alone, the rust-folk shooting arrow and spear at him. They were out of their tents now, screaming and yelling into the storm, arrows flying wild in the wind, heavy spears cutting through the storm with deadly accuracy. Janos stood resolute in his red tunic, unarmed, and waved his metal-clad hands gently as the arrows and spears that edged too close to him simply fell from the air.

Floré had rolled and punched and cut her way through the throng of goblins, the crow-man in close pursuit, and then she felt a numbing spark in her leg and glanced down and then up at the sky in horror. She skidded to a stop in the mulch and peat and the goblins caught up to her, circling and surrounding and jabbing crude stone weapons at her with frail arms. Snarling and accepting hit after hit from the surrounding goblins, sharp knapped edges cutting through her armour and biting at her legs and arms, Floré spun, casting her eyes over the scene, and then plunged her grey steel longsword into the ground. A moment later she felt the spark in her leg again, stronger, and she leapt through a throng of goblins, away and down into the stream where the rottroll had slept.

Behind her, the world exploded as a crash of thunder

exulted from above, from all around, and the purple lightning of the rotstorm sought a path to ground. The branching bolt cut through rain and sky and found her sword, and from there the goblins surrounding it and the crow-man looming over them. Floré pulled herself out of the stinking water, its acid taint burning at her eyes, to see a circle of blackened gore surrounding her blade. Forty yards away the final crow-man, the robed demon, snatched the amethyst shard from the air. The light stopped pulsing and it was just a lump of crystal, and the crow-man yelled something, but she couldn't hear any words, only noise. She wiped black peat from her mouth and glancing over her shoulder she saw Janos.

Across the mire, he cast his hands in an intricate pattern, weaving armoured fingers and hands in traces that left a glowing pattern of red light in the air. Through his tattered sleeves she saw his rune tattoos flare with red light as he called on the patterns remembered in each, the pattern in each tattoo calling to a pattern below that, within him, patterns he had sought and memorised and wrought over endless hours of meditation and study, days and months of energy reinforcing the design.

The two-dozen rust-folk surrounding him lunged forward as one at a yelled command of their leader, and by the light of their sentry's brand Floré watched them all die. Janos called on the skein, found the pattern that linked all things, and changed it. The charge faltered, and in a moment she knew what he had done. Janos had made salt. She had never seen it on this scale before, this change in the pattern. He said it was easy, the salt. The structure of the crystals was a pattern, and one he always seemed to be able to find. Even as she watched he fell to his knees, weeping and retching, and the grasses and reeds covering the ground at his feet wilted in an ever-expanding circle. He had taken from them, rather than be taken from.

Some of the surrounding attackers were consumed utterly, rust-folk turned to salt pillars that crumbled in moments in the whipping winds and driving rain. Others were not so wholly ensorcelled, single limbs or organs altered, the rest of them remaining the same. They died slower, but they fell as one. Screams cut through storm; twenty hardened warriors dead in as many heartbeats.

Floré turned back to the crow-man in front of her, and even as it turned to flee she was leaping forward. Surrounded by the dead and dying, she wrenched her burning sword from the ground. The simple red sword-knot from her hilt was charred away, and as she pulled at the hilt the blade broke off halfway down and the pulsing purple lightning lingering in the broken blade and hilt encompassed her gauntlet and then her hand, her arm, and she screamed and stumbled, but ahead of her the crow-man was fleeing, beginning to rise into the air. *If it escapes,* she thought, picturing her comrades dead in the swamp behind, *it was all for naught.*

Floré took three sharp steps and hurled the broken sword. It still sparked with the puissant light of the rotstorm lightning and the shard of blade was glowing white hot as it spun through the air and scored into the spine of the fleeing demon, who fell unceremoniously down, crashing to the fetid water of the swamp below the skull of the dead god. The eye socket of Lothal the Just that had not yet sunk into the mire stared down at her, empty and cavernous and dark.

Floré looked back towards Janos. His attackers had stopped moaning and fallen still, and he was on his knees in the mud, body shuddering as he sobbed. She felt the burning up her right arm, could feel where the lightning had traced her veins and ligaments and tendons and nerves and charred its way along them. Floré clenched her fists to stop her arm shaking and walked forward.

In the shadow of Lothal's bones Floré found the final demon. It was still trying to crawl away, dragging useless legs along behind it, one hand clutching the amethyst. Floré reached for Benazir's dagger at her belt and realised it was buried in a corpse thirty yards back, and when she glanced down at her broken sword in the bog, she couldn't bring herself to pick it up again. Reaching into a belt pouch she pulled out a silver coin stamped with the broken-chain crest of the Undal Protectorate and slotted it into the metalwork on the knuckle of her gauntlet, a notch made for just this purpose: *fire and silver and silver and fire*, to kill a demon. The demon's hood had fallen away revealing a face, a human face, a young man's face. His red hair was plastered to his forehead with rain, his skin pale, his eyes blue. He opened his mouth to say something and raised a hand but Floré didn't give him any chance to warp the skein or plead for mercy. Commander Starbeck's words whispered in her mind: *no trial for rust-folk*. She grabbed his slowly raising arm with her left hand and punched him with her right, turning his attempt at speech into a cry of pain.

The rain cascaded over her as she beat the demon to death, the silver raising burning welts wherever it found flesh, her fist crashing down again and again and again until she was gasping for air. The demon fell still. The rain washed the black blood from her armoured hands as she pulled her prize free, breathing heavily, slick with gore, trembling. The amethyst shard: the rotbud.

Floré returned to Janos with her broken sword and Benazir's silver dagger in her belt, her tunic torn, her thin chain mail shirt broken in a dozen places. They were still days from the Stormcastle, miles and miles of acid water and monsters, goblins and rottrolls, white crocodiles with a taste for human flesh, biting kelp and creeping vine, marauding rust-folk.

'Janos,' she said, shaking him until he turned to face her. The whites of his eyes were red, his rain-soaked face failing to hide his tears. Floré pulled him to his feet and embraced him, holding him close. Above, thunder rolled again and Floré flinched. She cast an eye around at the piles of slowly dissolving salt, and the bodies mixed between. At least twenty of them, dead at his will in a moment. It was a feat that should have shrivelled him to a husk as the skein drew from him to change the pattern, and yet he was hale, flush with health even as he wept. She looked at him again, up and down, the soft poet, her friend.

'No trial for rust-folk,' he said, his voice barely a whisper, and Floré shook her head at him.

'You owe me a joke,' she said, but Janos only fell back to his knees and wept. Floré blew out a breath through her nose, checked the straps on her gauntlets, and took a final look at the colossal bones, the ribs of the dead god reaching up into the sky just at the edge of her vision through the storm. She turned her gaze out to the mire beyond and the horrors to come. It was time to go to work.

ACT 1

ORBS OF LIGHT

Orbs of light
Dead of night
Hide your eye
Take your flight

'Sop for the mewling ones in the darkness that they might remember true fear and grow still.'
– Antian children's rhyme

1

LIGHTS IN THE FOREST

'Berren died, Anshuka slept, and for a hundred years of fire the empire spread forth. Tullen One-Eye rode the god-wolf Lothal into battle and together they broke Undalor, bowed the warmongers of Tessendorm and traders of Isken in the name of their empress. The years of war were followed by the slave generations, until the whitestaffs broke their chains and awoke Anshuka. The great mother woke from her sleep and slew the wolf and the army of Ferron. Anshuka in her wrath brought down the unending storm and ruined Ferron utterly. The owl fell into darkness, the bear slew the wolf, and Anshuka crossed the world trailing ice and pain and came to rest in Orubor. With the snows that year came the first Claw Winter, her nightmare as she slept.' – The Fall of Ferron, Whitestaff Anctus of Riven

Floré put down her tea and gripped her right wrist with her left hand and held tight, trying to keep the tremors in check. They came swift, and as sure as night follows day she felt the nausea, felt the pulse in her skull, and then the hot waves of pain coursing up her right arm deep down in the bone. She clenched her teeth and focused on her breathing for a long moment until the pain began to fade. She glanced along the kitchen, but Janos hadn't seen her tense, so she shook her head and forced herself to stay calm as the tremors passed. Janos was at the other end of the room half singing a song to himself as he prepared her a parcel of food for the road: a wedge of sharp cheese, a half loaf of dark bread, two apples. It was an old song: *Three daughters of the mist, unkind.* The melody was simple enough, and he sang quiet and off key. He bundled the food up in a cloth and tied it off primly then came to the table and slipped it into her pack.

'So they aren't sure what it is?' he said, feigning nonchalance, one hand on the chair and the other fidgeting with a button on his shirt. His voice was deep and his accent clipped, and Floré couldn't help but smile at him. He looked worried, always looked worried when she had to leave Hasselberry, and she loved the way his brow furrowed over his dark brown eyes. Janos was a slight man, with soft hands and a soft heart, prematurely grey hair with a high widow's peak tied loosely behind his head. His skin was a light brown, smooth and unblemished save for crinkles at the corner of his eyes. She let her grip slacken on her wrist and stood and went to him and kissed him gently.

The kitchen was lit by the low fire and the last light of the day, a safe space of wood and old iron. Janos wrapped his arms around Floré and they stood in silence for a long moment. His sleeves were rolled up and as he embraced her she glimpsed the sigils inked into his forearms, red and stark on soft skin. Outside the kitchen window the sun was skirting the treetops, and a wood pigeon called out from the forest.

She pulled herself away and returned to the table, to the weapons and armour laid across it, scanning them with a practised eye.

'It's a wee rottroll at worst, likely a few goblins,' she said, grinning at the idea of *action*, of blades in the night, and she started pulling on a light leather jerkin over her wool shirt. 'It's nothing much, my love, but Larchford have no Stormguard and so I must valiantly ride into the night!' Her smile faded as she remembered the pale farmer's boy telling his tale in the back room of the inn.

'The lad said five sheep gone last week,' she continued, sparing him the details. 'We'll get there before dawn and by the evening probably we'll be eating dinner in triumph in the inn, toast of the town.'

Janos nodded and cast about for a task, his eyes landing on Floré's scuffed and battered riding boots. He picked up the boots and tutted, and then opened the back door and sat down on a stool and went to work with a stiff brush on the muck encasing the heels as Floré took another mouthful of her tea and pulled the ties on her jerkin tight. The leather was thick but supple. She pulled her Stormguard Forest Watch tabard on over the top, the green fabric trimmed in gold and embroidered with a yellow lightning bolt in the centre of the chest.

With great care Floré drew her sword from its scabbard to rest on the table with its blade bare, and then buckled on her sword belt, her scabbard and old silvered dagger with its hilt of antler pulled tight to her hips, her dull copper rank buckle locking the belt in place. She lifted her bare longsword from the table and pulled it into a brief salute in front of her eyes before sheathing it, the smooth grey of the blade and the familiar weight at her side reassuring her. Tied around the pommel of the sword was an intricate knot of wet red silk, with a single white streak. The sword-knot did not drip, but was cool and moist to the touch, as it had been for a decade since she received it, as it had been for three centuries since the war of liberation.

As she hooked her heavy metal plate gauntlets onto a loop in her belt, Janos deposited the boots and went back to the kitchen. Floré took another mouthful of the bitter tea and watched him silently. He filled a waterskin and tied it to her pack and stared out the window for a few moments before disappearing to collect a rain cloak. Floré was pulling on her boots when he returned and was still pulling on her boots after he had packed the cloak, folding down the thigh guards of her boots so they rested just at the knee. He came and stood behind her chair and ran a hand through the cropped loose curls of her hair, the ashen grey lightening with every winter. She closed her eyes. She could tell Janos was about to speak, and so spoke ahead of him, smiling.

'No, love, Tyr can't go. He's too old, and past him it's just me and the cadets and they're all children.' Floré felt her husband stiffen as she spoke; clearly, he was bemused she'd so easily guessed his next words. 'Garrison promised us a few privates to round up our numbers start of summer, but no sign of them yet. They're waiting for someone to screw up badly enough.'

'You always know what I'm thinking, pretty one,' he

said, smiling. 'I reckon you're at least a bit Oruboro. Well. Teeth are sharp enough.'

Floré laughed and stood and kissed him again, first his mouth then his cheek and then she playfully bit his ear.

'If I'm Oruboro,' she whispered, 'then you would be my snack for the road, darling poet.'

Floré went through the kitchen to the front room and the door leading to the bedroom. She pressed a hand against it and pictured little Marta asleep inside, and then quietly walked to the back door of the house, swinging her pack to her shoulder as she went. The girl was a light sleeper, and as much as Floré would have loved to open the door or wake her to say farewell, Marta needed her rest more than most children. Every week there was another fever, another worry. She felt an ache in her gut at the idea of leaving her, but there was a thrill as well, a shiver down her spine at the idea of a sword and a forest and a monster. She blushed and blew through her nose, then went back across the room to Marta's door and gently opened it by an inch. The firelight from the hearth cast a dim light into Marta's room, and Floré smiled and felt the shiver disappear when she saw her daughter, her love, a shadow under blankets. She let the door close gently. Janos came with her down the garden path and kissed her once more at the gate.

'You'll be safe, mighty Bolt-Captain?' he said, and she laughed at his sincerity and her amber eyes flashed with mischief as she pushed against his chest with her strong right hand.

'I've killed more rottrolls than you've written soppy verses, dearest,' she said, 'and that is certainly saying something. Worry not. I'll take one of the young blades with me and rally a few sturdy folks from Larchford. No risks. It's hardly a night raid in the rotstorm.'

Janos winced at the mention of the rotstorm and rubbed at the tattoos on his arms absently. They pressed their foreheads together, both closing their eyes.

'Watch the little one, and write me a poem,' she said, and felt Janos gently nod.

'Eyes sharp, blades sharper,' he said sternly, with no hint of a smile, and she laughed again and went through the gate, stopping to snatch a sprig of lilac from the bushes bordering the fence. When she reached the end of lane she turned and threw a quick salute, the first two fingers of her right hand pressed to her forehead, and smiled at the sight of Janos leaning on the gate smelling his own sprig of lilac, arm raised. Their house sat behind him, the dark wood of the walls turned to burnt umber by the setting sun. Floré put a hand on her sword hilt and turned towards Hasselberry, fingers trailing gently against the deep green of the hedgerow as she walked.

~

The village of Hasselberry had no Stormguard garrison proper; the guardhouse was an old barn with a single cell in it for drunken millworkers, and three old horses that were tended by the cadets. Most of the equipment was held in Captain Tyr's house, a sturdy log cabin at the east end of town. Captain Tyr formed an informal council with the shaman, the whitestaff, and the leader of the millworkers, debating for long hours over minutiae of fence placement and fishing rights. As the ranking representative of the Stormguard in Hookstone forest he could dictate and demand, but instead he listened and debated. Floré liked that. The protectorate preached self-sufficiency and co-operation in equal measure, but whilst lumber left the forest every year, trade in return was sparse. The pine of Hookstone forest grew fast and wild, but the constant winds from the coast bent the boughs and trunks and kept most logging crews much further inland, north near Birchollow, in the sheltered forests where the wood grew fast and straight.

To the north of the village green sat the placid waters of Loch Hassel, and to the south-west were the shaman temple, the whitestaff's schoolhouse, Wheatgum's Provisions, and the Goat and Whistle Inn. There were maybe two dozen houses spread south of the green, and the bunkhouse for the lumber millworkers pressed up against the mill and the forest of dark pines behind. Floré knew the lad from Larchford was asleep at the Goat and Whistle; Captain Tyr had been visiting the Yulder farmstead to the east, so Floré had debriefed the boy that morning.

Marching into the village green, Floré saw the three Stormguard cadets fussing with their packs by the watch house. Petron was trying vainly to string a longbow that he certainly wouldn't be able to draw, and his brother Cuss was sat on a log trying to stuff a blanket into his overfull pack, sweating in the mild evening heat. The third cadet, Yselda, dour-faced and serious, was practising short sharp cuts with a training sword against the battered wooden training dummy leaning against the side wall of the barn. Floré raised an arm from across the green but kept walking towards the Goat and Whistle.

She found Captain Tyr at a trestle table on the village green; Shand from the inn left the tables out all summer from the last snowdrop to the first snow. The captain was in his fifties, a broad man with bowed legs and a barrel chest, thick salt-and-pepper mutton chops framing a wide face. He had the amber skin of the people of Cil-Marie, but in the Undal Protectorate that meant little; Floré certainly had a healthy measure of that herself. In Cil-Marie they would be sorted into castes by the shade of their skin, and in Tessendorm likely enslaved, but in Undal it was not important; they were a nation of slaves, the dregs and leftovers of a dozen countries and continents, raised from dirt. Mistress Water was always depicted hooded and robed, at her own request, to show she could have been any one of them. The protectorate didn't care spit where your stock was from, who you loved, who your people were before. If you were with them, they were with you. If you were against them or theirs, a sharp blade could always be found.

Tyr was sat playing chissick with three men from the village, and Floré nodded to them. They nodded back deferentially. The sound of Loch Hassel lapping at the thin beach north of the green turned her head; the long dock was bustling as the few small fishing skiffs were unloaded of their day's catch. There was a cold breeze coming off the water and Floré took a moment to revel in it, and the dying heat of the day, waiting for Tyr to speak first with a hard practised patience even as she wanted to speak, to push forward. Instead, she counted down from ten.

At four, Tyr took a long swig from his flagon, and when she saw him glance at her wet red sword-knot, she forced herself to be still, not to hide it away. She might be practising her patience, but she would not hide her sword-knot. Any captain of the Stormguard knew what the red and white signified. Tyr had never asked, and she knew he never would. Had he noticed the wetness, that strange unending damp that pervaded the red and white silk? Perhaps. He knew she had been something else before she came here, and even after five years of quiet service in Hasselberry she could tell he still had his pride and his worry. He saw in her his end, his replacement. His blade did not carry the red silk, let alone the white stripe, and the enduring wetness and all it connoted was rare enough to be rumour even amongst the elite. His sword hilt was bare, which was a story in itself; any captain would have, *must* have, at least one sword-knot, to commemorate their greatest deed. Floré had never asked, with an appreciation that he had never asked her.

The captain finished his swig and set down the flagon by the time Floré finished her ten-count, and then moved one of the chissick stones between him and the men to change the pattern. The figure immediately opposite was Rodram, father of Shand, old and grey with a bent back and wizened face. He muttered and peered at the altered pattern and Tyr smiled. Finally he turned his full attention to the woman standing at ease before him.

'Sergeant Artollen,' he said. 'You look geared up. Word from Larchford that bad?'

As Tyr spoke a serving boy from the Goat and Whistle refilled his flagon from a jug of thick brown ale, and Rodram started shuffling his own chissick stones, considering what to place. The other two men at the table stared with unabashed interest at the conversation before them; one was Tellen, a burly red-headed boss at the lumber mill, and the other was one of the outlying farmers. Floré thought his name was Essen, or Essom, or something like that. She frowned at the audience.

'Shall we head to the guardhouse and debrief, sir?' she asked, but Tyr waved a hand and took another gulp of ale.

'I've been out east at the Yulder's all arsing day, and it's hot. What's the boy got to say for himself? I put my head in but he was fast out.'

Floré shifted her feet and sighed. The rumour would spread in a matter of hours and all because Tyr wouldn't walk fifty feet to debrief in private. She wanted to say as much and would have done so five years ago. She scrunched up her eyes and forced herself to relax. *A rumour in Hasselberry doesn't matter,* she thought.

'Five sheep gone in the last week,' Floré said. 'One found mutilated. No meat taken and odd wounds. Sounds like a rottroll or a few goblins have them spooked most likely but might be something funny or *someone* funny. Last rotstorm surge we know of was early spring, so odd to still have goblins and trolls lingering; might be a delayed hatching. I'll take one of the cadets and march through tonight, give them a chance to practise their night navigation in the forest. Get a few likely hands from Larchford, and head out. We should be back within a day or two. Any delay past then or funny business and I'll send word. Do you approve, sir?'

Tyr nodded and ran a hand across his face, pensive.

'Good. Good,' he said, 'All sounds in order. I'll let the Larchford lad rest the day and he can follow you tomorrow. Oh, and don't be taking Petron. The whitestaff caught him using the skein to clean a pot, or summat similar. She had a face like a skelped arse. I reckon the lad has a day scrubbing ahead of him tomorrow.'

Tyr's three companions laughed at that and old Rodram placed a chissick stone and then let out a long sigh at his forlorn position on the board before turning to Tyr and Floré. Sizing up Floré he took a long draw from his ale and then let out an underwhelming belch.

'Tyr,' he said, his voice a rattle, 'tell the bonny lass about Yulder's fireflies!'

Floré grimaced at the old man and opened her mouth to tell him where to put his chissick stone, but Tyr interjected, tugging at his whiskers.

'She's a sergeant in the Stormguard, Rodram, not a "bonny lass". I'd remember that or you might find yourself swimming.'

Rodram bowed his head in deference, and the other two men grinned at Floré. Enough of their drunken companions had been laid out by her fists for causing trouble; they knew the risk of misbehaving far better than old Rodram. Hasselberry was quiet enough but the sergeant had earned a reputation for fists first, questions later, as was the way of the Stormguard. She was trying to learn patience, to look to a diplomatic answer, but only the week before she had broken the jaw of a seasonal worker who tried to rough up one of the old fishermen over a game of cards. She remembered the hot satisfaction in her heart when he hit the dirt after a single punch, and looked out at the loch, sickened with herself. *It is a sickness in me,* she thought, grimacing. The worker had taken the next carriage to Hookstone to seek a healer, since old Izelda said the wound was beyond her knack. Tyr took another sip of his ale and stared out at the flat waters of the loch and the pines on the northern shore.

'Yulder,' he said glacially, eyes not leaving the water, 'says last three nights there have been… strange lights, in the sky. Orbs. White lights, moving fast as a bird, but then hovering like a dragonfly over the trees. Orbs the size of wood wagons, silent and fast-flying. He reckons it's magic. And, his dog is gone.'

Floré blinked and screwed up her nose. She didn't know Yulder well, had only met the man a handful of times in passing. He had pale skin and was scrawny, tall, his face seemingly a permanent scowl. She thought a long moment for what lights in the sky could be.

'Does Yulder… like his ale?' She said at last, and Tellen and Rodram laughed but Tyr shook his head and shrugged. Taciturn Esson, or Essom, contemplated the chissick stones, nonplussed.

'Man's a stable one,' Tyr said, 'Mebbe a wee bit quiet since he lost his people in that business with the Marshlock, but a sensible lad. Swears down, lights last three nights, one or two, from the direction of the Unerdan. You know his farm?'

Floré shook her head. Tyr glanced at the millworker Tellen.

'The land's on the side of a hill,' Tellen offered. 'The cabin is at the top and the trees cleared back far enough that on a dark night to the west you can see the glow of Undal City and Hookstone Town and the lighthouses of the Star Coast to the south, down beyond the forest. A bonny place. Me and the team put it up ten years past.'

The four men sat in silence for a long moment and Floré tried to picture Undal as a distant glow instead of a vibrant presence. *When did I last see Undal?* she thought, and considered a ride out to the Yulder farm some night soon just to see it again, even from afar. Janos would like that, to see Undal again, to picture people reading his poems in that distant glow. Tyr looked troubled.

'I'll ask in Larchford if they've any word,' Floré said, 'and before I go, I'll speak to the whitestaff and see if she has any wisdom on this. Then I'll grab Cuss or Yselda and head off.'

Tyr nodded and picked up a chissick stone, turning it over in his hands. He turned to Floré at last.

'Go safe, Sergeant. Eyes sharp, blades sharper.'

'Eyes sharp, blades sharper,' Floré echoed. She saluted and turned and strode towards the whitestaff's house, the only stone building in town.

She had made it a dozen yards when Tyr called out, 'Get a blessing from Shaman Jule on the way out of town, aye?'

Floré raised a hand in acknowledgement but did not turn, her brow furrowing in annoyance. *No chance of that.* The shaman would say something seemingly profound if she went to him, quoting from his scripture or his heart, but it would do nothing. Shamans couldn't even touch the skein; how could he bring her any closer to Anshuka that she already was? Floré shook her head and kept striding.

~

The Whitestaff Izelda was smoking a long-stemmed pipe carved from a single piece of wood. She was sat in a rocking chair of rough wood in a simple homespun dress, her feet bare. Her Riven amulet, a green carved stone on a fine chain of silver, hung from her neck, but Floré could not see her staff anywhere. The whitestaff's house was just south of the village green, two storeys of dark stone with a thatched roof and a large vegetable garden surrounding it, as well as two tall apple trees.

She blew out a smoke ring as Floré walked up the garden path and raised a hand in greeting. Floré returned the wave.

'Ho, Whitestaff. All is well?'

'All is well, granddaughter,' Izelda said, and Floré determinedly did not let her expression change at the term even though she wanted to scowl. Izelda used it on anyone without grey in their hair or a stoop in their spine. Izelda's own hair had passed from grey to white to something translucent far before Floré had ever heard of Hasselberry, its wispy paleness in stark contrast to the wrinkled brown of her skin.

'I'm off to Larchford this night. Some sheep gone, one found mutilated with odd wounds. Clean cuts, no meat missing. Eyes cut out.'

Izelda nodded and took another breath from the pipe, letting the smoke languish behind wrinkled lips. She blew out another smoke ring, smaller this time.

'Goblins,' Izelda said with a dismissive hand, clearly uninterested. 'Was there anything else, Sergeant Floré? Your girl must be almost ready for my schoolhouse. I would be better for her than spending all day playing with toy swords and reciting... poetry.'

Floré ignored the statement and rested her hand gently on the pommel of her sword. She stared out from the whitestaff's garden towards the watch house. A whitestaff, even one in her dotage, was a powerful presence. The village benefited from her medicine and her storm prediction, and folks travelled from across the forest to seek Izelda's wisdom. Floré knew she should be deferential, but the old woman was a gossip and a prude. She made herself breathe in and out twice, deep and slow, and turned back to Izelda.

'I'll be taking a cadet,' she said. 'The captain said to leave Petron. Most likely it will be Yselda.'

The old woman nodded sagely as if she were granting assent, and Floré's sense of calm and respect left her in an instant. She cricked her neck to one side.

'Final thing, *mighty skein-mage*. Apparently Yulder has seen glowing orbs the size of carts, flying through the night sky from the Unerdan, out over the treetops. I figured that sounded like your kind of business. Heard of such a thing?'

Izelda considered Floré for a moment and then stood and laid her pipe on a small table next to her chair and walked inside wordlessly. *Probably shouldn't have called her 'mighty skein-mage'*, Floré thought, and she shrugged and waited an awkward minute. Surely it wasn't such a lapse in manners that the old woman would just walk off completely. The whitestaffs felt themselves as a people apart from most skein-mages, but Floré reckoned they were skein-mages nonetheless, and Janos said they were no different except in training. She ran her hand over the grip of her silvered dagger and was considering at what point she could just leave when the old woman appeared again in the doorway, clutching a heavy leather-bound book. Izelda sat down and put her pipe back in her mouth and opened the heavy tome.

'Why are you called the Stormguard?' she asked grimly, flipping pages, eyes down. Floré wrinkled her brow and blew air from her nose. She took a breath before speaking and tried to keep her tone even, trying not to betray her annoyance.

'After Ferron fell and the rotstorm rose,' she said, 'the slaves were freed, and the protectorate was founded on the bones of old Undalor. The Stormguard man the Stormwall, watch for demons and monsters, and protect the realm and those inside it. The City and Forest Watches keep peace, the Lancers guard our borders, and the Commandos keep the beasts of Ferron at bay. Freedom and protection for those who need it.'

Izelda nodded and then laid a finger on an illustration in the book she held and showed it to Floré. It showed a starlit sky over a calm sea, and above, two oblong shapes of grey-white.

'*Orbs of light, dead of night, hide your eye, take your flight.*'

The whitestaff closed her eyes as she spoke the words, her voice a sombre mantra, and then opened them and gave a snort.

'The only orbs of light I know, granddaughter, are the eyes of Ferron the mighty, that he used to seek out naughty boys and girls come Deadwinter!'

Izelda cackled and Floré huffed. She was being mocked, and as she peered closer, she could see the book in the whitestaff's lap was a collection of Antian tales; she recognised the heavy runic script. Her friend Voltos had tried to teach her, a lifetime ago, but she could never manage to decipher the intricacies of the runes.

'Good day, Whitestaff,' she said through clenched teeth, and started to stride down the garden path with a face as red as the old woman's tomatoes.

'Good day, granddaughter!' the old woman called, still laughing, 'Mind Ferron doesn't catch you!'

2

Night Fishing

'To ask the anatomy of a Judge is to utterly miss the point. They defy description, and each is individual. Anshuka, Berren, Lothal, Nessilitor; each is unique, each is like nothing else. To call Anshuka a bear is like calling a tree a leaf. Berren was not a man; Lothal was not a wolf; Nessilitor no more an owl than a man is a mouse.'
– *Pantheon of the Protectorate*, Campbell Torbén of Aber-Ouse

Floré could hear the whitestaff laughing until she was out of the garden, and she quickly strode to the guardhouse. The sun was almost below the trees completely now. Cuss, Petron, and Yselda were waiting in much the same manner she had seen them earlier and didn't notice her approach. Cuss was eating a heel of bread, his blanket successfully stuffed in his pack, and Petron was trying vainly to draw the now strung longbow, which was not Stormguard issue. They had shortbows inside; the longbow must have been his late father's. She knew his mother had no time for archery, had hardly time to breathe, hence her happiness to turn the two boys over to the Stormguard. Floré frowned at the brothers. Both had curly brown hair and dark skin of descendants of old Undalor, but Petron was slight and short where Cuss was tall and brawny. *Well, more round than brawny,* she thought.

Yselda was sat calmly on the grass, braiding her long black hair, her training sword neatly stowed, her shortsword sheathed on her lap. Her eyes were closed and her face turned to fading sun. Floré frowned at her too. At their age she had been working every hour of the day and more beyond, drilling with weapons and practising fieldcraft, helping repair the swamp-rotted boards of the wall. The fist and the blade and the guarded mind; the resilience needed to survive the rotstorm. Thinking of it drew her hands to her gauntlets; even now she couldn't bear to be without them.

Floré pictured the first time she truly trained with a sword, her and Benazir and the other new cadets at Stormcastle XIV, far in the north. The rotstorm was so close, and she had been so nervous; she could remember rubbing sweaty hands on her cadet tabard, feeling so weak compared to the others, so stupid compared to the cadets from cities and towns.

The sergeant had called them forward one at a time whilst the rest stood in ranks and watched. He had them attack a dummy with a practice sword, shoot a target with a shortbow, and then as a group run laps of the training yard until they fell. Floré swung the sword like a club; she had never touched a real sword before that day. The bow she thought she might do better with, but the pull on it was so heavy she could scarcely draw an arrow and her three shots went wild. The others were all much the same, chopping with abandon at the training dummy and shooting their arrows short or wild or both. Some of the Brek could shoot well, thick shafts of yew piercing the target, and the cadets all cheered. Finally Benazir was called forward; she had been lingering at the back.

Floré remembered watching her move with a sword, moving through forms, cutting fast and precise. The cadets had all fallen silent as Benazir continued, cold, calculated, silent, hitting the dummy with every conceivable combination of blows. The sergeant laughed when she finally stopped, face flushed and fringe sticking to her forehead, and sent her to the bows. All of her shafts flew true to the central target ring, and the cadets cheered as they had before.

'Fallow Fen,' a big lad next to Floré muttered to her. 'She's one of them Fallow Fen folk. Town got ate by the storm.'

Then it was the run. There were twenty cadets. After three laps of the yard some stopped running, wheezing, sweat pouring, clutching their sides. Benazir was amongst them; she retreated to the side of the training yard and watched from below her dark fringe as the rest ran on. Floré kept running. After five laps, more began to drop out. Soon it was only Floré and two others, one of the Brek lads and another she hadn't spoken to. They ran on and on and Floré had felt her legs burn so she slowed and fell back, but then a lap later the Brek lad peeled off to the side and stumbled to a stop, holding himself against the rough stone wall. Floré remembered feeling sweat and pain, but ignoring it. She could run. She could do the work. She ran and ran, ignoring the pain until the boy she'd not spoken to swore and fell off to the side and it was only her, and then she kept running, another lap, another, and eventually the sergeant waved her down and she slowed to a stop, her lungs on fire.

As she stopped running thunder tumbled through the sky and the edge of an arc of purple lightning cut through the storm high above them. All the cadets had stared up, except Benazir, who had stared down at the ground. When training was dismissed and they were sent for food, Floré went and sat opposite Benazir.

'You can fight,' she had said, and Benazir had simply stared at her.

'Could you teach me?' Floré had said, attempting a smile. 'I need to know how. Please.'

'The sergeant will show you,' Benazir said, unsmiling. They had both had long hair then, Floré a mass of loose curls pulled back from her face in a rough braid that was constantly spiralling out, Benazir silent and staring from beneath a fringe of straight black. Those were the first words she had heard Benazir say to anyone. The girl ate alone, and had kept to herself in the day since the cadets had assembled in Stormcastle XIV. Floré had tentatively spoken to a few of the others by that point, but she was unused to so many people and didn't know how to speak to them then, how to make friends. Floré remembered those first nights in the barracks, cold, forcing herself not to think of home.

'The sergeant will show us all,' Floré said, 'but I want to learn those sword things you did. The fancy stuff. We need to know how to fight. It'll be fun – we could train together. I'm Floré. From Tollen. Floré Artollen now, I guess. You're from Fallow Fen?'

Benazir had simply stared, and then left the table without another word.

Floré smiled at the memory, two awkward girls in a mess hall, her naiveté in thinking they'd have free time to train as they wished. Benazir's reticence. Training dummies and dulled swords and cold salt porridge every morning. She looked at the three cadets before her, in the calm of Hookstone forest, Cuss and Yselda older already by a year at least than she had been those first days. Within weeks of reaching Stormcastle XIV she had a sword always at her side, spending long days camped out along the wall fixing boards, learning to fight. Benazir always next to her.

Floré shook her head and frowned, and focused on the job in front of her. Larchford and sheep, pine trees bending in the wind.

'Right,' Floré said, 'fall in, cadets.'

The three rushed to their feet to stand in a ragged line. Floré took a few moments to adjust their stances, tapping legs and arms and chins and backs. They all wore cadets' tabards, like her own but with no lightning slash across the chest and no border of gold, only plain green material.

'Petron?'

'Aye, Sarge?'

'Aye, Sergeant. The words, if you please.'

The boy straightened and cleared his throat. 'Stormguard, preserve the freedom of all people in the realm. Suffer no tyrant; forge no chain; lead in servitude.'

He ended with a passable salute with the first two fingers of his right hand to the centre of his forehead, which Floré, Yselda, and Cuss matched.

'Well enough, Cadet,' Floré said. 'Now stow your gear,

put that ridiculous bow back before your mother catches you, and get out of my sight. Word is the whitestaff caught you cleaning pots with the skein.'

The boy winced and looked at his feet. They all stood in silence for a moment and he sniffed. Floré blew a breath out through her nose and heard Janos chiding her in the back of her mind. She so quickly slipped back to old habits that were fit for trained soldiers, not village children. Petron raised his gaze from the dirt and started to stammer a response, but no words came out. Floré silenced him with a raised hand.

'Calm down, lad. Listen to the briefing, then stow your gear, get some sleep. A day scrubbing pots for Izelda won't kill you. If you can clean pots with the skein at twelve summers, you might end up a fire-slinging skein-mage of the Stormguard proper one day. If you want to learn the longbow, we will set aside some time, but an unfamiliar weapon on duty is apt to end in disaster. Aye?'

Petron gripped the bow and managed something like a smile, his eyes watering, and nodded his head. Yselda sniggered but stopped when Floré cut her a glare. Cuss looked forlorn on behalf of his brother. Floré knew from the whitestaff that aside from Petron none of the children in the Hookstone forest villages were much shake with the skein, but Cuss never seemed jealous of his younger brother. Janos said Petron seemed strong enough to go to Stormwall next year if he wanted. His mother could certainly use the money. The idea of that boy standing on the wall, heading into the rotstorm surrounded by armoured commandos to hunt a rottroll made her stomach tense. Floré sighed as she turned and looked Cuss up and down.

'Five sheep missing in Larchford,' she said, 'another found mutilated, clean cuts, eyes missing. What do you think?'

Cuss swallowed hard and glanced at Yselda, who stayed patiently quiet and kept her gaze forward, off into the distance.

'Could it be... goblins?' he said at last. Floré shook her head at him and turned to look across the village green.

'Could it be goblins, *Sergeant*, Cadet. Speak with some steel in your spine for pity's sake.'

'Sorry,' he said, and Yselda elbowed him in the ribs, thinking herself beyond Floré's sight. His eyes widened and he quickly corrected himself. Floré continued to gaze at the village green, not letting on she had seen Yselda's arm move.

'Sorry, Sergeant!'

'Cadet Grantimber,' she said, turning back to him, 'are you still holding half a loaf of bread?'

'Aye, Sergeant,' Cuss said, taking one arm clutching a half-chewed loaf from behind his back. Floré turned to look towards the darkness of the trees. The boy was not fit enough to keep pace if she was going to make Larchford by dawn, and his sword work wasn't the best either. He had good strength in his arms and his guard was not bad, but his archery was barely passable even for a village boy, and he was slow and prone to clumsiness. Goblins were easy to kill but a mistake could still turn things rotten, and if there was a rottroll... Her eyes took in the loch, the forest, the hills to the east.

'Why is it unlikely it is goblins, Cadet Hollow?' she asked, and the girl raised her chin and took a moment to think before speaking. Floré nodded in approval at the pause.

Yselda's voice was quiet, barely above a murmur, and her eyes focused on the ground at Floré's feet as she spoke.

'Sergeant, there has been no rotstorm surge this summer. A few thunderstorms, but no surge, so no wet-lightning; no wet-lightning, so no seeds buried by the strikes; no seeds, no goblins or trollspawn or other rotstorm… things.'

Floré nodded her assent and turned to Cuss.

'Cadet Grantimber,' she said. 'Tomorrow you are on Stormguard duty. Gear up, and head to Yulder's farm. There have been strange lights in the sky up that way last few nights. Spooky stuff. Head out early, get there by noon, and spend a few hours seeing if you can find any clue or trace of what is happening. Captain went out today, but I want you to speak to Yulder. I want a map drawn, I want a report, and I want to hear your thoughts. Aye?'

That ought to keep him occupied, at least, and away from his mother's kitchen. The boy stood up straight as a spear, beaming. 'Aye, Sergeant!'

'Good,' she said. 'Now the two of you grab your gear and get out of here. Yselda and I are marching to Larchford through the forest, and she is leading the way.'

Yselda's eyes widened at Floré's announcement. She had surely been expecting a horseback ride in the morning and a warm welcome, rather than a night of whipping branches and river crossings and sore feet. She held up a hand hesitantly, still not meeting Floré's eyes. Floré nodded at the girl to speak.

'If it *is* a goblin, Sergeant, we kill them, but what do we do, what if it's trollspawn or a full rottroll or a stormblight or something worse? Send to Hookstone for the garrison?'

Floré clapped a hand on the girl's shoulder as the sun

finally gave up and fell at last behind the treetops. She gripped her sword hilt with her other hand and felt the wetness of the red and white sword-knot under her fingers and held still until Yselda looked up and met her eyes. Cuss and Petron looked on expectantly, each holding their own bag, Cuss holding his loaf in his mouth.

'There is never only one goblin. If it is goblins, or trollspawn, or rottrolls, or something worse, Cadet Hollow, it is simple, and it is the same,' she said.

'We kill them all.'

~

Later, they were meant to be asleep, but Petron and Cuss bobbed on Loch Hassel in an old rowboat out around the reeds where nobody from town should see. Nobody was meant to fish the loch at night, but Petron had heard old Rodram talking about how much better the catch was at night, and so he and Cuss had gone out once a span all summer long. No night birds disturbed the quiet, only the lapping water and the hum of bugs.

'Reckon the old fella is about?' Petron asked, and Cuss sniffed in response, leaning over the cold water. 'You saw him with Pa, didn't you? I'd like to see him.'

Cuss ran his tongue over his teeth and looked back at his younger brother. Petron asked about their father only rarely. He always wanted to hear the same story: Cuss's glimpse of the bogle at the bottom of Loch Hassel, and he wasn't sure why Petron kept asking over and over. Cuss sat back, leaning on the side of the boat, and turned his gaze to the water.

'Just a bogle, the old fella,' he said. 'I only got a glimpse.

Yellow and sparkling like it was made of coins, green teeth, jaws the size of your hands. Pa called it Hassel, like the loch. Biggest eel in the world, he said.'

Petron watched as he shifted uncomfortably and both remembered what Cuss had told him another night, about their father dropping coins and fish in offering, slow and desperate, muttering wishes. They didn't need to talk of that again.

'The old fella won't be out tonight,' Cuss said at last, 'not this close to shore. He stays deep, out at the heart of the loch. Let's focus on getting a good catch for Ma.'

They fished in silence, casting lines and drawing them back, baiting, tying hooks to floats and flies. It was a sporadic technique, the combination of what Cuss had learned from his Pa, and Shand in town, and what he'd pieced together himself. After long hours and little luck with their hooks and lines, Petron closed his eyes and held his free hand out towards the black water. Screwing up his face and muttering a prayer to Anshuka, he focused his will.

He breathed slowly and methodically as the whitestaff had taught him and he visualised the skein of energy that connected the water, the air, the two boys in their boat, his rod and his line. He felt the thrum of energy as his mind followed familiar pathways and gripped fully onto to the skein, felt his awareness spread out to knots of energy in the darting small fish and a pulsing presence in Cuss next to him in the boat, felt the sparks of the bugs on the surface of the water and... there! Just below the water far to the side of his hook and line, Petron could visualise a tangle of power within the faint outline of a large fish, an abstract geometric pattern like a fish that had been drawn out but only using straight lines, showing its insides and out all at once.

The skein looked like a writhing morass of lines and connections, all made of pulsing lights of every colour he could name and a few he couldn't begin to articulate. The fish was right at the edge of his awareness, perhaps ten or twelve feet away. Petron smiled; only last summer Whitestaff Izelda had said he'd never be able to reach past his own nose. He opened his eyes and raised his hand slowly. He could see the skein layered over his regular vision of the starlit loch at night and could feel beads of sweat running down his neck and face from the strain of gripping it with his mind. He gasped with the effort and let his rod fall to the bottom of the rowboat, steadying himself on his bench seat with one hand and with the other extended he closed his fist, clenched, gripped hard, and under his fingers he felt something cold and wet.

Petron raised his hand and ten feet out from the boat, the loch surface broke and a fish rose from the water writhing and gasping and began to float towards them.

Next to Petron, Cuss laughed, and the boat rocked as he reached out with a net on a long pole and caught the floating fish as Petron drew it closer. Petron slumped back onto his seat and wiped his brow.

'I reckon the whitestaff might boil your heid if she saw you using the "almighty skein" to catch fish,' Cuss said, and Petron grinned at his brother and ruffled Cuss's curly hair.

'Well we best no tell her then, lovely Cuss. 'Sides, I've seen Izelda use the skein to light her pipe when she thought I wasn't looking. They only tell us all that balance tripe to stop us getting into what they reckon we shouldn't.

Whitestaffs worry about balance, but I'm going to be a skein-wreck!'

Cuss wrinkled his nose at the wriggling fish, and he let the net drop to the bottom of the boat. He quickly retrieved the lead bar the boys called 'the shaman' from the back of the boat and brought it down with one swift motion on the fish's skull. The lead bar's mottled grey was the same as the village shaman's cloak, and folks always said, the shaman was the last thing you saw before you died. The fish stopped writhing and the loch was still again except for their breathing and the water against the wooden hull. Petron gazed proudly at the fish; it was a fat trout, easily larger by half again than any of the half-dozen fish the two boys had managed to catch thus far that night. He let his grip on the skein drop and felt a sense of relief as the world returned to muted grey and silver of moonlight.

Cuss snorted and shook his head at the fish, and his brother's strange powers, settling himself on the boat and staring back across the loch to the dim lights of Hasselberry.

'You all right, Petro?' he asked, and the younger boy cricked his neck and then blinked a few times and nodded.

'It ain't easy, Cuss,' he said, 'and Izelda says it's harder the more you try and do, but easier the more you practise. Ihm-Phogn could turn a building to dust and fly across Cil-Marie in a single day. Izelda says Ihm-Phogn once slew a sea monster with a harpoon made of star metal, skein-threw it so hard it went right to the bottom of the sea. But if you don't get the channel right, it uses you instead of you using it. Got to be careful, but I know what I'm doing.'

Cuss nodded and the boys were silent. The village was almost entirely dark at this hour, but there were still some faint traces of yellow light from behind loose curtains. The night was hot and plenty of windows had been left wide open, and as the breeze on Loch Hassel flirted with light summer curtains brief motes of candlelight spilled out across the water. Petron and Cuss kept fishing another hour and caught nothing. They sat happy in their boat, warm and content in the quiet.

~

Deep in the forest Yselda was trying to keep her calm. Behind her Sergeant Artollen patiently followed, and Yselda knew she was watching. Now a few miles from Hasselberry the forest was mature, with widely spaced pines towering upward, high branches curved from the ceaseless wind from the coast, and the occasional copse of smaller trees and bushes to contend with. Thick brambles and beds of nettles always ready to catch and sting, yellow gorse flowers turned grey in moonlight and protected by a thousand thousand barbs. The blanket of ferns and old pine needles softened their footfalls, and the pair trudged onward, Yselda always in the lead. She held her shortbow with an arrow nocked but not drawn. She startled at every noise for the first hour of walking, but slowly her senses attuned to the forest and she felt herself calm. She kept picturing goblins, pebbled grey skin and black orb eyes and stone knives, sinewy arms, teeth like nightmares, dropping from the boughs above or reaching for her ankle from the shadows.

The sergeant had shown them a goblin corpse the summer before, and she had seen one Captain Tyr had captured when she was a little girl, but she had never fought one or really been close to one. They were lucky in Hasselberry;

the rotsurges rarely passed over Hookstone forest. Yselda had never really fought anything before except Cuss and Petron and the sergeant – not really. She forced herself to think about goblins, not the other things, the things she truly feared. The night was still warm, the summer still high, and the thick ferns twisted and turned her path as she tried to stay straight.

Yselda knew that to reach Larchford cross-country from Hasselberry she had to steer them east, parallel to the Star Coast. It was perhaps only eight miles as the crow flew to Larchford, but those eight miles of ridges and forest and streams and hills and rocks were a daunting task. There was a road of course. Yselda had taken it the previous summer with the innkeeper Shand and his wife Esme, her adopted family these last eight years, to Larchford for the summer fayre. The road followed the river Hassel from the east end of the loch and looped north and east around the worst of the hills in the forest, passing Plompton Rocks and Greenfields before finally reaching Larchford where it ended. Yselda was instead leading them straight east, aiming for a bare hill known as Father's Pate. Floré patiently watched but did not interject as Yselda climbed trees, checked the stars, and oriented them by landmarks in the forest. She spent a few minutes looking at the moss on a tree to confirm which way was south, but the moss seemed to be just as thick on all sides.

They passed an outlying homestead, and Yselda knew a tow-headed boy lived there with dimples and dark eyes; his name was Culver. She had seen him around town, always sullen and quiet. The pair passed the homestead within a hundred feet, but the two dogs asleep in the neat vegetable garden did not so much as twitch their ears.

Another hour in the forest and they reached the waterfalls and diving pools at Black Dog Rock, the eponymous black stone sat squat in the centre of the pools, slick with spray from the short falls, darker by far than the grey rock surrounding the pools. They stopped to refill their waterskins. Yselda had never been there at night before. Two weeks prior all the village's children had come for a day's swimming and splashing. She had splashed and wrestled with Culver and Cuss and Petron and Three-Tun and Strachan, but at night it seemed utterly different, the water bleak and unfriendly, the stone an almost malicious presence. Yselda thought it didn't look much like a dog in the daytime, and at night the similarity was gone completely. When they were swimming, they had taken turns to push and climb up the rock, to dive off. The stone was slippery with lichen and the water below so cold, but with the sun out it had been perfect.

As she knelt by the cold water, she jumped as Sergeant Artollen's hand gently tapped her shoulder. The older woman nodded down at the muddy bank of the pool and Yselda felt her pulse quicken as she recognised the impressions all around the bank. Wolf tracks. Her eyes widened and she looked back at the sergeant, who shrugged and handed her waterskin to Yselda. As Yselda filled the second skin, the sergeant stared outward towards the woods. Yselda's hands were shaking and she felt dizzy. She hurriedly tied both waterskins to her pack and shouldered it, and then picked up her bow and nocked an arrow.

'Are they here?' she whispered, and the sergeant shook her head, eyes roving across the shadowed treeline. Yselda could hear howls in her mind, could smell smoke and see flame, and in her mind's eye could see her mother's face. She exhaled hard and stared at the print; it was huge, as large as her hand span.

'How do you know?' she asked, her voice almost breaking, and Sergeant Artollen glanced back at her, and seeing her distress held her gaze. The sergeant looked calm, almost bored, but Yselda saw that her gauntleted hand was gripping the handle of her longsword.

'Rain in the tracks,' Floré said, 'last rain was… yesterday morning? They might still be about but unlikely.'

The sergeant reached out and let both of her hands weigh on the Yselda's shoulders.

'If they are this close, means no bear or goblin within a few miles,' she said. 'Stow your bow. An arrow might take one wolf but another two will be on you before you draw again. Hand on hilt; eyes on woods.'

Yselda nodded and did as she was told but her hand shook and her bladder fluttered. From the reference of the Black Dog pools, she knew it was three more miles to Larchford, and she knew the direction. There was a game trail that would take them more than halfway. *How fast could I run there? Could I run faster than the sergeant if they came?* Her face burned with shame at the thought. The pair stepped into the trees and kept walking, and Yselda kept her hand on the hilt of the old shortsword she had been issued. Her eyes flicked from shadow to shadow and she was breathing fast. With every step she evaluated another tree to climb.

The forest had an air of expectancy. It was not quite asleep even so late into the night; so far into summer the forest never really slept. It was ripe and bursting, berries and fruit, rabbits and foxes and owls hinted at in whispers of grass and the faint crunch of the pine debris. Everything seemed to come alive after the pools, but it was perhaps only her heightened senses. The thin sliver of a moon casting across them turned both to wraiths of grey. After the wolf tracks, the sergeant stuck closer to Yselda.

As they walked Sergeant Artollen drew closer still until they walked only a few feet apart and began to talk, quietly. Her voice was rich, not low but strong.

'My friend Benazir,' she began, 'was deadly, and smart, and beautiful, and funny. We met when we were a wee bit younger than you. We trained together for five years, and we served together for ten more.'

Yselda forced herself not to turn and stare. Floré, the stern Sergeant Artollen, never spoke about what she did before she moved to Hasselberry. They crossed a stream, scrambling up the loose stone and dirt of the far bank.

'She had green eyes, green as a summer leaf,' the sergeant continued, 'her hair was blacker than the Black Dog Rock, and her skin was as brown as a conker. She could throw a dagger as well as any man alive.'

Yselda kept watching the forest, kept marching, but she felt a current of excitement cut through her fear. Petron, Cuss, and Yselda would spend whole evenings conjuring stories about the sergeant. She was a princess fleeing her evil father. She was a war criminal from the eastern kingdom of Tessendorm; she was a Stormguard lancer exiled from the Antian front; a mercenary adventurer retired after a job gone wrong. The woman herself gave no word in clue until now.

'She came from Fallow Fen,' Floré continued, 'farther west than you could imagine. Out there the rotstorm isn't a tale for children. The rotstorm is the sky at night, the Stormwall visible at the edge of sight. Their town had high walls, a hundred hundred soldiers garrisoned. You remember Gil, the juggler from last autumn? Gil was a Fen man. They make fine men, in the fen.'

Yselda blushed at the sergeant's joke; Yselda had followed the juggler moonstruck for his few days in town, much to the amusement of Shand and the sergeant. She hadn't realised how obvious she had been in her infatuation until Gil was gone, and she was left to the jokes. They walked on in silence for long moments, pushing through the dense undergrowth, low branches snagging at their hair and tabards.

'Benazir was sweet on a girl. She was a year younger than you are now. She went to meet her, late at night. It's never truly dark by the rotstorm. They met beyond the city wall, towards the east, rode horses to a quiet meadow.'

Floré stopped walking and Yselda turned to her.

'That night the town was overrun. Gifts from old Ferron, aye? A surge of demons from the blight; true monsters, Yselda, stormblight and rottrolls. There was even a wyrm, so they say.'

The sergeant ran a gauntlet-covered hand through her hair and closed her eyes, and Yselda pictured a town ablaze, a black-haired girl with green eyes watching.

'Fallow Fen was made ruin that night. No more than a handful survived, by chance or providence. She was east, so she and her sweet girl got on their horses, and they fled.'

Floré moved close to her charge and reached out, halting her, straightened Yselda's tunic, tugged her sword belt tight, and rubbed dirt from her face.

'Ten years after Fallow Fen fell, I stood shoulder to

shoulder with Benazir and we drew our swords, and we marched across the ruin of Fallow Fen into the rotstorm with a thousand of our kin.'

Yselda looked away from the sergeant's intense gaze, but the woman waited patiently until she met her eye again.

'Stormguard has always taken orphans, or those who need help,' she said, 'and the Stormguard always will; but we *do not fear* what put us here.'

She drew the shortsword from Yselda's belt and handed it to her hilt first.

'I know about the last Claw Winter. I know about your parents and your brother. The timber wolves; the frozen loch. I know the tale, though I don't claim to know all of what you saw or did.'

Yselda felt the breath catch in her chest and the burning of tears in her eyes. The villagers didn't speak about the Claw Winters, never. Anshuka's nightmares, a season of horror. There would be drifts of snow taller than a man that came with autumn and stayed until summer, ice and wind and hunger, so much worse than a normal winter. Bandits and beasts driven mad by the hunger and cold. When the ground was thawed enough to dig, there would always be fresh holes in the shaman temple's boneyard.

She stared at the ground for a long moment but the weight of the blade in her hand gave her strength. She forced herself to stare at this woman who would draw comparison, who would claim to know anything at all. Her eyes blazed as she raised her head.

Floré was staring back and smiling.

'Good,' she said. 'Anger is good.'

Floré drew her own sword and touched its tip to Yselda's.

'We are Stormguard, little sister. We don't fear wolves, or demons, or the dark things of the storm.'

She swung her sword through the night air between them and brought it up to a perfect salute, held high by her chest, blade against her cheek. 'They fear us.'

Yselda started to copy the salute but faltered and dropped her sword as the forest was flooded with white light. She recoiled and fell backward over a tree root.

The glare pushed through the upper layers of the thick pine to the south, and the forest floor was as bright as day but the light was a sterile cold white, and the shadows moved and danced. Yselda scrambled for her sword and felt herself yell but no sound came, and the sergeant fell into a defensive stance, standing over her as the light passed over them, seemingly above the trees. Accompanying the light was a pressure of air that utterly silenced the forest; not a creaking branch could be heard, though Yselda could see them sway in the night breeze. She saw Floré scuff her foot against the pine needles and say something but heard neither, and her ears began to ache.

The light passed slowly, heading west and north towards Hasselberry.

Both women stared after it the dissipating glow, and the forest slowly came back to life as the wan moonlight reasserted itself and sound returned, the gnarled pines of Hookstone rustling in the wind, branch touching branch, a murmur of pine needles pressing against one another and then swaying away. Each tree seemed to sway individually, and Yselda felt sick as she stared up at them. She pulled herself to her feet and cleaned the dirt from her blade on her tabard and gripped it tight. They stood in silence for a long time.

'Sergeant Artollen,' she said, her voice a tiny thing in the vastness of the forest, 'what was that?'

Floré sheathed her blade and stared north and south and east and west and Yselda found bile in her mouth as she saw the answer that did not need to be spoken.

Yselda could see the sergeant did not know. She saw that the sergeant was afraid.

3

HOOKSTONE FOREST

'The rotstorm defies the sages' laws. Three hundred years on, it should have dissipated or calmed. It remains ever the same, the flow of surges and calms according to no pattern or design our wisest can discern. In the name of the protectorate I sent fifty Stormguard commandos in today, seeking a rumoured rotbud. I find now I pray not firstly for their success, but for their return. Anshuka, forgive me, I must find strength.' – Private Diary, Commander Salem Starbeck

Janos sat with a cup of whisky by the dead fire and sipped slowly and tried not to worry. He had a book on his lap but was not pretending to read any longer, lost in thought. The embers still held a memory of heat and light. The door to the bedroom opened slowly and he saw her there, little Marta. The girl was wearing a simple white cotton night dress, her hair, which had been washed and braided so recently, unspooling into loose tendrils. She started to pad to the kitchen, stepping with ostentatious care, and Janos smiled.

'Are you hungry, Marta?' he asked, and she yelped.

'Papa!' she said, and ran over to him, jumping up onto his lap. He held his glass out wide, safe from her flailing arms, and gave her a squeeze with his other hand.

'What are you doing up so late, little one? It is only owls and Antian awake at this hour.'

The girl wrinkled her nose, just like her mother did, and Janos felt another pang of worry. She had the same ashen hair and amber eyes as her mother, but Janos could see himself in her crooked nose and the dun reddish-brown of her skin.

'I was thirsty,' Marta said, using her 'grown-up' voice. 'Where's Mama?'

Janos picked her up and set her on the rug.

'Mama had to go to Larchford. She'll be back tomorrow. She kissed you goodbye, but you were sleeping.'

Marta harrumphed at that, and Janos smiled at her.

'Come on, petal. Let's get you a drink of water and then we will both get to our beds and our dreams. Sound all right?'

Marta nodded, and led her father through the dark house to the kitchen. Janos poured water from the ewer into a clay cup and passed it down, and tapped his whisky to her water, and together they drank in the cool quiet of the kitchen.

'Tell me about Tullen One-Eye again,' Marta said, and Janos smiled and finished his drink. He refilled the glass from the bottle hidden away in the back of the kitchen, a slow trickle of gold and a scent of peat and fire. Just the mention of Tullen made his tattoos itch.

'A little late for a story, isn't it?' he said, and the girl replied with a stern frown he couldn't help but sigh at.

Janos nodded in acquiescence and held out a hand, and Marta led him to the front room and sat on the rug next to his favourite chair. He lowered himself down slowly into the chair and stared at the whisky. It was a rough drink, distilled from fermented barley by the Brek up in the Great Glen. He silently raised his glass to Fingal and Yonifer, the brother and sister from Brek who had first introduced him to the taste, and he took a long swig as Marta rubbed at her nose with her finger and drank from her water. He pictured Fingal and Yonifer alive, laughing, clay cups and the heat of a peat fire, shouts and roars and songs and dancing. He let the heat of it fill his mouth, could feel it in his nose, and then cascading down the back of his throat. The whisky gave a purifying burn that spread across his chest and made him shiver. He took a deep breath and turned to Marta, and he began to talk.

'Tullen was the most handsome, most smart, most charming skein-mage to ever live. Ever! He could use the skein to put out a forest fire, to spot a wiggly worm a mile away in the dirt, or even fly!'

Marta nodded along; he had told her the tale often enough.

'Tullen had an idea though. The best ever skein-mages, except wonderfully clever Tullen, were the Antian. The mole-dog people, you remember?'

'Like Mummy's friend Voltos!' Marta said, and Janos smiled.

'Mummy and Daddy's friend Voltos, yes. Just like Voltos. Well, brave clever Tullen wanted to see the skein even clearer, so he went past the Antian wall and all the way to mysterious Glen Driech, in the shadow of the Blue Wolf Mountains. And you know what he did?'

Marta nodded gleefully.

'He popped his eye out,' Janos said, clutching at his own eye and grimacing, 'and said to an Antian witch, *I'll give you my eye, and a bag of rubies, for your eye, that I might see the skein better!* And the witch was very greedy, so she popped out her own eye, grabbed the rubies and Tullen's eye, and ran off. Now Tullen put that Antian witch-eye right in his head, and you know what he saw?'

Marta giggled as he clasped a hand to his eye and started blinking wildly. 'Nothing!' she said.

Janos smiled. 'That's right, petal. Nothing, because Antian witches are all blind!'

She squinted one eye closed and growled at him, reaching both hands up and scrunching up her face, and he reached down to tickle her. She giggled and squirmed but then began to cough, a hacking cough that turned to a retch. Janos sank to his knees and he held her close until it had passed, hushing and humming and saying quiet nonsense to placate her, speaking into the tangle of her hair. Finally she was calm.

'Sorry, Daddy,' she said, breathing fast, 'I'm better now, I promise. I haven't been doing it much.'

Janos shook his head and stroked her hair, over and over. They sat together like that in silence for long moments, and then Janos reached down one hand and picked up his cup from the floor by the chair and sipped the final sliver of golden liquor.

'You're better now,' he said. 'I know, petal.'

There was a faint glow out the window, and he turned his head sharply, feeling every instinct in him scream at once. Within seconds the room filled with light, white light, bright and jarring. They both stared for a long breathless moment and Janos felt the air drop in pressure, as if a storm were coming. He felt the sigils on his arm start to burn and dropped his cup and didn't hear it bounce and he leaned forward and grabbed Marta and lifted her close to his chest. In one movement he was standing and then running, and he flung open the door and ran for the forest. He could not hear Marta crying in his arms. His heart raced and his blood boiled. He ran behind the house, into the forest, and behind him there was light and that awful pressured silence, the silence of a too-loud noise. The sigils on his arms and chest pulsed with black light and with Marta in his arms he did what he had sworn not to do. He reached for the skein.

Janos reached for the skein and could not find the pattern within it. Where the pattern should be was only chaos. His felt his heart racing as he stumbled over root and branch, trying to find the pattern in the skein through the chaos. It was a chaos he had felt before, beyond the Stormwall. The chaos brought by crow-men.

Janos ran, and remembered Starbeck and Primus Thum-Pho pleading, cajoling, threatening, and remembered his resolve to never use the skein.

He ran, and remembered this chaos taking him over before, long hands and knifes reaching for him, and then Benazir's blade and the commandos, eyes sharp and blades sharper, a ring of steel and silver and fire around him as Floré stood over him, sword drawn.

Janos remembered Floré, after Urforren, after the salt and the fire, telling him it would be all right, cradling his head in her arms. Janos ran, and remembered running before, long ago.

~

When the lights came, they came they came from the south, over the miles of thick pine that separated Hasselberry from the Star Coast road and the Wind Sea beyond. The first they knew of it the sound of the insects stopped and the loch was awash in what looked like moonlight amplified a thousand-fold. The light was a harsh white. The two boys leaned over in their small boat and stared at the water, moments before black, awash with a pure glow. Cuss dipped his finger, but it felt just like water. Turning to each other, they both gaped in amazement, and turning back to the village they nearly fell out of the boat. Over the village of Hasselberry an orb the size of a carriage floated perfectly still above the treetops, utterly silent and unmoving.

Cuss put down his rod and lifted an oar to his chest, his eyes locked on the orb. Petron dropped his fishing rod in the water but it seemed to make no noise, no splash, and he fumbled at the bottom of the boat and his hand gripped the lead shaman. It was slick with fish blood and scales. He couldn't tear his eyes from the orb, a perfect oblong of pearlescent light. He could see the treetops sway in the breeze but the orb did not move with them. It hung in the air as if it had been there forever and would be forevermore. Petron opened his mouth to scream but no noise emerged; the world seemed to have been muted, as if they were all far underwater.

After a long moment a feeling made the two boys look directly above them. It was like the kick of a huge drum into their chests, but silent, and pushing downward. Above the boat a hundred feet up was another orb.

The two boys stared and Petron started to tremble. He could almost hear Cuss shouting, but the words weren't reaching him. *Jana,* Petron thought, *we need to get to Jana and mother.* Despite this insistent thought he could not bring himself to look away from the orb above the boat. Neither of them heard the shouting in Hasselberry as the watch bells rang. Neither of them saw the flames engulf the whitestaff's house, the orange flame lost in the sea of white light pushing out from the orbs.

As the boys watched a dark iris opened in the base of the orb above, and from it a figure began to descend. Petron had seen a travelling whitestaff perform a feat of levitation at the summer fayre in Hookstone once when he was little, where the young man leapt from the shaman temple spire and half fell, half flew to the ground. Petron knew this figure descending with measured levitation was no whitestaff; there was no staff, no white cloak, and no Riven amulet. The figure was perhaps seven feet tall, wiry and lean, with oddly angled arms and legs as if they held too many joints. It was clothed in a black cloak and a tight-fitting cloth robe of black, hands covered in dark gloves. Absently Petron felt Cuss tugging at his shirt, and almost heard the words his brother yelled.

The figure's leather boots touched down on the boat and the vessel bobbed, and Cuss leapt into action, his oar swinging and his mouth open in a silent roar. Petron blinked and the boat rocked and Cuss was in the water, ashen face up, thrashing, and the opalescent sheen of the water was broken with thick streams of red from his chest. The figure held in a gloved hand a metal rod pointed at Cuss, the end glowing blue. It turned to Petron but he could not see a face, only the deep shadows of the cloak.

The shadowed creature lowered itself into Cuss's seat, and Petron was sure he was wailing but the world was still silent. He swung the lead shaman but the figure batted it from his hand idly and it spun into the water. Desperate, Petron called on the skein and threw the hook of his mind at it and in his horror he latched to the skein and opened his eyes and he could see it all, Hasselberry and its people, the woods, the loch, fire and fear, hearts racing, tangles of life everywhere; he felt Jana and his mother and somehow knew it was them, but the pattern of the skein was *wrong* – there was no order to it. Everything was recognisable but somehow disjointed, chaotic. He felt his temples pound with pain and his stomach began to wrench.

When Petron turned his gaze to the figure before him, there was only an empty space surrounded by chaos, and then his body was rising towards the orb and the figure was with him so close and it raised a hand to Petron's face and its fingers were so long. Petron felt himself begin to weep – *Oh, Anshuka, its fingers, what is it?* – and then it was touching his face and he saw nothing at all, and he screamed but heard no sound, and he writhed but did not move.

~

Janos ran, clutching Marta, and after a hundred yards the chaos in the skein began to fade behind him and he felt the pattern again. He kept running another fifty yards through the thick pine, towards the shore of the loch, one hand over the back of Marta's head as the other held her close. The low branches of the pines pulled at him but he did not slow. He could feel the runes and patterns tattooed on his chest and arms itching with potential, could feel the tangle of chaos behind. The forest was oddly lit by the pale white light cast by the orb that still hovered over their house; glancing back as he ran he could make it out between the trees, an ellipsoid of steady cold light shining through the darkness.

They crashed through ferns and bushes and reached the shore of Loch Hassel, north of home, a beach of golden sand separated from the village by a rocky promontory. Janos heard his own breath ragged and Marta's sobs and realised he was free from the silence. He rushed Marta to a heavy pine trunk that was washed onto the sand, a log they had sat on so many times in the sun. Glancing behind him at the pale orb floating in the sky above the treeline, he squeezed her hands and pressed her down behind the log, down low.

'Stay still, my love. Stay silent for Papa.'

Marta coughed and squeezed her eyes shut and put her hands over her ears, pressing herself down into the cold sand. Janos knelt beside her and stared back at the forest and the light above. It was like nothing he had ever seen before. He had been as deep in the rotstorm as any alive; he had seen every monster the world could produce. This was something else, something beyond mere flesh. *Ferron*, he thought. *It must be Ferron.* He let his awareness spread until it encompassed the beach, the forest, the village. He could sense the buildings, the trees, the people, but over the loch and over his home there were breaks in the pattern, fields of chaos he could not penetrate perhaps a hundred feet in diameter each. He had felt that chaos before; *crow-men*. Focusing his awareness he turned his eyes to the forest sharply, feeling knots in the skein moving towards them, breaking from the chaos, and entering the world he could sense.

From the treeline, silhouettes emerged, squat figures clad in black with blades glinting in their hands. *Goblins*. Behind them and above, a hundred and fifty yards now back in the forest, Janos saw the Orb that hovered over his house let out a great stream of flame, directly down. He rose to his feet and felt his stomach twist as through the trees he saw his home burn. In a flash he remembered a burning cottage in a rainstorm; remembered a burning mill surrounded by roiling clouds of red and black; remembered a city aflame. The burst of fire stopped and then a pulse of purple light, a beam, pressed down thrice from the orb in a staccato surge. No noise escaped the destruction, but Janos watched with clear eyes as the trees nearest the house collapsed and shattered, broken to so much dead wood. He felt an aching weariness wash across him. Home was gone, again. Goblins on the beach stalking towards him, towards *his daughter*. Some unknown enemy in the sky over his village.

Janos did not get angry. He sighed, resigned to play his role, and fell further into the skein. A river of pattern and connection opened to him, a web, a spiral of connections, a net of light connecting all things. He no longer saw it as a layer over his sight, rather it was sight itself. The dozen goblins were screaming now, black orb eyes and rough grey skin, gaunt faces and rows of serrated teeth. They started sprinting across the beach towards him as soon as he stood. His eyes did not leave the orb. As the goblins ran, he waved a hand, and the rune tattoo on his left arm pulsed with red light as he called to the pattern in it, and the pattern below. The endless hours of effort and memorisation and understanding, the pattern that called *flame*. It did not take from him. He extended his awareness and drew energy from the world, from the skein, from the liminal space between knots and pattern that even he could scarcely see after a lifetime of study.

From his hand, a cone of white fire spat forth, a stream of flame that seared his eyebrows. When his hand lowered the dozen goblins were char and smoke and twisted meat, and his own palm blistered and scorched where his control had faltered. Over the forest the orb was raising slightly, as if to move, and Janos spared a glance down at Marta. Her hands were still over her ears and her eyes were blessedly closed, her breath coming in short sharp bursts. He knelt quickly and placed his uninjured hand on her chest.

'Calm, my heart,' he said. 'Papa's here.'

Janos kissed her head and stood again, raising his hands to shoulder height and focusing on the orb. Pushing his awareness in the skein out to the orb, as soon as his eye drew close to the light he felt the familiar taint of chaos: *crow-men*. Demons from the rotstorm. He could not allow them to come closer; all his power came from the pattern, and he had seen too many skein-mages cut down by swords or a crow-man's black fire, desperately calling for a pattern they couldn't find.

The orb dipped and rose, and then seemed to move towards them. *What would Floré do?* he thought, and bit his lip. He had no choice. He looked at the pattern and the orb and the dancing flames through the treeline, his home, and he spat on the sand and *pulled*. A fifty-foot pine tree ripped out its roots and hurled at the orb, point first.

It rose trailing dirt and needles, dead branches and cones trailing below it. When the tree hit the orb, the blazing white light fell back and seemed to wobble in the sky, but then the tree was falling away down to the ground and the orb was still flying.

Marta, her hands over her ears and her head peeking over the log, shrieked, and Janos snarled. His eyes locked on the orb and he called on everything he had. A bolt of lightning flew from one hand, pure power cutting through the sky, but the orb was moving already towards them, impossibly fast, and the bolt flew past the orb and streaked out into the sky. Raising one arm he pulled trees upward again, impossible battering rams, not one pine but five, six, a dozen, all hurtling towards the orb.

The orb veered up and cut through the air like a fish in a fast stream, dodging up and down and around and darting its way forward. At least two of the trees found their mark, silently smashing against the burning white light of the orb's exterior. Another tree was torn from the sky by a bolt of purple light that shot out from the orb, exploded to splinters as it careened through the sky, but the orb was still flying, and flying closer. Behind it his thrown trees fell to the forest below, but he did not hear them land. As the orb crossed the treeline to the beach Janos pulled everything he had into another bolt of white lightning and this one connected with the orb, his straight lightning striking into the burning white but... the orb did not slow.

Janos bit his lip and shut his eyes at what he must do. He could not impose his will on the chaos, but he could change the world around it. Reaching, he felt the ragged edges of the field of chaos spiralling out from the ship, and felt the sky beyond it. He felt the currents of wind and air so insubstantial, and he pushed his senses until he could feel the air in a column a mile over the orb, a column of air he could *change*. He felt the air resist him as he reached for the pattern for flame, for a heat beyond anything this world had seen since—

Something hit his leg and Janos blinked, faltering, and the vision was gone, the pattern was gone, and he was gasping. Marta had sprawled forward and clutched at his leg, squeezing tight. She was crying and speaking and Janos screamed in frustration but then he couldn't hear himself screaming, or her speaking, and he lost the pattern completely. Chaos enveloped him along with pressure and silence and white light, and the pattern and the pattern beneath it were both gone. He sank to his knees, slick with sweat, and pulled Marta close to his face. He yelled at her to hide, to hide and run, but her eyes were closed and he couldn't hear himself, couldn't hear anything.

The orb stopped fifty feet above them, and a dark portal in its base opened and two figures began to descend, gently floating downward. Janos felt sick, felt his heart beating too fast. *Crow-men*, demons only stoppable with fire or silver. Demons who could hold him from the skein. Demons who would kill him, for all he had done. Both figures were over six foot tall, cloaked and clad in black, clutching what seemed to be wands of iron tipped with coloured gems.

I am going to die, Janos said, but did not hear himself say it. As the figures landed not ten feet from them, he grabbed Marta roughly and forced her hands from her ears and her eyes open with his fingers. She was screaming or saying something but he couldn't hear, couldn't make it out. He pulled her to her feet and shook her until she stilled, a violent shake as he never had inflicted before and then he pushed her away from him towards the forest.

Run, he silently screamed, and he pointed, and he ran with her a few steps until she began, stumbling, to head towards the treeline, eyes streaming.

Janos did not follow her. They were there for him, not her. She would be safe with her mother. Turning, he faced the two crow-men on the beach. They stared at him and did not approach closer as he tore free his shirt, showing the runes and patterns tattooed all across his chest and arms, stark red against his brown skin, some of them pulsing weakly now with black light as the chaos the crow-men brought to the pattern sought to infest them.

One of the figures raised its wand like a sword and drew back into a duelling stance, but the other only stared, and then slowly lowered its hood. The face below was human, red-haired, youthful, freckled, mouth parted in consternation, brow furrowed in concentration. Her face twisted in what might have been fear and with a finger she pulled on the skein, amidst the chaos, and in the sand between the crow-men and Janos she drew a rough rune, her finger tracing the air and the sand parting six feet ahead of her, a circle cut through the centre with a line: Ø. The Ferron rune for salt.

Janos rubbed his nose with his thumb, and clenched his fists, remembering Floré teaching him to punch, Benazir teaching him to dodge, both of them teaching him he was useless in a fist-fight. The demon gestured at the rune, and Janos drew himself tall and nodded. Salt. He was the

Salt-Man. Who else alive in all Undal could throw a forest? *Floré, forgive me.*

The two demons looked at each other, and Janos sprang at them. He made it three steps before a bolt of blue light hit him from the right-hand demon's wand, and he felt his leg crumple as if cut to the bone. He fell to the sand and saw the blood pooling, streaming from his leg. The silence and pressure encompassing them all consumed his scream. All he could think of was the pain, and Marta. *She must be free, must be gone, must have run.* He deserved this.

He dragged himself to his knees as they came for him, and they both had their hoods down now. The second crow-man had an aged face, wrinkled and grey and worn, a shock of white hair above. Both demons were weeping, fresh tears falling openly down their faces, turning to each other as if to be sure this was real, that it was truly him. He swung his fist, lunging forward on his good leg, but the woman levelled her own wand and its bolt of blue light hit him in the stomach. He felt flesh tear and he fell to the sand. They were on him in a moment, fists and boots, a flurry of blows. He could see them yelling, in the silence, could see their faces twisted in hate.

The beating stopped. Janos lay in the sand, and managed to turn his head enough to see the reason. Marta. *Marta.* She was clutching a branch, her face strewn with mud and tears, and she threw her whole body furiously behind the wild swings she took with her branch at the nearest demon. She was yelling, but he could not hear. With a burning effort and a wave of pain he reached an arm towards her as the aged crow-man wrenched the branch from her hand and produced from his robes another wand, ending in a gem of faceted green crystal. A burst of green light, and Marta crumpled, and Janos felt every sinew in him tauten as he tried to throw himself towards her. It did no good. All he managed was to turn himself onto his back. The crow-man slung Marta over his shoulder and sheathed his wands. The red-haired woman gestured to him, and he spat on Janos but then nodded and began to rise, up towards the floating orb above, away through the silence.

As Marta rose, the crow-man with the red hair got to her knees and leaned close to Janos, her face to his face, and stared into his eyes as she sank her dagger into his stomach and wrenched it. He felt pain, new pain, a dislocation in the core of his being beyond anything he had ever experienced, and high above him saw Marta enter the dark portal in the base of the glowing orb. Janos wept and retched and tried to say, *Leave her, it's me, only me you want,* but he couldn't form words, could only scream into the silence that the orb pressed down. The red-haired woman tore her knife free slowly and stood and spat on him, and made sure she caught his eye as she said a single word, dagger soaked in his blood clutched to her chest. He could not hear the word she said as she did it, but he knew what it was. *Urforren.* She turned and rose to the sky, arms open, to the embrace of the orb of light above.

The orbs left as they came, silent and fast, and the light from the burning village of Hasselberry washed over the loch. The abnormal quiet was broken by screams and wails from the village as a lone boat bobbed in the water listlessly, with nobody to guide it. On a sheltered beach past town, Janos screamed. He reached for the pattern, but all he could see were stars and smoke, and all he could feel was pain.

~

Floré's lungs were burning as she crested Father's Pate, jogging past the treeline. She could hear Yselda fifty yards behind her, breathing hard. The girl was drenched in sweat. They had been running since the lights in the dead of night, had been running for an hour or more. Hints of the dawn were starting to rise off to the south and east, and as Floré picked her way up the rocky summit she was finally granted a view beyond the pines. Panting herself, she turned immediately towards Hasselberry. She could see no lights in the sky. Thick smoke languished in spirals in the still air over the town. She could see no buildings from this point, not even the tip of the shaman temple tower, but could make out the far end of Loch Hassel. The waters looked calm, but at least half a dozen streams of white smoke were rising from different points where she knew Hasselberry sat. The pre-dawn light was enough to discern the spirals of white and grey.

'Berren's black blood,' she said, and felt a tightness in her chest. 'Marta. Janos…'

She drew her sword without realising, and began to pace the top of the hill, looking for sign of Larchford and the other hamlets. Towards Plompton Rocks and Greenfields, there was no smoke. Far south and west towards Undal, the faint smog of industry hazed the air beyond the forest, but nothing unusual. Towards the east the Cimber hills rose, blanketed in pine and stillness. South, a scant few miles from the coast, all she could see were trees. Yselda reached her as she peered over the forest, looking for Larchford. She heard Yselda's soft cry behind her but forced herself to focus. *There*. Half a mile distant to the east there was a thin trail of smoke, the ghost of a wisp. That must be it.

'Sergeant,' Yselda said, gulping air. 'Sergeant, what's happening?'

Floré shook her head. 'I don't know,' she said, 'but something is wrong in Hasselberry. Dead sheep can wait.'

She started downhill at a jog towards Larchford. Yselda blinked, startled, and called out, 'Wait! Aren't we going back?'

Floré skidded to a stop and loose scree tumbled down below her, towards the treeline. She glanced back at Yselda and saw a girl in shadow, eyes fearful. She extended a hand and waited for Yselda to scramble down from the peak of the hill to her side. She nodded to her, tried to think what an endless stream of trainers and commanders had done to help her overcome her own fears, but she could dredge up no wisdom. All she could think of were smoke spirals, Janos, *Marta*. Floré flexed her right hand and spat on the ground, feeling the sweat on her brow and back cooling already. She didn't have time to coddle.

'Horses from Larchford, straight onto the forest road, we ride hard,' she said, her voice stone. 'Plompton Rocks and Greenfields look calm. We ride straight through, faster than the forest. We go, now!'

4

THE BROKEN STAFF

'Berren was fairest of the Judges, and the Ferron gave thanks to him for all the beauty in the world. He was the first Judge to fall, and the great bear Anshuka wept such tears that floods swept the world. Cities drowned, and three Judges remained.' – The Fall of Ferron, Whitestaff Anctus of Riven

The sergeant was still holding her sword, and it was all Yselda could do to keep her in sight as they ran through the forest. The morning sun caught the dark grey blade as it rose and fell with the sergeant's arm, and Yselda fixed it in her mind, pushed herself to keep it close. The half mile to Larchford passed in a blur of whipping branches and trampled ferns, tripping over knotted roots and splashing through streams without ever slowing pace. Yselda's knees ached and her heart pounded fast, and she was drenched in sweat that was cold in the weak light of the dawn as they passed the first outlying farmhouse.

The farmhouse was silent, and the sergeant ignored it,

heading towards the hamlet square; there was a farmhouse there that doubled as an inn called the Naga's Tooth that must have some horses. The sergeant slowed her pace to allow Yselda to catch up as they approached.

'Sword out, Cadet,' she said. 'No telling what waits for us.'

Yselda could only gasp and nod, her lungs burning. As they cut through a garden and into the village square, Yselda saw the narwhal horn hung from a chain over the door of a squat wooden building and recognised it as the inn. 'There!' she shouted, and then stopped dead. The sergeant stopped next to her. In front of the inn, a man lay face down in the dirt, surrounded by a pool of blood. Yselda recognised the innkeeper from her visit to the summer fayre. His name was Garton and he made pastries that he gave to the children, sweet pastries. She remembered the taste, the way the pastry would flake away with every bite. She started to hyperventilate, taking in sharp breaths.

The sergeant turned her head up and down the street and grimaced and Yselda followed her gaze. She could see another body to the left, and a pair in front of a farmhouse to the right. There was so much blood!

'Are they dead?' she said, and felt stupid even as she said it, even as she stared at the blood, at the stillness. The sergeant put a hand on her back and started guiding her behind the inn.

'Barn,' she growled, 'horses. Quiet like.'

They turned the corner at the side of the inn and saw the wolves. There were three of them, rangy, huge grey and brown mottled beasts. The wolves were feasting on a woman who lay dead in the lane behind the inn, their jaws wrenching her body back and forth, kicking up dried earth and dirt and worse things. The woman's dress was ripped to shreds and she lay face down, dark hair wet with blood. Yselda felt the world start to spin. She stared at the wolves and pictured her parents, her brother. *It was always going to end with wolves,* she thought.

The wolves lifted their muzzles, dripping with viscera, and in concert growled at the two women. Behind them Yselda could see the barn, could hear horses whickering inside. She swayed and felt herself shaking and the sergeant put a hand on her arm and squeezed hard enough to make her wince. The pain brought her focus back. Neither of them took their eyes from the wolves.

'Watch my back, little sister. Use your sword, remember your training. Eyes sharp, blade sharper.'

With that the sergeant threw herself towards the beasts, charging forward with her sword raised to her shoulder, fast strides closing the space between them in moments. One backed away, startled by her rush, but the other two leapt to meet her. Yselda gave a wail as a long two-handed sweep of Floré's blade cut deep into the shoulder of the first wolf, throwing it against the wall of the inn, but that left her other side open to the second wolf that leapt at her throat.

The sergeant pulled back one arm and managed to intercept its jaws with a gauntleted hand, a swift backhand punch into the mouth that broke teeth and sent it yelping back. Yselda took half a step forward with her sword and felt her arms shaking, and the blade fell to the ground. She heard screaming. *Was it her own voice?* She saw the wolves, again, the other wolves, so long ago, heard her mother's voice telling her to run, and she dropped her pack and took a step backward.

Fifteen feet in front of her, the sergeant pulled her blade from the shoulder of the writhing wolf on the ground just long enough to drive it deep into its stomach, pushing her whole weight into the strike. Her sword sank through and into the dirt of the road below just as the third wolf leapt atop her.

The sergeant was forced to her knees, one hand protecting her head from the wolf's snapping jaws, the other desperately trying to draw her silvered dagger. She managed to shoulder it in the ribs and push it half off her, but then the one with the broken teeth was there and the two of them forced her back on her heels and then her back.

There was a sound of tearing paper, and then it came a second time accompanied by a yelp, and the wolf tearing and snapping at the sergeant's throat tumbled off. Quick as a snake she thrust her silvered dagger into the mouth of the second wolf snapping at her, deep and hard, her other hand coming behind its head and pulling it towards her. The rune on the dagger blade flared with white light and flame roiled from the blade as it pierced the beast's flesh. Together they rolled on the ground and the wolf grew still, its mouth and head a mess of blood and burning fur that spread quickly until its whole body was aflame.

The sergeant pushed the burning wolf off herself and got to her feet, retrieving her sword. The last wolf was crawling along the ground, an arrow buried to the feathers deep in its gut. The sergeant stalked over and swung her sword hard at the head of the dying wolf, and then allowed herself a long exhalation and turned to Yselda.

Yselda stood in open shortbow stance, turned side on, her pack at her feet and her sword in lying in the dirt. She had a third arrow nocked and half drawn. Her tabard was muddied and her boots and trousers caked in dirt. She had sweated through her shirt and strands of black hair that had escaped her braid were plastered across her face. Her eyes were wild as they flicked to every shadow, and her fingers were raw where she had caught them on the bowstring. She could feel everything, could feel every muscle in her body tensed and ready for whatever was next. She stared at the burning wolf.

The sergeant nodded at her and wiped her sword blade on the fur of one of the wolves. She kept the blade unsheathed and rolled her shoulders. Yselda did not relax but once the sergeant drew close she stared at the older woman and tried to make a mental inventory of her wounds. It was that, or think about herself, and she couldn't do that. The sergeant was covered in so much blood it was hard to tell if she was hurt, and her tabard was charred and scorched from whatever that flame had been. Yselda allowed herself to clutch her bow to her chest and turned her gaze to the wolf she had killed.

'I said to use your sword for the wolves,' the sergeant said, picking up her own fallen pack and slinging it over her shoulder.

'You did,' Yselda said, and lowered her bow. She felt the strength go from her legs and her bow and arrow fell to the ground, and then she was on her knees and clutching at her hair. After long moment of shaking she forced herself to breathe deep and slow. She gave herself five breaths. *Five breaths; you can do anything with five breaths to prepare.*

When her legs stopped shaking and she looked up, the sergeant was bent over inspecting the arrow buried deep in the dead wolf in front of her. She caught Yselda's gaze and glanced down the alley to the second arrow, which had skipped off a wall and lay broken in the street. Yselda climbed to her feet and rubbed at her eyes with her shirt sleeve, pushed her sweat-plastered hair back from her forehead, and blew out a long breath.

'Either of those arrows could have had my end written on them,' the sergeant said, her voice steel. 'Positions can change in a melee in a heartbeat. You rolled the dice with my blood on each shot.'

Yselda blinked and the corners of her mouth dropped.

'I'm sorry,' she said, her breathing still coming fast, tears running down her cheeks. 'I'm sorry.'

The sergeant wiped her fists on the haunch of one of the dead wolves, leaving a trail of blood and broken tooth chips. She spat on the ground and rolled her shoulders again, and some of the fury seemed to fall from her face.

'The wolf is dead and I'm not. Don't be too sorry,' she said. 'You did well, Cadet.'

She gestured for Yselda to gather her things, and she did so as quickly as she could, wiping her muddied sword blade on her tunic before sheathing it. Together they went to the barn, and within five minutes were racing out of Larchford on horseback, out into Hookstone forest proper, on the long forest road looping back towards Hasselberry.

As they broke the horses into a gallop, in Larchford wolves began to howl.

~

Cuss awoke in the glare of the sun. Consciousness came upon him with a horrifying rapidity, and he found himself gulping mouthfuls half of air, half of brackish loch water. Thrashing, he found himself on his back deep in the reeds at the edge of Loch Hassel. He could see the dock of Hasselberry village a hundred yards off, but all else was obscured by the reeds. He could see his overturned boat out on the water, half sunken, aimlessly drifting. Grunting and aching, Cuss pulled his shivering form through the reeds and up the bank of the loch. His head was pulsing, and his chest burned. The reeds cut at his hands and he felt cold to his core.

'Petron!' he yelled, though his voice seemed no stronger than a whisper. 'Petron!'

There was no answer. Cuss sobbed and fell into the reeds and they cut at him and he pulled himself up again, forced himself forward, weeping, until he made it past the water and onto the bank of the loch. He pulled off his ruined shirt, letting out grunts of pain as it touched his chest. His chest hurt and with every movement he could feel skin tearing. With his shirt off, he could see four deep cuts in his pallid flesh, intricate shapes cut deep. It felt like they reached all the way to his sternum. Blood seeped from them steadily, a dark red, and Cuss felt woozy. He lay back on the bank and coughed and said his brother's name again, and again. He forced himself to look at the sky, and to breathe, and that was when Tellen appeared at the edge of his vision, running round the edge of the loch past the reeds. Cuss knew Tellen, from the mill. Tellen had fixed their back door last winter after Cuss and Petron had broken it wrestling.

'Tellen!'

The man stopped short and yelled over his shoulder, 'Cuss is here; he's hurt!'

He ran to the boy and pulled him further from the water's edge and sat him down.

'We thought you were dead, boy. Judge be praised, Anshuka must love you.'

Cuss spewed a great gallon of loch water and bile, tinged with blood. He coughed and wiped at his mouth with his wet arm and felt himself start to cry again.

'Tellen. Tellen. Tellen, what happened? My mother, Jana, are they okay?'

The man sat next to him on the muddy bank and pulled him close and did not meet his eye.

'Tellen? Are they okay? The thing, the thing it... I think it took Petron. The lights! We were night fishing and they came over the forest...'

Cuss trailed off as he pictured Petron staring spellbound at the figure descending from the orb. He remembered swinging, and then he was on his back in the water and he had a glimpse of Petron and the figure rising upward, towards the light, and then pain and then this. Cuss coughed and winced as the tears in his chest pulled wider. Tellen ripped a sleeve from his shirt and pressed it to the wound. Cuss could hear running footsteps towards them from around the reeds, from the town.

'I'm sorry, Cuss,' Tellen said. 'I truly am.'

~

Petron dreamt of a spire of golden stone, nestled in grey mountain on an island shrouded in mist. He was there in a cell of stone and a blindfolded white-haired woman asked him questions, but he could not understand the language she spoke. Then he was floating, flying, rising above the golden spire, above the mountains. He could picture the world below him as if he were a star nestled in the night sky. North of him were ice and snow, great glaciers and mountains impassable. The rotstorm to the east raged with light and sound, and behind it Old Ferron masked in dark; below him the Blue Wolf Mountains and the hillfolk; the Antian wall, half destroyed; the walled forest of Orubor and the storm fens; the great city Undal, and east of there the Hookstone forest. Could he see Hasselberry? South was the Star Coast dotted with fallen stars, huge lumps of metal and stone, and resolute lighthouses from another age guarding ships against the brutal shore.

He strained towards Hasselberry but could not move closer. He could see south of the coast the Wind Sea spreading across half the world, storms scudding across it, strange lands and strange peoples beyond; jutting from the waters was Shardkin, the reef city of the Tullioch the size of a mountain.

Nestled in the waters south of Undal, past barrier islands with more of the ancient lighthouses, a crescent island: Iskander, the island of the whitestaffs. Beyond that, open water, and beyond that, hints of shadow and land. Petron strained himself towards Hasselberry and then in an instant was back in the golden spire, in a bare room with walls of dark stone, the blindfolded white-haired woman shaking her head and saying things in a language he could not comprehend.

'Please,' he said, but when he spoke no sound came. He reached for the skein and felt as if a nail was being driven through his consciousness. Instantly he stopped, and slumped, his head pounding but otherwise almost no sensation in his body. He did not feel... physical. It was a dream, surely a dream.

Below the blindfold the white-haired woman had a kindly face that was wrinkled with age. He sat on his heels and rocked gently back and forth. Again, she asked her questions, always the same three sentences, but he did not understand.

'Please,' he said again, and again no sound came, but he could hear her questions. They did not stop, but he could not answer.

'Please.'

~

Floré and Yselda passed through Greenfields at speed in the soft morning light, hooves thundering through the quiet village. The village appeared normal, two dozen houses and swathes of cleared forest with crops planted. Livestock milled, and villagers waved hands in greeting. The sergeant made her horse slow down to a trot and yelled at one waving farmer, 'Larchford has been attacked, and a wolf pack is about. Keep watch. Garrison will be out soon!'

She kicked her horse onward and as Yselda raced to follow she did not hear the man's reply, if he made one. Yselda's thighs ached and she was exhausted, but she held her course and managed to keep up with the sergeant. Her eyes itched and ached from the tears, but the sergeant rode ahead and Yselda was determined to keep her composure. Sergeant Artollen was driving her horse determinedly, but she knew it could not gallop all the way to Hasselberry.

They ran in surges, galloping, and then drawing back to a trot and a canter as the horses' wind would allow.

At one point she slowed them to a walk and she made Yselda eat an apple and some bread and cheese from her pack. As the sergeant undid a neat package of food only slightly crushed in her fight with the wolves, Yselda saw the panic and fear running across the older woman's face when she thought it was hidden from view. Larchford was dead, an entire hamlet dead.

'We should have inspected the bodies,' she said to Yselda as they walked alongside the horses, 'to see what happened.'

Yselda shook her head and drank long from her waterskin to wash down the bread and cheese. She felt so tired, but the food and water were steadying her. She kept her eyes on the forest edges as she replied.

'You heard them howl as we rode out? Three wolves aren't a pack, Sergeant. We were right to flee. They would have killed us.'

They pressed on. The forest road was well kept and wide, bordered by deep ditches and steep banks, shaded from the morning sun by the endless soaring pines.

Plompton Rocks was much the same as Greenfields, a small cluster of dwellings around some strange rock towers, and the sergeant stopped long enough to refill their waterskins and let the horses stand still.

'What's going on here?' a voice said, and Yselda started and spilled her water. 'Sergeant Artollen, isn't it?'

The question asker was a middle-aged man dressed like a farmer, with thinning red hair and a broad face. The sergeant passed her waterskin to Yselda, who started hauling the well bucket back up.

'Larchford has been attacked,' she said, voice flat. 'Unclear by what. Many are dead. There is a wolf pack in the Hookstone forest, perhaps worse. We need to get to Hasselberry and then Hookstone to rouse the garrison. Can you spread the word? Prepare the village?'

The man stared open-mouthed for a second, then nodded.

'You'll want fresh horses. Wait five minutes and I'll have you our two best.'

He quickly turned and gave instructions to a boy and girl lurking nearby. As they waited for the horses, they washed their faces with the well water and Yselda watched the sergeant wince as blood and dirt cleared from her scalp. She gasped as she saw the sergeant's shaking hand reaching up, and she realised that perhaps half of the sergeant's right ear was gone.

The red-haired farmer brought them some cloth bandages as they waited for the fresh horses. Floré let Yselda wind one around her head, wincing again as the adrenaline began to wear off.

'We need to get going. Where are the horses?' she said, and the man waved his hand towards a barn.

'Two minutes, Sergeant, two minutes,' he said, and then he hesitated. 'Tell me, does this have something to do with… those lights last night? They lingered above us a long time.'

The sergeant stared into the forest and did not answer, and he eventually dropped his gaze and walked away. Yselda tied off the bandage and used another to try to clean a few other accessible wounds, but the sergeant wouldn't take off her gauntlets or armour. As they waited, Floré reached down to the hem of her grey cloak and cut a strip of cloth six inches in length and one wide.

'Your sword,' she said, and Yselda passed across her shortsword in its sheath. The sergeant tied the scrap of grey cloth to the pommel and then passed it back.

'A sword-knot marks our victory, reminds us of our deeds and our courage,' the sergeant said quietly, eyes on the trees, and Yselda stared at the sergeant's own sword-knot, the red silk with the white stripe. It looked damp.

'You killed a wolf today,' she continued. 'You protected your comrade. You did well.'

Yselda couldn't speak, so she just nodded and put her sword belt back on, her fingers lingering on the grey cloth.

'I'll get you a proper one,' the sergeant said, rubbing the torn hem of her cloak in her fingers, but Yselda shook her head.

'It's perfect,' she said, and the sergeant almost smiled.

When the farmer brought the fresh horses Yselda found a moment alone with the horse that had taken her from Larchford. It was tired and shaken. The horse was a dappled brown, taller than her by a long way. She held its muscular cheek in one hand and hugged its neck and whispered in its ear a quiet thanks.

They rode out of Plompton Rocks fast and hard, leaving panic in their wake.

~

Floré leapt from her horse as soon as she emerged from the forest road to Hasselberry. She stepped forward and stopped, aghast. The whitestaff's house, which doubled as the schoolhouse, was burned to cinders, a pile of broken stone and charred timber. Fires still raged in the ruin, but it was clearly beyond saving. The shaman temple spire was broken off and lay shattered on the churned grass and dirt of the village green. On the green itself she saw burly red-haired Tellen, his farmer friend Esson, and half a dozen villagers and workers from the mill labouring in silence. On the heat-cracked grass, two dozen bedsheets covered still bodies beneath. As she watched she saw Tellen pull a sheet over the broken form of old Rodram. Some of the sheets were spotted with dark blood and other viscera, and some of the forms were much smaller than others. Floré felt the tremors begin in her right arm and clenched her fist and ground her teeth. She didn't have time for old pain.

The Shaman Jule was there in his mottled grey cloak, wandering amongst the dead and clutching at a talisman, muttering to himself. She had seen that talisman before, a simple branched figure he claimed represented a facet of the great Anshuka. When he saw Floré he furrowed his thick black eyebrows and started walking back towards his shattered temple. Jule had the walk of a heron, long legs picking a careful path. His bald head was pale and red in the afternoon sun, his lips thin. He looked old for one so young, younger than her easily. He stalked away and she shook him from her mind and stepped forward into the green fully.

The Goat and Whistle stood staunchly undamaged, and Floré could hear the wailing of children in there. At least a dozen houses were burned to ruin, with one more blazing wildly. Wheatgum's Provisions had half collapsed. She could see Cuss and a few others lying on the outdoor tables of the inn being tended to by a village girl whose name she couldn't remember. Those on the tables looked hurt but not dead; Cuss lay flat, staring at the sky through red eyes, skin like wax. Bandages wrapped his stocky chest.

Floré marched forward into the square, having forgotten the borrowed horse in an instant; it was too tired to wander far, and seemed grateful to have a moment of stillness.

'Tellen,' she called, and when he turned the look of fear on his face at seeing her made her wince. His clothes were torn, one sleeve missing, and all of him coated in blood and ash. His eyes were hooded. 'Tellen. Janos and Marta. Where are they?'

Tellen stared at her for a long second and then looked down, and Floré felt a shiver run up her spine. She turned sharply.

'Yselda,' she called over her shoulder, 'find Captain Tyr and let him know we are back, and check on Cuss and Petron.'

'Aye, Sergeant,' the girl answered, her voice thin as she hopped down from her horse. She quickly tied up her horse outside the inn and retrieved Floré's horse and tied it up as well before starting to walk away.

'Wait,' Tellen said, his voice a millstone.

'Sergeant,' he said, and then stopped. 'Floré...'

Floré spat and reached forward and grabbed him by the shirt, hauling him to his tiptoes. The lithe muscles of Floré's arm tightened and bunched and she pulled him close.

'Ashes and blood, Tellen: my husband and my daughter. Are they alive?'

'I... we went there this morning, Floré. House is gone. Forest there is all torn up. We found Janos on the beach past the woods, hurt bad. He is alive, but he... he ain't looking good.'

Tellen flinched and turned to stare at Cuss, lying on the table nearby. Janos was not one of those on the tables being treated. Floré tightened her grip on his shirt and felt the plates of her gauntlets digging into his chest.

He looked back to her.

'He said she was gone, Floré. That they took her. The orbs. Same thing the boy Cuss said about Petron. Figures, cloaks, they came from the orbs. Demons, he said.'

Floré let him go and her hands dropped to her blades.

'*Cuss* said demons or *Janos* said demons?' she asked, brow furrowing.

Gone, she thought.

'Janos said demons,' Tellen said.

Jule the Shaman stood silent and still by the temple door, across the green. The millworkers and surviving villagers had all stopped what they were doing, and were looking to her. Yselda stood next to Floré, sweat-stained and coated in dust from the road, swaying slightly.

'Tellen,' Floré said, 'I've been gone less than a day. What in all the hells happened?'

The man looked out to the still waters of the loch and shame flashed over his face.

'Captain Tyr is dead,' he said, and Yselda gasped. Floré did not break her gaze.

'The... the lights came last night,' Tellen continued. 'It all went silent. The size of lumber carts, glowing white and flying through the air, hovering like dragonflies. I ain't seen nothing like that afore. A bunch of folks came outside. Some of us fled to the woods, those you see alive. The rest who stayed are dead. Those who tried to fight back, or didn't run fast enough, all dead, houses burned. Whitestaff Izelda did something with the skein; there were lights. I think she tried to make them leave but… one of them came down from the orb. It broke her staff, and… it killed her. Took her green stone. Tyr tried to help her; it got him too. I don't know how. Strange cuts to his chest like Cuss's, but deeper. He died an hour ago.'

Tellen sounded half defiant as he spoke of fleeing. Floré's expression did not change. She looked down at the trampled and charred grass and saw a dandelion. She stared at it.

Gone, she thought, *and Janos said demons.*

Tellen pulled something from his pocket and handed it to her. It was Captain Tyr's rank badge, an oval disc of steel with a bolt of lightning over a crown and four horizontal slashes, and on the back his rank, name, and number.

'Me and the team from the mill have done our best here. Far as we can tell all are accounted for or dead, except Petron and Marta. A few folks in the houses that… well. They ain't alive. No word from outlying farms but no smoke thataways. Floré, you understand what I was saying? Cuss said they took Petron into one of them orbs, and Janos said Marta got took too. Alive.'

Floré stared down at the rank badge in her hand and remembered holding another, with the same symbol, with the rotstorm high above her and Benazir next to her, the stench of blight thick in her throat. Her right hand trembled.

'Tyr said,' Tellen started, and stopped to cough and cover the lump in his throat, 'before he passed, he said, congratulations on the promotion, and to get your arse to Hookstone. Janos is in the temple. The shaman has been making him… comfortable.'

Floré nodded, but her eyes strayed from the rank badge back to the lone dandelion pushing up from the dirt.

Gone, she thought again, *and Janos said demons.*

She made herself blink, made herself breathe, made herself think. Long lectures in Stormcastle XII came back to her. Civilians in danger, infrastructure destroyed. *Janos said demons.* What should she do? *Gone.* The village survivors were pressing closer now, looking to her to lead. Floré closed her eyes a long moment and pictured Janos leaning against their gate with lilac in his hand, a smile on his lips; Janos on the Stormwall reading poetry aloud to her as they patrolled, his deep voice. She felt a trace of pain up her right arm and shivered. There was work to be done. She opened her eyes.

'Tellen,' she said. 'Good work, keep it going. Get some people to check that fire spreads no further. I want a count of the dead and a count of the living; see if anyone else is missing. That is the priority. I want everyone left alive armed and barracked in the Goat and Whistle tonight. Wolves are on the road so we can't leave these bodies like this. Get them into the guardhouse, and set men to digging at the edge of the forest. Yselda, check on Cuss and then I need provisions and fresh clothes. Tellen, I need to get the garrison from Hookstone. I need you to take charge here until then. I'll be back tomorrow aye?'

The big man nodded, his face grim and grey. She could see the look of hope returning to the survivors' eyes, the hope borne of purpose. She had seen it before, deep behind the rotstorm. No matter how bleak a situation, a task can hold off despair, regardless of its utility.

'Shand,' Yselda said behind her, her voice quiet. 'Esme

and Shand and the girls. Tellen. Tellen, are they in the inn? Lorrie, Lorrie and Nat – are they in the inn?'

His mouth opened but no words came out. He could not hold Yselda's gaze and looked at his feet as he shook his head.

Yselda rocked on her heels and Floré swore under her breath and then turned and gripped her hard.

'Cadet Yselda, I need you to help Tellen. Distribute weapons from the Stormguard stores. Advise on best ways to fortify. Help with the sick. Take three men with you and check the outlying farms tomorrow morning. There isn't time to get back by dark today.'

Yselda didn't nod or acknowledge her at all. Instead she sat on the ground and hugged her knees. Floré turned back to the ashen figure of Tellen before her.

'Have we got fresh horses?' she asked, and Tellen shook his head and looked nauseated.

'Horses are all dead. Strange wounds, same as the captain and the boy Cuss. Same thing with the dogs, and Jule's old goat, and even some of the chickens. Almost no livestock left. Everything that stayed in the town met the same fate.'

Floré glanced at the horses she and Yselda had taken from Plompton. Both looked tired.

Get your arse to Hookstone, Tyr's voice said in her mind. *Raise the garrison. Protect the people.*

Tellen half reached a hand to her shoulder before pulling it back.

Marta is gone. The thought seemed ridiculous. Her Marta, a wriggle of limbs and questions and wild hair. Gone. Her stomach churned at the thought of it. She couldn't conceive of it, not really. *How could Marta be gone?*

'Floré,' Tellen said, quietly so the meagre crowd could not hear, 'you need to go to Janos, in the shaman temple. There may not be much time.'

Floré slowly nodded, and Tellen turned and immediately was all business. A decade managing the lumber mill had given him a voice like a thunderclap, and it was swiftly put to use organising work crews. The surviving villagers all looked tired, but none refused the suggested orders. They were happy to have work to occupy them.

Yselda waited a moment for them to leave, and then looked up from the ground at Floré's feet and asked, voice breaking, 'What are we going to do, Sergeant? I think, I think Shand is dead, and Esme, and little Lorrie and Nat. I don't know what to do. It's happening again.'

Yselda was staring at the white sheets covering the bodies on the village green. Floré ran a grimy gauntlet through her sweat-slick hair and screwed her eyes shut for two breaths before they opened, sharp, ready.

'I'm sorry, Yselda,' she said. 'They were good people. You need to do what I asked. Check on Cuss, and then I need provisions, fresh clothes, and I'll be on horseback to Hookstone in the hour. I'm going to rouse the garrison, and we're going to find out what is going on. I need to find Marta, and Petron. You will grieve for them, but for now, I need you.'

They both knew it would take until the dead of night to reach Hookstone, and no help would reach Hasselberry until at least the next afternoon.

'Sergeant,' the girl said, '... what do I do if they come back?'

Floré reached down a hand, and when Yselda accepted

it she pulled the girl to her feet and tapped her quiver and scabbard with her gauntlets. She brushed dirt from the cadet's shoulder and straightened her tabard, trying to keep the lightning in her mind and the red-raw fear in her heart from showing. *It's always easier to be strong for others than for ourselves,* Benazir's voice said in her head.

'I saw you kill a wolf today, Cadet. A Hookstone timber wolf that would have made a Stormguard lancer shit their trousers. I know you can do the necessary,' she said, and turned her gaze to the sky, 'but in this case, this enemy is beyond us. If the lights come back you take the children; you get into the forest. Today you make sure everyone knows. Scatter to the forest and hide.'

Yselda nodded. 'You'll be back soon?' she asked.

Floré ignored the question and continued to gaze up at the sky. 'You know how to kill a demon, Yselda?'

The girl stared wide-eyed.

'Fire or silver,' Floré said. 'Silver or fire.'

She undid her belt and pulled the sheathed silver dagger from it, handed it to the girl, then retied the belt. The dagger had a hilt of antler and a hint of the silver blade showed above the sheath.

'Eye's sharp, blades sharper,' Floré said, and gave the girl a half-hearted wave. Yselda nodded and moved off, clutching the dagger to her chest. Floré pictured Benazir and felt the tremors in her arm begin anew. She was left alone. She knew she had to find Janos, and she knew she had to get moving. As she breathed methodically to calm the tremors her eyes spotted something odd next to one of the sheets, ashen and broken on the grass. It was Izelda's staff, taken from the great white tree of Riven itself. The focus a whitestaff could use to feel and manipulate the skein, a mark of office and respect.

The staff was snapped in two, each half twisted and charred. Floré made herself shift her eyes from the broken staff to the shaman temple and started moving.

She had to find Marta. She felt fear and sorrow and an ache in her soul and wanted to weep, to fall to her knees. Around all of that, an anger, a cold rage that anyone would hurt her daughter. She embraced the anger, let it fill her, and clenched her fists. She would find Marta and she would kill the demons who had dared to take her.

5

THE HARD LAYER

'Anshuka the bear; Berren most fair; Lothal the Just; Nessilitor the Lover. Strength and art and justice and love were the purview of Ferron's Judges. Lothal the wolf held the empire's excesses in check; Anshuka protected it. Berren inspired them to greatness, and Nessilitor led them to raise up the humble and see to each of their needs. The Antian and Tullioch and even the wild Orubor respected Ferron's borders. The death of the Emperor Ferron led to stagnation; the death of Berren to scarcity; and an empire grew, and fell, as empires are wont to do.' – Pantheon of the Protectorate, Campbell Torbén of Aber-Ouse

Floré skirted the village green and approached the temple. Up close she could see how extensive the damage was. The shaman temple was a simple affair, a long rectangular room with a two-storey spire at the front end over the double doors. That spire was broken now, landed in a shamble on the green a dozen feet from the temple door.

Floré could see the four symbols of the Judges: the claw Y, the feather X, the eye ↑, the flower F. The symbols were intricately carved in dark wood and had sat above the four copper bells. The bells sat cracked in the dirt and rubble, their bell ropes tangled and rising to the ruined spire above. The largest bell marked with Anshuka's claw was split entirely in two.

Jule stood silent by the front doors. Floré went to the doors but the shaman stepped before her, his mottled grey cloak and robes swirling. He held a hand to bar her way and Floré stopped, flaring her nostrils.

'Where is he, Jule?' she said, and the shaman looked at her sternly.

'You did not come for Anshuka's blessing before you left with the girl,' Jule said, staring at her intently, but Floré did not look away. She had held the gaze of better and worse men than he. Jule's eyes widened with anger as she refused to be cowed.

'You are meant to be a protector,' he sputtered, 'but you deny the aid of the god-bear. The protectorate exists only at her whim. You would deny that?'

Floré curled her lip, and Jule slammed his fist into the timber of the door.

'Your husband lies dying and your daughter is gone, woman, because you do not show humili—'

Floré's gauntleted left hand batted into his face, a quick jab to gauge distance, and before he could fall or draw his own hands up in protection her other hand swung in fast. She followed her weight through on that strike, and heard his nose or cheekbone crack, the heft of her steel-plated gauntlets sending him reeling. Jule fell back to the door

93

and tumbled to the ground, coughing, his face streaming blood.

Floré picked him up by the front of his mottled robe and held him off his feet, pressed against the wall. Glowering through swelling eyes and a split nose and lip, Jule did not struggle. 'You are not above judgement, *Sergeant*.'

'You claim to speak for Anshuka, *shaman*,' Floré spat, 'but all you do is take coin from peasants to send to your church. You don't contribute. Judges need no priests, and I don't need you.'

Floré slammed him against the wall twice and then let him drop to the dirt and walked into the shaman temple, breathing hard and flexing her hands.

The pews had been lifted to the side of the room. Straw coated the floor, and blood coated indentations showed where the dying had lain. Janos lay alone on a patch of straw on the stone floor, his body layered in cloth clotted with blood. His shirt had been removed and through blood and cloth she could see the sigil and rune tattoos coating his arms and the parts of his chest not pressed tight with stained dressings. A solitary candle by his head lit the room. One of the village women, Siobhan, was pressing a damp cloth to his head from a basin of water. Seeing Floré she cast her eyes down and quickly left. She paused by Floré's shoulder as if to say something, but then she was gone. Floré stared, and then slowly she went to his side and down to her knees. She pulled her gauntlets off and dropped them on the floor and put her hands in his.

'Janos,' she said, but he did not respond. His chest rose and fell in stuttering syncopation. His skin was stiff, the usual light brown faded to grey. She could see no wound to his head or face, but from his shoulders down the bandages and sheets were a deep crimson. Gingerly she peeled them back with her free hand. She had pulled the sheet a scant few inches when she stopped. The wounds were grievous, deep and open and clearly mortal. With a dozen whitestaffs in Riven itself he would not survive this. He should not be alive even now. She could feel her grip on the world slipping, and her hands began to shake. *Guard him well,* Starbeck had said, after Urforren, *keep him safe until he is needed.*

I need you now, she thought, her hand cupping his cheek.

The world dropped away from Floré and she was standing with Benazir and Janos on the ramparts of Stormcastle XII. Benazir and Floré wore gleaming mail armour and tabards of red and gold. The three of them stood and stared at the rotstorm, a half mile past the Stormcastle ramparts. The endless roiling cloud and lightning, the burst of light and colour, the roaring and howling at the edge of language of a malevolent, almost sentient wind; they stood and let it all wash over them.

Janos had a tabard, but no armour. He wore simple cloth and leather, a nobleman's hunting outfit as was stylish in Ossen-Tyr. His hair was brown then and cropped short, but his smile was the same. He pulled a flask from a pocket and held it up.

'Tomorrow, we roll the dice!' he said, smiling, and took a drink. He passed it to Floré.

'Tomorrow, we fight,' she said, sombre, staring at the rotstorm. She took a drink and winced at the potency of the spirit within, a hooch made from kitchen scraps, potato peels and gods knew what else. She passed the flask to Benazir.

'Tomorrow, we stand together,' Benazir said, and raised the flask in salute to her comrades. That brought a smile to Floré's face, and Janos laughed.

'Well, you two stand together,' he had said. 'I'll be fifty foot back or so if that is all right...'

Floré squeezed her eyes shut and was back, back in Hasselberry, the cold waters of the loch lapping against the long dock, the cursing of the shaman outside, the laboured breathing of Janos in front of her. Light poured through thick windows stained with paint and dye into crude tableaux of the four Judges.

'Janos,' she whispered, 'I'm sorry, Janos. My love, forgive me. I'm so sorry.'

She pressed her face to his hand and wept for a long time.

'... Floré?'

His voice was a breeze on the reeds, the spectre of a whisper. One of his eyes half opened and it focused on her.

'Floré,' he said, and she squeezed his hand, 'Floré. It took Marta. A demon. Crow-man.'

Floré felt her head sway and reel at the words. *A crow-man? That was impossible. This was all impossible.* She had seen him hurt before, but never like this. Gods, she had seen him *broken* before, but only in spirit, never injured and beaten and *torn* and... Janos interrupted her, lurching up a few inches, straining, fresh blood blossoming on the bandages covering his torso, and his other eye shot open, blood-filled and sightless.

'A demon, a crow-man! Floré, a demon! Silver and fire. My love. Marta. I'm sorry. Find Marta.'

Floré cradled his face and lowered his head back to the cold stone of the temple floor.

'Rest easy, love. A demon, I know. Fire and silver and silver and fire. I'm so sorry.'

He nodded, perhaps, and was silent a while longer.

'I love you,' he said at last. 'Marta. You must find her. I kept her from it where I could, but she reaches. Find Marta. Benazir will help you.'

Floré winced. Marta reached for the skein, stronger than most skein-mages, stronger than Janos when he was fully grown. She reached out with the skein as naturally as Floré would with her hand, but whenever she touched it and changed the pattern it took from her, and so she weakened and she sickened. Janos kept her from it, where he could. *What can I do? What could Benazir do?* All Floré had were her fists.

She made herself smile at him, and kissed his hand.

'I know, my poet, I know. Hush now. It will be all right. I will find her, and when I do I will keep it from her.'

Janos looked at her and clarity came to his vision, and she saw him understand. Tear tracks cut through the ash and dirt caking his face.

'They went north,' he said, and she nodded and kissed him.

'I will get her back, Janos,' she said.

He smiled and closed his eyes. 'I know you will. I know. Hold me one more moment, soldier,' he said. 'One more moment.'

~

Floré left the shaman temple. She stood before the door and let the soft light of the afternoon engulf her. She slipped Janos's blood-caked silver wedding band onto her index finger on her left hand and pulled her gauntlets back on. The thick leather and steel plate of the gloves were crusted in dried wolf blood with a wet smear of shaman blood on top. Of Shaman Jule there was no sign.

She could see a column of smoke rising from behind the hedges and trees in the direction of her house and knew there would be nothing left, and she couldn't bear it. Instead she walked towards Captain Tyr's house. As she approached, she saw Yselda on the village green, sat cross-legged on the grass with a hand on one of the sheet-covered bodies. Shand, most likely; the innkeeper had given her hearth and home since the last Claw Winter when her family perished. The girl had washed her face and hands and changed into fresh cloth beneath her leather jerkin, with a clean Stormguard cadet's tabard on top. *How long was I with Janos?* Floré wondered. She took it to be a good sign the girl was dressed for action. The silvered dagger was on her belt and her shortsword in its scabbard beside her, next to a restocked quiver of arrows and her bow. Yselda's head was bowed, and she was speaking in a low voice to the dead man in front of her, and did not see Floré cross the green towards the captain's house.

It felt sacrosanct to enter the captain's house unbidden, but Floré steeled herself. She pushed open the door and the calm inside compared to the charnel and ruin of Hasselberry was jarring.

'I got you a washbasin!' Cuss said from behind her, and she swore. The boy jumped in response, and almost dropped the ewer of water clutched in both hands.

'Sorry,' he said, grimacing. 'Yselda said I could help. I got fresh clothes from the miller Sandy, and the supplies you wanted are all through in the kitchen.'

Floré followed Cuss through to the captain's kitchen where her own pack sat, looking stuffed with food and with full waterskins strapped to each side. He must have taken it from the horse.

Cuss poured the ewer of water into a tin basin sat on the heavy wood table, then quickly put down the jug and absently rubbed at his chest. Floré could see the thick bandages padding beneath his light shirt. His eyes were red and ringed in shadow and there was a frantic energy to his movements that bordered on mania.

'Cuss,' she said. 'What happened to Petron? Are your mother and sister all right?'

He did not meet her eye, instead looking out at the water of the loch through the open kitchen window.

'The orb took him. A... man, but not a man. It flew. I... I tried, Sergeant.'

Floré nodded, noted the way he did not mention his mother or sister, heard the way his voice came so close to breaking on those last words.

'I will find them, Cuss.'

The boy nodded and they both stood in silence for a long moment, and then he tugged at his shirt sleeves.

'Yselda told me about the wolves, Sergeant. I can maybe clean your jerkin and get a whetstone to your blade while you get ready? Is there anything else I can do?'

Floré sighed and unbuckled her sword belt. She pulled her charred and blood-tarnished tabard over her head and laid it over a chair, the green and gold turned to brown and black by the dust and sweat and blood and flame.

With much more hesitance she unlaced her thick leather jerkin and gingerly removed it. A wolf tooth fell from the leather and tapped to the flagstone floor of the kitchen, and beneath the jerkin her shirt was torn and stiff with dried blood and sweat. Floré bundled her jerkin, sword, and gauntlets together and handed them to the boy. As she did, she felt a long wound on her left shoulder open and begin to seep fresh blood.

'Deal with these quick,' she said, 'and get back here.'

Cuss nodded, his eyes flitting across her bandaged head and bloodied body, and he left her. Floré closed the kitchen curtain and door and undressed fully. She peeled the bandage from her head and what was left of her ear began to bleed. Silently she moved her hands across her whole body, cataloguing wounds, scratches, bruises. She pressed her strong hands against her arms and felt the thin layer of softness before the hardened sinew and muscle below. The softness was a Hasselberry softness, a new thing. Motherhood had changed her body; inertia in this village had changed her body. She felt tired and weak, but Floré pressed down hard until she felt the strength below pushing back. Strength won through a lifetime of training and horror. Strength to fight, to protect. It was still there, the hard layer.

~

The blade of the sword was beaten silver, and endless runes were etched upon it overlapping, folded into the blade itself. It had a simple handle of antler. Ashbringer knew the story of the stag that antler had come from. She had been told it over and over, as a child. She brought the blade up close to her eyes, examining it in the light of the fire. It was broken – a foot from the hilt, the blade had been snapped cleanly. The pale blue skin of Ashbringer's face was etched with red rune scars, and her eyes were orbs of dark gold with no pupil and no iris visible. She squinted at the blade, reading the pattern in the runes, looking for a clue as to the weakness it held, focusing on the runes nearest the breaking point. The six Highmothers of Orubor sat around the fire, in the shadow of the forest's only mountain, and took it in turn to speak a truth about her prey. They did this whenever Ashbringer returned, defeated again; they had done this for her ancestors stretching back three hundred years.

'No blade will pierce his skin,' said Highmother Ash.

'No fire will burn or rock will crush,' said Highmother Elm.

'Smoke will not drive the air from his lungs, and no poison will harm him,' said Highmother Oak.

'He does not age. He does not weaken,' said Highmother Beech, and her tone was bitter, her voice a whisper.

'He has killed more men than there are stars in the sky,' said Highmother Pine.

'He has killed gods,' said Highmother Willow.

'*A* god,' corrected Highmother Pine, and Willow sniffed.

Ashbringer looked up from the broken blade to the night sky above, the great river of stars, running a hand over the cool skin of her scalp. *Every star a soul,* her mother had told her. The souls could guide you home. Her father had taught her the names the Baal-spawn gave, meaningless patterns read into the sky. The wheel, the goat, the sea serpent, on and on, Char the Warrior. The Baal-spawn read pattern in everything. Ashbringer blinked and lowered her gaze from the souls of her ancestors, ashamed.

'I am sorry, Highmothers,' she said, her voice weak, 'I have failed you yet again.'

The Highmothers were silent, save Willow. Highmother Willow was the eldest of them, leader of the Orubor enclave that was her namesake. Like the others she sat cross-legged on the soft bed of grass and flowers that covered the clearing.

'Child,' she said, 'none expected success. You hunt Deathless. One who has power beyond any man who has ever lived. Only Anshuka's intervention stopped him before. It has been three hundred and twelve years since the Ferron Empire fell, and still he wanders, still he seeks. He is bound by the curse of the bear-mother to endure, until he can be punished. He will face judgement. Tell us what happened.'

Ashbringer nodded solemnly and pulled her cloak tighter. It was a cold night, and whilst the towering pines surrounding them blocked the worst of the wind, she was tired.

'I found him south and east, this time,' she started, 'near the border of Isken. It was Moonday, market day for the Isken, and I knew he would seek information and supplies. I'd spent flower and flame following rumour and scant sign, but come harvest I knew I was closing in. South of the Cimber hills at the border of Isken stand the Watchful Brothers. Two statues, each a hundred feet tall. The Ferron built them when Isken bowed; one is a Ferron noble, a hand raised in welcome, the other arm heavy with scrolls and fruit and coin. The brother boon. The other is a Ferron knight, armoured, grim-faced. They are seamless, heavy black rock the same as the Ferron slave roads and the overseers' forts they built themselves across old Undalor.'

Highmother Beech handed Ashbringer a wooden cup full of steaming tea, and she gratefully drank. She closed her eyes.

'At the foot of the Watchful Brothers, the Undal trade with the Isken. There is no town there, on the border, but every day traders come from Wedderburn or nearer villages on the Undal side and Flous-tar on the Isken side and a great market appears. The Isken are meticulous in noting what enters their realm. The Undal act as they always do, indifferent until someone impinges the freedom of one of their traders. Deathless was there. He looks the same as last time, the same as ever. Green robes, a green cloak. He has swapped his eyepatch for a cloth strip. His skin is the same dark brown as usual, not lightened like it was at the time of the incident in Fallow Fen. I caught sight of a forearm, and his rune tattoos are still in place, though faded. A heavy black moustache and black hair streaked with grey knotted and twisted into long locks he ties behind his head. He was seeking supplies, but also rumours and information. Apparently orbs of light have been seen at night far over the Wind Sea, over the Tullioch clan waters. He sought rumour of those and spent coin freely. I am not sure what he wanted with this information, or what this means, Highmothers.'

Ashbringer kept her eyes closed and felt the heat of the fire against her face. She did not tell them how he seemed utterly unsurprised and unafraid. She did not mention his mocking smile. She opened her eyes and looked at the Highmothers one by one.

'I trailed him, and when we were on the periphery of the market, behind some lumber wagons, I passed down the decree of the bear-mother. For his crimes, his life. I struck at his neck, and he did not resist, but... the blade broke. He was unharmed. He allowed me to live, again.'

The Highmothers stared at her, and Highmother Ash lit a pipe and swore softly.

'Orbs of fire, Ferron's ire,' Highmother Ash intoned, and the others nodded solemnly.

'Deathless,' she said, 'always it has been this. I am sorry, granddaughter. Sorry for this burden.'

Ashbringer bowed her head.

'We cannot keep doing this,' Highmother Beech said, and the others turned cold eyes to her. Orubor eyes with no pupil or iris, each a different shade, each marbled with insinuations of colour and shadow. Eyebrows were raised at her proclamation.

'What do you mean, Highmother Beech?' asked Highmother Elm. 'We were given this task by Anshuka herself. To cease our efforts is heresy.'

Highmothers Elm, Ash, Beech, Oak, and Pine all began to talk at once. Ashbringer stared at the broken blade in her hand and felt her mouth go dry.

'Calm,' said Highmother Willow, 'calm.'

The women stilled and, in the forest, an owl called out. Highmother Willow looked up at the rocky outcrop to their north, towering over the pines and blocking out the stars on the northern horizon.

'Orbs of fire, Ferron's ire. Deathless must be brought to justice,' she said. 'In this none disagree. The runesmiths of Elm and Beech will reforge the sword, and we will try again.

In the meantime, however, Ashbringer is a resource we must not waste, and we must find the truth of these rumours.'

Ashbringer lifted her gaze and the green of Highmother Willow's eyes seemed to pierce straight to her core. The other Highmothers muttered their assent to Willow's plan.

'Ashbringer,' she said, 'you are a weapon of the Orubor. You are Anshuka's weapon in this world, her waking claw. You are the eyes of the Orubor beyond our border. If Deathless seeks information on these orbs of light, we shall know why.

'Orbs of fire; this is not an unknown enemy to us,' Highmother Willow continued, and Ashbringer heard pain in her voice. 'Our memories go further than Baal's children. Before the empress and the wolf Lothal enslaved half the world, Ferron built himself an empire in the west. Orbs of light, wands of fire and death, power beyond anything the empress and Deathless ever wielded when they went to war with the world. Power to call the judges to him. If the orbs of Ferron have returned, we must prepare ourselves for worse to follow.'

On the fire a log cracked, and a plume of sparks flew upward. Around them, the tall pines of southern Orubor pressed in close, a familiar and calming presence.

Ashbringer held the broken blade and turned to the south, towards the distant Wind Sea and the broken Tullioch Shard beyond.

'Rest tonight, Ashbringer,' said Highmother Ash.

'Seek the truth of the orbs among the Tullioch,' said Highmother Elm.

'Hide your skin, hide your teeth, hide your eye,' said Highmother Oak.

'Anshuka remembers, and we remember,' said Highmother Beech.

'If Deathless seeks it, we shall find it first,' said Highmother Pine.

'You are our eye and our blade, Ashbringer. Take the eye of the forest to the land of Baal's children, and the Tullioch beyond. We will reforge the blade, stronger again, ever stronger,' said Highmother Willow.

Ashbringer nodded, feeling the forest floor beneath her bare feet, the presence of life all around, the weight of Anshuka's will. She gazed at the mountain, the rock and soil and tree and grass and root and stone that covered her sleeping god, and she bared her teeth.

'I will find the truth of the orbs of fire,' she said, bowing her head in deference, 'and then I will kill Tullen One-Eye.'

~

Floré washed herself. With a wet cloth pressed against her face she allowed herself a long moment of silence and stillness, pressing her hands against her eyes. She had been awake far longer in the rotstorm, and in preparation before; days and days at a time with only snatched moments of sleep, functioning on fear and desperation. She could feel it now, the heightening edge, but knew it was a lie. She felt the wisp of a cold draught running over her wet body, heard birds landing on the loch, and her body felt receptive to the world, but her mind was slowing.

Floré stood a long moment on the cold flagstones, naked and silent, eyes closed. She was trying to feel which of her wounds was open enough to need care before she left.

She dried herself and pulled on some of the miller's

clothes. The woman was a similar height, though more curved than Floré. The clothes were adequate but close in places, loose in others. She went and found a healer's kit in the store of Stormguard miscellany the captain had kept in his back room. She wrapped a bandage tight around her head, and then slipped a dressing under her shirt and pressed it against her shoulder. There were some basic swords and weaponry in the storeroom, but she knew he must have some reserves held back.

Tyr had fought at least a campaign in the Lancers before coming back to Hookstone forest and had acquitted himself well if rumour in the village was to be believed. If he was a lancer and a captain, he would have a sword-knot. If he had a sword-knot, she was duty-bound to return it to his superior along with his rank badge.

She checked his living room and back room and kitchen but there was no obvious place where such mementoes might hide. Floré went upstairs to the captain's bedroom and found a wooden chest sat beneath a knitted rug in the corner of the room, and inside she found his treasures. A locket full with a knot of dark, thick hair wrapped in tissue paper; a sword-knot of black, with a yellow streak; a silvered dagger with no rune; a pair of knuckledusters; and finally, a faded blue-and-gold Stormguard Lancer tabard.

There was also an obsidian spearhead, still attached to the top two inches of a broken spear haft, and Floré laughed aloud, turning it over in her hands. She picked up the sword-knot and considered it for a long moment before pocketing it. Black meant he had fought in the second Antian campaign and the yellow streak... the siege of Aber-Ouse? Her Watch Commander at Storm Castle XII had told her tales of that siege: sickness, starvation, fighting from the sewers to the tower tops of the mountain town. Floré considered the tabard and the weapons and the rumours and tried to picture a young Captain Tyr half-starved and street fighting an Antian warrior, a wild-haired dog-man with ceramic armour and obsidian spear. She smiled.

Cuss was in the kitchen fussing with her pack when she came downstairs. On the table sat her clean jerkin, though she could see now several holes in it. Her sword sheathed and belt ready, her gauntlets free from the worst of the gore but unpolished. With them was a clean Stormguard Forest Watch tabard, and sat on top of it her badge of rank and Captain Tyr's alongside it. In the Stormguard Lancers and Commandos, their ranks were sewn into the tabard and etched into their plate armour, but in the Forest Watch the simple rank buckles threaded into belts were deemed enough. Floré looked at the green-and-gold tabard and remembered the day she had been given the red and gold, stood between Janos and Benazir, a lightning-torn sky, Commander Starbeck placing a hand on her shoulder.

They had graduated together after four long years of training as cadets, Benazir, Janos, and her. The night before graduation, there was a tradition all the cadets did every year. The commander would pretend not to know, but really it could only happen with his support. After nightfall, the cadets would sneak up the garrison, past the commander's office and the primus-mage's rooms and into the tallest tower. The tower top was covered with a tiled pyramid, below which was a space open on all sides to the storm and the countryside. This was where the commander could survey his domain, and if the weather was clear you could see the dark blurs of the next Stormcastle in each direction down the wall. There were twenty of them graduating that year from Stormcastle XII. They lit a fire in a stone hearth placed there to warm the commander's own feet, and sat high above the castle and waited for the storm.

Floré and Benazir sat on a stone bench drinking wine from clay mugs, and Janos had approached them. He was skinny then, hair cut short.

'A peace offering,' he had said with a faltering smile, proffering a dark bottle forward. Floré had nodded and held out her cup, but Benazir turned away from him.

'The mighty skein-mage speaks, Floré,' she had said. 'We should get parchment and quill, make notes of his wisdom.'

Floré had laughed, but drank what Janos had offered. Benazir had turned back to Janos and wrinkled her nose.

'You are still here. Is something wrong, mighty skein-mage? Is there something we mortals could possibly help you with?'

Janos had sat down on the next stone bench along and looked out at the storm. As they had sat drinking, it had slowly ebbed outward from the swamp and mire until it almost encompassed the Stormwall. The winds had been strong, and Floré remembered the black and purple and red of the clouds, writhing together in the darkness.

'I'm sorry, Benazir,' he had said, but Benazir just shook her head in response. Then the storm sparked, and lightning struck.

The first blast arced down from the rotstorm into the mire beyond the wall, a bolt of fractal purple dancing downward. Thunder engulfed them all, and the wind howling around the tower pulled at the cadets. It was time to begin.

One of the lads from Brek got to his feet and went to the rampart and spat over the wall towards the storm, and then took a huge pull of wine from his cup.

'For Brek!' he said, and they all cheered. It was another minute before the next bolt hit, and the next cadet stepped forward. She spat over the wall as the thunder was still echoing in Floré's ears. She couldn't remember what place that cadet had named. Slowly, as the lightning hit, they took their turns. When it was Floré, she spat, downed her cup of wine, and then turned and spat that too, into the storm.

'For Tollen!' she screamed, and she had never screamed so loud in her life. The cadets roared with her.

Benazir was unsteady on her feet when it was her turn, drunk and reeling in the wind, and Floré had to help her stand straight at the wall. A bolt of arcing light and heat burst down from the roiling cloud above and hit the swamp east of the wall, and before the thunder even reached them a second bolt in almost the same spot. Benazir waited for the thunder to roll over and then she spat into the storm.

'For Fallow Fen,' she said, and took a sip of her drink. The cadets didn't cheer for that. For Fallow Fen they all raised their glasses.

Floré remembered her arm around Benazir on the stone bench, the cold wind whipping rain through the sides of the tower. Janos was one of the last to go. He waited for a bolt, and then he spat and he mumbled, his words lost to the wind and thunder, and he drank and sat down.

'Skein-mage can't even yell right,' Benazir said, and Floré had sighed.

'You could give him a chance,' she had said, and Benazir had laughed and taken another drink.

The next morning, in the cold of the courtyard in front of the Stormgate, Floré stood in her cadets' tabard with Janos on one side and Benazir on the other and Starbeck walked the line. He stopped at each one, and said something.

'You do our people proud,' he said to Benazir, who grimaced and nodded.

'You will keep our people safe,' he said to Floré, and she remembered she had tears in her eyes. His hand went to her shoulder, and she blinked them away. The sergeant following Starbeck handed her the tabard of the Stormguard Commando, blood red with a trim of gold and a bolt of lightning across the chest. Starbeck moved on.

'The pattern will protect us,' he had said to Janos, and afterward, when it was all done, the cadets had roared and hugged and twirled each other, and she and Benazir had spent a long moment of silence together. They had made it. She had hugged Janos then for the first time, the prickly skein-mage who was always so easily offended, who bickered endlessly with Benazir on any point under the sun.

'We made it,' she had said, and he had smiled at her.

In Captain Tyr's house in Hookstone, Floré clutched the fabric of the Forest Watch tabard in her hands and pictured that smile. She heard a scuff and realised Cuss was standing behind her, waiting for some sort of order.

'Do you know how to stitch a wound, Cuss?' she asked, reaching her hand to her shoulder, and he shook his head rapidly, his eyes widening. Floré rolled her shoulder and grimaced.

'Berren's blood, bugger it then,' she said. 'I've wasted enough time.'

She pulled the jerkin on, and it caught her bandaged ear,

and it pressed at her padded shoulder. She tied it tight. She donned the tabard and sword belt and looped Captain Tyr's sheathed silver dagger opposite her sword after checking its blade. It had no fire-sigil, unlike the blade she had passed to Yselda, but a well-worn wooden grip and a well-kept blade. She considered giving the blade to Cuss, as she had given her own dagger to Yselda, but decided against it. Better he run than think he stood a chance against a demon.

She slipped the rank badges onto her belt and pulled it tight and then slipped on her gauntlets and grabbed her pack. At the door of the house she paused and turned to the boy. He gazed at the floor. She grabbed his chin and forced his face up.

'Cuss,' she said. 'They took Marta, as well as Petron.'

The boy's eyes started to water. Floré let go of his face and handed him the heavy knuckledusters she had found upstairs.

'I'm going to get the garrison,' she said, voice flat, 'and then I'm going to find them, Cuss. They're alive, and I will find them.'

She strode away. Across the green, she could see the Goat and Whistle where Yselda stood by two horses. She turned instead towards the lane with the hedgerow so tall, towards the smoke that lazily spiralled upward from her own home. She glanced back briefly and saw in the doorway of the captain's house Cuss staring down at the knuckledusters and rubbing a hand over the bandaged wounds on his chest.

'They are alive,' she said to herself again as the boy slipped his fingers into the knuckledusters, feeling the weight of them. The scant few dozen steps down the lane from the green to her home felt like the path to the gallows.

On either side the ancient hedgerows bordering the path loomed over her, and then there was the gate and lilac blooming in bursts beside it.

She stood at the gate and felt tears rolling down her cheeks. The cottage was destroyed. The base stones were still in place, but the roof had collapsed into ash and cinders. The door lay in pieces on the path outside the front of the house, and the window shutters were either burned away or lying broken on the ground. Her home was ash. A tree lay half through one wall, and the forest behind the house was a chaos of trunk and branch, whole pines uprooted and fallen into one another.

Floré pushed through the gate and stepped forward and saw the whole west wall had collapsed. She tried to picture Marta, her little Marta. She tried to picture her cool kitchen and the stuffed chair by the hearth, the bed she and Janos had slept in every night now for five long years in Hasselberry. *Guard him well,* Starbeck had said, but what was there to guard from on the banks of Loch Hassel? Glinting in the grass she found a pewter spoon, flung from the kitchen by whatever force had destroyed the house. The orbs: the orbs had destroyed her home, killed her husband, taken her child. *Crow-man,* Janos had said, and she knew exactly what that meant. It meant Ferron. Rust-folk. The enemy.

Floré placed a hand on the doorframe and then she turned and walked down the garden path, over the splintered remnants of the front door. Her view here was the same as it ever had been, a gate and a hedgerow, lilac on all sides. She pushed the gate open and snagged a sprig of lilac and remembered Janos the night before, leaning there, smiling at her. Alone in the forest, Floré smelled the sprig of lilac and sat on the ground and wept.

Later, clear-eyed, when she made it across the village green Floré mounted immediately the horse she had taken from Larchford and made no mention of Yselda doing the same on the horse next to her. The girl had been waiting grim-faced, a pack by her side, bow and quiver on her back and sword on her belt, ready for an argument. Floré didn't bother. One girl would make no difference, here or there. All that mattered was Marta. Seeing the two of them prepare to leave, Tellen approached. Floré checked her reins and adjusted her jerkin.

'Yselda is coming with me,' Floré said, and he nodded.

'Ride well, Captain Artollen,' Tellen said, and Floré heard those same four words in Janos's voice, in Benazir's, in Commander Starbeck's. She felt her right arm start to shake and her heart begin to pound. There was only ever one way to calm it.

Action.

She kicked her horse and sped into the forest, and did not look back.

6

GRIM BINDLE

'Command is a duty to those in your care, and a duty to the Stormguard. I send these young men and women to their deaths in a wall of lightning, a nightmare of colour and sound, acid clouds. I do this because what emerges is stronger than what grows within. We strike it before it can grow strong. When the wet-lightning of the rotstorm builds, there is a moment of charge on the ground before the beam strikes. This is when you thrust your sword into the dirt and you roll away. The Stormguard act; we do not react.' – Private Diary, Commander Salem Starbeck

Floré rode hard and did not wait for Yselda. The girl was a less experienced rider, but the Hookstone forest road from Hasselberry to Hookstone Town was well maintained, a long arcing curve. Side-tracks led off to logging grounds, a quarry, and a dozen farmsteads, but nothing Yselda would mistakenly follow over the wide and maintained forest road, and so Floré felt no need to wait. She did not want company.

The horse pushed at the world and sped forward. The Hookstone forest was thick with pine and ferns, and the road was littered with dead needles that muffled the sound of the hoof beats. She kept a sharp eye on the woods for timber wolves, but it was unlikely even a pack would harry a rider on horseback, especially when Larchford was an unguarded and uncontested meal. Floré rode and did not think about Marta and Janos, about Petron, about the people who made up so much of her life in tiny moments of shared company in Hasselberry, who even then were being dragged to the guardhouse by Tellen.

Instead she composed in her head her report to the commander of the Hookstone garrison, Bardon Mears. Hours passed and the sun set far to the west. In the east, darkness spread over Father's Pate and the distant Cimber hills. Floré felt herself tiring, and again and again went over her report, always changing words and forcing herself to memorise the new version. It was a trick Benazir had taught her, taught to her in turn by some schoolmaster in Fallow Fen. *An occupied mind has no time for troubles,* Benazir would say, sharpening her runed silver knife, or practising the same movements over and over in the training yard. When the road occasionally crested hills, Floré found her eyes lingering over views of those western plains awash in the amber dying light, the faint glow of Undal City beyond, and to the south the forest began to thin. There was salt on the air. The Wind Sea was close, and before then Hookstone Town. She could not hear Yselda behind her. *Commander Mears,* she began again in her head—

Her eyes caught the unnatural movement, and in a heartbeat one hand was already moving for her sword.

A goblin leapt from the bushes alongside the road and threw a crude spear and Floré leaned forward instinctively, digging her heels into her horse and pushing it to go faster. She was past the slavering monster in three heartbeats. The spear missed her by six feet at least. She was about to push forward when a second spear flew past her from the side and she remembered Yselda an unknown distance behind. *Goblins on the Hookstone road,* she thought. *Anshuka be bloody praised.* Most goblins spawned in the rotstorm, but whenever a rare storm surge burst forward from the rotstorm and crossed the protectorate, raining down acid and wet-lightning, seeds were sown and blight-nodes would bubble beneath the ground. From them would climb goblins, or worse.

Sometimes, rarely, they would sit dormant a month, a year, a decade, and from them, goblins and trollspawn and rottrolls and worse would emerge. *A gift from old Ferron,* the farmers called it. Every farmer had a heavy axe and shield, or old longsword they could take to hand as needs be. A nest of teeth and skin and claws growing in the earth like a tumour until the horror within found form and crawled out, in an instant, or a span or season. Floré wheeled the horse around in a quick, tight turn.

Three goblins spilled out from the dense undergrowth at the side of the road and stood in a loose rank across the road, squinting against the last vestiges of sunlight cutting through the trees. Ranging three to four feet tall, they raised their spears and screamed at her, shark-like teeth and lolling tongues below black orb eyes with no pupils, their smooth earless heads smeared in dirt and viscera. They were dressed in ragged animal skins that still bore wet flesh where they had been crudely harvested, and the sunset gleamed faintly across their rough, sandpaper-like skin, a dappled grey and blue. A fourth was half in the bushes, gazing out. The goblin in the bushes and one of the trio in the road held crudely hewn wooden spears, more sharpened branches really, and the two who had thrown their spears were reaching for stone knives secreted in their animal skins. They gabbled at her in Ferron.

'*Eat your heart,*' is what Floré caught – her Ferron was rusty, and they spoke over each other. Her horse whickered and sidestepped. The tongue was harsh and guttural, but Floré always thought of the language as refined. Her Ferron teacher had been a noble of Ossen-Tyr with an accent to match, reciting epic poems in the dark stone classroom below Stormcastle XIV. *Janos wrote me a love poem in Ferron,* she thought.

Her nostrils flared and she felt a hot fury fill her at the thought of Janos. She kicked her horse forward in a burst of speed and muscle and crashed through the central trio. Two dodged, leaping aside, but the one in the middle was trampled by heavy hooves. She kept riding, and twenty yards past the dead goblin slowed her mount and leapt down, drawing her sword and slapping the horse to send it running back up the road. A mount untrained for battle was a liability in a situation like this; hopefully Yselda would catch it.

She stood for a second to take in the scene. The goblin entangled in the bushes was now free, and those unarmed had retrieved their spears. Floré raised her sword and sprinted at them before they could have time to prepare. One had run up the road and retrieved its already thrown spear and threw it again as it ran back to its brethren, and she didn't bother to dodge as it went wide. The other two were smarter, but as the spear-thrower reached for its knife Floré was already there and with a heavy swing batted two guarding spears aside. With a quick backhand she caught one of the goblins in the side of the head, her blade biting deep and lifting it off its feet. She let go of her sword and grabbed the second spear-wielding goblin's weapon by the shaft as it swung back around towards her. She wrenched it from the beast's weak grip easily and kicked out with her riding boot at the knife-wielding grey-skinned wretch slowly approaching from the left side, sending it spinning back into the dirt. With a twirl the spear was point first at its owner, and she left it embedded in the goblin's shallow chest.

Retrieving her sword from the dead goblin's head, she walked towards the one lying in the dirt.

It turned and threw its stone knife at her face, and she twitched her head to the side, the blade sailing past and into the forest. She felt the wound in her shoulder throb, and she grimaced.

'*Lightning-child, this is not your world,*' she said in old Ferron, and the goblin lurched at her. Her sword cut across and took its head off in a clean blow.

When Yselda arrived twenty minutes later with Floré's horse trailing behind her, it was to a blood-spattered road. The sun was gone and moonlight played on the fresh pools of claret. There were no bodies on the road, but Floré held a crude spear and from it four goblin heads dangled, tied on by rough twine threaded through holes she had cut in their skin.

'Thank you for getting my horse,' Floré said, mounting up as Yselda looked at her wide-eyed.

'There are goblins in the woods,' she said. 'We should ride together these last few miles.'

Yselda nodded mutely and gazed at the goblin heads, and Floré saw the girl's mouth twist with disgust. Floré mounted her horse and led on, and Yselda followed close. The four heads on the spear over Floré's shoulder jostled and bounced, dead black eyes looking out at the forest behind them.

~

The forest thinned, and soon they were riding their horses under starlight and scudding clouds, the salt breeze pressing against them from the Star Coast. They passed the outlying farmsteads and Yselda noted barred doors and chained dogs that barked as they passed. *Have the orbs been here?* The night birds called out and owls and bats cut through the sky. She thought of wolves and teeth and she and was glad to be beyond the forest.

After the forest the land was rock and scrub, but at the farmsteads rows of maintained crops cut the plateau into irregular shapes. Thick hedgerows and lonely trees separated field and farmsteads, occasional short orchards and brooks breaking the monotony. Hookstone Town sat atop a low hill behind a wooden palisade. Torches should have marked the gates, but against the speckled shade of the night the walls and watchtowers were visible only by an absence of stars.

Yselda had only been to Hookstone once before, and never outside of the palisade at night. She was tired, but the sight of the town pulled her interest; it was something to think of other than Shand's smile, the girls, something other than wolf teeth and hot blood. She rubbed her fingertips together, feeling the raw skin where her bowstring had grazed them. She remembered the feeling of letting go of the arrow; the noise of it as it sank into the wolf so very deep. Yselda blinked and made herself focus on the town, the palisade, the farms – anything and everything other than the wolves, but her fingers strayed to the knot of grey cloth tied around the pommel of her sword.

They ran the horses past the final farmsteads and headed towards the thin moat but pulled up short. Across twenty foot of thin air, the gates of Hookstone were shut. The town was low, but beyond the wooden wall she could perhaps make out the tower of the whitestaff hall, the shaman high temple, and the sharp tip of the Stormguard garrison tower. Past the town the distant sea whispered unseen.

'Berren's blood and ash and storms and shit,' Floré said, and Yselda raised her eyebrows in surprise at the language. 'Never seen the bridge up before; torches dark, bridge up. Something is wrong here.'

Yselda moved her horse closer and gazed down into the moat. Her only other trip to Hookstone had been midwinter three years past, and the water fifteen foot below had been frozen. She had dropped stones with Cuss and Petron, and watched the cracks spread from the centre. Cuss and she had made a game of it, teasing Petron, who seemed so much younger than them then, who could never drop his stones in the right place. One dropped a stone, and the others had to get theirs into the hole in the ice without cracking it any more. Now, in the depths of summer, the water buzzed with insects and reeked like a midden. She pictured Petron and ice and felt her stomach twist.

'What do we do?' she asked, turning back to the sergeant, who was already dismounting.

'We do our job. Hasselberry needs healers, guards. We need to report.'

She paused a moment and flexed her right arm, the way she did when she was angry, and then turned to Yselda.

'I need to know what they know of the orbs,' she said, and Yselda felt the hairs on the back of her neck rise at the desperation in the sergeant's tone.

The sergeant dropped the spear with the goblin heads and tied her horse to a post near the indent where the heavy bridge would fall. She pulled off her right gauntlet and stuck two fingers in her mouth, and a piercing whistle cut through the night. Two short, three long, the simple distress call taught to all cadets.

After a few seconds there was a clatter and a sally door in the watchtower next to the gates opened, a crumpled red face peering out backlit by torch.

'Moron has lit himself up,' Floré said, shaking her head. 'Judges forgive us. Remember that, girl. Never just open the bloody gate, no matter the signal. Check.'

'Who's there?' the voice called, and Yselda peered into the darkness, glaring at the shadows. The man's voice was full of fear.

'Stormguard Forest Watch, Sergeant Artollen, Hasselberry,' Floré said, and Yselda thought, *Captain Artollen, now*. Floré's voice was hard and clipped and cut through the still night. 'Lower the bridge. I need to speak to Commander Mears.'

It was an order, rather than a request. A second guard emerged and the two conferred. After a few moments, where Yselda could see the sergeant – *captain* – clenching her fists, they planted their torch into a sconce by the sally door and started heaving on coiled chains. Those chains did not lower the drawbridge and open the gate; instead they raised from the wet and murk of the moat two more wrist-thick chains. They were connected to posts buried in the thick grass on the side of the moat opposite the sally door, and matching posts anchored the chains the guards pulled, slick with scum and fetid water. When the guards pulled them taut and cleated them off, the chains crossed the moat five foot down from bridge level. Yselda got off her horse and looked at the black water below.

'Oh for pity's sake,' Floré hissed, hitting her hand against her hip, 'lower the bridge, you arses!'

She shouted that last part, but the guards ignored her. One of them clambered down and put his feet on the lower chains and pulled his torso in tight to the higher. Slowly he edged across the moat and Yselda could see the captain's growing impatience, a pacing and measured series of exhalations. Her gauntlets were back on and she tugged Tyr's rank badge from the side of her belt to the front.

The man pulled himself up the moat edge finally, out of breath, wiping slime onto his trousers.

'Evening, Sergeant,' he began, and Floré cut him off.

'I said open the gate.' Her voice was ice. 'Not arse around playing siege.'

The man opened his mouth to speak but Floré silenced him with a half-raised hand and picked up her grim bindle of goblin heads and shouldered it.

'An officer of the Stormguard ordered you to open the gate. We've been awake two days, dozens are dead, and I don't have time for this nonsense. Tell your man to lower the gate. I need to see Commander Mears, now.'

If the man was cowed, he didn't show it. Instead, he glanced at the goblin heads and sighed and looked out towards the distant forest.

'The orbs came to Hasselberry?' he said, and the look on their faces answered the question. He nodded. He wasn't a handsome man, or well built. His skin was dark, his hair and beard darker, and his teeth were crooked yellow stumps. He looked tired, and Floré noticed that his grey City Watch tabard was tainted with ash, and maybe worse. 'That changes things, I guess. You aren't the only ones having a bad day, so maybe stow the tone. Mears is dead. You want Bannon, she's at the smithy last I heard.'

'Mears is dead?' Floré said, turning to look at the dark town. 'Here too?'

He went to run a hand through his hair and stopped himself when his slime-coated fingers got close. He sighed again heavily, not making eye contact.

'For what it's worth, I'm sorry,' he said, and then turned and clapped three times fast. Across the moat the other guard hollered an order, and the bridge began to lower. The gates opened and, beyond them, Yselda and Floré could flickering braziers lighting rubble and ash and ruin. Yselda felt a weight in her stomach. *Is it everywhere?* They mounted their horses and Floré led on into the silence and dark of Hookstone.

~

Petron dreamt again of a spire of gold, nestled in grey mountains and shrouded in mist. He was still there in the cell of dark polished stone and the blindfolded white-haired woman asked him questions, but he could not understand what she said, as if his head was deep underwater. The dream seemed endless, and then there was darkness, and then a cold that bit his bones.

He awoke naked and wet, his mind already within the skein. His head ached. The skein lay over his ordinary senses like a film of oil on clear water beneath, distorting. Sight and sound were diffuse, tendrils of skein energy writhing and growing, fading, entangling. The old woman from his dream had removed her blindfold and she stared at him as he floated taut in the centre of a bare chamber. Three others were with her, staring silent, two men and a woman. They were aged, wrinkled and wizened and half bent, white hair and black robes. The ceiling glowed dimly, bare and seamless, a yellow light. They paced around him and he could sense them with his eyes and ears, could even smell lemon and oiled leather, but in the skein they were utterly absent. The skein itself was a fractured thing, hints of pattern obscured or broken.

'How old are you, boy?' one of them said in Isken, and Petron spat and cursed. He went on a long time, through all four Judges and their excrement, through every word he'd heard a drunken millworker mutter. Finally he was spent, breathing hard, and still he floated. He could just about turn his head and could speak, but any other movement was impossible. He felt as if every inch of him was bound.

In the blank stone wall, a hole grew from nothing and stretched organically, asymmetrically, the stone melting back as if liquid. Through the opening a hooded man stepped. He was tall, cloaked and robed in black, with gloves and boots of brown leather. At his black belt, a dagger with a handle of white twisted wood or bone, a green gemstone at the pommel, a blade dark as night bare against leather and cloth.

'Hello, young fellow,' the man said. Petron strained his eyes in the dim light and tried to disconnect from the skein to see the man better. Like the old people, the man was an oddity in the skein. The pattern moved around him and seemed fractured and chaotic where it neared him. Petron could see the skein as he normally could, but with these people nearby he couldn't seem to grasp any patterns or make any sense of it all. His head pounded, every heartbeat bringing a stab of pain at his temples. The figures' limbs and fingers were oddly jointed and overlong. Petron could feel himself sweating, breathing hard, could feel muscles twitching and pulling but no movement. The figure, a man if that was what it was, circled the floating boy and then waved a hand, the old women and men left through the hole in the wall, and Petron was left in silence.

The man leaned over so his head was above Petron's face, and pulled his hood back. The face below was benign in feature; soft, pale hair framing a smiling face.

The boy stopped breathing when he saw the eyes though, for in beautiful green irises pupils danced and writhed and split and reformed, coruscating and bursting into fractals.

'My name is Varratim,' the man said. 'Don't be afraid. Tell me. Tell me. There was confusion. I was not expecting him to be there, and two of my kin made... a mistake, perhaps. What is your father called?'

Petron screwed up his face.

'My father is dead, and I'll not speak his name to you, demon.'

Varratim laughed, a soft noise. The eyes writhed, scrutinising, and Petron tried to recoil.

'I think you are too old,' he said slowly, 'to be the child of the Salt-Man. Yes, yes, too old unless you were begat at the Stormwall. Any child of his must be able to touch the skein, so if not you, is it the little girl? Marta? She won't speak to me.'

Petron tried to hurl his whole body towards Varratim, and his floating form twitched forward.

'You hurt her I'll... I'll... I'll kill you.'

Varratim smiled. 'Good! Very good. A skein-mage in training eh? A disciple of Skein-wreck Janos, the mighty Salt-Man? What secrets did he tell you, little one? How to take, without giving?'

Varratim trailed a gloved hand across Petron's arm as he spoke and the boy shivered.

Janos? He didn't understand. Sergeant Artollen's husband was a poet. The quiet man, who tended their garden. Petron had never seen him so much as lift a sword, let alone touch the skein. A skein-wreck was a skein-mage of horrible power, like Tullen One-Eye or Ihm-Phogn from the stories. A skein-wreck destroyed the Tullioch spire, broke a coral spire the size of a mountain clean in half!

Janos baked pies with the apples from his garden. He taught Cuss how to fly-fish, and brought their mother pinches of spice wrapped in wax paper, and dishes of extra food when he made too much. He helped the boys chop wood last autumn. He taught Petron how to bake his first apple pie one long wet afternoon when the sergeant was busy, the whitestaff ill, his mother tired. When the wolves were in the wood, or goblins and rottrolls spawned from a surge, he stayed in the Goat and Whistle whilst Sergeant Artollen led a posse. The idea of Janos as a skein-wreck!

Petron laughed, and laughed, and Varratim stood up and his face went still.

'I will know what he taught you, boy. I will know every word.'

Petron focused on the skein and probed, and looked for a knot, looked for others, looked for pattern. There was only a fractured chaos, shadows of shape that slipped from him. Nothing. Nothing. Nothing. And yet... Marta was alive, somewhere. He had to keep this creature from her.

'I'll tell you none of my father's secrets, monster,' he said, and tried to sound convincing.

Varratim considered him a long time, and then looked at the wall. His pupils continued to gyrate and mosaic, shrunk and grew, spun, ever moving. Except for the pupils he was still, tense. He smiled an easy smile again.

'I will not torture a child, Petron. I am not a monster. We will speak, and in time you will understand the wrongs your father did. I understand he likely told you of his campaigns and triumphs against the rust-folk, but I would ask you keep an open mind. There are always two sides to a story, and where I am from the Salt-Man is a tale to scare children; to humble the strong; to caution the bold. His death is a tragedy to you, but there will be dancing in the streets when news reaches home.'

Varratim gestured and Petron fell hard to the cold floor.

'You will be brought clothes, and food. Books, perhaps. We will speak again.'

He left as he had arrived, and behind him the stone wall closed and Petron was alive, alone. He let the skein unhook from his mind, and the effort of having it active for so long made his muscles shiver with fatigue. He pictured Cuss and his mother and his sister and wrapped his arms around his legs and cried for a long time.

INTERLUDES:
SUFFER NO TYRANT

HISTORY OF THE SKEIN-WRECKS

'*Before the whitestaffs began to self-mythologise, there were four: Mistress Tree, Master Soil, Master Wall, and Mistress Water. Four mighty skein-users, slaves of Ferron, four who rose from shackles and helped guide the Undal Council in revolution. They did not throw fire, or break stone. They listened to the skein. They awoke the sleeping bear and brought forth the storm.*' – History of the Skein-Wrecks, Campbell Torbén of Aber-Ouse

Janos spent every moment of free time in the orphanage at Inverbar studying the skein, wandering the libraries of the shaman monastery. When he passed his twelfth summer the abbot himself wrote a recommendation for the master of the whitestaffs, and Brother Guhn accompanied Janos south to Ossen-Tyr for the high harvest festival when the whitestaff would be considering applicants to head to the island of Iskander to serve the protectorate.

Janos walked with Brother Guhn, who was not a kindly

man. The boy tried to speak of what they passed, the people on the road, the broken fire-blackened stone of the ruined Antian wall, the marshes becoming glens becoming hills as they neared Ossen-Tyr. Brother Guhn would speak of only one topic, that which he had devoted his life to: the Judges.

'You know the bogle down in the old orchard, boy?' he asked, and Janos scuffed his feet on the dirt road, kicking away stones. He hated being called boy. They were days still from Ossen-Tyr, and the road was quiet, hemmed at the sides by thick woods of birch and ash.

'I know it, Brother Guhn,' he dutifully replied. 'The rabbit bigger than the other rabbits, with the green eyes. Sister Marin told me it was just a hare.'

Guhn sniffed at that. Janos was looking, ever looking at what they passed even after three days on the road. He had never seen hills like these before, or trees so straight and tall and so lush. Not at all like the gnarled swamp trees that rose from the salt marsh around Inverbar.

'Sister Marin,' Guhn said, 'should spend more time thinking on the Judges and less time fretting over villagers with scraped knees. The bogle of Inverbar forest is not a hare; it is a power. Every place has a power, boy, every place in the world. The skein is a web connecting all things, but some places are a nexus. A joining point. In a place like that, a power may come to be. Have they taught you this yet? Do you understand?'

Janos squinted at a squirrel hanging upside down on a grand oak, twenty feet in the air. Its ears were fluffier than the Inverbar squirrels, and its coat had a black-and-grey mottle that was much different to the red squirrels in the north.

'I understand, Brother Guhn. So the judges are big bogles, not hares?'

Guhn clipped his ear, of course.

'More than that, boy,' he said, 'much more than that.'

The brother ceased his sermon, and Janos went back to thinking on skein-wrecks, trying to remember his stories. Tullen One-Eye had burned down the old town of Ossen when Ferron conquered Undalor, but since the rotstorm and the fall of the empire he had never heard mention of the town in any of the skein-mage and skein-wreck stories he had read. The old town of Ossen was a motte and bailey fort of a corrupt Undalor Chieftain, Ossen of the Ice, but Tullen One-Eye had got himself invited to dinner and then... *rescued a princess? Something like that.* Janos couldn't remember, but the story had ended with Tullen riding away on his horse Thunderbolt, a princess on the saddle behind him and the town aflame on the horizon. Sister Marin let him read the old Tullen stories, but once Brother Sebalt had seen him reading a copy of Campbell Torbén's *History of the Skein-Wrecks* and had made Janos spend two hours scrubbing chamber pots, and write a three-page essay on the crimes of the skein-wreck of Ferron.

The pair travelled onward, wending up through the hills leading the donkey Sweet Jon and the small cart of trade goods from the monastery behind, tapestries and intricately illuminated manuscripts piled next to shaman idols blessed by the abbot. They camped by a stream, and Janos watched the stars reel above. He saw a shooting star head towards the coast far to the south. In the west, he convinced himself he could see a faint glow, the mighty rotstorm, Anshuka's wrath incarnate. Before sleep took him he mumbled a prayer to Anshuka to watch over his parents, wherever they were. Janos slept on the hard ground and dreamt of a princess on a horse, and a town aflame on the horizon.

The next day they reached Ossen-Tyr and Janos was overwhelmed. Despite his distaste for Guhn's endless droning about mighty Anshuka, he found himself sticking close to the shaman as they entered the town. Guards in grey tabards wielding tall spears manned the gates, a stout man with a huge red beard and pale skin and a tall woman with tightly braided hair and light brown skin like his own. He smiled nervously at her and she smiled back and nodded her head. Both guards wore chain mail beneath their grey tabards and seemed alert as they cast their eyes over everyone entering and leaving through the city gate. Brother Guhn led Sweet Jon the donkey up into the town, and Janos scurried behind.

'Ferron architecture,' Guhn said, sniffing and pointing at a huge stone building a few streets away. It towered over the nearer wooden houses and shops, a monolith of grey stone similar to the city walls but utterly distinct from the rough timber of the more modern buildings. They headed straight towards it. The streets thronged with people, revellers preparing for the High Harvest festivities. Janos remembered High Harvest at home, his sisters and his mother preparing intricate breads, a day free from farm work. High Harvest at the shaman monastery in Inverbar was a solemn affair, with long readings from the Book of Judges and recitations of the lessons of the god-bear. Here, people laughed and smiled, sang. They passed drunk men and women even though the sun was not yet high, and

Janos found himself blushing as a chain of dancing maidens passed him in a swirl of twirling skirts and hair and smiles.

'Boy!' Guhn called, and Janos realised he had fallen behind. Dutifully he rushed through the crowd to join Brother Guhn and Sweet Jon.

'Focus your mind, boy. The abbot wants you off to Iskander to think big thoughts. To do that, you need to impress this whitestaff. So stop smiling at girls and start thinking on Anshuka's twelve blessings.'

Hours later and Janos was sat on a cold stone bench inside the grey building. Guhn had deposited him at the heavy wooden door with the abbot's letter.

'Anshuka bless you, boy,' Guhn said as he made to depart. 'If it goes well, then you go well, and know our prayers go with you. If not, I'll be at the shaman temple. You should be able to find it easy enough – the tall tower. Ask a guard if you cannot find it. Either way, Judges guide you. The abbot has great faith in you. Do not let him down.'

The old man stalked away, half-dragging Sweet Jon and the cart behind. He clearly didn't want anything to do with the whitestaffs, a point he had made at least once a day on their journey.

'The skein is for the Judges,' he had said, over and over, and Janos had nodded. Now, alone in the stone corridor sat on the cold bench with a small pack with all his worldly belongings inside, Janos allowed himself a breath, a breath free of the judgement and constant critique of the shamans.

The dark wooden door in front of him creaked open, and behind it in a dimly lit room an old man sat. He couldn't see who had opened the door. Was this the skein? Had he just *seen* somebody using the skein?

'Enter, child,' the man said, and Janos stepped through. The room was lit by three candles in ornate stands, and the floor was covered in heavy rugs. The man wore elaborate white robes that engulfed him as he sat in a high-backed stuffed chair, a book resting on his lap. His head was completely bald, but from his ears great tufts of grey hair spiralled outward, and his eyebrows were thick and wild. His eyes were dark beads atop a short nose, and his skin was wrinkled and weathered. Janos felt the blood start coursing around his body as he saw the green amulet, *a real Riven amulet,* on the man's chest. It was a large stone of jade, shaped like a river pebble, and a chain of silver encased it. Casually leaning against the chair was a staff of grey wood, smooth and thick. The man leaned forward and squinted.

'Hmmph. Ona stock, by those eyes,' he said, his voice deep and slow. 'You have a letter, I'm told?'

Janos nodded and handed the letter across and then stood very still. The man inspected the seal and then tore open the envelope, his eyes scanning the paper.

'Sharp mind, keen interest in the skein, orphan, and so on. Janos, eh? Janos of Garioch, Janos of Inverbar. And you want to be Janos of Iskander – is that it?'

Janos nodded and the man glowered.

'I'm busy today, Janos of Inverbar. Tell me three things. Firstly, have you ever used the skein? Secondly, why are the whitestaffs important? And thirdly, who is the greatest skein user to ever live? Answer me these three questions. Be succinct. Be complete. You may proceed.'

Janos felt his stomach roil. He had expected this.

'Thank you for the opportunity, sir,' he started, and the old man waved his hand.

'The questions, boy,' he said, and Janos winced. *Boy. Always boy.*

'Sir,' he began, 'firstly, I have not used the skein. We have no whitestaff in Inverbar who might have taught me. However, I have focused all of my studies on the skein and its application and practice. Regarding your second question, sir, the whitestaff order were instrumental in establishing the Undal Protectorate from the slaves freed after the Ferron Empire fell; their role is to advise the protectorate on threats only the skein can combat, to seek out those who might aid the protectorate as skein-mages or as whitestaffs, and to aid and support the people of the Undal Protectorate. To lead through servitude.'

The old man was staring languidly at Janos, who took a breath and glanced at his feet, forced himself to unclench his hands.

'Thirdly, the greatest skein-user to ever live is debatable depending on how you define the word greatest, but Mistress Water—'

'No.'

Janos blinked rapidly and bit his lip.

'No, sir?'

'No, Janos of Garioch, Janos of Inverbar. Semantics will not see you through this. I don't care how well you can argue. A man can argue any point, if he is clever enough. I can see you are clever. I want to know how you think. Bear in mind I am a whitestaff, boy. I can read a lie like a sailor reads the sea. Every applicant says Mistress Water. Answer me true. I will know if you lie. Who do you believe is the most powerful skein-user to ever live, boy? Master Wall, Master Soil, Mistress Tree? Hussain the Blue? Ihm-Phogn?'

The beady eyes fixed hard and Janos felt himself start to wilt. He closed his eyes for a moment and pictured his mother holding him close, whispering words in his ear, words only for him. He pictured the storm, the goblins and the trollspawn and the rottroll itself, the slaughter in Garioch. He remembered running in the dark. Janos clenched his jaw and stared back at the whitestaff.

'Tullen One-Eye,' he said, firmly, and then found himself smiling.

The old man sat back and licked his lips.

'Tullen One-Eye, boy? The man who broke the Tullioch spire? The man who burned old Undalor and its chieftains to ash? The forger of chains? Tullen One-Eye, who killed Nessilitor the Lover?'

Janos nodded. A gust from below the door sent one of the candles guttering. The old man fixed an eye on Janos and leaned forward, his face stone.

'Why, boy? You will tell me why you would say the name Tullen One-Eye to a whitestaff. An order whose entire work has been undoing that devil's harm.'

The old whitestaff stood and picked up his staff and slammed the butt of it on the ground, and sparks flew from the tip of it. He suddenly seemed much taller and younger. The three candles began to burn more brightly.

'You will tell me, idiot boy,' the old man roared, 'and then you will leave, and you will never set foot on Iskander, and you will *never* touch the skein.'

Janos bowed stiffly. He could feel a white-hot ball of anger in his stomach. This old whitestaff, so sure of his answers, so sure and then so shocked that Janos maybe didn't want this. In his small pack in the hallway were a single change of clothes, and a single book: Campbell Torbén's *History of the Skein-Wrecks*. He pictured Garioch and how it could have been. Would a whitestaff have made a difference? *No.* Tullen would have made a difference, or Ihm-Phogn, or the nameless knight of the Tullioch. Ihm-Phogn was an emperor, Hussain the Blue a mighty warrior. The Tullioch knight was, well, a Tullioch! Tullen had been a farmer's son, and he had changed the world.

'Tullen One-Eye could use the skein at no cost to himself,' he heard himself say. 'He never ran. He protected his people. He was a skein-wreck, not a skein-mage like the whitesta—'

The blow caught him on the side of his head, and then he was on the floor vision spinning. Another blow cracked into his back – *was it a boot?* With each kick, the whitestaff grunted one of the precepts of the Undal Protectorate.

'Suffer no tyrant.' A kick to the back.

'Forge no chain.' A kick to the guts.

'Lead through servitude.' A kick to the face.

Janos felt his mind detach, and there was a tangle, a burst of light and a layer of energy over everything, tendrils and roots probing and pulsing, a pattern of knots and connection. His head pounded. A hand gripped Janos by the shoulder and dragged him to the door and flung him into the corridor. The tangle faded as quickly as it had appeared. Janos pictured Tullen One-Eye bloodied and battered but never defeated; Deathless, he had called himself.

Janos coughed and felt hot blood on his face, and he grabbed his pack and he ran.

A Balanced Blade

'Forge no chain. What about the maddened murderer? The unrepentant thief? The forebears of the protectorate came from the Ferron plantations, the mines. They came from a hell of masters. So we forge no chain; there are no prisons in Undal. Only the cold blade and the firm word. Fifty lashes today for Cadet Campbell who slept at his post. If he does it again, I'll take a finger and send him away. We forge no chain, but there must always be consequence.' – Private Diary, Commander Salem Starbeck

Benazir spat blood and licked her lips. The lower was roughly split; she could feel the tear with her tongue. The blood was hot in her mouth, rich with salt. She grimaced and clenched her fists, altered her stance.

'I'm not trying to punch your face,' Floré said, smiling, her sweat-soaked curls falling across her eyes. 'I'm trying to punch the back of your head *through* your face.'

Benazir rushed at Floré, head low, a wild swing from the right arm. Floré easily twisted away, her muscular shoulders pivoting and her own arm coming down hard to jab into Benazir's bare right forearm, punching it down and away. Their fists were padded in cloth and leather for the fight. Benazir stumbled past and then they were facing each other again.

'I don't need lessons from you, dearest comrade,'

Benazir said, skin burning, and she rushed in again. This time she feigned a lunge and when Floré responded with the same downward jab, suddenly Benazir's left fist was driving into her thigh. The two clashed in a relentless tirade of blows, a kick, a knee, a jab, each woman pushing back and forth across the sand of the training courtyard. They wore identical training outfits, plain heavy cloth vests and trousers that had once been blue but were now washed pale with age, bare feet, cotton-padded fists and wrists wrapped tight with wound cloth and leather strips. Benazir's long black hair was braided; Floré's was chopped roughly short save her wild fringe of curls. The blows landed or were deflected. The women spun and kicked and grappled.

Finally, they halted and faced each other. Benazir's lip was bleeding, and Floré's left eye beginning to swell. Both were breathing hard; both coated with a slick of sweat and dust. The training courtyard fell silent again. Along the west wall and south walls, covered racks of weaponry sat alongside archery targets and wooden dummies with red paint daubed on their vitals. The east wall had the well and some low benches, and the north wall doors leading to the dormitories and kitchens of Stormcastle XII.

'You still rely too much on your fists,' Benazir said, feeling at her jaw and relaxing her stance, and Floré rolled her shoulders and gave a hawkish grin.

'It was a fist fight, Benny,' Floré said. 'With fists like mine, why wouldn't I?'

'You never kick. You barely grapple. It's a boxing match with you every time.'

Floré shook her head and laughed. 'I know my strengths,

and I strengthen my strengths. Don't get mopey because your feet are slow.'

Benazir flexed her fingers and moved her jaw again, then looked up and squinted at the pale sky where a tendril of purple cloud from the rotstorm was snaking eastward, dissipating slowly in the fresh winds of Undal.

'Enough for today, I think, Captain Artollen. You have bested me with your mighty fists and now I must commiserate with wine, and revelry. *I'm not trying to punch your face, I'm trying to punch the back of your head through your face,*' she said, and after a pause continued, 'Honestly, you've been spending too much time with the fire-slinger. You're getting almost poetic.'

Floré blushed and Benazir leaned forward and gave her a soft jab in the shoulder, then the chin.

'Eyes sharp. That's me, Floré. You could have told me.'

'Sorry, Benny.'

'No matter. He is too skinny for me anyway, not at all my type.'

'I mean about...' Floré started, but Benazir cut her off with a wave.

'Forget it,' she said, and Floré nodded slowly, not meeting Benazir's eyes.

The two women went and sat on the low bench by the well in the training courtyard. Biting flies warily approached and were swatted away. The air was thick with humidity. The constant winds of the rotstorm twisted through the sky above their heads, clashing and pushing at the Undal winds that pressed across the plains to the east, but the air in the courtyard was still, protected on all sides by high stone walls. Here at Stormcastle XII the wall was high and strong, sandstone and wood and earth palisades, a deep ditch on the far side. From the courtyard, leaning her back against the wall, Floré could see the watchtower high above, the faint impression of figures navigating around the unlit beacon on top. Benazir, her green eyes focused, watched Floré watching the tower.

'Starbeck wants an incursion to round out the summer of fun,' she said, and Floré frowned, turning to her friend.

'Who is going to lead? Lilith won't be fighting anytime soon after that rottroll.'

Benazir shrugged and took a long draw from her waterskin, then passed it to Floré.

'One of *us*, sister,' she said. 'Has to be. Yute is still at castle eleven, Lilith has a broken leg as you say, and Fat Mannon is only fit for running drills with the cadets these days. The rest are corporals and privates. If the spooky brigade think there is something worth chasing, Starbeck will have to either wait, which you know he won't, send one of us, or go himself – and since that business with the crow-men at Howling Dell the Commander won't go back, I reckon. He's lost his bottle.'

Floré scratched her neck and batted at a midge fly that was circling her face.

'Well,' she said. 'What do you think? The balanced blade or the gauntlet?'

Benazir smiled at that and rubbed at her collarbone, feeling the fresh swelling from one of Floré's heavy blows.

'It will be the balanced blade, darling Floré,' she said, 'but I think you are less about the gauntlet than the fist beneath. Even without metal you still manage to get the job done.'

Floré laughed and Benazir finished the waterskin. They

sat in silence a long moment and Benazir stared across the courtyard. Slowly she moved her hand and entwined her fingers with Floré's.

'I'm not mad,' she said quietly. 'I'm really not, Floré. He makes you laugh, even if he is an arse.'

She felt Floré squeeze her hand and they sat there in the silence, watching the clouds.

A wooden door set in the north side of the courtyard opened and the two women pulled their hands apart, and in stepped four cadets wearing training clothing and carrying practice halberd, long staffs with weighted heads wrapped in padding. Seeing Benazir and Floré they paused and pulled scrappy salutes, hindered by the long polearms.

Benazir waved to them lazily but Floré stood and returned the salute.

One of the older cadets, the orphan Guil with the freckles from a farm village somewhere to the south, held up a hand. Her teeth were crooked and her arms were toned and her hair cropped in a soldier's cut.

'Captain Arfallow,' she said, 'can you, would you... can you show the others what you showed me yesterday?'

Floré turned to Benazir with a questioning look, the corners of her mouth turning up in a near imperceptible smile.

Benazir furrowed her brow admonishingly at Floré's implication and then stood up and brushed off her training vest. She grabbed her weapons belt from the bench and strapped it on, and Floré followed suit. They went to the cadets and stood at ease in front of them.

'Sergeant Mannon asked you to drill with polearms, in this weather?' Benazir asked, and the cadets wouldn't meet her eye except for the girl with the freckles, Guil, who looked up and gave a frown.

'Punishment duty, sir.'

Benazir hid her smile and nodded solemnly. She and Floré had drilled with polearms many a hot afternoon, and many a cold one. She shook her head exaggeratedly at the cadets.

'Punishment duty, but you want to see knife tricks, Guil? My, oh my.'

She tutted and walked to the southern courtyard door with Floré. As Benazir walked, Floré silently passed Benazir the steel dagger from her belt. Benazir's father's dagger with its handle of antler and its silvered blade was firmly sheathed at her hip.

Just as they reached the door and heard the cadets start to hit their polearms together, Benazir turned and with a flick of the wrist the heavy steel knife flew out, spinning through the air to stick three inches deep in the weighted wooden end of the freckled cadet's practice halberd.

Guil dropped her halberd, and she and her team turned and stared at Benazir with wide eyes.

'Cadet,' she said. 'Please return Captain Artollen's dagger.'

The girl clumsily pulled the heavy dagger from the wood of the halberd and ran it across to Floré, who sheathed it and gave a nod of thanks.

'All of you,' Benazir said, 'practise your polearms. It's hotter past the Stormwall. And if Sergeant Mannon is pleased, we will see about teaching you the art of the balanced blade.'

Benazir and Floré left the training courtyard, smiling, conspiring where to find a bottle of wine, and high above them rotstorm winds blew but they were safe behind stone and wood and earth.

~

Hovarth from Fallow Fen brought Benazir a bottle of rum from Cil-Marie, a ridiculous delicacy. His caravan wended its way from the port at First Light to the port at Final Light, following the Stormwall where it stood and cutting inland to the safer roads where the wall had fallen, like the mess at Fallow Fen. He had known her father, back before Fallow Fen fell, back before Benazir had come to the Stormwall, and now whenever he passed by Stormcastle XII he always brought her a gift. Hovarth was the one who found out her family's fate, in the end, a tale passed from a scarred survivor in a tavern in Aber-Ouse to a trader who went to Ollen and told a herder from Brek… The chain of communication was meaningless to Benazir. All that mattered was she had some finality to the story of her mother, her father, her brother. They were all dead.

'This is too much,' she told Hovarth, but he just smiled and gave her a hug. She embraced him, the bear of a man who dressed and spoke and acted so like her endless uncles back in Fallow Fen, where an uncle was any man your parents trusted.

'Have to keep spirits high at the Stormwall,' he said. 'Now 'specially with the rumours. Will you be going, next summer? Hard to go back, but a righteous thing. Lancers from here back to First Light are mobilising. Grand Council and the whitestaffs in full agreement, according to a crier in Laga. It is to be war against whatever we find, until Fallow Fen is back in safe hands, Anshuka be praised.'

They were stood awkwardly in a hall outside the main kitchens, Hovarth having finished his business with the quartermaster and in the process of readying himself to leave. Benazir had heard the caravan had arrived but had been expecting them to stay overnight so had only sought out the trader when one of the cadets mentioned they were leaving before nightfall. Her lip was still bleeding and her clothes still sweat-soaked when she found Hovarth outside the kitchens, sweet-talking the bakers. She felt the pain in her right eye, her lip, and the stiffness in her shoulders, smelled baking bread and the dust from the road on Hovarth's heavy cloak.

'You have to leave now?' she asked, and he shook his head sadly.

'Time is a thief in the night, little one,' he said, 'and we are turning east to Ossen-Tyr. Many hard miles ahead, and a hard job is one best started soon.'

His men were all survivors of Fallow Fen as well, and as they moved past Benazir and Hovarth the few who knew of her gave her curt upward nods of familiarity and solidarity. Benazir licked her lips and shook her head, looking away, but Hovarth pressed on.

'They mean it, Benny,' he said. 'Next summer, Fallow Fen, a thousand lancers, every skein-mage they can muster. It will be a great battle.'

'I've heard nothing, Hovarth,' she said, and even as she spoke, she knew the lie of it. There were rumours of deployments, rumours of early graduation for cadets. Where else was there to be going this side of the country with a thousand lancers other than Fallow Fen, or into the storm itself? The council knew no army would survive past the wall. She hadn't heard, not officially, but a part of her had known the liberation of Fallow Fen was coming.

Hovarth put a hand under her chin and raised her head so their eyes met. His thick moustaches were slick with oil but his cheeks and chin were shaved clean, and his eyes had lost none of their brightness in the year since he had last passed by Stormcastle XII.

'I know you, girl,' he said. 'I know your bones. Your mother had those bones, and her mother before her. You are a Fallow Fen girl back since before the empire fell. This is your land. You'll be all right. Anshuka will watch over you, and your father will too.'

With that last he gestured to the antler-hilted blade at her waist, a dagger most soldiers would kill for and most commanders would lust after. Silver blades were expensive and meted out only to the elite commandos. Rune-blades were rare enough that at Stormcastle XII hers was one of only three: Commander Starbeck had a shortsword with a flame rune to match the rune on her dagger, and one of the commandos had a longsword with a handle of bone that pulsed acid across its blade, retrieved from an ancient Ferron warrior's skeleton in the shadow of Lothal's bones if the rumours were true. Benazir did not even begin to believe that; everybody knew Lothal's bones were so deep in the rotstorm that they were impossible to reach.

'It's my father's knife,' she said quietly. 'Not my own. I'm only a captain, Hovarth.'

Hovarth laughed at that and squeezed her shoulder, and then started leading her out from the dingy kitchen corridors and into the main courtyard of the castle.

'*You* are your father's knife, Benazir,' he said, squinting in the sun as they emerged, 'and the fact he gave you his blade means he knew that as well as I can see it now. Only a captain? Only a captain in the Stormguard Commandos, the greatest fighters ever to live! I do not worry for you, Benazir; you are stronger than you know. I worry for the lancers who are used to chasing smugglers or lining up against Tessendorm barbarians with their clubs, suddenly facing rottrolls and gods know what else.'

They stood in silence for a long moment in the courtyard and Benazir tried to imagine returning to Fallow Fen. She could think of no words for kind Hovarth.

'I must leave this night,' he said at last. 'Rest easy, drink the rum with your friends, and when you march on Fallow Fen, give the sisters my regards.'

Benazir smiled at that, hugged and thanked Hovarth a final time and went to her rooms. The sisters were two willows that had grown by the river Wyndle in Fallow Fen, two willows that had over centuries intertwined to become as one with a beautiful canopy trailing down over a clearing below. She remembered them well: the sisters were a spot for dreaming, for star-crossed lovers.

Benazir made it to her room and her bed and then she took the dagger from her belt and put it on the floor. She sat by it and stared at it, the intricate runes on the blade, the silver edge, remembering her father's face. She drank the rum, all of it, and pictured Fallow Fen aflame, and her in the arms of a girl from the mill village Rooknouse east of the city, sitting up from the meadow grass where they had lain and looking back as hell and flame ate her city. At her belt was her father's magic dagger, a trinket borrowed to make a farm girl swoon, and in the burning city the parents she was at war with met their fate.

The Altar & The Blade

'The whale!
The salmon!
The squid!
The seal!
The shark!
The shell!
The eel!
The bone!'

– Tullioch hunting chorus

The circular altar was an uncompromising black stone except for four incandescent runes inscribed around its edge. The flat-topped altar stone absorbed all light, a slick black that emerged from the wet grey of the floor. The runes burned with a white-hot intensity and the prisoners shackled to the cavern walls averted their eyes, looking anywhere but at those four lights that seemed to leave an impression not only on the eyes but on the mind beneath; a sickly image burned into the deepest recess of thought. Other than the glare from the runes the cavern was lit only by the dull glow of luminescent fungi, a pallid grey light that felt wet and cold.

The prisoners huddled and waited, for what they knew was coming. They did not look at the altar, or the runes, or their fellow captive now tied and bound to that abnormal stone.

The Tullioch tied to the altar strained taut muscles against her bonds, and the rope cut deep into her scales but she felt no give in the restraints. Her head was resting face down by one of the runes – she recognised it as the old Ferron tongue, but did not know its meaning. She knew only the four runes of their Judges, inscribed on standing stones at the northern coast of her people's land at the border of Old Ferron. Her clan had captured one of the stones during the great revolt, the season the blight waters came and the rotstorm rose, hundreds of years before. It sat in the clan hall. She had played with coloured shells in the shadow of the captured menhir and knew those runes, the runes of the Ferron Judges, as well as her own language. The rune carved in the altar was something complex and angular and foreign.

The rune had burned into her mind as the nameless figures bound her to the altar; grey-skinned goblins with black orb eyes scarpering around the feet of the tall humans who secured her bonds, limbs oddly jointed and stretched, hands strong. She had been carried limp from her shackles against the cavern wall under the effect of some skein-spell, but once she was bound she felt the will return to her movements and again and again she strained. Tullioch were powerfully built, and she knew herself to be the pride of her clan – fully seven foot tall, she was heavily muscled beneath a thick scaled hide, with three long claws and a thumb-spike on each webbed hand, and a powerful tail. Her head still bore the yellow crest of a juvenile.

None of her strength helped against the bindings, which seemed to tighten whenever she moved. Hissing behind a thick cloth gag with the exertion and the pain, she finally grew still, and stared into the black stone of the altar, away from the rune. It was almost as if she could see distant points of light in the black stone, immeasurably deep, like blazefish in the water off the reef on the night of the new moon – specks hinting at something more in the darkness. The new moon was always the best night to hunt, when the light was dim and the fish and beasts hid in their holes, trapped. It was also the night when she would pray to the great whale to protect her, for Tullioch were not the only ones who hungered in the depths. She remembered hunting with her father and her broodmates, cutting through cool water. She felt so dry, sick with the air, so long from the water and her family. She closed her eyes and for a long moment there was stillness.

Minutes or hours later, she tensed as a figure approached. She could not move her head enough to see the figure but could hear the delicate footsteps. All she could see was the black of the altar stone and the wall of the cavern where a dozen prisoners sagged in their manacles and chains, held fast against the wall, almost all dolefully avoiding her gaze. They were mostly human, a few Antian. There was one other Tullioch there, of a different clan. Her chest was mottled with the green scales of the Deepfarrow. The Deepfarrow Tullioch met her eyes – she had a purple crest on her head and a deep cut across her brow, a smear of half-dried blood across her face. It was a comfort to see her. In the reefs of the Wind Sea they might have met with blow or blades, clan against clan and claw against claw, but here there was only Tullioch, prisoners, and monsters, and the two held each other's gaze for a long moment.

'There is no point in struggling, Deepkin,' the figure said from behind her, and she snorted. The figure spoke in carefully enunciated Isken, the trade tongue of the seas and lands along the Star Coast. 'There is no escape from this place.'

Gagged as she was the Tullioch could not speak, could not curse the figure in the name of her ancestors. She could do nothing. She tried to open her mind to the true current as her broodmother had taught her, to find that place of control and awareness where she could hook herself to the energy infused in everything, to find the pattern, but when she reached... there was no pattern. Nothing was there but chaos, energy and life and power in tangles of randomness she could not break through. Columns of discordant power exuded upward from the runes on the altar, and with her secret eye open she could feel them and see them as tendrils of wavering light; from the robed figure a tangle of chaos emerged, tendrils of disharmony pushing beyond it, engulfing her and everything she could see.

Neither of these were the pattern her broodmother had led her to so many times. She could not find it; it was as if the currents of the ocean were torn by a great storm above. She felt her heart pounding and bile in her throat at the effort of seeking it, and finally she let her mind relax from the pattern and there was only a cavern and a figure and an altar.

She despaired, and her nostrils flared as she tried to breathe deep to steady herself. The air was damp, but not the cool salt wet of the Wind Sea. This was old damp – water that had been still too long. How many days had she been here, shackled and beaten by the beasts and their masters?

She had lost count. She had lost count of how many times she had seen a fellow prisoner dragged to the altar. She had lost count of how many times she had reached for the pattern, or prayed to the great whale. She knew what was coming, and so she flexed her claws and tried to twitch her tail, breathed that old damp in again and again as the figure stood behind her, silent. She tried to focus on picturing her father, her broodmates, her home, but her mind would not obey – it focused her every sense on the danger beside her.

Eventually the figure circled around and squatted down to meet her gaze. They were clad in a black cloak hiding their face in shadow, a close-fitting black robe, and dark brown leather boots and gloves. Their arms and legs seemed overlong and oddly bent for a human, as did their fingers. The cloaked figure leaned forward and the Tullioch recoiled the scant inch she could. She remembered the orb of light over the chop and surf of home reef, a similarly clad trio of figures descending on a column of white light through sea spray and rain, and then blackness. She felt so very far from the embrace of the reef, and clenched her jaw in determination; she would not allow herself to show fear.

'Did you know Tullioch were prized warriors, in Ferron?' the figure said, and its voice was soft. She did not respond, would not respond.

'Held in high esteem, in the first era! The spire was unbroken, then. They were not slaves, as in Tessendorm, or scraping survival from the wrecks of the Wind Sea, hunting squid and farming weeds. They were proud warriors, powerful shamans: some were even skein-mages of great renown.'

The figure drew a dagger from within its robes, a wicked

straight blade of obsidian with a cross-guard and handle of twisted bone. At the pommel, a green gem set in the bone glittered in the light of the burning runes. She felt her eyes focus on the blade, on its edge, and her breathing came in sharp bursts.

'I am going to kill you now, Deepkin-Tullioch,' the figure said, and the prisoners against the wall began to murmur and shuffle, 'and for that I am truly sorry – but it is *necessary*. I will allow you a last word as is custom; do not waste it on pleas, I pray.'

The figure stood and removed the gag from the Tullioch's mouth, dropped it to the cavern floor and readied the dagger against her back. She felt the cold of its tip against her scales.

The Tullioch's eyes blazed. She strained once more with all she had, but it was futile. She was bound and had no defence. She made herself stare into the darkness of the strange figure's hood.

'I am Hassin, daughter of Heasin, of Shardkin-Tullioch,' she said, and her voice stayed strong, the heavy sibilant speech of her people forcing itself around the trade tongue. 'I have seen the rotstorm; I swam the blight-waters. I do not fear you, Baal-spawn. Say your name that I might hunt you in the afterlife.'

The figure nodded slowly. 'Good, that was good. That was an honourable thing to say. Your clan would be proud. This is not so bad a death, Hassin, daughter of Heasin. Your ancestors would not turn their eyes.'

In a single motion the figure plunged the dagger deep into Hassin's back until the bone hilt pressed to her scales and she gasped with a pain so cold, so sharp – a breaking so utter it filled her veins with acid and her heart with fire. Leaning down close to her head the figure twisted the blade and Hassin could not help but scream. She was still screaming as the figure whispered to her, so softly, 'I have seen the rotstorm too, Hassin, daughter of Heasin, of Shardkin-Tullioch. I am not Baal-spawn, not some brute from Tessendorm, not some Isken dullard. I am Varratim, of Ferron.'

As Hassin's green blood pooled over the black stone altar the rune by her head flared with a blinding light and searing heat and her mind went to that place, sought the pattern. Her broodmother had shown her the pattern in the reef; in the wild waters of the Wind Sea; in the movement of a shoal of fish chasing shadows; in the beating of a heart. Her mind went to the true current, and she felt a pattern within herself emerge, and there was chaos and pain as the runes beside her flared and the pattern at her core began to crack and dissipate. The runes flared, and the dagger buried in her back pulsed with power and her eyes lost focus on the blackness of the stone. The cavern was a tumult of wails as the prisoners tried their best to turn away, chains rattling, moans escaping every throat.

Varratim stood tall by the black altar, his face in shadow, and he stared for a long moment at the burning runes and the bloodied knife before reaching down with a gloved hand to delicately close the eyes of his sacrifice.

ACT 2

DEAD OF NIGHT

Suffer no tyrant
Forge no chain
Lead in servitude

Precepts of the Undal Protectorate

7

HEARTH

'*After Berren died, the flooding, the failed crops, and the violent winds brought harshness to Ferron. With full fields and coffers they were peaceable traders, but hunger put an edge to their blades. The Empress Seraphina sent forth her armies, and the third Ferron War began – though it was the first that could be said to be begun by the Ferron themselves. Lothal the god-wolf took to the field of battle, and Undalor was destroyed, its people enslaved; Tessendorm and Isken bowed; the Tullioch Shard was broken by the skein-wreck Tullen One-Eye. Still Ferron hungered. Across the sea, Cil-Marie and Ona and the strait kingdoms did what they could to prepare. The world of Morost waited with bated breath.*' – *The Fall of Ferron*, Whitestaff Anctus of Riven

The guard took their horses and started to give directions, but Floré waved him off. She had been to Hookstone before, on her way to Hasselberry five years before. She had reported to Commander Mears and then she and Janos had spent the day wandering the town, fresh spring blossom of white and pink and lurid red hanging from the trees that shaded the twisted streets. They had gotten drunk in an inn whose name she couldn't remember, but she remembered the market square and the hulking smithy house that took up almost an entire side of the square.

She remembered the bed at the inn with its dozens of blankets, and Janos lying there with a bottle of wine in one hand reading her his poetry. One side the temple, one side the Stormguard garrison, one side the smithy, and the fourth side trees, a fountain, and houses. A troupe of musicians were playing in the square as she drank wine from Cil-Marie that reminded her of her father and his tales of the land of mists and heat to the south, and Janos read her poems by moonlight casting through open windows as they lay together that night.

She felt herself shiver and her knees begin to weaken at the thought of him, picturing him swathed in blood and stillness in the shaman temple of Hasselberry, so she bit her lip until the pain made her shake and forced her to focus on the task at hand.

She led Yselda through the coiling streets of the outer town, grimacing. Doors were bolted, windows boarded up hastily. Scared faces peered from behind curtains, from high windows. Thick and pungent peat smoke from hearth fires rose from clay chimneys, but no light spilled onto the street. They walked up towards the market square and Floré stopped short, aghast. The mighty garrison hall of Hookstone that had stood eight hundred years, the white marble edifice that the Ferron had raised as their seat to pass judgement and trade in blood and flesh and grain and power… it lay in ruin. Columns toppled, marble veneer cracked over stone walls. The roof was collapsed and the entrance blocked with timber and rubble. The wooden shaman temple had its doors wide and lamps lit and people rushed out and in, carrying bandages, stretchers with sheet-covered bodies. The whole town was coated in dust and ash. The trees she remembered to the south of the plaza, facing the south Wind Sea, were scorched. The fountain was cracked.

Yselda shook her from her stupor.

'Is that it, Captain?' she asked, and Floré shook her head and focused. The smithy – men and women in Stormguard City Watch uniforms stood staunchly in front of it with halberd and spear, more being dispatched to the walls with bows. Every one of them was armed to the teeth, and they looked tired. She saw a half a dozen blue tabards amongst the grey of the City Watch – a lancer patrol must be in town as well. They approached and nobody questioned their entrance.

Inside, the forge was unlit and on the anvil a map of Hookstone and its surrounds was spread. Surrounding it were three figures: a woman in a City Watch tabard who looked ragged and tired was arguing with a round-faced young man in a lancer tabard who was swearing and pointing at the third figure who had its back to Floré; the third figure was a black-haired Antian, one of the short dog-like creatures who held their tiny sunken kingdom under the lands north of Orubor. Armoured in thick silks with ceramic plates sewn in, the Antian was patiently standing as the lancer held forth. Floré felt Yselda tense up next to her, hand reaching for sword, and she held her own hand out in signal of calm. The fat lancer slammed his fist on the map and continued his tirade.

'An Antian arrives and next day half the garrison is dead, Bannon, and you tell me you have had other Antian *living* in town for years? We should have this one's head on a spike, not be asking its advice on—'

Bannon saw Floré and Yselda at the door and held up a hand and the man fell silent. She locked eyes with Floré and nodded, and the lancer turned around too.

'Commander Bannon,' she said, gesturing to herself. 'You are Forest Watch?'

Floré opened her mouth to answer but then the Antian turned around and she saw the flecks of grey in his coat, the spectacles precariously perched on its muzzle, one ear upright and alert and the other half folded over, the piercing blue eyes.

She was across the room in a heartbeat and on her knees, bringing her to a height with the four-foot creature. She wrapped her arms around him with a strangled yell and he did the same, and Bannon and the fat lancer each took a startled step back. Yselda went for her sword, and then she realised that Floré was laughing and smiling and crying all at once.

'Voltos,' Floré said, 'Voltos. All the stars in the bastard sky, Voltos Thirdskin, it is good to see you!'

The Antian Voltos pulled back a little and bowed stiffly, first to Floré, then to Yselda. Yselda felt her hand drop from her sword hilt. The lancer puffed out a breath and straightened his tunic.

'You've heard my thoughts, Bannon. I'll be with my men. This isn't over.'

He stormed from the room and Voltos gave a lazy wave and then turned to Bannon.

'It seems I am at an advantage,' he said, his voice raspy and deep. 'Please, allow me to introduce you. Commander Bannon, this is Bolt-Captain Artollen of the Stormguard commando, Stormcastle XII. *Exactly* who I am here to see.'

Floré reeled back and her face flushed, and Yselda's eyes widened.

All four of them turned as a match struck, and from the shadows in the corner of the room, a light flared as a tall man lit a pipe. He puffed on it, and emerged into the light of the room, sharp features smiling around a neat dark beard. He was clad in simply cut black clothing beneath a red Stormguard commando tabard.

'This is all very fun,' he said, his tone light, 'but I think much talking is about to happen. There is wine and food in the hearth room. I suggest we make use of it.'

With a quick step he passed the three women, nodding to Bannon.

Voltos sighed. 'Always so dramatic,' he said, shaking his head as the man left the room. 'That is Tomas-mage, the new Primus of Storm Castle XII.'

The Antian ran his long tongue across his whiskers and adjusted his glasses, and gave something resembling a smile to the three women before turning to follow the skein-mage. Commander Bannon followed, her deep frown unwavering.

Floré got to her feet and gestured for Yselda to join her, and together they followed Voltos to the hearth room of Hookstone forge.

~

Cuss tightened his belt again and gingerly touched his chest. He had his Stormguard Forest Watch tabard over a leather jerkin over a homespun shirt, and below all of that a thick layer of bandages. He was sweating already. He had a shortsword from the Forest Watch shed sheathed at his hip, and his right hand was slipped through one of the heavy knuckledusters Sergeant Floré had passed him. Cuss trudged.

Whenever he thought about Jana or his mother he found himself on his knees, heaving with sobs, unable to breathe, or suddenly lying down. He lost long minutes. So he didn't think about them. Shaman Jule had taken him aside and said some words about Jana, and his mother, and Petron, but Cuss didn't listen. Sergeant Artollen was going to bring back Petron; the orbs had taken Petron; Yulder knew something about the orbs. *Judges might be gods,* the sergeant used to say, *but shamans aren't Judges.* Cuss had thanked the shaman and then made his plan. Mother and Jana he couldn't help but that monster had Petron, and Cuss wouldn't leave his little brother. *So what to do?*

The day before, Sergeant Artollen had told Cuss to go to Yulder's farm to investigate the lights in the sky. Yulder was the only one who knew about the orbs of light before the attack: Cuss figured he might have seen where they were heading, or know something at least.

So Cuss geared up. He didn't dare return again to the cabin he shared with his mother and sister and brother; he couldn't face it. First he went to Captain Tyr's house and filled a pack with bread and cheese and apples. Yselda had mentioned wolves, but Cuss could climb a tree as fast as any boy in the Hookstone forest, even if it maybe tired him out a little more – he had a lot of Cuss to lift after all. Truth be told Cuss was terrified of the idea of a forest full of wolves, but he made himself gear up nonetheless, and then checked everything over twice. Sergeant Artollen always said: *Courage is the preserve of the ill-prepared.* When she explained it a bit simpler, Cuss understood. You didn't need to be brave if you were ready for anything. You only needed to be brave if you weren't ready; so be ready. She always said, *Cuss, for pity's sake, check your gear; if you've forgotten your sword again I'll have you drawn and quartered.*

'Courage is the preserve of the ill-prepared,' he said to himself, over and over like a prayer.

So as the sun set Cuss had food, water, weapons, a travelling cloak, and the knuckledusters the sergeant had given him. He practised punching with them; jab with the left to gauge distance, cross with the right, *put your shoulder into it.* He knew he was useless with a sword but he remembered sparring with Yselda and Kellen and Petron and Ged and a few of the village children in a competition on the village green last year – a few of the millworkers' lads had laughed at him; they always laughed at him. His mother said it was because he let them laugh at him. Petron had beaten one boy bloody for calling Cuss a pig, but last summer, Cuss didn't need his little brother to fight his fights. Before they started the sergeant had leaned down to him and said, *Keep your guard high, jab and cross, and be patient. Remember to move your feet.*

Cuss had won the sparring competition on the green, had won against boys bigger than him, smaller than him, stronger than him. Jab, then cross. Guard high, and be patient. Everyone loses their patience eventually, and when they come you jab, and you cross, you move your feet, and they go down. *Back of the head,* Cuss thought as he practised punching in the silence of Captain Tyr's house. *Don't punch them in the face – punch them in the back of the head, through their face.*

The knuckledusters were heavy metal, a dark iron with thin strips of leather and cotton padding on the inside of the thick rings. Cuss flexed his fingers as he left the captain's house, and he stared across the village green. He had gone to the ruins of his own house earlier. He would not let himself dwell on that, the blackened timber and the piles of soot and ash. His mother and Jana were inside, still; inside forever now. His chest ached from the wounds, and something else. He felt as if he was floating, felt every sensation heightened. He was at the bottom of the loch and there was so much weight on him that he could barely move unless he focused on the next task, the next right thing to do.

The grave at the edge of town was already being filled in. Tellen was with a gang of men and women from the mill assessing the Whitestaff Izelda's house; the stone lower wall was still intact, the rest burned and collapsed, lazy tendrils of smoke still curling from the ruin. Her intricate garden was in disarray.

Cuss went to them and forced himself to interrupt.

'Mister Tellen,' he said, to no response. Tellen was pointing at a wooden beam and muttering to a man with a pockmarked face.

'Mister Tellen!' Cuss repeated, and the men turned.

'Cuss, lad,' Tellen started, but Cuss spoke fast – adults always thought they knew what you were going to say, so you had to say your thing first, sometimes, before they'd said what they thought and already made up their minds.

'Mister Tellen – you have this under control. The sergeant wanted me to check out strange lights seen up at Yulder's farm. I'm going now. If he has an idea where the lights were heading, the sergeant needs to know so she can find Marta, and… and Petron.'

Tellen put a hand to the back of his neck – he looked tired, dark circles under his eyes.

'Cuss, lad, the morning—'

'No,' Cuss interrupted. 'No, Mister Tellen. I need to go now. If the sergeant is going to find my brother and Marta, she needs to know where those orbs went. And Yulder is the only person who saw them before… before last night. I need to go.'

The pockmarked man reached down and plucked a tomato from a fallen vine in Izelda's garden. He chewed on it as Tellen and Cuss stared at each other.

'No horses, lad,' the man said. 'Orbs killed 'em.'

Cuss shrugged. 'I've got legs.'

The man laughed. 'Balls too.'

Cuss blushed and Tellen smiled.

'Go then, lad,' Tellen said. 'Nash, will you go with him?'

Cuss opened his mouth to object, but Tellen stayed him with a hand.

'I don't doubt you, lad. But if you find anything useful you might need to run off to Hookstone Town quick fast to catch the sergeant, and Nash can come back tell us. And two sets of eyes are better than one when wolves are about, aye?'

Nash stood and brushed ash and dirt from his jerkin.

'I'll get me axe, lad,' he said, 'and then a night-time stroll sounds just fine.'

~

Ashbringer pulled her cloak close with gloved hands as the fisherman made fast on the island reef south of Wedderburn. The boat was scarcely ten foot long, a single sail pulling them forward across black water. The island was a sand bank three miles from shore, where the deep current on the Wind Sea that followed the south coast of the Undal Protectorate lost its strength, and the Tullioch reefs began. It was dark save for starlight and a thin crescent of moon. The fisherman gazed at her whenever she turned her head away. She was cloaked heavily in black, gloved, but he could tell something was wrong from the way she moved. He ran the boat up into the sandbank and leapt across the prow, dropping a short anchor chain onto the sand and holding the boat steady for her.

'Five silver pieces as we agreed, with my thanks,' she said, stepping out into knee-deep water and walking through the low surf to the stillness of the sandbank. She breathed in the smell of the sand, the salt, the air, and licked her lips. It had been too long since she had been at sea.

'Aye,' he said, 'and your thanks is sure to be appreciated. How long are we... staying, if you don't mind me asking? Easy sail back now, but in a few hours tide will turn and it'll be a hard press. You need long for your birdwatching?'

Ashbringer turned to him and tossed him a pouch she had filled with five gold pieces and an assortment of small coins of silver and copper. She started to pace up and down the sandbank, peering south to see if the stub of the Tullioch spire was visible. She could not make it out over the grey and black of the water.

'You should leave now, good boatman. You should row and catch your wind and be home and safe in bed. I have business here. I will make my own way, away.'

Ashbringer stopped her pacing and stared south at a patch of water.

'Tullioch are coming, boatman,' she said. 'You leave now.'

The boatman slipped the coin into his bag and then scratched at his beard.

'Can't be leaving you here, lady,' he said. 'This sandbar will be under water by dawn. Won't do it. Ain't right. Tullioch won't harm Undal folk, don't you be worrying.'

Ashbringer turned to stare at him and took three sharp steps forward until the blackness beneath her hood was inches from his face.

'You take a lone woman clad in black to a deserted sandbar, on a dark and silent night. You ask no questions, you take your money, and you leave. Do not complicate things, good boatman.'

He pressed back on his heels and his face reddened. He peered around them, at the lapping water, the stars above, and seemed to find his resolve.

'You said birdwatching! Night birds! I ain't done nothing wrong here. I don't care for your business, woman, and I'll have you back in that boat in one hour and safe to Wedderburn by dawn.'

Ashbringer lowered her hood and smiled at him, showing her serrated teeth, the orbs of gold that were her eyes. The starlight played across her blue skin scarred with stark red runes, her shaven head, the points of her ears pressing away from her head. The boatman fell silent.

'Go,' she said, and then he was splashing and pushing, throwing his anchor aboard and launching his boat out into the water. As it bobbed in the waves and he set his sail, he looked at her, and she smiled. Then the sail caught a luff of wind and he was gone and she was alone on the sandbar.

Ashbringer waited a long hour in the cold. She could sense the Tullioch just offshore watching her, and she made no aggressive movement, simply sat cross-legged on the sand and watched the stars, the ancestors. They danced for her. There were no clouds. Finally, one of the Tullioch emerged from the water.

'Hail, Deepkin,' Ashbringer said in Isken, bowing her head. The Tullioch moved up the beach, striding from the water. It was a female, she thought, seven foot of muscle and sinew. Black scales and a crest of gold. It turned its head so one eye could coldly appraise her, a trident of black iron slung across its back. Its chest was a mottled green.

'Long has it been,' the Tullioch hissed, its tongue wrapping around foreign Isken trade tongue, 'since an Orubor saw the reefs.'

'I seek lights in the sky,' Ashbringer said, and the Tullioch nodded and came to her.

'There is much to say, then,' the Tullioch said, and together they sat beneath the stars and talked long into the night. The Tullioch told her of lights in the sky, children snatched in the night. Whispers of a darkness returned.

In the darkest hour of the night, together they fell silent and watched as from the north orbs of light, no bigger than a mote at such distance, flew across the sky. The orbs flitted, one across Hookstone forest, one near Undal itself, and more still west towards the Stormwall and Ferron and the rotstorm beyond. Eventually they retreated, all to the north, and Ashbringer sighed.

'Stay strong, Deepkin,' she said at last, when dawn's light came.

'I will take my leave, friend Orubor,' the Tullioch said, nodding in response. 'You are welcome in the reefs, by the word of the Deepfarrow. Know this, and go safely.'

Ashbringer inclined her head, but held out a hand to pause.

'Wait a little, Tullioch,' she said, smiling. 'You may take heart in the manner of my leaving.'

Ashbringer began to sing to the spirit of the place in the language of her people, her voice high. For long minutes she sang, her voice mingling with the murmurs of the surf, and then with a throaty call a seabird came arcing over the grey seas and circled over her. It was small, its wings white and its body black, its white head turning to her as it spun spirals high above. She gestured at the Tullioch to step back, and she kept singing, the poem of this place, and the poem of where she would go. She reached out to the pattern and called to it, and to the great mother. The bird flew closer, and she could see that behind it trailed a wake of silver light, and its beak was wrought of jade, as were its eyes. Ashbringer rose to her feet and continued her song and the little god circled, and the sand at her feet began to glow with the fire of the dawn sun and then it was not sand but the long grass and bulrushes of the swamp.

Ashbringer raised a hand to the Tullioch, who stood impassively at the edge of the sandbar, watching the bird circle over her, and then there was a flash of white light and she was gone and there was only sand once more. The bird circled twice more and let out its throaty cry and then cut away over the waves. The Tullioch waited for the sun to fully rise, and then she clicked her teeth and slid back into the cool water of the Wind Sea.

~

Commander Bannon took charge as soon as they settled in the hearth room. She sent a boy to bring hot wine and a tray of food.

'I admit I'm confused. Voltos claims you as bolt-captain in the Stormguard Commando, but you wear a Forest Watch tabard, and Commander Mears' records have you as a sergeant in the Forest Watch based in Hasselberry,' she said. 'Regardless, I need a report on Hookstone forest; then you can talk with the Antian and the skein-mage.'

The captain stood and gave a coldly clinical account of the events of the last few days, and Yselda found herself focusing on anything but those words. The boy brought back wine, which she drank. Yselda's mind was caught in a tumult, a barrage of ideas and thoughts tumbling over one another to bury the underlying scream – Shand, Esme, the girls Lorrie and Nat, her mother and father, her brothers on the frozen loch, Petron, little Marta – she squeezed her eyes shut and did not think of them. She took another sip. The wine was sweet, not like any she had had before. She had never seen an Antian, and watched from the corner of her eyes as Voltos listened patiently and lapped at his wine. He did not look ferocious, but like a fat dog, or a muscular giant mole, or some mix of the two.

She cast a few sidelong glances at the handsome skein-mage Tomas, and felt blood rushing to her cheeks fiercely when his eyes caught hers and held her gaze and he gave a lazy smile. She looked down at her wine as Floré finished her official report. Shand didn't let her drink wine, but Esme slipped her a glass every now and then. Yselda forced herself to count her breaths, forced herself not to submit to it all. *A little flower can weather a mighty storm,* her mother had always said.

'Thank you,' Bannon said when the sergeant – *captain* – had finished. 'We will send what help we can. As you can see we suffered similar trials here. Our resident three whitestaffs all killed, as well as a dozen of the City Watch and our two skein-mages, and many civilians. Three children taken that we can tell. Horses and cattle killed sporadically for a half-day ride in every direction.'

The captain nodded and opened her mouth to speak. Yselda's head was thumping.

'Commander,' the captain said. 'My report. The children taken... I was not... clear. One was a cadet in the Stormguard Forest Watch, Petron Grantimber. He is my responsibility. The other, Marta...'

She threw a sidelong glance at Voltos and swallowed visibly.

'The other was my daughter.'

Tomas spat out a mouthful a wine and Voltos and Bannon both made to speak but Floré held up a hand and Yselda squirmed in her chair.

'Please. Commander. Captain Tyr wished my promotion to Captain of the Forest Watch, which would give me responsibility for Hookstone forest and its people. I ask you to pass this to someone else, from the garrison. I need to follow the orbs. I need to find my daughter.'

Bannon bit her lip, breathed a heavy sigh. She looked out of the window, at the dying sunset.

'Captain, we know nothing of these orbs, their destination, their source, their power. *Nothing.* There are whispers of rumours that they head north. I had a rider this morning from Undal City – the council mean to send an expedition. They will find your daughter, and the boy Petron, and our three children, if they are to be found. The people of Hookstone need command, and safety. Packs of wolves with no fear of people, goblins this late after the last rotsurge? With our horses dead and our herds attacked, we will struggle to mount anything like an effective defence of what we have, should we need to. Hells, if this continues we will struggle even to *feed* our people.'

Bannon drained her wine and everyone in the room could see how drawn she was, stretched near to breaking.

'It is madness, all of it – and if lights in the sky aren't enough, there are reports of bandits on the Star Coast road near the Cimber hills on the Isken border. They might enter the forest at any moment. We have lost an entire village, you say, at Larchford; we need a strong hand in there. I'm sorry. I truly am sorry. Your place is with the Forest Watch, for the best of the people.'

The captain stared at her and the pewter goblet in her hand creaked as she squeezed her fist. The room grew tense and silent. Yselda's mouth was dry, and she felt as if she were falling. She needed to help the captain find Petron. She couldn't face going back to Hasselberry, not now – maybe not ever. From his chair in the corner of the hearth room

Tomas inhaled deeply from his pipe and blew out a smoke ring.

'Well!' he said, smiling. 'Well. Lovely. Really. But I'm afraid Bolt-Captain Artollen is being recalled to her primary regiment at Stormcastle XII. She was only ever on temporary secondment, special dispensation from the Grand Council. She and the Skein-wreck Janos, the mighty Salt-Man himself, are needed at the front. So you must do without, I'm afraid, dear Commander Bannon.'

The captain stared at him, and then Voltos, and did not speak. She put her goblet of wine of the map table. Yselda sat silently and tried to parse what was going on – *skein-wreck?* She had heard of skein-wrecks of course, like Ihm-Phogn across the sea in Cil-Marie, or the nameless knight of the Tullioch, Hussain the Blue who threw back the Tessendorm legions when her grandparents were young. They were skein-mages of terrible power who were capable of wondrous feats. Tullen One-Eye, the skein-wreck consort of the Empress Seraphina, had enslaved half the world. But… *Janos?* She pictured the captain's husband, the quiet poet who always had a book in his hand, who spoke so gently, who spent long hours walking the woods or staring at the waters of the loch. Yselda shook her head, unable to link the two ideas. Janos was a gentle man.

Bannon seemed to deflate, resting back into her chair and sighing, and then taking a long drink from her cup. Voltos refilled his own goblet from the steaming jug of wine the boy had left and sniffed at it. He looked at it when he spoke.

'Commander Benazir is in dire need of assistance, and all of these threads are of one tapestry,' he said, eyes not leaving his wine. 'Where is Janos? We need him, Floré, and you as well. Forces are gathering near the wastes of Urforren, crow-men and worse. These lights are not only a problem here at the east. They've been seen in the Slow Marsh, as far north as Dun Fen and as far south as Laph. They've been seen crossing the Stormwall and into the rotsurge itself.'

The captain stood and went to the window. She drew the curtains open and looked out into the night, and did not speak.

Voltos looked to Yselda, and again made that strange face, his canine features approximating a human smile. She felt herself shrink back in her chair, and hoped he couldn't tell.

'Do you know anything of Skein-wreck Janos, Cadet?' he asked. Yselda looked to Floré by the window, who nodded without looking back. *Skein-wreck Janos?* She didn't understand.

'Mister Janos died in the attack on Hasselberry, sir. He was trying to protect Marta, they said.'

Tomas dropped his pipe, and Voltos dropped his goblet of wine. Bannon stared between them, and Floré did not leave the window.

'The Salt-Man is dead?' Tomas said, eyes wide, and Voltos turned to look at Floré.

'What is going on?' Bannon demanded. 'I don't understand any of this.'

Voltos picked up his dropped goblet and placed it carefully on the table. The spilled wine pooled on the flagstones of the hearth room floor, dark except for the flickering reflection of the hearth fire, pooling across the stone and into joins and cracks.

'I'm sorry, Commander. Janos was a highly valued member of the Stormguard who has been on... extended leave. A skein-wreck – a true one! The council's last line of defence. We were hoping to bring him back with us.'

Voltos turned his head to the captain and then back to Yselda, and his shoulders sagged.

'He was a friend, as well. Thank you, Cadet... Yselda, was it?'

'Yes, Mister Voltos. Cadet Yselda Hollow of Hasselberry,' she said, dipping her head in a slight bow. Voltos smiled at her.

'Mister Voltos. I like that. Floré,' he said, turning back to the captain, 'this news changes things. Is the child his?'

The captain pulled her gauntlets from her belt and slipped them on and turned to face Voltos with cold eyes.

'The child is *mine*,' she said, her voice steel, 'and I am going to find her, and the boy Petron. If I must cut through the council themselves I will do it. If I must fight the Stormguard and Anshuka herself I will do it. If I must tear down the Tullioch Shard by hand I will do it. I will not be distracted by Benazir jumping at shadows in the rotstorm or Starbeck's auguries of doom; I will not waste time sharpening swords in Hookstone forest, or peering at crow-men over the Stormwall. Urforren is *salt*, Voltos. We killed them all.'

Commander Bannon grimaced and glanced from Floré to Tomas; as a skein-mage of the Stormguard commando, Primus of a whole Stormcastle, he outranked everyone present. Yselda found herself overwhelmed between them – the City Watch Commander, the foreign Antian, the Stormguard skein-mage from the Stormwall itself – and in their centre, Floré Artollen with gauntlets donned, rage and anguish visible in every line of her face.

Tomas refilled his goblet slowly from the jug of warmed wine and raised it.

'Calm, Bolt-Captain. Calm. All threads in one tapestry, as you say, Voltos. We seek the truth of these orbs. If the Salt-Man's daughter needs rescuing, and your friend Bolt-Captain Floré needs our help, who are we to deny her? I am sorry, Bolt-Captain. I met Janos-Wreck only once, during the Fallow Fen offensive, but it was certainly memorable. He was an inspiration, and will be greatly missed.'

Voltos began to wring his hands. Tomas tipped his glass to Floré and Yselda and then drained it.

'If we can find a whitestaff, we can track the girl with your blood, if she lives,' Tomas said, looking at Floré, and Yselda felt a clenching in her guts. The mage's eyes were pale and his gaze was intense. The spark of hope that flitted across the captain's face was brief, but plain for all to see.

Bannon stood suddenly, held up a hand and clenched it into a fist.

'Quiet, all of you,' she said, and when Voltos went to speak she shushed him and cocked her head. Her face paled, framed by her dark hair grimy with smoke and sweat and worse.

'No no no no no,' she said, and ran from the room. Voltos's ears raised and then he said something guttural in his own tongue and let out what seemed to be an involuntary whine.

Tomas put his pipe in his pocket and started flexing his fingers, pulling on leather gloves, and the captain drew her sword and stretched her wounded shoulder.

'Captain,' Yselda said quietly. 'Captain, what is it?'

The captain looked at the girl and sighed, and rain began to fall in a torrent and outside the shouting started. Yselda found herself breathing heavily and she drew her own sword. The first bolt of wet-lightning hit somewhere close enough that tremors shook the smithy and thunder filled the room. The captain didn't need to tell her. Yselda knew what this was.

Rotsurge.

8

ROTSURGE

'There are spirits of places, many spirits, but the Judges are unique in their scale and power; unique in their scope. They are spirits of a concept, rather than a place. The Tullioch claim the Bird and the Whale are Judges, but none but the Tullioch have seen them, and no Tullioch will tell of their concepts. It has been said oft: a place has a spirit; a spirit can be fed; what is fed will grow. Do the Judges differ from the forest bogle and the sprite of a forgotten well only in their diet?' – *Pantheon of the Protectorate*, Campbell Torbén of Aber-Ouse

Commander Bannon led the charge from the smithy out into the storm. Floré followed grim, blade bare, pausing only to push Yselda back into the room. 'Stay here,' she snarled, and Yselda found herself quaking and nodding. The noise from the rain had swollen in only a few moments to a constant roar, a rush of water pounding roof and wall and street and window. Wind screamed down the twisted roads of Hookstone village.

The Antian Voltos followed Floré a few paces behind, drawing his black-bladed dagger, the hilt a twist of what looked to Yselda like white wood. There was a black stone in its pommel, a rough lump of dark quartz. His ears flattened close to his head as he passed. The skein-mage Tomas rose from his chair and strode to the door slowly with no change in his demeanour. As he passed her he laid a gentle hand on her shoulder and Yselda recoiled.

He leaned in and winked at her, his pale eyes twinkling.

'Only a rotsurge, Cadet Hollow,' he said. 'Keep the wine warmed.'

Then he was gone, and Yselda was alone. She could hear the shouts of the men and women of the City Watch. Someone screamed, streets away, and it cut through the wind and rain, a blade of sound that pierced her core. She had never been in a rotsurge before without weeks of warning, without hours of boarding windows and preparation. The wet-lightning would hit, the seeds would be planted. Goblins and trollspawn and even perhaps a rottroll would spew out, now or later, growing wildly fast and spilling up from the ground, and the insidious rotvine would slowly spread unless burned and hacked back. The storm would bring banks of red mist that would turn skin red and burn the lungs. The downpour of rain lashed the windows of the hearth room. Rotsurges came only once or twice a year at most, Yselda knew, always heralded in advance by swift riders and divinations from the whitestaff council in Iskander.

The last rotsurge had been two summers past. In advance for two spans of days Hasselberry was preparing weapons, long spears, battered sword and axes being sharpened.

The night it came, the whole village had sheltered in either the mill building or the Goat and Whistle, pressed in close together. The storm was unlike anything Yselda had ever seen – purple lightning, thunder that rumbled and rolled far longer than seemed possible. The clouds themselves were low and strange, black and purple and red, a roiling mass a mile wide that clung together and moved straight, regardless of the winds around it. They had watched it come, rolling across the tops of the forest, and that night Esme had slept with Yselda and little Nat and Lorrie. They had pressed in together in one big bed whilst Shand stayed downstairs, watching the barred doors and windows.

Shand had joined the posse the next morning, riding out with Captain Tyr and Sergeant Floré. All summer long the posse rode out whenever another seed was found, a gang of goblins, and even a rottroll that Yselda heard they brought down with longbows and burned in a pit near Plompton Rocks. All summer long Esme and Shand had her and the girls stay close, never far from the village green. There was no swimming at the Black Dog Rock that year, and Yselda remembered chafing under the rules until they heard about the girl in Greenfields who wandered into the wood alone. The goblins had taken her, and Shand said all that was found was a single shoe. Yselda stayed close after that.

Hearing the storm outside now, she sat on a stool by the hearth huddled away from the windows. She drew the dagger Captain Floré had given her. The hilt was brown-and-white antler, and the blade was fine silver that caught the light. From the base of the blade to the tip a line was etched, and in the centre of the blade it spread into a continuous pattern, a sigil of power, a twining circle chasing itself, crossing itself, encasing itself. At its heart was a single and simple rune, perfectly carved: ‹, the rune of fire. As she held the blade she felt its potency, and knew a drop of blood would call forth a gout of flame. These blades were what Ferron slavers used to punish runaway slaves. These blades were what Stormguard commandos took as trophies from crow-men. New knives were forged in Cil-Marie, but the one in her hand felt so very ancient. *Why did she give it to me?*

Yselda listened to the howling wind and driving rain and didn't allow herself to think about Shand and Esme and Nat and Lorrie. She had lost a family before, a home before; she knew thinking wouldn't help, not now. *What would the captain do?* She thought for a long moment, and found herself almost smiling. She sheathed the blade at her belt and found their packs and brought them close to the hearth. She began her inventory, checking food supplies. She checked her bowstring was dry and the fletching was undamaged on her arrows, and oiled and wiped down her sword blade and the silver dagger. Finally, she filled their waterskins from the pewter ewers on the side table. She splashed her face with water and held her hands to her eyes for a long moment, and outside the storm raged.

~

Floré stood in the rain and watched as the chaos unfolded. The rain felt good against her skin, cold and battering and pure. The wind was howling down the streets, toppling carts and ripping shutters from doors and windows. Most of the city had pulled themselves indoors. The only people outside on the square were City Watch and the lancer patrol she had seen earlier. The lancers were desperately wrestling with a half-dozen horses, trying to force them into the stables of the inn, but the horses were mad with the storm, bucking and rearing.

Floré ignored that, ignored Commander Bannon and her directions to the City Watch. Floré ignored it all, save the storm. Purple lightning cut down from the storm, and she ignored it even as it tore chunks from spires and roofs. She was waiting for the wet-lightning, the bolts black and red the storm would send, and what was carried inside. Finally, after a long minute standing still in the rain with Voltos beside her, she saw a spark down an alley to her left and then a blast of arcing black-and-red lightning was cutting between buildings. The sound of it was an explosion this close, enough to shake her organs and her teeth and make her want to scream. Floré grinned, and ran into the alley.

The lightning had burst through the cobbles, a pit of dirt five foot wide charred and blackened below. Floré drew her sword and stalked forward, and behind her in the distance heard another crack as more lightning hit. From the charred pit where the wet-lightning had struck, a grey hand with jagged yellow claws pushed up through the dirt, and another, and the scrabbling torso of a rottroll emerged. Its head pushed free of the dirt, mouth snapping. It was similar in form to the goblins though much larger, grey and pebbled and devoid of ears, with lank hair matted across its scalp.

With a great haul of scrabbling too-long arms it pulled its torso from the dirt and roared at her, rows of serrated teeth and a tongue like an eel thrashing in the rain. The troll turned its eyes onto her, orbs of black, and started to push at the ground, grunting as it struggled to pull its legs clear. Floré heard Voltos behind her calling out that they should send for help, but then she was running, running on cobbles in the rain, the wind in her face, and her sword in her hand. The rottroll raised an arm to block her first swing, the sword biting deep into thick keratinous hide but barely drawing blood. It jerked back that arm and swung the other at her, and Floré ducked low, pulling her sword with her.

She knew rottroll anatomy. Their hide was thick as armour on the arms and legs and spine and shoulder, the crown of their head. Elsewhere it was thick too, thick enough to withstand a single blow from any normal sword. Floré circled the beast, harrying at its arms, trying to stop it from pulling its legs free of the dirt below. It managed to get one leg out and then swung a vicious backhand at her, snarling. Floré blocked with her sword but the weight of the blow sent her sprawling, and then the rottroll was free.

With the rain and wind lashing around it, and more bolts of lightning crashing in the streets beyond, it leaned back its head and roared. Floré pushed up into a crouch and dropped her sword and from her belt grabbed Captain Tyr's silver knife. She drew her arm back and threw the blade, as she'd thrown so many endless knives in endless practice yards and countless battles. The blade spun, catching the light from glass-covered oil lamps that lit the street, and sank into the roaring open mouth of the troll. It staggered and squinted down at her, spitting a mouthful of blood, and then she was rolling to avoid its heavy hands as they slammed into the ground where she had crouched.

As Floré rolled she grabbed her sword and then ducked in close, to the back of the knees, a short hacking blow at each. She danced back again as it fell to its knees, and then pushed herself flat against a building as a lancer running up behind her in a blue tabard nearly took her head off with the follow-through of a swing with a halberd after he missed the rottroll by at least four yards.

'Moron!' she yelled, but the lancer was down now, the weight of his halberd having spun him off his feet. Behind him, another half dozen lancers were there with polearms, along with Bannon and Voltos. The rottroll lunged its arms forward and grabbed one of them, its long hands encircling the man's waist. The others jabbed at it with spears but it ignored them, pulling the screaming man back from their rank. Floré leapt forward to hack at its wrist before it could squeeze the life from him. As she did, Bannon yelled an order in the darkness and the lancers as one charged with long spears. Four of them hit true, and the rottroll collapsed back into the charred hole it had crawled from.

Floré hacked again and again and its hand fell open, the lancer rolling free to the street with a wet thud. Grinning, Floré breathed hard and reached her gauntleted hand into the mouth of the fallen rottroll, retrieving Captain Tyr's silver dagger. She wiped it on her sleeve, and turned to the others.

'More?' she yelled, and Bannon nodded. Floré spun her sword in a circle and followed the commander.

~

Tomas returned as Yselda was wiping her face dry with a cloth that had been left by the wine. She had sat listening to the storm with her head in her hands for perhaps twenty minutes, but the winds were calming and she'd realised her face was still wet.

'Well,' he said. 'Pretty under all the mud and blood. Pretty girls in the Forest Watch – wonders never cease!'

Yselda didn't know how to react to that, and she felt the tips of her ears burning and her gaze turning downward. Tomas breezed past her and found his wine, and returned to his seat. He was completely dry. *Had he even gone outside?* Floré and Voltos came next, closing the door behind them. Both were soaked. Outside the hearth-room door Yselda could hear Bannon shouting orders.

Floré took off her gauntlets and rubbed at her eyes.

'It is done,' she said. 'The wet-lightning only struck thrice. Only one rottroll, and a few goblins. Now it is only the rain, the wind, the mist, the lightning. Bannon has it under control.'

'Captain,' Yselda said, 'it's been two days and two nights. If we are going to head north, we should rest now. We can't travel in the rotsurge. After the rain, the acid mists. We should rest.'

Voltos patted at his soaked silk armour with a cloth and tutted.

'Cadet Hollow is right, Floré,' he said, 'and Tomas was right as well. If we find a whitestaff, we should be able to get a bearing on your daughter. Bannon said the whitestaffs in Undal have been recalled to Iskander for a conclave – that means those in Ossen-Tyr must be heading south as well. Perhaps we can catch them on the road and not lose any time.'

Voltos retrieved his wine and lowered himself stiffly to a chair, and Yselda noticed the dappling of grey in his otherwise black muzzle, but she found herself struggling to remember how old Antians really got. Voltos stared into his wine and the room fell silent but for the crackle of the fire, and the incessant wind and rain outside. The walls vibrated as a thunderclap cut through the town – more wet-lightning, and close. Floré stared at the pelting rain through the window and Yselda stared at Floré.

'The loss of Janos-Wreck pains me,' Voltos said at last. 'You know he and I were close. I would not leave your daughter. We will find her – Marta – and then we will help Benazir, yes?'

Floré shrugged, and turned to the skein-mage, Tomas, who watched her steadily with his twinkling eyes. Floré's eyes were shadowed and tired, and Yselda saw her shoulders slump a little with resignation as she reached her decision. She turned back to Voltos.

'You find my daughter,' she said, 'and I'll hold Benny's hand so she can go over the Stormwall. Whatever you need.'

~

Cuss and Nash reached Yulder's farm after the sun had set. The pockmarked woodsman wore a rain cloak and carried his axe at the ready, and Cuss walked beside him, his chest aching and his legs tired. They did not talk on the way, and as night fell Cuss was grateful that a thin slice of moon was casting light through the pine. Even with only the moon to light their way, the path was not so bad, a wide cart trail of compacted earth that wound uphill away from town to the east, gaining elevation quickly. The trees this close to town had largely been cut back decades past, so the forest was new growth, twisted by the wind from the sea to the south, rather than the towering pines of the deeper forest.

Nash pulled back his hood when they reached the edge of

the treeline, and Cuss blinked at the sight before them and he felt his breath catch. Yulder's house sat on the north side of a steep hill, the trees cleared back in a hundred feet in every direction. There was a paddock and a barn, a chicken run and a sty. None of that caught Cuss's attention; what he saw was over the top of the treeline, a landscape beyond anything he had imagined. In the distant west, there was a faint glow from what must be Undal City itself. Casting his gaze south, he could see the blinking lighthouses that lined the Star Coast, at least three of them. Craning his neck, Cuss looked for the lights of Hookstone Town, and recoiled as he saw a tempest of purple and black clouds hanging low in that direction. The rest of the sky was dark but clear.

'That,' Nash said, 'really doesn't look good. Is that a wee rotsurge?'

Cuss shrugged and grimaced, and the two exchanged glances and then stared back out at the miles-distant maelstrom.

'Right,' Nash said, shaking his head and looking away from the storm and up again at the farmhouse. 'Right, sword out, eh lad? No smoke from his chimney, no lights. I can see a horse and some chickens though so might be he is all right.'

Cuss nodded and stepped forward, drawing his shortsword.

'Yulder!' he called out, and beside him Nash shook his head slightly and worried at his axe handle.

'Quieter might have been better, lad,' he said, and Cuss could only shrug. There was no response from the house, so the two approached. At the door Cuss glanced at the older man and then at the paddock where two dark shapes lay in the short grass and flowers. Horses, Cuss saw. They were utterly still. *Dead,* he thought, picturing the horses at Hasselberry, the cows in the south field. *All dead.* Nash took a step that way and squinted at the horses as Cuss raised his sword to rap the pommel on the door, frowning. Before he could knock, the door flew open inwards.

From the darkness of the open door a sharpened iron bar jabbed forward and Cuss tumbled back, falling off the porch and onto his pack. His chest flared in pain but it was the wounds from the night before rather than any new injury – the spear had missed by a fraction of an inch. From the doorway a goblin leapt forward, raising its spear to finish the boy rolling on the ground, black orb eyes and pebbled grey skin seeming to absorb the moonlight. It was wearing an oversized tunic of simple wool and it chittered in a language Cuss could not understand as it hopped forward and raised its spear two-handed to strike down and impale him.

Off to the side of the door, there was a twitch as Nash's grey-green rain cloak was pushed aside and his body turned and his axe swung out with a practised aim. Nash's axe cleaved the goblin; the woodsman's blade was built for splitting logs, and the axe head buried deep through the shoulder and back of the goblin, coming to rest in its chest. The iron bar spear fell from limp hands to tumble to the dirt next to Cuss, who rose to his feet, breathing hard.

'Ashes and spit, Nash,' he said, as Nash pulled his axe free from the goblin corpse and peered tentatively in the door. Nash sniffed, and his hands on the axe grip.

'Light a torch boy,' he said. 'That one didn't see me, but might be more of the little bastards.'

Cuss fumbled to pull a torch from the side of his pack and to find the flint and steel in his belt pouch. Within a few moments he had the torch lit. Nash nodded to him, and the boy took a tentative step towards the door, torch in one hand and shortsword in the other. He stepped over the dead goblin – *he had never seen a live goblin before*! The torch cast a ring of light behind them and as he passed Nash he could see the woodsman keeping a watchful eye on the forest.

The cabin was empty. Cupboards were open and stripped, and a clothes trunk lay almost empty at the end of the bed. Cuss frowned and looked around – there were clearly no other goblins. *Why would there be a single goblin here?* None of it made sense to him.

'Boy!' Nash called, and Cuss spun and ran outside to join the woodsman. He only made it a step and then he stopped, and felt his gut quiver and his chest burn. Slowly he lowered the torch and sword, and his mouth opened soundlessly.

To the east, over the Cimber hills beyond Hookstone forest, an orb of light flew. It was the size of a firefly from here, but it burned bright. Cuss felt Nash's hand on his shoulder guiding him to look west, and he could see another, off near the broken mountain at Bow, west of the river at the edge of the horizon. In a panic Cuss cast about, behind them, above, and felt cold sweat on his back and forehead as he remembered the night before on the loch; the orb had appeared then from nowhere, without warning. He could see no other lights.

The two of them stood and watched as the orbs flew as high as clouds, both of them north, and soon they could see them both at once without turning as they seemed to meet over the Great Glen and then north still until they were too small to follow.

'Well,' Nash said. 'That ain't great news.'

Cuss nodded. 'The sergeant needs to know,' he said quietly. 'They both went north. Past the Great Glen at least, but definitely north, towards Orubor or the mountains past it.'

Nash wiped the goblin blood from his axe on a shirt that was lying on the floor by the door and exhaled slowly.

'What's the plan then lad?' he said at last, and Cuss looked up from the goblin corpse and screwed up his eyes.

'I… need to find the sergeant. She went to Hookstone, but… she might leave before I get there. If I take the forest trail west I can head to the ford at… Ollen? That way I can follow the road south to Hookstone, but if they've already headed north somehow I shouldn't miss them. If they've already passed I can follow.'

Nash eyed the boy for a long moment.

'You mean to follow these things north, Cuss?' he asked, and Cuss felt his cheeks redden. He set his jaw and forced himself to make eye contact with the gaunt woodsman.

'They have my wee brother,' he said, and to his surprise Nash didn't argue with him or order him back to the village, but simply nodded.

'You need to sleep first, lad,' he said. 'Sleep and prepare. I'll sort the goblin. We'll leave at dawn.'

Cuss tilted his head and looked back in the direction of Hasselberry.

'Don't you need to let Tellen know Yulder's gone, and there are goblins?'

Nash smiled, and put a hand on the boy's shoulder.

'Tellen ain't stupid,' he said, 'and they'll be ready for any goblins. Like you say, most important is making sure the sergeant and whoever is looking has all the facts. I'll come with you to the ford and then swing past Hookstone on my way back to Hasselberry, pick up some supplies and whatnot.'

Looking down, Nash prodded the goblin corpse with his foot and curled his lip.

'Besides, lad,' he said, 'I don't want to be out in the woods alone right now any more than you do.'

~

Floré dreamt of Marta, and Janos. It was a dream that was more like a memory, or a whirling concatenation of a hundred memories, the cottage with lilac bushes in the garden and thick thatch above, the gentle smell of wood smoke from the hearth.

Marta was a babe in arms, Marta was crawling, Marta sat with coloured blocks or carved toys. Marta smiled and gurgled, or used her words. Janos was a constant presence at the kitchen table, writing his poems or by the fire reading the poems of others, always reading aloud.

'A poem written down is an egg,' he had told Marta, 'but a poem read out loud is a fabulous chicken.'

Marta had loved that.

'Time for chicken,' she would say, and Janos would sit her on his knee and read her a poem from a book, or invent one on the spot, iterations of themes recurring.

Floré dreamt of home, of the simplicity of a sword in a scabbard on a belt on a hook behind the door, a tabard with no lingering bloodstains.

Marta was in her sickbed then, a babe, a toddler, coughing and pale for weeks on end, always reaching for the skein and too young to understand it was drawing from her, hurting her. In the dream Floré could not comfort her as she had in life. Whenever she reached for her, something was in her way: a goblin, a rottroll, her mother, her old training sergeant, a fence, a door, iron bars.

She awoke sweating and heard the rain battering against the window of the hearth room. Casting about quickly, she could see that Tomas and Voltos were asleep, as was Yselda.

She should send the girl back, she knew, but found it hard to bring her thoughts to bear. Back to what? Would she have wanted to go back to Hasselberry, to mourn and grieve, when she was fifteen?

Floré almost smiled at that. When she was Yselda's age she had been with Benny at Stormcastle XII, flirting with the other cadets and slaughtering goblins, stealing wine. When she was fifteen she had met Janos.

They were already two years into the commando training when they met him: as a skein-mage, Janos had it easier than they; or so they told him every day. He would spend hours with Thum-Pho and Nostul and the old woman Hurien, the one the cadets called the witch. They would speak and lecture and meditate, Janos and four other skein-mage hopefuls. Meanwhile Floré and Benazir were sparring and running, and tracking through the marshes for two long years. Dozens of them would range east for weeks at a time into the Slow Marsh on the safe side of the wall, sent on war games against each other to capture flags. In the third and fourth years the skein-mages began to join them, and that was when Floré and Benazir were put in a patrol with Janos.

'Couldn't track a bear in a barn,' Floré had said their first day out with Janos, watching this gangly teen utterly fail to draw any conclusions from obvious trail sign. Benazir laughed, the other cadets laughed, and Janos fumed in silence. Later that afternoon, he lifted a grass snake silently from the reeds and dropped it on her head, and she would have broken his nose if Benazir hadn't grabbed her arm, laughing.

'Play nice,' Benazir said to her then. Four days later, when the rain came and they were all soaked through and sheltered in an abandoned crofter's hut, Janos lit a fire with wet wood and no tinder using only his hand, and Benazir produced a bottle of rough spirit she had gotten from one of the cooks. They had huddled close, drinking.

'You're from Fallow Fen,' he said to Benazir, later that night when the talk was low, and Floré remembered the chill in her spine, remembered the look in Benazir's eyes. Benazir didn't talk about Fallow Fen.

'It's a shame,' he continued, the drink loosening his tongue. 'It's a real shame what happened there. Preventable, of course.'

Benazir stared at him and Floré had stirred in the dirt but Benazir held out a hand to stop her from intervening.

'Preventable?' Benazir asked, her voice steady, and Janos smiled at her.

'The garrison was weaker than it should have been, the signalling systems were all out of date. Hurien said, if Commander Hallfast hadn't died there, the Grand Council would have hung him.'

'Hanged,' said Benazir, her voice quiet. Beyond them the Slow Marsh, the buzz of insects, the cool breeze, and Floré had tried to intervene.

'We should turn in,' she had said, but Benazir ignored her and Janos carried on, oblivious.

'Hallfast was a fool. He ran Fallow Fen like a playground, not a border city. No discipline. It'll be different when we're in charge!'

'My name is Benazir Arfallow,' Benazir said, slowly. 'You understand the Stormguard name, for orphans? Artollen, from Tollen. Argarioch, from Garioch.'

She nodded to each of them in turn, and then leaned forward in the darkness and drew the silver dagger from her waist, with the hilt of antler and the runed blade, and pointed it at Janos. His face fell.

'I don't understand,' he said, at last, and Floré tried to tell him with her eyes to be still, to *be quiet*.

'I am Arfallow,' Benazir continued, moving forward now and pressing the tip of the silver knife against Janos's chest. 'I *was* Benazir Hallfast. If you speak my father's name again, oh wise and all-knowing skein-mage, I'll burn you to ash.'

Benazir stalked from the fire and Janos opened his mouth to apologise but Floré kicked his shin.

'Best not,' she had said, and had left him there with his fire and his warmth, to find her friend.

Looking out of the window in Hookstone now, Floré watched the rivulets of water coursing down, and let the sound of the coursing wind overtake her. She could not move through the storm to find Marta. She could plan no further than she had.

Floré allowed herself a moment of decadence, of weakness. She cried silently into her bedroll, for Janos, her ward. Janos, her husband. Janos, her daughter's father. Janos, her love.

By the time the sky began to lighten and the winds began to calm she had run out of tears, and she gripped herself hard on each arm. The hard layer was there, the layer she had worked so long to put away. Callousness, a brutality borne of necessity, a willingness to break and be broken to do what must be done.

She would use it.

'I will find you,' she said, and closed her eyes.

9

EYES SHARP, BLADES SHARPER

'The Stormwall is our burden and our pride. From First Light in the north to Final Light in the south, it wends across marsh and rock and hill. So we build, we repair, we patrol, and we push forth into the rotstorm to ensure no remnant of Ferron threatens our people ever again.' – Private Diary, Commander Salem Starbeck

In the darkness of the night the rotstorm eased as it passed, headed east along the coast towards the Watchful Brothers that marked the border between the Undal Protectorate and Isken beyond. Yselda awoke on her sleeping roll to find the captain already washed, dressed, and armoured. The captain passed her a bowl of porridge and sat back down on her own sleeping roll, which had been next to Yselda's.

'Where are Voltos and Tomas?' she asked, and Floré glanced out to the smithy beyond. Bannon had returned after organising the City Watch to respond to any nearby wet-lightning strikes, and had offered them the hearth room for the night.

'They will be back soon,' Floré said. 'They are getting supplies.'

Floré gave Yselda a scrutinising glance and Yselda rubbed at her eyes.

'I'm sorry, Captain, I'll be ready to go—'

The captain cut her off with a wave, and chewed the lumps on her porridge thoughtfully, still eyeing Yselda.

'You don't have to come,' she said, her voice quiet, and pushed through though Yselda opened her mouth to interrupt. 'It is good you want to help Petron. But there is no knowing what we go into, if we find anything at all, and it will be danger and death at worst, or days or weeks on the road to no avail. You don't need to do this. Hasselberry is your home. You can go there and help them rebuild.'

Yselda set aside the porridge and stood and began to don her clothing, and then pulled on her leather jerkin and her Forest Watch tabard. As she dressed she saw the captain's right fist tensing and fingers spasming, her jaw clenching.

'I won't be a burden,' Yselda said. 'I *won't*.'

Floré rolled her eyes at that. 'I know that, girl, I taught you to shoot myself—'

'No!' Yselda said. 'No. Not to you. I know I can help you where you are going, and you know I want to find Marta and Petron, and… and bring the blade to whatever it is that did all that to Hasselberry, to Shand and Esme and the girls. I won't be a burden to the town. I won't go back a lost girl to sit at another home fire and wake up crying every night. I want to *fight*.'

Floré's fist relaxed and the pain in her eyes seemed to diminish. She nodded.

'All right, then,' she said, 'I'll not turn down your sword, little sister. But listen close and listen true – Voltos and Tomas are playing their own game. The Stormguard's game. They want to find out about the orbs, but not for Marta and Petron. You understand me?'

Yselda nodded, though in truth she did not see how those aims would ever lead to anything but the same. Tomas was of the Stormguard; he wouldn't leave Marta and Petron behind, no more than she would.

It was another hour by the time they left Hookstone – the lancer captain was in the square when they left, and he stared at Voltos with a smouldering anger. His men were soaked with mud and rain from a long night hunting wet-lightning strikes, trying to find any seeds planted that might sprout rotvine or goblins or a rottroll. Most of the horses in town were killed in the attack, burned or asphyxiated or cut deep with strange rune scars, but Voltos and Tomas had arrived after the attack and Yselda and Floré still had their mounts from Plompton Rocks. Their horses were stabled in an otherwise empty barn, but they whinnied and tossed their heads and were clearly upset. The stable smelled of blood.

'Why are they killing horses?' Yselda asked, a hand on the cheek of the dappled mare who had carried her from the forest.

'Five sheep gone,' the captain muttered, cinching tight the girth of her horse's saddle, and Yselda frowned and turned to Tomas and Voltos.

'Kill them now and they can't be ridden to war, or eaten later,' Tomas said, shrugging. His own horse was a black-coated beast sixteen hands high, its eyes wild. Two grooms were settling it as he watched.

'It is a precept of every war ever fought, Cadet. Resources, whatever they are, must be controlled or denied. We do the same thing past the Stormwall,' he continued, stroking his beard. 'Kill any livestock we come across, scatter herds where we can't kill. Salt every well and patch of earth that might grow a crop. Any resource, no matter what, is controlled or denied.'

He turned to face the captain and they held eye contact for a long moment, and then Floré mounted her horse and rode from the stable without another word, and Yselda watched her go, out into the light of the morning.

'Of course,' Voltos added, feeding an apple to a sturdy horse scarcely larger than a pony, 'it could be something else entirely. This threat seems linked to the Ferron, to be sure, but the rust-folk are a primitive assortment. They are scarcely surviving. This is something else, and the motives behind these actions may be beyond our ken. For the moment, at least.'

He turned to follow Yselda's gaze out into the light and mud beyond the stable doors, the smouldering ruin and wet stone of Hookstone.

'Or they want us to think so,' he continued, quietly, both ears dropping down, 'and it is all just a game of charades so we spend our time guarding livestock and herding horses when we should be looking elsewhere.'

Yselda heaved herself onto her horse, and looked back at the empty stables, the blood on the air still tangible, the dark patches in the hay where the dead horses had lain. She shivered.

The four rode out through the west gate and spent the morning hugging close to the hilltops, following the Ferron slave road towards Undal City. From the hard stone of the road they could see south and down to the Wind Sea, and when they passed the Dal lighthouse, the mighty stone beacon of the Star Coast was impressive even in the daytime. Past the fields pale beaches were pounded by heavy surges of surf, and a hundred yards into the water the Dal lighthouse rose from waves, a hundred feet straight up, the same dark seamless stone as the Ferron roads, topped with an opaque glass orb that blazed all night with a warm yellow light. In the cool of the morning, the glass orb was dim.

Yselda had glanced at it before when down near Hookstone, but had never been west of there before and never seen it so close. She found herself biting her lip as she rode, unable to draw her eyes from it. The glass orb, in shape, seemed so similar to the flying orbs they had seen over Hookstone forest; but she had seen the light of the Dal tower before, on so many nights, and it was a calm and yellow beacon, not that blazing white heat of the orbs. Still, her gaze lingered.

They rode on, and at the village of Dal turned north without delay; a City Watch guard tried to hail them but the captain ignored him and rode on. Voltos and Yselda followed, but Tomas lingered back to speak to the man. Yselda gazed at the unfamiliar village; the stone walls of the harbour, the stout cottages by the shore with their nets hung out to dry and their slate roofs. There was a shaman tower with four bells and dark-stained wood. It was a normal village, untainted by the corpses that littered the roads of Larchford, or the fire and wreckage of Hasselberry and Hookstone Town. They rode ever on, and by turning north at Dal they avoided Undal City, which was only a scant dozen miles past the harbour village. If it had been night, Yselda might have seen it – seen *Undal City itself!* She found herself smiling and then weeping in her saddle as she remembered Esme and Nat and Lorrie discussing plans to venture into the capital one day for High Harvest or the Deadwinter festival.

As the sun reached the top of the sky they were riding dead north, Unerdan River on their left and Hookstone forest a glowering presence to the right. They stopped to let the horses drink and eat, and took a brief meal and rest themselves. Yselda tried to braid her hair, which had come loose in their wild ride, whipped by the winds blowing in from the sea. Her legs were bruised and her muscles knotted painfully from the day's hard ride, but she knew the captain would press them further and she would not allow herself to complain. *I will not be a burden.* Tomas seemed disgruntled to be travelling so fast and hard, but the Antian Voltos was unperturbed – his saddle was different to theirs, allowing him to partially lounge, with a cushioned seat, more support for his back, and wooden protrusions upon which he could rest his arms. Yselda had never seen anything quite like it. His small sturdy horse had kept pace with them all day, utterly unconcerned by the pace or terrain.

The captain was off checking the horses when Voltos approached Yselda.

'Cadet Hollow,' he said, 'I wondered if I might ask you something?'

Yselda made herself smile, though she was disconcerted to be alone with an armoured Antian, even if he did seem so scholarly and friendly.

'You spoke to the survivors in your village, Cadet,' he

said, slowly. 'Tell me, where do *you* think these orbs come from?'

Yselda glanced over at the captain, who was perhaps two dozen yards away, brushing down her horse with swift, efficient strokes. She swallowed the lump in her throat and pushed a stray lock of her hair behind her ear.

'Cuss,' she said, 'Cuss... Cuss is another cadet. His wee brother was taken, Petron? Cuss said someone came down from the orb. I saw them, the orbs I mean. In the forest. Each one is as big as a lumber wagon, at least. If someone came down, are there people inside? Or something inside? If it is like a ship, a ship in the sky, then...'

Yselda pictured the lighthouse at Dal with its orb that glowed every night, with its smooth glass top and seamless stone sides. She glanced away from the Antian's probing gaze, down at her feet, and bit at her lip again.

'It seems Ferron, Mister Voltos. Like the Dal lighthouse. Things we don't understand. The Whitestaff Izelda showed me books with drawings and paintings of towns and people and carts and ships from Ona, from Cil-Marie, from the strait kingdoms and Tessendorm. I've met Isken trade caravans, and no offence, Mister Voltos, but I've now met you and seen your... saddle. Your armour.'

Voltos nodded sagely and looked out west towards the river, the Unerdan bubbling and rushing over rock.

'I mean to say,' Yselda continued, 'they are all different, all of them. But the things from Ferron, the slave roads and the lighthouses, the Watchful Brothers, even the overseer forts – they are foreign in a way I can't describe. Seamless stone and strange glass. The orbs felt like that. Different.'

Voltos continued to stare at the river.

'I think you might be right, Cadet,' he said, 'but I certainly hope you are not.'

~

Petron dreamt once again of a spire of gold, nestled in grey mountains shrouded in mist. He awoke in his cell of bare dark stone, and there was a tray of food and a bundle of clothing. He pulled on the clothing, a strange one-piece suit of a dark material he did not know. It had no pockets, no buttons, no ties, but when he had pulled it on the fabric seemed to adhere to itself to keep from flapping open or falling down. He rubbed at the material with his fingers, soft and stretchy, and he made a sour face.

'Not even real clothes,' Petron said, and blew out a long breath, 'not even real clothes, Cuss. Berren's knees, this is trouble.'

He was alone in his cell of course, and he sat down to eat soon enough. Bread and some sort of porridge, a clay cup of water. He had dreamt of the spire of gold, and the blindfolded white-haired woman asked him questions but again he could not understand what she said.

Once he had eaten, he prowled the walls of his cell. When he could find no trace of the organic opening in the stone that had admitted his captors the previous day, he reached for the skein, but could feel nothing, no pattern, no power. Instead, there was only a tangle of chaos and disorder. His stomach churned.

Varratim came for him a few hours later. He had spent the time inspecting his room, and trying not to think about his mother and Jana and Cuss. The wall opened like an eye parting, a seam appeared where none had been before and then there was an opening and beyond a dark corridor of metal and rock. Varratim had the same disconcerting gentle smile, and his pupils gyrated and split and reformed and danced within green irises as he stared at Petron.

'Is my brother alive?' Petron asked immediately, and Varratim frowned.

'Your brother?'

'He was with me, in the boat, when you took me. He tried to save me and you did something and... he fell into the water. Does he live?'

Varratim rubbed at his chin.

'I do not know, Petron,' he said, 'and you are confused. I did not take you. I am not alone, in this endeavour. One of the others took you, and brought you to me. They also took Marta, and I'm happy to say we sorted out that Janos-Wreck business. They are clear. They cut him down, the girl in his arms. So you are not his son, but a village boy with a knack for the skein.'

Petron looked away as Varratim spoke, terrified he would give something away. How could he help Marta? *Crow-men*, he thought, *crow-men are the monsters that live in the rotstorm.*

'My master taught me many things,' he found himself saying, and made himself make stare into the oscillating madness of Varratim's eyes. 'He taught me many things, and if you let her go I will tell you everything.'

Varratim laughed and gestured for Petron to stand.

'I find myself liking you, boy. A brother is an important thing. I hope yours is alive.'

With that, Varratim turned on his heel and strode out. Petron stared after him, and widened his eyes in surprise when the wall remained open.

'Come along, my boy,' Varratim called, 'there is much to see, and much to understand.'

Petron hurried after him, bare feet cold on the stone floor. He tried to picture wrestling the knife from Varratim's belt. He could kill the man, find Marta, and then...

He turned a corner and Varratim was before him, his hands resting on a metal railing, and beyond him a huge cavern.

'Isn't it wonderful, Petron?' he said, and Petron could only gape. Down from the railing, the cavern spread wide, at least two hundred feet across and twice that in depth. At the far end daylight cut through hanging vines and falling streams of water that obscured a huge cavern mouth. The roof of the cavern was studded with stalactites and trailing moss and occasional motes of light seemed to float between them, cascading a gentle glow across the rest of the space.

Down on the floor, six orbs of dark stone sat on spindly metal legs on a smooth rock floor. Each was larger than a lumber wagon, with a band of hazy glass around their centre, and a convex disc of round dark stone above and below the glass, giving each orb the silhouette of an eye. Around them and over them were goblins, dozens of them, wiping at the floor with rags or carrying bundles. They were clad in short black robes, barefooted, and directed by a handful of men and women in the same severe black uniform as Varratim; the uniform Petron realised he was wearing himself. Varratim turned to him and smiled.

'Welcome,' he said, 'to the mountains of the Blue Wolf.'

~

Cuss and Nash reached the ford at Ollen by late afternoon, having wound down the narrow game paths from Yulder's cabin through Hookstone forest. As they headed deeper into the forest the trees grew wilder and taller, and Cuss kept one hand on his sword hilt and glanced back every few moments. The sergeant and Yselda had told them about the wolves. Would there be any here, in the north-west of Hookstone forest?

The landscape soon grew rockier, the trees slightly more spaced, and soon they were clambering through beds of ferns and long grasses as they lowered in elevation. By noon they reached the edge of the forest and emerged onto grazing land, startling a flock of black-wooled sheep that scattered over grass and hillocks.

'Nash,' Cuss asked, 'have you been to Ollen before?'

'I have,' Nash said, smiling. 'I certainly have. There is not much there but the ferry and a market every Judgeday, except one wonderful thing: the Ollen Wheel. Best inn this side of Undal City, I reckon.'

They rejoined the road and then it was only a final mile to Ollen, and Cuss found himself staring wildly at the sight. To the west of town the river Unerdan cut a line through the world from north to south, three hundred feet across and running slow compared to its wild white waters between the steep rocky banks to the north and south of the town. The ferry was a simple wooden platform forty foot in length, tied to a static guiding chain that was anchored to a tall oak on the far side, and a huge boulder on the Ollen side. From the platform ropes led to teams of horses on each side that would pull the ferry across. Cuss could see the horses waiting patiently as the ferry was loaded with carts and passengers. The ground around the ferry landing was churned to mud, and even more caravans of goods were tied up just north of the ferry, where a waterwheel stuck out on a spindly arm from the first floor of a wooden inn. The Ollen Wheel.

Cuss followed Nash as the woodsman led them around the inn, but as they tied up their horses outside, Nash suddenly held out a hand and tilted his head. Cuss followed suit – above the rushing of the water and the din of the ferry being loaded, there was a... roaring?

'Something ain't right here,' Nash said, and Cuss followed the woodsman as he stepped cautiously to the back of the inn.

'Baal's spit,' Nash said, and Cuss drew his sword as they stumbled straight into a crowd of people holding axes and bottles and hoes, a mixture of traders and farmers; presumably, the customers of the Ollen Wheel and the traders hoping to cross the river.

As one the crowd turned to them, and Cuss let out a low curse as he saw what they were doing. Beneath a tall tree in the open space behind the inn, a Tullioch was noosed and tied by a dozen ropes. The creature was at least seven foot tall, hands ending in thick talons, scales a dark iridescent green-black. It was stripped to a loincloth and bleeding from a dozen small wounds, a rope around each wrist and another thick noose around its neck. A heavy tail was lashing behind it, and the crowd of men and women were keeping well clear.

One of them, a fat woman in middle age with a cascade of brown curling hair, gestured at the group to be still.

'Forest Watch!' she said, pointing at Cuss's tunic. 'Forest

Watch! We've caught a Tullioch, we have! A wild Tullioch from the sea!'

A murmur of assent rose from the crowd.

'Wait,' the Tullioch said, and Nash dropped his pack. Cuss cleared his throat and looked back at the woodsman, and Nash stretched his neck and stepped forward.

'What's going on?' he said, and pointed his axe handle at the woman. 'You – what's going on? Simple like.'

The woman frowned at him.

'We caught a Tullioch! You heard about them flying balls of fire? That's not human business – Tullioch or Antian. We caught this one, and we're going to deal with him!'

'Wait,' the Tullioch said again, its voice thick and deep, and someone threw a bottle at it. It bounced off the creature's muscled shoulder and it roared again.

'Law-man!' it said, looking at Cuss. 'Law-man, these take my coin, my blade when I sleep. I am traveller, no crime. No crime here. I keep the concords!'

Cuss opened his mouth and stepped forward but the fat woman held out a stout arm.

'Not going to be trusting a lizard, are ye? We'll have him hung quick fast, don't you worry,' she said, and beside Cuss Nash nervously glanced around the crowd the crowd. Cuss cleared his throat again to speak.

'You *can't* hang him,' he said, and the woman stuck out her bottom lip.

'There's been orbs of fire!' one man said, a red-haired man with a long beard. 'My whole herd got burned up not ten miles away!'

'Aye,' said another. 'My cousin's daughter was stolen in the night, and all their horses dead, out Laga way!'

Cuss tried to speak again but they were all shouting and he found himself taking a step back.

'He ain't Forest Watch,' a red-haired woman said. 'He's a cadet...'

There was a long moment of stillness and Cuss curled his lips into a sickly smile and raised his hands to placate the mob, and then there was swearing as three men rushed Nash. In a moment the woodsman was held tight, still holding his axe but his arms pinned to his sides. They didn't even bother to restrain Cuss.

The fat woman gestured at a man beside her, a farmer with a heavy wood cudgel, and he stepped towards Cuss.

'We're hanging him,' the man said. 'Now ye gonna drop that pretty sword and watch and join us for a drink after? Or we going to beat you two bloody and leave ye across the river?'

Cuss took another step back and drew his sword and raised his fists, one clutching his sword and the other with the knuckleduster slipped on tight.

'You can't hang him,' he said, and felt all the blood in his body rushing to his head. 'You can't kill him! By... by order of the Forest Watch, stand down!'

'Well,' Floré said, stepping around the side of the inn, 'I'd agree with that.'

Floré stepped towards Cuss fluidly and never slowed down, and Cuss felt a wave of relief as behind the sergeant he saw Yselda draw her shortbow. A thin, black-robed man with a red Stormguard commando tabard stood beside her, and closing his eyes he raised hands wreathed in green flame. Between them, an Antian stood holding a black-bladed dagger in a reverse grip, face drawn into a snarl.

The sergeant strode forward and past Cuss and in a single motion her fist came up and with one punch she knocked the farmer with the cudgel flat onto his back, and the crack of his cheekbone snapping under her gauntlet cut through the sudden stillness of the crowd. He fell back to the mud.

'Forest Watch,' she said, drawing her longsword and flourishing it. The dark grey of the blade drew every eye.

'That Tullioch is *mine*.'

10

The Blind Beggar

'Berren was found dead in the valley garden of the Iron Desert. His wounds were not visible, but he ceased, and when he ceased the people of Ferron lost their grace. The Eternal Emperor Ferron passed his mantle to his daughter, Seraphina, and he went north and north and north, never to be seen again. Without Berren's favour or Ferron's genius, the crop yields failed, and hunger drove the empire outward – they needed farmland, and bodies to work it. Ferron expanded by fire and steel and for four centuries the world wept.' – The Fall of Ferron, Whitestaff Anctus of Riven

The atmosphere in the Ollen Wheel was not convivial. Floré had drawn her sword and pointed the tip at the two men holding Nash, who released him and stepped back into the crowd, and the traders and farmers were silent as she stepped forward and cut the Tullioch free. Sheathing her blade she bowed briefly to the hulking lizardman, and then turned to the crowd and with a look demanded they disperse. As the crowd stepped back to whisper in groups of two or three, torches and pitchforks lowering, Floré led them straight into the inn. Tomas was saying something to the crowd, waving his burning hands around, but Floré didn't wait for him. The fat woman with the curling hair followed her, mumbling excuses and apologies, but Floré was in no mood. A peat fire smouldered in the hearth of the inn, and the window shutters were open to let in what remained of the afternoon light. Her stomach growled as she glanced around, measuring exits.

'Does the mail coach run overnight to Ossen-Tyr?' she asked, and the innkeeper's eyes narrowed, seeing a chance of escaping punishment by dint of her usefulness.

'Yes, sir, yes, it leaves in about an hour—'

'No,' Floré cut in. 'It leaves when we're ready. Tell them this is at the command of the Stormguard Tomas-Mage, Primus of Stormcastle XII. They will drive us overnight to Ossen-Tyr with no other stops, but first we need to eat and to speak to this Tullioch. You will bring hot food and you will resupply our stores – bread, cheese and meat for the road. Refill the waterskins. Understood?'

'Of course,' the woman said, giving a slight bow. 'I can explain what happened, you see—'

'No,' Floré said, her voice brooking no dissent. 'Go.'

Yselda and Cuss hugged each other briefly as the rest sat down around the table.

'I'm glad you're safe,' Yselda said to him, and Floré rubbed at her eyes and glanced over her young cadet. Cuss was almost as tall as her now, and he was shaking from the adrenaline. Floré absently patted him on the shoulder and gave him a small smile when he turned. The sight of one of her cadets, of *Cuss*, facing down a mob for the sheer right of it warmed her heart. The boy smiled back nervously and stilled a little.

'I had coin,' the Tullioch said gruffly beside her. 'Weapons and clothing; my pack.'

Floré nodded at him, leaning back in her chair.

'I'm sorry,' she said, and then took off her gauntlets and laid them on the table, ran her hands through her hair and tipped her head back to look at the ceiling. She exhaled and looked down. Nash, Cuss, Yselda, Tomas, and Voltos all stared at her expectantly. *Of course they did.* The Tullioch looked warily at all of them, and his gaze kept on lingering on Voltos. Floré was fairly sure he was a male; the display ridges down the spine were usually a giveaway, though this Tullioch's were black and matte compared to the vibrant ridges she had seen previously.

'Yselda, Tomas, go speak to the innkeeper and let her know that if all the Tullioch's possessions aren't ready for him by the time we leave I will be staying overnight to personally find every last one of that mob and I'll be exacting the Grand Council's judgement. Cuss and... Nash, isn't it? I need a report on Hasselberry and why in all hell you are here at all – and, sir, I'm afraid I didn't catch you name?'

Yselda left the table, but Tomas sat stolidly by and shook his head at her request, eying the Tullioch. The Tullioch slicked his forked tongue from his mouth and hissed softly.

'I am Heasin son of Luasin, of Shardkin Tullioch. I am in your debt, Law-man.'

'My thanks, Heasin son of Luasin. I am sorry this has happened. There have been strange occurrences the last few days, the people are on edge, but of course Undal does not seek to break the Tullioch Concords, and you have a right to safe passage.'

Heasin flexed the claws on his fingertips and leaned across the table, the lone candle casting shadows across his face as he turned to them each in turn and then back to Floré.

'You mean the orbs of fire,' he said, and turned his gaze around the table. 'The orbs have come. They have... taken children. They go north.'

Floré pictured Marta sitting on the rug before their hearth, with Janos beside her, and she closed her eyes tight, and the pain came, the tremors in her arm and her right foot now, and she clenched her jaw and put her hands under the table and gripped her right hand with her left and breathed in and out, head bowed, her heart racing. She could smell the acid of the rotstorm; she could hear the screaming, almost. Forcing her eyes open she stared back at the Tullioch.

'Do you know what they are?' she managed to ask at last, and Heasin shook his head.

'Curse,' he said. 'Memory. Ferron, again. Chain and whip, again, perhaps. This is how it started last time, I am told, before the empress. The memory of the elders is long. Before the shard broke. Before the cyclops, and the chains.'

Heasin pulled back his claws, leaving long gouges in the table, and tensed his arms. Tomas lit his pipe and stretched a casual arm along the back of his chair in what Floré assumed was feigned nonchalance. The Tullioch let out a long hiss.

'Hassin is the daughter of Heasin. Hassin, daughter of Heasin, of Shardkin Tullioch was taken, as were others. We hunted. We sought. We crossed the reef to the blight waters in the west, and the depths and darkness of the east and south. They go north, it is said, up the river you call Unerdan. So Heasin is here. They took all our young who could touch the... pattern. If you seek orbs, Heasin would join you.'

Floré could feel a pain in her head starting to build so she gripped her fingers into her leg beneath the table and swallowed three times. *Weakness is decadent.* She had to be strong for Marta. The innkeeper returned with a bottle of wine, followed by a serving girl laden with plates of steaming stew, lumps of beef and potato and carrot cooked so long they had formed one cohesive mound.

'Well,' Nash said, casting a glance at the hulking Tullioch and then the bottle of wine, 'I for one could use a drink.'

~

Cuss watched as Nash rode south into darkness, a strange feeling of loss coming over him. He barely knew the woodsman, a seasonal worker in the village who kept to himself, but the man had been kinder to Cuss than most of the true locals and had saved him from that goblin.

'Stay safe, lad,' he had said, and had slipped Cuss a whole silver piece when the sergeant – *captain* – wasn't looking. 'Your boss wants me to head to Undal to let them know where you lot are going. Sounds like a heavy mess, so eyes sharp and knife sharper. That's it right?'

Cuss had smiled, but then Nash was gone and smiling seemed hard again. He looked at the silver piece, turning it over in his hands. It was emblazoned with the broken chain on one side and the symbol of the Grand Council on the other, a sword and staff crossed beneath a four-pointed star.

'Get aboard,' the sergeant – *no, captain* – said, and Cuss hurried to clamber into the mail coach. He was sat squeezed tight next to Yselda and the strange Antian, and opposite them the Tullioch Heasin sat calmly next to a clearly awkward Tomas. Heasin's belongings had been returned, and he now wore a heavy dagger at his belt with a blade of pale rock and a handle of coral, and a loose-fitting blue robe that covered the rest of him.

'This is not going to be a comfortable night, is it?' Tomas said, looking at Cuss. 'You wouldn't mind a swap would you?'

Yselda seemed to twist uncomfortably at that, and before Cuss could think of an answer – *he certainly didn't want to sit next to the Tullioch* – Floré climbed in and wedged herself beside Tomas, pressing him even closer to Heasin, slamming the door closed behind her.

They crossed the ferry as the sun fell, a team of horses on the far side pulling it across waters that looked calm but tugged incessantly at the ferry barge, trying to take them downriver to Undal City. Cuss was very aware of the proximity of Yselda at his side, and aware that after two days' hard travel he smelled ripe. He held himself close and tried to focus out of the window, and thought about what he would tell Petron – *a ferry so big ten horses pull it; a Tullioch with claws and a rock dagger; a real Antian, but no spear; a skein-mage, a real one from the Stormwall itself!*

He lulled himself with this inner monologue, describing to his little brother all he had seen, committing it to memory, especially the skein-mage; he memorised all he could of his robes, his manner of speech, his tall boots and delicate hands, for Petron would surely love to hear of that.

Tomas-Mage, Primus of Stormcastle XII, was right: it was not a comfortable night, but Cuss still managed to sleep through most of it. The lantern guiding the coach cast a dim glow back into the passengers' compartment, and the gentle trundle of the wheels and the hooves of the team of horses soon lulled him. Behind the coach, the horses that the captain and the rest had ridden from Hookstone followed in a loose train.

He dreamt they were crossing the ferry at Ollen again but this time in heavy white water, the river in spate, and this time Petron was with them and Whitestaff Izelda was instructing them on proper diving form. He was too afraid to jump in the water, but Petron leapt with great shouts of joy, in and out like a fish.

Cuss awoke with Yselda's head on his shoulder, and so he sat very still. Her hair was knotted and matted and she seemed small pressed up against him. He woke intermittently at the creaking of the axle below, the rumble of the wheels over stone. After a particularly large bump, he found himself fully awake, looking in the dim light at the other side of the carriage where Voltos slept with his mouth open, wet pink tongue lolling out, a patch of drool growing on his silk armour.

'Are you okay, Cuss?' the captain asked him quietly, and he almost gave a start. He hadn't realised she was awake. Everyone else was asleep, nestled and still.

'Captain!' he whispered. 'Yes, thank you. My chest is sore still, but it itches, which means it is healing – that's what the whitestaff always says.'

The captain continued to stare at him.

'Are... are you okay, Captain?'

She turned away, looking out the window at the rising dawn. They were west of the Unerdan River, following the Ossen tributary up into the red clay hills. The trees were shorter and sparser here, no towering pines but smaller copses of silver-limbed trees with wide leaves.

'It doesn't matter if I'm okay,' the captain said, 'not until we have Marta and Petron back. Until then I am... hurt, not injured. Do you understand? Does that make sense, Cuss? We must be functional, for them. We have to be strong.'

Cuss followed her gaze out over the rolling hills, the dawn rising over heather and rock, and felt himself nodding.

~

Yselda woke with the carriage almost light, and thankfully they stopped soon after that for a short break to water the horses at a brook. She clambered out of the coach and stretched her legs and checked on her gear. Her eyes peered into the woods and moors off the track, but she could see no sign. She was looking for wolf eyes, yellow slits staring back at her, and as soon as she realised that she made herself stop. Back in the coach, Tomas was complaining about the lack of breakfast and Voltos was showing Cuss his obsidian dagger. She climbed back aboard, and wondered how far the captain would let them come. *Will she leave us in Ossen-Tyr?* Yselda didn't want to be left behind.

The coach climbed another hour up winding switchbacks past boulders of pale rock that dotted a thick red clay – they had risen above the peat bogs that followed the river on either side in the lowlands. Burns and brooks cascaded across the road occasionally, their water turned red by the ground beneath. The day carried onward, and the

Antian Voltos was schooling Cuss on the differences in the Stormguard: the City Watch, the Forest Watch, the Lancers, and the Commandos.

'The City Watch keep guard,' he said in an avuncular manner. 'Tabards of grey, truncheons of oak, iron helms and light chain shirts. Some ceremonial spears and halberds and swords, normally a few longbows to drive goblins and the like from the walls. The Forest Watch you know of course, green tabards, leather armour and shortswords and bows for ranging in the woods, to move silent and fast.'

She watched as Cuss fingered at his own cadet's tabard, and his sheathed sword, unaware of his hands moving as he listened with rapt attention to the Antian whose voice had a wet quality, as if speaking through a mouthful of saliva at all times. Yselda looked back out of the window at the sheep dotting the hillsides, the smoke from morning fires rising from croft chimneys.

'The Lancers are the bulk of the Stormguard,' Voltos continued, ignoring an ostentatious yawn from Tomas. 'Soldiers with lance and longbow, pike and sword and heavy shield. They patrol the borders, man the Stormwall, and hunt bandits and slavers in the wilds between the protectorate and Tessendorm to the north-east. Blue tabards, chain mail or half-plate armour, a variety of weapons and tactics at their disposal, mounted cavalry and the like. A mixed bunch. And then the Commandos...'

Yselda followed the Antian's gaze to the captain, who stared resolutely out of the window.

'They fight monsters in the rotstorm,' Cuss said. 'Red tabards, right?'

'Correct,' Voltos said, cleaning his eyeglasses on a loose

patch of silk fished from a pocket. 'They go into the rotstorm itself, and fight goblins and rottrolls and wyrms and worse, crow-men, demons; the remnants of Old Ferron. They push back, and strike early, that our lands might know peace.'

Yselda hadn't taken her eyes from the captain, and saw the tight set in her jaw.

'They wear the red, and light armour so that they can move through the swamps and mire and heat and hell of the rotstorm. They wear masks over their faces to keep out the burning clouds, long sleeves of thick leather to push back thorns. Silver daggers in their belts for the demons, steel in their scabbards for the monsters, and most important of all, the metal gauntlets on their fists.'

Cuss turned his gaze to the captain's hands, covered in their heavy gauntlets of intricate steel and leather, resting on her knee. Yselda nudged him and he looked away and down at the floor, then back at Voltos.

'Why the gauntlets?' he asked, and Tomas snorted. Voltos gave him a weary look and then smiled at Cuss and Yselda.

'In the rotstorm,' he explained, 'the ground itself will burn your hands. Every tree has a thorn, every vine a stinging tendril. Every patch of moss has a burning sickness or a poison needle. Rare copses of peace exist, hidden and safe. A Stormguard commando keeps their gauntlets, so they can keep their fists beneath. And they need to keep their fists to swing their swords!'

He gestured to Floré, who rolled her eyes and took off one gauntlet begrudgingly, passing it to Cuss. He ran his fingers over the intricate steel joints, the supple but thick leather beneath, the scratches and scars on the knuckle plate.

'What are the ridges for?' Yselda asked, taking the gauntlet from Cuss and prodding at three sharp ridges on the back of the hand, raised and oddly worked.

'Nothing,' said the captain, and took back the gauntlet and slipped it onto her hand, cinching tight the leather strap at her wrist. She gave a hard stare at Voltos, who nodded and turned to look out of the window, and Yselda blew through her nose and turned away herself, frustrated with the endless taciturn silences that made up the captain's existence.

'You are forgetting the skein-mages, Voltos,' Tomas said in the ensuing silence, and Voltos nodded in acknowledgement and stroked his whiskers.

'The skein-mages,' he told Cuss. 'Artillery, sniper, force multiplier. A clever skein-mage can knock an arrow from the sky; place a spark *just right* to turn a building to flame. A clever skein-mage can do many things.'

Yselda shifted in her seat and scratched at her nose.

'There is a price,' said the captain, and they all turned to look at her.

'A price?' Yselda said, and the captain nodded, looking at Tomas-Mage but not focusing her eyes particularly.

'To touch the skein, to bend it to your will, takes strength. It saps the mage. A clever skein-mage can knock an arrow from the sky, and afterward feel as if he had run a mile. The better the skein-mage, the less taxing their magics, as they understand the nuance of how to... interact with it all.'

Heasin flicked out his tongue and turned his head side on, his beady eye focusing on Tomas-Mage.

'This is why my people prefer the blade,' he said, one

hand moving to his knife hilt. 'To touch the pattern needs time, and… what is the word? *Focus*. Focus.'

He turned to face Cuss and Yselda and opened his mouth in what might have been a smile and clicked his long teeth together, and Yselda shuddered.

'There is not always time,' he said, 'and there is not always *focus*.'

~

Hours later, Yselda was worrying at a loose nail in the carriage seat when they finally reached Ossen-Tyr. It loomed from between two rounded peaks of rough rock, and Yselda found herself staring grimly at the stone watchtowers and wooden palisades. *They were no help to Hookstone,* she thought. *What is the use in a palisade if you can simply fly over it?*

The gates were open, and the coach trundled through with no remark and pulled to a stop in a market square where some traders were already set up for the day, stalls of vegetables and meat and skins and whatnot. They disembarked and Heasin drew glances immediately. Heasin with Voltos next to him was enough to make people stop what they were doing and openly watch, lowering crates of vegetables and grabbing their colleagues to point and whisper.

'This,' Voltos said, 'might get tiring. My burly friend, would you consider donning your hood that we might move somewhat surreptitiously? Tullioch are not so common, this far from the sea.'

Heasin stared down at the diminutive Antian and shrugged, and then pulled the cowl of his robes up.

'I think,' he said sibilantly, 'they will see me anyway. We are not common as it is dry here. Too dry, I am thinking.'

He sniffed at the air and flicked his tongue out, and Yselda shivered. The Tullioch spoke Isken well enough, but his gestures felt so foreign to her. She could never tell quite what he was thinking.

'We need to go to the garrison to find the whitestaffs,' the captain said. 'Heasin, Voltos, Tomas, with me. Cuss, Yselda, Ossen-Tyr doesn't seem to have been hit yet, so see what rumours you can find in the market: directions of the orbs, any strange activity. Meet us at the garrison at noon.'

With that, Floré shouldered her pack and went to speak a few words to the coach driver, and then the four adults departed. They were alone. Yselda looked at Cuss and blew out a breath.

'What do you think, Cadet Grantimber?' she asked, and Cuss grinned, eying the market stalls.

'... breakfast, Cadet Hollow?'

They shouldered their packs and left the east gate market square where the mail coach had deposited them, heading into the town proper and the centre where there should be more fare and folk. Ossen-Tyr was an old mining town; Yselda knew the Ferron had used it as a centre for their mining operation in Undal, and from the nightmare of the Ossen-Tyr mines some of the first resistances to the occupation had sparked. There was an overseer's building that was now the Stormguard garrison, but aside from that and the hard slave road connecting Ossen-Tyr to Undal in the south and Aber-Ouse in the far north, there wasn't much from Ferron left, or old Undalor even. The Ferron had pulled down the castle of whatever lord or chief from

Old Undalor had ruled the place, but whoever that was their name was lost now.

Tall buildings of quarried pale stone were thatched and well maintained, and the main streets were cobbled and kept clear of rubbish. The people were well dressed, with slightly finer clothing than she was used to. In Ossen-Tyr, there were fewer people dressed in functional hard-wearing leather and rough-spun fabric and wool, and more colours and layers, women in dresses and hats with wide brims. She saw some people from Brek wandering the town in their garishly bright cloaks. They were north of the great glen now and the hill tribes that farmed it; the Ferron had never pacified them. If you listened to the Brek folk who occasionally worked a season in the mill in Hasselberry, that was because they were such hardy fighters, but the Whitestaff Izelda had told her it was because they had no ore to be mined, good land to be farmed, or wood to be felled.

'Nothing but sheep dung and peatbogs and endless rain,' Izelda had said. Yselda smiled at the memory of the sour old woman and felt a shiver in her core at the memory of the broken staff on the village green in Hasselberry.

Following their noses and the general flow of people the two cadets soon found a food market, a few streets from the imposing Stormguard garrison – and even better, it was Starday and so the peddlers and jugglers were out as well as the food traders. Yselda only had a few coppers in her pouch, but they soon got themselves hot seeded rolls and fresh milk. They walked as they ate and did not talk much, watching the stall holders for a long while. Slowly the market began to fill and the jugglers and tumblers began to vie for attention. It was a hot morning, even though they had climbed so high to reach the hilltop town. Yselda felt strange, and wasn't sure why, but finally she realised; there were no trees in Ossen-Tyr, even in the market squares and wider avenues. She felt herself shiver.

'Never thought I'd see Ossen-Tyr,' Yselda said as they watched a young man stand on his hands. He moved back and forth hesitantly, and the crowd gave a scattered applause.

'I did,' Cuss said, and Yselda turned sharply to him.

'*You* thought you'd come to Ossen-Tyr?' she asked, and Cuss blushed.

'It's not that far from Hookstone forest,' he responded, 'and my dad was a miner, in Laga. I thought I might... take up the family trade if the Stormguard didn't want me.'

Yselda didn't know what to say to that, but the idea of the broad and tall Cuss down a mine made her nose wrinkle. She tousled his hair.

'You'd hit your head every five minutes. Besides, Cuss, the girls prefer a Stormguard tunic to a miner's hat.'

With that Yselda pointed to a group of girls from Ossen-Tyr who were down to watch the jugglers same as they, who were clearly eyeing the pair of them, conspicuous as they were in their green Forest Watch tabards. One of the girls giggled and said something behind a raised hand and Yselda laughed as Cuss blinked rapidly.

'We should find some information for the captain,' he said, frowning, and she rolled her eyes as he led her further into the market.

They paused in front of a puppet show; a cart had been turned on its side and the puppeteers behind it raised simple creations of wood and cloth for a crowd of children, accompanied by an old man with a drum and a tin whistle. Yselda frowned at the cloth puppets: Tullen One-Eye with a magnificent cloak fighting a troll with tricks and magic. She shook her head.

'I don't understand why people hate Ferron so much,' she whispered, 'but Tullen One-Eye is still the hero of all the stories.'

Cuss chewed thoughtfully on his bread as the puppet troll was set ablaze, the fire symbolised by flowing red ribbons that twirled around the puppets. The children gasped in appreciation.

'Mister Janos told me Tullen stories,' Cuss responded, and Yselda saw his face crinkle with the thought of Janos. 'I asked him that once, why is Tullen One-Eye the hero when he did all those bad things, enslaved everyone, broke the big spire thing in the sea?'

The old man trilled on his whistle and the next story began, the Tullen puppet's cloak being stolen by crafty thieves all in black. Yselda felt hot tears in her eyes without warning as for a moment she thought of Shand and Lorrie and the girls, a warm hearth and a story of Tullen One-Eye and his thrice-stolen cloak.

'Mister Janos said that Tullen isn't the hero. But he said the stories are still about Tullen, even though folks hate him, because he came from nothing. He was a farmer's son. He wasn't rich, or a prince or something. He was the hero because he did things, rather than letting things happen to him. Mister Janos said Tullen was always chasing magic or old stories, adventure. I don't know. Even if you hate him, he traded his eye with the Antian witches, he rode the giant wolf into battles against great armies, he *did* stuff. The whitestaffs don't like it and the Stormguard don't like it, but the folk do. *I* do.'

Behind the cart, the uncloaked Tullen now clad in black had gained the thieves' trust and joined their guild, and then revealed that he was the owner of the magical cloak they were all desperately trying to understand. The thieves turned on him with swords bared, and Yselda pulled at Cuss's sleeve and took him away from the show.

'He was a bad man,' she said, and Cuss shrugged. They walked on, exploring the stalls, talking about Tullen One-Eye rather than Hasselberry, Shand or Petron, Jana or Lorrie or the girls, Izelda. The list of things she could not talk about had grown so long now the Yselda found it simpler to talk of tall tales, sorcerers, and demons long dead and gone.

Eventually they found themselves at a quieter corner, back a dozen steps from the hubbub of the market, a blind beggar on one side and a man selling hot nuts on the other.

'How do you think we should find out about the orbs?' Cuss asked, and before Yselda could answer, the blind beggar intervened.

'Orbs of light, dead of night, hide your eye, take your flight!' he said, his voice deep and rumbling. He had golden skin like the captain's, and long black hair cascaded to his shoulders. He was dressed in a shabby off-white shirt and breeches, barefoot, and sat cross-legged on the stone street. His eyes were wrapped in a white bandage and his face was smooth.

'What did you say?' Yselda asked, and a grin split the beggar's face. His teeth were crooked and yellowed.

'What do you seek, girl? Answers? Auren the White knows all answers. Auren trained at Riven, on Iskander itself!'

Cuss and Yselda stepped closer, and the beggar raised his hands; the fingers were callused and dirty, and the knuckles split.

'These hands have clutched a staff of white oak from the Riven tree,' he whispered. 'I am fallen, but I remember. Ask me your questions, any questions, and I will answer... for a fair price.'

Yselda went to step forward even closer, but Cuss held her arm.

'It's a trick, isn't it? Why would a whitestaff be a beggar?'

Auren the White turned his face towards Cuss and leaned forward an inch.

'Forest Watch, in the mining hills? Stranger and stranger...'

Cuss breathed in and pulled Yselda close.

'He knows I'm Forest Watch, but he's blind! How can he know?'

Yselda batted Cuss's arm away and leaned forward.

'A copper piece if you tell me about the orbs of fire that have been seen flying at night,' she said, and she tried to emulate the nonchalance of Tomas-Mage as she spoke, tried to project the authority the captain put into her every word.

'I'm paying for gossip, Auren the White, not magic.'

Auren bowed his head and licked his lips, pausing a moment before he began. 'They cut across the sky like fire. They leave behind dead horses, dead cattle, dead... whitestaffs. Rumours are that the Tullioch sent them, or Cil-Marie is stirring for war. *Rumour* is that maybe the

Stormguard are flying them, to keep the people afraid enough to keep their junta in power.'

He smiled sickeningly at them and licked his lips.

'*Gossip* is that villages have been vanished, or burned, or nothing at all. That some people have disappeared suddenly on horseback or started painting runes on their neighbour's doors. I heard farmers for twenty miles are locking their doors and sharpening their axes, is what I heard, girl. People go to bed, and in the morning where they slept is a goblin, hungry for fresh meat and thirsty for blood.'

Yselda drew back from the man and looked again at his ragged white clothing, his wrapped eyes. In the distance, a bell began to toll the hour.

'Berren's black breath,' Cuss said, 'that's noon; we need to get to the garrison.'

The two went to leave and then stopped as a flash of flame as small as a gnat appeared in front of them. They turned, mouths wide in shock. The beggar Auren held out a hand in their direction.

'The girl said a copper for the gossip,' he said, his voice unsteady, his face grim and drawn. 'And I've a thirst a copper would slake.'

Yselda threw a coin back down at him, face pale, and he snatched it from the air and bit it.

'Good copper,' Auren called as they ran, 'good copper is always welcome. Find me at The Hanged Man if you need more gossip, or the answers to your questions, girl and boy!'

11

GOLDEN SPIRE

'Berren died and then for a decade the crop was sparse, and Nessilitor grew distant. Anshuka was asleep, but Lothal was awake, and he aided the Empress Seraphina, and Ferron, as they pushed out. Tullen One-Eye whispered in the great wolf's ear, and Lothal grew as hungry as the people. The expansion began, and the world bled.' – Pantheon of the Protectorate, Campbell Torbén of Aber-Ouse

Floré paced back and forth in front of the commander's desk and tried to think. She could feel her face flushing. Though it was mid-morning, the commander's office was dim. The morning light tried to brighten the room but it was a drab place in a cold and old building of dark stone, once a Ferron overseer building, now repurposed but still inexorably grim. Every wall bore a scar of a shackle hook or post that had been wrenched free; the Ferron loved their chains, and the Undal loved nothing more than to rip them out.

'How can they all be gone, and you don't know where they are?' she asked, again, and the Ossen-Tyr Commander frowned at her, hearing the incredulity and admonishment in her tone.

'You forget yourself, Captain,' he said, and Floré forced herself to be still, not to let his nasal voice drive her to madness. Tomas-Mage stepped smoothly forward and she stepped back to let him argue their case, biting her lip to keep from grabbing the fool of a commander. They'd waited over an hour in an antechamber in the garrison. Despite the heat of summer outside, it was cold. The walls were a thick grey stone unmarred by seam or join and held the heat of the morning at bay.

'Tensions are high,' Tomas said, and Commander Hearns sat back further in his chair, rubbing a hand in his greying whiskers. Hearns pursed his lips and gestured to his second in command.

'Yarrow, bring maps of the lands north of here, up to Aber-Ouse,' he said, and then as his whip-like second left to fetch the maps he leaned forward and crinkled his nose.

'So... a Tullioch, a skein-mage commando, an Antian, and a Forest Watch Captain. You understand my confusion, I assume. I am an old man. Tell me again: why do you want a whitestaff?'

Tomas smiled and widened his arms, palms outward in a gesture of supplication.

'Commander,' he started, 'you know of the orbs. I realise they have not yet attacked Ossen-Tyr, but rumours of abductions and slaughter in outlying farms are spreading like wildfire. On behalf of the Stormguard we—'

The commander cleared his throat officiously.

'On behalf of the Stormguard?' he asked. 'Truly? On behalf of the Grand Council in Undal City? Or is this a jaunt you have chosen yourself?'

The commander shook his head and drank from a pewter goblet, and then wiped at his whiskers with his sleeve, blinking slowly.

'I think you'd best be heading to Undal City,' he said, 'and seeking the wisdom of the council on this.'

Tomas's smile faltered at that. He turned to Floré and gave a slight shrug. Clearly he had expected his red tabard to grant him some special treatment, but the Ossen-Tyr commander wore the grey of the City Watch and commanded a garrison of blue Lancers. The Commandos meant little to him.

'Sometimes,' Tomas began, slowly, 'we must act independently of the council when speed is of the essence—'

Floré blew a breath through her nose and cut him off, pushing him aside firmly with one hand.

'Commander Hearns,' she said, bowing slightly. 'We were not properly introduced, not fully. I was Sergeant Artollen of the Forest Watch, yes, but that is not who I am. I am Bolt-Captain Artollen of Stormcastle XII, Stormguard Commando. My duty is to guard the Skein-wreck Janos, the Salt-Man, the only skein-wreck the Undal have known in three generations since Hussain the Blue fell to the disciples of Ihm-Phogn. I am his sworn blade.'

With a flourish she pulled her sword free and into a crisp salute, and allowed herself a twitch at the corner of her lips as she saw the commander's eyes flick to her sword-knot, the red silk with the white stripe, damp, forever damp. She sheathed the blade.

'We seek the orbs of light. Heasin son of Luasin, of Shardkin Tullioch, seeks youths abducted from the reefs of the Wind Sea. He has been sent by his people to investigate. Every youth taken from them was a skein-adept, and they lost livestock and farmers to this menace. The Antian Voltos Thirdskin was military advisor to Knight-Commander Starbeck, who now sits on the Grand Council, and Thirdskin now advises Commander Benazir Arfallow who leads Stormcastle XII; it was Commander Starbeck who promoted me to Bolt-Captain, and who presented me with the red-and-white knot of Mistress Water's silk for my actions beyond the wall at Lothal's bones. I was there at the reclamation of Fallow Fen. I was there at the fall of Urforren.'

She waited a moment for him to think that through. What happened at Urforren was rumour and legend in the Stormguard. She saw his jaw move as he thought on it.

'We are not trifling, sir,' she said, evenly, 'or playing at adventure. We need information; fresh horses; supplies.'

Floré stood at ease, and felt a surety of purpose, an iron in her voice. It was like being back, back at the wall with Benny and Janos and a team of men and women waiting for her word, any word, waiting with heavy fists and sure hearts, silver daggers in their belts, steel on their hands. She hated herself for the thrill that ran through her, a thrill that in Hasselberry had faded with each passing day of peace. *I am doing this for Marta,* she thought. *I won't go back.*

'Suffer no tyrant, Commander. This threat stinks of Ferron. We need a whitestaff, so we can track the orbs. They are killing entire villages; they are stealing children in the night, each child a skein-adept if we are correct. You say the whitestaffs have left the city. When? Headed where? Are none left at all?'

The commander sat back and looked appraisingly at Floré, and she held his gaze. Yarrow returned with the requested maps, and Commander Hearns gestured to a long table at the side of the room.

'We are on the same side,' he said slowly. 'I meant no offence. I did not perhaps realise it was so... urgent as all that.'

They gathered around the maps showing Ossen-Tyr and the country to the north – farmsteads, small market villages, mile upon mile of hill and dale, high moors cut by streams and valleys. It was perhaps fifty miles of hard country before the ruins of the old Antian tunnel; east of there the Antian had their surface redoubt. North again were many more miles of sparsely populated grazing lands, and then the citadel town of Aber-Ouse. Yarrow brought candlesticks and weighted the corners of the map down, the yellow light of the beeswax candles casting flickering shadows across the landscapes of ink and parchment.

'Here, here, here, and here,' Commander Hearns said, leaning down and pointing at small hamlets and villages. 'Each of these villages has reported orbs of fire in the sky. Livestock dead at those first two, strange bloody wounds, deep, cuts like runes but not a language we know. Always the orbs of fire or light seen in the night. A child missing from the third village. Two older women missing from the northernmost village the night after the orbs were seen, and in their beds, the Forest Watch found goblins. North, the witnesses all said.'

Drawing his finger up north of Ossen-Tyr, past the Antian redoubt, following the river Unerdan, his hand stopped when he was pointing at the mountains east of Aber-Ouse.

'North towards the Blue Wolf Mountains,' he said, 'past the Antian, and Aber-Ouse. A boat from Blue river port said they had seen lights in the sky east of there, towards Glen Driech, but there has been no word from the town there, none I've heard.'

Hearns stood straight and stretched his back, and cast a sidelong glance at Heasin, who loomed over an entire edge of the table, flexing his claws and tilting his head to get a good view of the map. Floré stared at the mountains on the thick parchment, jags of dark ink. She had seen the Blue Wolf Mountains once, at a distance, when she spent a summer on the Tessendorm border embedded with the Lancers. Six months of skirmishing with slavers and bandits weighted down by cumbersome armour and shield, six months away from Benazir and Janos. She remembered the mountains, granite teeth rising from the plains, wreathed in cloud. Squinting at the map, just north of where they were now at Ossen-Tyr, she saw Tollen. *Home.* She had not been back there since she was a child. She did not allow herself a moment to dwell on it. *Hasselberry and Janos and Marta are home,* she thought, and bit her lip.

'The whitestaffs?' Floré said, not looking away from the map, and the commander rubbed his hands together.

'I don't know,' he said quietly, 'truly. These reports all came in the last three days. Two days ago, after we met to discuss the first report, the whitestaffs left in the night. I'd had some of them advising on... all of this. Gate guard said they were headed south on horseback, fast, but since they left, no rider I've sent has found them or word of them. The road south to Undal City, perhaps, but for them to leave with no word worries me greatly. I have sent riders to Undal City in pursuit of answers, but no word back yet. There was a whitestaff north of here, in a town servicing the folks on the high moors, but he is nowhere to be found. The man I sent looking found an empty house.'

Heasin said something sibilant and slow in some dialect of Tullioch and stalked away from the table, flexing his claws, and Voltos removed his eyeglasses and rubbed at them worriedly.

'What are we going to do?' he said at last, looking at Floré and Tomas, but Floré ignored him, staring at the maps.

'Floré,' he continued, 'maybe north isn't the right move. We might need more soldiers, whitestaffs, skein-mages to deal with this. We might need an army. We should go to Benazir. You know she would help you.'

Floré kept staring at the map and did not answer, and Tomas let a heavy breath out. The commander looked at them all and then at the map again.

'I can't give you the lancers,' he said. 'If these orbs come here we must be able to defend the mines, and if they are attacking the villages we will be overrun with refugees within a week. I could give you a squad at most, and supplies of course.'

'If they come,' Tomas said, 'you should shelter in the mines. Lancers won't stop what is coming, by all reports.'

The commander rubbed at his whiskers and frowned. Floré just stared at the map, and tried to picture finding Marta alive.

'I go north,' she said.

~

Benazir stared out across the Slow Marsh from the tower atop Stormcastle XII. Night had long since fallen, and with it all heat had fled from the air. The winds of the rotstorm to the west of her pushed out and tugged at her tunic and cloak but she ignored them, did not give the storm the satisfaction of a glance. It roiled and tumbled behind her, majestic and horrifying as always, but instead she stared at the peace of the Slow Marsh, the isolated specks of distant crofts through the fen and bog.

'Wine, Commander?' her squire asked, and Benazir did not turn around.

'Leave it with the maps, Whent,' she said, 'and then I have no further need of you tonight.'

'My thanks, Commander,' he replied, and within seconds her warmed wine was poured and he was hurrying down the steps, doubtless planning on helping himself to the rest of the carafe. Benazir smiled, and went to the table.

The tower was roofed in wood and tile but open on all sides, a stone rampart scarcely chest high even on her frame and then open air beyond. A stone fireplace was full of warmth and flame, surrounded by stone benches, and past those Benazir had set a table on one side, a map of the protectorate weighed down by her silver dagger, her gauntlets, and a stone. Her wine steamed in a pewter mug next to it, and Benazir went and squinted in the firelight at the map as behind her a peal of thunder rolled through the rotstorm and dissipated out across the Slow Marsh.

Affording the storm a glance Benazir saw it churn, but the winds were mild as they went, and the lightning not so frequent. She smiled at the memory of spitting from this tower wall, cursing the storm with her fellow cadets. She had been drunk that night, drunk as she'd perhaps ever been. Floré had kept her steady.

Benazir's smile faded. Turning, she briefly checked from her vantage up and down the Stormwall. *Repairs to the breach by XI*, she thought, *third patrol tomorrow north need to meet with the cadets from XII.* The list in her head was endless, the machinations of a castle on siege footing against the very rotstorm itself. Food, water, repairs to the castle, repairs to the Stormwall. Training for cadets, training for soldiers, training for officers. Discipline for all. Starbeck's cryptic warnings from the Grand Council of forces gathering in the storm, but no intelligence shared. And now the new threat...

Benazir sat on a stone bench by the fire and drank her wine, facing east over the protectorate, and she waited as she had the last three nights. They came, eventually.

The orbs were flitting embers on the periphery of her vision, one to the north that appeared and then seemed to be gone, barely a spark. Another, closer, to the south and east – *perhaps near Laga?* That one danced and spun, but then away it sped to the north. Benazir rose and went to the wall and peered into the darkness, and then two figures emerged from the stairs to join her.

It was the skein-mage Nostul, and the Lady Kelvin. Nostul bowed slightly to her, showing her the top of his thinning red hair, and the Lady Kelvin grinned and waved. She was young, only eighteen summers, and wearing leggings and some sort of velvet doublet. The style was apparently all the rage in the City.

'Mind if we join, Boss?' Nostul asked, and she waved them to her side. The three of them stood facing the Slow Marsh in silence, and Benazir finished her wine. It was a sour red, a bad vintage from the east of Isken. She had been gifted the bottle by old Hovarth on his now annual caravan along the wall, but the sentiment and exoticism weren't enough to hide the sour taste. She still drank it, and apologised her squire had taken the rest and there was none for the skein-mages. Perhaps another ten minutes passed, Benazir poring over her maps as the skein-mages watched the stars, and then the Lady Kelvin let out a low whistle.

'There!' she said. 'North and east!'

She pointed into the darkness and Benazir rushed to the wall, Nostul straining his eyes.

'Do you mind if I kill the fire, Boss? Might see better.'

She nodded and the skein-mage whipped around, his slight frame curling elegantly down to the ground. Without a moment of hesitation he reached a fist into the flame and then the fire was gone, only a tendril of smoke remaining. Smiling, Nostul returned to the two women at the rampart and the three of them watched the orb.

This one flew closer, far closer than distant sparks. It grew in the eye, first a spark then a mote and then a thumbnail.

'Closest yet,' Benazir said, and Lady Kelvin let out a whoop.

'It might come to visit!' she said, grinning. 'Whatever it is, I want a look!'

'Perhaps best not to wish that,' Nostul said, staring out at the orb. It was the size of a fist now, and seemed to be heading straight towards them, growing in size unerringly fast. The Lady Kelvin's face fell and Benazir reached for her wine but it was empty.

'What is it Voltos said when he left?' she said, eyes not leaving the orb. It was the size of a cartwheel now, north of them, still over the scrub hill and rock north of the Slow Marsh, but heading towards the wall.

'Orbs of light, dead of night, hide your eye, something something.'

Nostul closed his eyes for a long moment then shook his head.

'Can't feel it. And it was *take your flight*, Commander, that last line. Take your flight.'

Benazir nodded and the orb suddenly was closer, again, larger, again, and growing.

'Shit,' she said. 'Shit. Kelvin, wake the mages! Nostul, rouse the troops! I want the wall manned and everyone armed and sharp. This thing is too close for my liking.'

The two mages nodded and moved to run to the stairs but then Benazir saw the orb cut west, towards the Stormwall. It was still north of the Stormcastle, but how close was impossible to say. This was as close as one had ever been, cold white light glowing from it. She had read the reports, of course...

'Wait,' she said, 'a moment more...'

And then without ceremony the orb cut across the Stormwall, and into the rotstorm beyond.

The three of them stood in silence for a long moment, and Benazir licked her lips. She could still taste the sour Isken wine.

'Belay that last,' she said, 'but double the watch tonight,

and from now on. I don't like this. A mage with every watch, as well.'

Nostul nodded and departed, and the Lady Kelvin sat on one of the low benches and scratched at her nose.

'What does it mean, Commander?' she asked at last, poking the ashes of the hearth-fire with the tip of her boots.

Benazir stared into the rotstorm and down at the wall below her, such a flimsy thing. Stone at the castle, stone and palisades of wood north and south. Strong here, but so weak elsewhere.

It crosses our border, she thought. *It doesn't care for us at all. As if we weren't even here.*

'I don't know what it means, Kelvin,' she said at last, and found herself to be utterly tired. 'I don't think anyone knows.'

~

Petron eyed the dagger at Varratim's belt, but couldn't bring himself to lunge at it. He still couldn't feel the skein except as a jumble of chaos, and the man before him was so utterly calm it unnerved him. *Patience,* he thought, *patience.* Cuss was always the patient one, slow where Petron was quick. He had always thought it a weakness of his brother but here in this place he could imagine Cuss calmer than he, patient and slow and methodical.

After showing Petron the cavern from the balcony where they had emerged from the cells, Varratim led him down a steep rock stairway and they walked among the black-clad men and women with the wizened faces, and the goblins dressed in shorter black robes attending to the bizarre stone discs, each the size of a wagon, each standing on thick legs of metal.

'What are they?' Petron asked, his gaze cutting between the humans, the goblins, and the strange metal discs, and Varratim gave him a long stare.

'They are my people's past, Petron, and your people's future,' he said calmly, and pointed at the black-robed men and women wandering between the discs, inspecting them and directing the goblins in opaque tasks.

'You see my brothers and sisters?'

Petron nodded and Varratim gripped the nearest strut supporting a disc, gripping the metal and pressing against it. It did not move. He looked so young, Petron thought, compared to all the others.

'It takes a toll, to fly the orbs of Ferron across the sky, to shoot the flame and the force. It takes a toll, all from the pilot. My brothers and sisters take that toll willingly, Petron. They do so because they understand it is *necessary.*'

Petron looked again at the disc of dark stone. *Was Varratim saying that these were the orbs he had seen flying over Hasselberry?* One of the goblins ran to Varratim and spoke quickly at him in a language Petron did not understand. Petron leaned back and took half a step behind Varratim; he had never seen a live goblin before. Its black orb eyes shone wetly, and its slate grey skin was scaled and rough. It was short and stunted, arms twisted, and its fingers were bent and crooked, but it was wearing black cloth robes unlike the pelts and skins Petron had seen on the dead goblins Sergeant Artollen had shown him last autumn back home. Its nostrils were slits, and there was no hair on its head, small holes instead of ears. It turned to him briefly but seemed focused on Varratim.

Varratim reached forward and pressed a hand to the goblin's face gently, almost lovingly, his long fingers cupping its angular cheek. It looked up at him and its mouth opened slowly, a thick black tongue slipping out over rows and rows of jagged teeth.

'Vosh, Russ,' Varratim said, and the goblin closed its mouth and scarpered away.

They continued to walk, past the strange discs, and a door in the stone wall coruscated open wetly, revealing a small figure beyond sat on a thick rug.

'Petron!'

The voice was high and soft, and then Petron was on his knees wrapping his arms around her and felt great breaths and sobs as she gripped at his chest.

'Marta, little one,' he said. 'Oh, Marta. Are you hurt?'

He held her at arm's length to take stock of her, wiping the tears from his eyes with the back of his sleeve. The strange fabric of the clothing he had been given was soft against his face. Marta was dressed in the same black strange cloth as himself, similarly barefoot. Her ashen hair had been cropped almost completely away, and her amber eyes welled with tears as she looked at him.

'Petron... my Papa,' she said, '... he's not okay.'

Her lip began to wobble and he pulled her close and tight.

'I'm sorry,' he said, 'I'm so sorry, but I'm here, Marta, I'm here.'

The chamber behind Marta was simple, walls of dark stone and the floor covered in rugs, a low bed and a water jug, some coloured wooden blocks and a chamber pot. Patches of the stone ceiling glowed dimly with white light.

'She is not hurt,' Varratim said. 'She is fed, and safe.'

Petron turned his gaze to the angular man behind him, the dagger at his belt, the odd bend to his arms and legs. *If it is the last thing I do,* he thought, *I will kill this man.*

'Who *are* you? What do you want with us?' he asked, and Varratim sighed and reached out a hand.

'Come,' he said, 'you may return each day, if you obey.'

Petron sat a long moment more holding Marta, but he could see past Varratim, could see a dozen or more goblins, *monsters*, could see the men and women, some young but most so incredibly aged, clad in black, all tall and severe. He had no power here.

'I'll be back tomorrow,' he told Marta, and she began to weep and clutched to him.

'Please,' she whispered, 'please. We need Mama. I can't feel the shapes – they're all wrong. Papa said I shouldn't but now I *can't*.' Petron could scarcely believe it but he found himself prying her hands from his clothes, pressing her back to the rug. *We need Mama.*

'Tomorrow,' he promised, and held her cheeks in his hands until she looked at him.

'Tomorrow,' Marta said.

He stepped back and back again, not taking his eyes off the girl, and then the metal door swirled closed in front of his face and he let out a breath he hadn't realised he was holding. He turned to Varratim, who was standing so *close*, and he looked up into the mesmerising sunken eyes of his captor, the insanity of the ever-moving pupils that split and re-formed and gyrated and danced inside steady irises.

'I will kill you if you hurt her,' he said, and though his voice broke with the strain of it all Varratim did not laugh or recriminate.

'That,' he said, 'is fair. That was a good thing to say, Petron of Hookstone forest. Now come with me and I will show you a truth, the first of many.'

He led Petron on, past the stone discs on their metal legs, and into a passage of stone that sloped down deep, curving and twisting. It was dark in the passage, and Petron felt the air grow humid. The only light came from small white and green mushrooms that glowed, casting a sickly hue across the stone that made the loose stone beneath his feet just visible enough.

After a long minute heading deeper into the stone and darkness, the passage opened into a cavern. More of the mushrooms grew around the edges of the cavern, a wide space with a roof studded with stalactites. Petron felt a low moan leave his lips as his eyes adjusted and he stumbled back.

In the centre of the cavern next to a pool of brackish water stood an altar of perfectly black stone, resting atop a short pillar. Something on top of it was burning with white-hot light, and he could feel his stomach turn as the light seemed to pierce his very core. It was not that which so unnerved him; beyond the altar chained to the wall with thick manacles of steel there were perhaps two dozen prisoners. They were mainly human, some Antian, and there was even a hulking Tullioch among them. The humans and the Antian were small, young. *Children.*

'Oh Judges,' Petron said, 'oh Judges…'

Varratim grabbed his shoulder and pulled him into the room.

'I want to be clear, Petron,' he said. 'I want you to *understand*, do you hear? I show you this as a kindness.'

His tone was light but there was an edge in there. He drew the dagger from his belt and across the cavern some of the shackled prisoners began to weep, to avert their gaze. Others stared stolidly at the ground, unfazed, broken beyond fear.

'I will kill you,' he said. 'I will take your pattern, and I will hone my blade with it.'

He gestured at the prisoners by the wall with his blade.

'I will kill them,' he continued, 'until my blade is sharpened with their focus. Do you know what the Stormguard do, past the wall, Petron? Do you know what Ferron was before the bear destroyed it? Do you know what the bear did to our people, punishment for their sins, the curse she bestowed? *No trial for rust-folk* – that is what your soldiers say as they burn and kill, as they drive children weeping into a god's nightmare.'

His eyes were dizzying, the pupils spiralling and splitting and coalescing. He gripped Petron's shoulder tighter and pushed him towards the altar until Petron could see the runes carved in the black stone, could feel the heat and light from those runes pushing at his mind. He began to weep.

'Please,' he said, 'please no, please.'

Varratim pressed his blade against Petron's neck and leaned in closer.

'I have seen remnants, and wonders. I have spoken to the Deathless one. I *know*, Petron, I know how the third Judge died. The blade that killed the third can kill the last.'

Petron strained but Varratim held him fast, and so he

reached for the skein and it wasn't there, just a pulsing of energy, a chaos wave. There was no pattern.

Varratim smiled and pulled away his dagger.

'I know many things, Petron,' he said. 'The skein is a pattern, and the crow-men can change the pattern. *I* can change it, change it to chaos so you cannot use it, or I can remove it from your reach completely. I know many things, but I do not know the secrets of the skein-wrecks. I do not know what Ihm-Phogn knew, or Hussain the Blue, or the Unnamed Knight, or Janos the Salt-Man. Deathless Tullen One-Eye said it could not be taught, that pattern below the pattern, to take without giving something back. In Urforren, before the end, they did not know. I have travelled to Tessendorm, to Isken, to far Cil-Marie; they did not know.'

Varratim sheathed his blade and stroked Petron ever so gently on the cheek with his gloved hand.

'You will tell me what you know, what Janos the Salt-Man taught you,' he said, his voice barely a whisper. 'You will tell me or Marta will join the rest of them, in chains, and her pattern and her focus will hone my blade.'

12

The Death of Nessilitor the Lover

'I have cut down women, and children. I have killed babes in arms. I have burned homes, and farms, and mills. I do not ask my soldiers to do anything I have not done. Every one of the rust-folk is a potential knife in the ribs, now or in the future. If they will not flee, they will die. We drive them back into the storm. Let Anshuka's wrath judge them.' – Private Diary, Commander Salem Starbeck

Cuss was out of breath and leaning his arms on his thighs in the shadow of the garrison entrance when the captain and the others emerged. Heasin pulled his hood up and stared up into the cloudless sky as if searching for something.

'Well,' Voltos said, 'if it is north, we might see my kin as we pass the tunnels. There are Antian here in Ossen-Tyr. With your consent, Captain, Primus Tomas-mage, I will seek what information they have; there may be rumours amongst the Antian as to what is going on. We could aim to depart tomorrow morning, which should give us time to requisition the necessary supplies, do you think?'

Captain Artollen dipped her head in agreement.

'A good plan Voltos,' she said, 'but you and I need to have a discussion at some point about Benazir. And Janos, I suppose.'

The Antian licked his lips and looked from Floré to Tomas, and Cuss thought it all seemed awkward.

'What's the plan?' Yselda asked Captain Artollen, but it was Tomas who smiled and responded as the captain glowered.

'North,' he said, 'but no whitestaffs to be had so we have to do this the old-fashioned way.'

Yselda looked to Cuss and raised her eyebrows, and he wrinkled his face. *She couldn't mean the blind beggar,* he thought, *surely not.* He shook his head slightly.

'There was an inn we passed,' Floré said. 'Boro's Drum. We go there. I will get horses and supplies from the commander here ready for the morning. Cuss, Yselda, wash up and rest up. Tomas, can you speak to the skein-mages in the garrison to see if there is any rumour beyond what the commander told us?'

Tomas passed his pack to Cuss and with a half-wave slowly wandered back into the garrison, stopping on the way to bend and inspect a flowering shrub. They all watched him go, his red tabard a stark contrast to his black robes. Voltos shouldered his own bag and headed off into the town with a curt nod of farewell.

'I can help,' Heasin said flatly, breaking the silence, and the captain turned to him and clapped him on the shoulder.

'I am sure you will. Rest,' she said, 'it will surely be a long time before we have the chance again.'

She passed Yselda a pouch of coins and gave her a

few more instructions, but Cuss was watching Heasin, specifically the way his eyes seemed to blink *sideways*.

The captain left and Yselda began to lead them back to the inn with Cuss trailing behind and Heasin next to him. Cuss was struggling with Tomas's pack in his arms as well as his own on his back, and the Tullioch reached an arm across and lifted it easily.

'Thank you,' Cuss said, and realised he was staring again, so made himself look ahead. The street was long and cobbled and busy with carts and people everywhere, small shops and businesses and children running about underfoot. It was Starday, a market day, and only a span away from the Flame festival to celebrate the height of summer. People traded bright fabrics, gossiped of flowers and dances.

'You did not know they were going to come,' Heasin said after a few moments of quiet walking, and Cuss looked at him quizzically.

'What do you mean?' he said, and Yselda slowed to walk in line with them, clearly curious.

'They had me noosed,' Heasin said, 'noosed and tied, and you told them to stop. I thought you were a law-man; you are big enough to be a grown human. You are a... cadet, yes? A youth? A broodling.'

Cuss nodded, unsure where this was going. The road was getting even busier and there were people everywhere – fine clothes and colour and noise – and he wished he was in the forest, with trees and green and nothing to worry about.

'You saw what they did not,' the Tullioch continued, 'that this was a wrong thing. You and the man Nash – I owe each of you. You stood before them, though they were many, and they were angered, and they held weapons. I will not forget, Cadet Cuss. Heasin pays his debts.'

Cuss felt himself frowning.

'You really don't owe me anything,' he said. 'Really, sir.'

Heasin gave an approximation of a shrug, his tail swishing behind him.

'That is not for you to say.'

Cuss didn't know how to respond to that, but wished Petron was there to see Ossen-Tyr and all its people, or Nash was here. Nash wouldn't be overwhelmed.

'You're so big,' said Yselda, 'and you have claws! How is it you ended up in that situation, Heasin?'

The Tullioch opened his lizard-mouth wide and let out a series of sharp hisses; Cuss thought that might be a laugh, or something close. He reached out his claws and flexed them in the sun, and a passing child dropped an apple and began to shout in fear, pelting off into the crowd. A few people stopped to look, but Cuss puffed out his chest and felt a swell of pride when they glanced at their tabards and turned back to their business.

'I seek my daughter Hassin,' Heasin responded. 'I have no quarrel with the children of Baal. They were upset about the orbs, and I thought resisting would only give them cause, and then things had gone... too far, I think this is right? My Isken is not perfect. I apologise.'

As he finished speaking, the inn came into view, the sign a huge drum of tin and the name above painted on wood.

'It's better than my Tullioch,' Yselda said, and Cuss smiled at her.

Heasin hissed again and clicked his teeth together.

'You are young, and there is time,' he said. 'Perhaps you will learn the Spire Tongue.'

~

That night they ate in a private room. Voltos had not returned, and Yselda found it odd to be around the captain and the skein-mage when both were not in armour and tabard, but simple shirts and trousers. The innkeeper was solicitous, a barrel-chested man named Julius. When he saw Tomas's red tabard, he insisted on giving them the private room and an extra bottle of orange wine from Cil-Marie on the house.

'My lad Gunter was at the wall,' he said, 'a lancer at the port at Final Light. A good lad, Gunter. Crow-man got him, in the end, but he suffered no tyrant, no sirs. Did his duty to the people. Stormguard Commando don't pay for drinks in my inn.'

Tomas smiled broadly and frowned appropriately as the innkeeper told his tale, and even insisted he join them in a toast to Gunter, and all the fallen Stormguard.

'To Gunter,' they echoed, and Julius had to leave the room, clearly overwrought.

'So,' Tomas said as they ate. 'North it is. A pity we don't have a whitestaff, a pity, a pity. Though, at least we won't have preaching about balance all day and night, so perhaps it is for the best.'

He smiled at Floré and Yselda, and ignored Cuss and Heasin. Yselda felt a knot in her stomach when his eyes lingered on hers. She did not like Tomas, Primus of Stormcastle XII, skein-mage. He had an oily quality to his actions, and his constant smiles felt false in comparison to the truth of the captain's constant scowls.

They ate largely in silence, Heasin and Cuss discussing Tullioch food awkwardly and briefly. Tomas drank his wine down, and another glass, and poured a third. There were thick bowls of barley broth followed by roast chicken and mashed potatoes, all suffused with garlic in the style of the Brek. Yselda was sure she would smell for days.

'Artollen,' Tomas said, nursing his third glass of wine, and Yselda watched as the captain flexed her right hand and exhaled before looking up.

'Yes?'

'I would know the fate of Janos-Wreck. His death is a tragedy, and potentially a disaster.'

'Janos was retired,' Floré replied. 'There is nothing more to say. Retired and dead are... close enough as far as the Stormguard are concerned.'

Yselda made meaningful eye contact with Cuss. They had discussed this oddity briefly that morning as they ate breakfast and watched the jugglers and tumblers. Why was everyone so interested in Janos, the poet? They were unsure, but Yselda thought it was because he was a skein-mage. He couldn't be a skein-wreck, *surely*. There hadn't been a skein-wreck in the Undal Protectorate since Hussain the Blue was killed.

'He still bore the pattern,' Tomas said, and he was no longer smiling. He rolled up his shirtsleeves slowly to show red sigils and runes etched deep in his pale skin, some fresh, some faded.

Yselda leaned across her plate to look at the sigils. She had seen them before, or very similar ones at least; Janos had had them all over his arms and chest. Yselda had been there when Petron had asked the captain about them once the summer before, and the captain had said they were tattoos, relics of a misspent youth, and not in a tone that allowed for more questions.

Tomas sat back and drained his wine and pulled his fringe back from his face.

'Do they know?' he asked Floré, looking only at her. 'Do they know what your man was, what you were?'

Floré took a spoonful of steaming potatoes and blew on them. Cuss and Heasin were both looking back and forth from Tomas to Floré, one wide-eyed, the other with a darting tongue.

'I was a soldier,' Floré said between mouthfuls, without looking up from her plate, 'and Janos was a skein-mage. He was a skein-wreck in fact, far more powerful than any mere skein-mage.'

She took a mouthful of chicken and looked up at Tomas, chewing carefully. After she swallowed, she drank some wine. Yselda could hear singing in the common room of the inn next door.

'We led in servitude,' Floré continued, still staring at Tomas, 'and were granted retirement after... a hard campaign in the rotstorm. The liberation of Fallow Fen, and an unpleasant scenario with crow-men in Urforren.'

Yselda dropped the piece of bread she was holding and Heasin leaned forward, staring more intently at Floré. She knew Urforren. Urforren was the demon city of Ferron, in the rotstorm. Urforren was destroyed by the Stormguard, six years before. A crier had ridden into Hasselberry, all the way from Undal City, bidden to ride to every town and village and tell the tale. *A city of demons,* he had said, *but we have prevailed, and they are brought low. The protectorate is safe*. Captain Tyr had been drunk; there had been dancing all night. Yselda had been so much younger, but she remembered the dancing on the green outside the inn. Remembered Shand and Esme dancing. She stared down at the table, and Tomas refilled his glass and took a deep mouthful.

'The Salt-Man Janos turned the sky to ash and the earth to salt for a mile around the town,' he said. His stare bored at the captain and she held his gaze and Yselda poured herself a glass of water and tried to keep up. The captain had been *inside the rotstorm*? It was insane – the rotstorm was acid clouds and deadly plants, goblins and rust-folk and crow-men and rottrolls and wyrms and endless wind and choking fog. *How can she do it?* Yselda thought. *And I'm afraid of a wolf in the pine forest?*

'Nothing will grow there,' Tomas continued, 'not ever again, not even the rotvine or the bite-kelp. A circle a mile wide of ever burning salt. The forward fortress of the crow-men, a living city with a thousand rust-folk, men, women, children, gone in a heartbeat in a pyre of burning salt.'

They sat in silence and Floré drank her wine and Heasin picked at the meal in front of him, sniffing at the chicken suspiciously. Yselda furrowed her brow, desperate to know more but sensing the captain's anger, seeing the whites of her knuckles on her cutlery.

'Primus Tomas-Mage,' she said, 'what is the difference between a whitestaff and a skein-mage and... a crow-man?'

Cuss gave her a little smile as Floré and Tomas visibly relaxed, each leaning back, having leaned so far forward in the terse discussion so far. Tomas tore at some bread and pushed his wine away, instead taking water.

'Quite, Cadet,' he said. 'I forget myself, and perhaps my audience. In the simplest terms, if the skein is a river, the skein-mage directs the current to create new streams. This takes energy. The whitestaff does the same thing, really, though they will tell you it is different. They... find the current that is already there. The training is different, one to make a new stream, one to find an already existing stream. Some claim to be able to master both, but none I've ever met. Does that make sense?'

He must have seen from her face it did not. Cuss reached across the table and grabbed a fresh roll of dark bread.

'Petron told me it's a pattern,' he said quietly, 'and a skein mage draws a new pattern, for fire, for a... push, for whatever. A whitestaff takes the pattern already there and pulls more threads towards it, like... how Izelda's tomatoes were so big.'

Tomas snorted at that.

'Big tomatoes,' he said, 'just about sums up the whitestaffs. But they have their uses. Those trained at Riven can investigate the pattern in more depth than any skein-mage, can heal a wound, sense a truth, can... find things, even at great distance. Which would have made all this much easier. With a whitestaff, we could use the captain's or Cuss's blood to track Marta or Cuss's brother.'

Yselda nodded to herself.

'I,' she started, 'we, I mean, Cuss and I, this morning... there was a beggar. He wore white and claimed he was trained at Riven, he... knew some things he shouldn't have, about us. Auren the White, a blind beggar. We were seeking gossip as you told us, Captain. He said he can be found at the Hanged Man. I didn't think he was a whitestaff, but he did make a little spark when we went to leave so I think he can touch the skein. Do you think he could help?'

Tomas drained his glass stared at her for a long moment, and then stood.

'Probably not,' he said, 'but with no whitestaff it will be weeks of wandering the mountains fighting wolves and bandits and Judges knows what else. The Hanged Man you say?'

She nodded, and caught the captain eying her appraisingly. Floré stood as well.

'Tomas and I will go,' she said, 'and see what truth there is in this.'

Heasin stood and his chair toppled.

'I join,' he said, and he walked from the room, the door swinging. The humans looked at each other.

'Well,' said Tomas, 'I suppose "he join". Keep an eye out for the furry one, you two.'

As the captain and Tomas went to leave Yselda screwed up one eye suddenly.

'Wait,' she said, 'Primus Tomas, what about crow-men?'

He turned back and gave her a slight smile and leaned forward until his face was close to hers.

'Crow-men,' he said in a stage whisper, 'are rust-folk who use the skein. Twisted by the blight, they can cut your senses from your mind, throw lightning, fly through the winds. They eat human flesh. They wear the faces of those you love most so you won't strike them down. They—'

'Enough,' Floré said, placing a heavy hand on the skein-mage's shoulder and pulling him upright. Her knuckles were thick, knotted things, the skin broken and healed so many times, and Yselda took comfort in the scarred skin of her captain's hands.

'Let us go and find this blind beggar,' she said, 'and perhaps some luck.'

~

It had been a day of pain, and Petron wept.

'You said you wouldn't torture me,' he gasped finally between the sobs, and Varratim stepped back and rubbed at his jaw.

'I did say that, didn't I,' he mused, 'but then you wouldn't tell me what I need to know, so what choice do you leave me? This pains me a great deal, I hope you know. It is a lesser evil, but evil nonetheless.'

Petron was stripped and tied to a bench of cold dark stone, his wrists and ankles bound. All his skin burned, a lattice of fresh cuts each only a hair's breadth deep, but all pulling at each other when he moved, tearing with every breath. Varratim held in one hand a thick metal-and-wood rod with a rune-inscribed blue gemstone at one end.

'Once more, and then another chat,' he said, and then he pointed the rod at Petron's stomach. A beam of coruscating blue light shot out through the faceted gem, hitting him on his already tender stomach. He could feel a dozen cuts as the runes on the gem were incised into his flesh. Varratim had explained the runewand to him, a focus of skein-energy, an artefact of the Ferron Empire.

'A remarkable tool,' he said, 'one of so many lost in the darkness after Ferron left us, before Empress Seraphina built the empire. The skein is a pattern, Petron, and your skein-mages use it by creating a new pattern and pouring energy into it. They take their tattoos and their scars and their meditation, they try so hard to draw these patterns. It is effort, all of it. My ancestors realised we could simplify that, by creating a pattern that was ready. How much simpler, how much more efficient – all you need to do is make the connection, and supply the strength from yourself.'

He aimed the rod at a wooden chest in the corner of the room, and when the beam of light hit it the chest was blasted apart into a hundred pieces. As it did so, his face paled and he winced.

'I won't use it on full power on you, of course,' he had said, 'but you will have to talk eventually and I really am short on time. It is tiring, so tiring. It is less tiring than flying the orbs of course, but there is always a price to be paid.'

That had been the morning, and Petron did not know how long it had been since. A layer of runes cut onto his arm, another on his leg, then the arm again, runes overlapping runes, leaving intricate patterns of pain. The wounds were so shallow they barely bled but they stung, and as Varratim's anger grew he could feel them cutting deeper. His face, his legs, his fingertips. He howled and cried and none of it made a difference; he was stoic and still it happened.

Finally Varratim left him, and he lay as still as he could, his breathing shallow, feeling a layer of wetness, a thin film of blood covering everything. *I can't do this,* he thought, *Mum, Cuss, Jana, I'm going to die.* He fell into unconsciousness, and awoke to the sound of his captor's voice.

'I told you, I am short on time,' Varratim said, and Petron turned his head and at his side was Marta, a blindfold around her face, standing by the table and sniffling.

'No,' Petron said, 'no.'

'Petron?' she said. 'Petron I can't feel the shapes; it's not right. Petron?'

'You are not in a position to say no,' Varratim said, ignoring Marta, 'but you can make a choice. What I have done to you I will do to her, or, you tell me. You tell me all of it.'

Petron felt tears on his cheek, the salt stinging in the filigree of cuts, and he nodded.

Marta was taken away, and Varratim came to him and Petron told him everything: the sergeant and her husband the poet, the red sigil tattoos, lessons from a village whitestaff but not a skein-mage, let alone a skein-wreck. Janos the poet; Janos the neighbour; Janos teaching him to bake in a kitchen warm and safe. He wept.

Varratim sat in silence for a long time once Petron had finished, wringing his hands on the metal runewand. Petron lay on the stone table in the stone chamber and apologised over and over in his head to the sergeant, to Janos, to Marta, but what else could he do?

Varratim stood, kicking over his chair and blasting it with the runewand, and then the walls, the carpets, the light globes. Beams of light shot from the rod as he laid waste to the walls, the thick rugs, the sparse furniture.

'Wasted time,' he said, slumping, 'again and again, wasted time. Do you understand yet what I am trying to do, boy?'

Petron could not answer, could only breathe and shake with the pain.

'Anshuka killed Lothal the wolf, Lothal the Just. Anshuka awoke, and saw what Ferron had achieved, what *we* had achieved, and she fought the wolf. Nessilitor tried to intervene... but Tullen One-Eye killed her. Killed a Judge! A god-incarnate slain. Anshuka killed Lothal the wolf, Lothal the Just, and in her rage the bear-bitch ran to Orubor.'

Varratim whistled sharply, and the black-clad goblin with the lolling tongue came into the room. He reached a hand out and stroked its cheek.

'Vosh, Russ,' he said. 'Vosh. Look at him, Petron. What do you see?'

Petron stammered with the effort of speaking, but he could not disobey; Varratim still clutched the runewand tight.

'A... a g-goblin,' he said, and Varratim stared into his eyes.

'Anshuka killed Lothal, and Anshuka cursed the Ferron people. She raised the rotstorm, and within it... there are nightmares beyond what you can imagine. She cursed Tullen One-Eye to watch forever more the ruin of his people. Forsaken as we are to live in the endless storm. Those who try to flee the storm are cut down by your *protectors*, your shining knights of Undal with their blade and judgement. Those who stay, those who are not strong enough to live... are transformed.'

Varratim looked down and sighed at the goblin who stared up at him patiently. He held its hand and stood.

'This is Russich,' he said, 'once as human as you or me until the rotstorm corrupted him.'

Petron stared wide-eyed at the goblin, who stared back, mouth ever open, tongue slavering over rows of jagged teeth. The huge black orbs of its eyes reflected his own face and he could see the intricate cuts and wounds covering him, and he let out a fresh wave of sobs.

'When Nessilitor the Lover was killed by the Deathless

one, all the winged-god's great works were undone,' Varratim continued, unfazed, 'the light sculptures of Jurron faded to nothing, the arches of the Nillen Gate crumbled. When Berren the Fair died, his cultivations and crops died with him, the great valley gardens rotting away, the tree city of Hunesh collapsing away. When Lothal died, the armies of Ferron that bore his mark felt his strength leave them and became men instead of wolf-touched warrior princes. They fell to blade and bow and rock and club.

'This,' he said, pointing to the knife at his belt, the knife of bone and obsidian with the green gem at its pommel, 'is the blade that killed Nessilitor the Lover. I took it from Tullen One-Eye, but Anshuka has broken him. He is of no use to me. He cannot teach me. And so I go to use it, to free my people, without the secrets of a skein-wreck. If I kill her, the storm will end. Her works will be undone. My brother will be human again, not cursed, not broken. What would you do for your brother, Petron? What would he do for you?'

Petron pictured Cuss then, Cuss swinging an oar at a crow-man and being blasted into the water by a runewand. *Is he even alive?*

'Artollen,' Varratim said at last, to himself. 'You say her name is Artollen, and the girl has her blood. So be it. I will find her and ask her. It is her, or nobody. Either way, the bear will die.'

Varratim left the room, and Petron heard words in a language he didn't know and then the goblins were there, a dozen of them, and the table lowered and they surrounded him and reached for him with their crooked fingers and as he screamed he saw nothing but blackness.

INTERLUDES: FORGE NO CHAIN

THE RUST-CHILD

'*Rust-folk live there, actually live there, inside the storm but outside the Ferron ruins. It beggars belief. Less than two-dozen homes, they seem to be farming the bite-kelp. We found the place when looking for a crow-man who attacked one of XI's patrols. He was hiding in one of their barns. Town is burned, fields are salted, locals scattered.*' – *Report on Hop-Vasser*, Sergeant Pripyat Boon, Stormcastle XII

Russich and Varratim ran back laughing before the bite-kelp could tangle them. The air was acrid and thick, clouds of fume and spores hanging languidly. When the winds came, and they always came, those clouds would dance and spiral and come together, but on this rare day the wind was still in Hop-Vasser mire.

The bite-kelp grew up from the mire of brown water and peat. The fronds reached and probed, puckered purple flowers sniffing at the air and whipping out at passing insects, rodents, birds. They struck fast, thick thorns biting hard and drawing their prey back below the water to whatever lay beneath. The boys ran close and back, a game of daring. Russich would shy first, dropping his stick to mark his bravery. Varratim would run past it and drop his own stick, always a step beyond his brother. Another stick lay unmoved many yards past; the neighbour boy Brandt had been daring, but not smart, and now his stick lay still.

Their mother Taran was gone three winters at that point. She had sickened, and there had not been enough, never enough food in Hop-Vasser. Their father had struck out with a pouch of copper and skins to trade, and a heavy stave, through the bleak snow and ceaseless winter wind. Three days and nights the boys sat and sang to their mother and played games, and she faded into her bed, flesh wasting, skin turgid. One the fourth day, Taran coughed blood. It was not to be a quiet end. It was an end full of the indignities of death, and Varratim held Russich back from the worst of it where he could. None of the others in their hamlet came to aid. There was no succour they could provide, and the wasting that ate at Taran could be catching, after all. Their house was shunned. Father returned on the fifth day with medicine from Urforren town to a silent home.

On the windless summer day, the boys dared the bite-kelp and dodged the listless red clouds of burning mist. Russich pulled down the cloth wrap he habitually wore around his face and tugged at his elder brother's sleeve.

'Is it safe?' he asked, and Varratim nodded, pulling down his own cloth mask. Both brothers had green eyes, pale hair, slender builds.

'A still-day, little brother. A day for adventure and exploration, not for dragging up swamp-root for dinner!'

Russich smiled crookedly. His teeth were misshapen and he had a pigeon chest, sallow skin. He looked so like their mother, Varratim found himself checking his brother for signs of the wasting, of blight-plague.

'Could we go to the river?' Russich asked, and did not look at Varratim as he did, instead picking up a rough stone and tossing it in his slender gloved hands. He knew they were not meant to go to the river.

'What about the goblins, Russ?' Varratim said. He raised his arms and contorted his face into a snarl. 'What about the rottrolls, and the crow-men from Urforren? What about the swamp snakes, and the cloud wolves, and Old Ferron in his orb?' He leaned in close and whispered conspiratorially. 'What if the Storm-knights come and burn us all, little Russ?'

Varratim laughed and Russich scowled and stepped back. He threw his stone towards a clump of bite-kelp. They were standing on a path just past the centre of Hop-Vasser, a thin dirt wend that raised across the stinking peat. Stands of bite-kelp and bulrushes rose from the fetid water, and occasional sickly trees stood as lonely sentinels on harder patches of ground. The sky above was an old bruise of purple and green, hints of dark orange sun cutting in beams through the ever-present blight cloud hanging over them. From the water, through the rushes, the occasional mote of blight would roll like mist. The boys stepped casually aside as one small blight mote emerged through a clump of bulrushes and rolled past them at chest height.

Russich turned to his brother.

'It's a still-day. It hasn't been a still-day since mid-winter, and summer is almost past.'

He didn't need to say any more. Varratim led the way, stopping to break two bulrushes. He ripped the heads and roots from them and passed the light hollow stem remaining to his brother. The rushes weighed almost nothing, but each boy held it as if it were a mighty blade. The boys were both armed with short cudgels tucked into rope belts, heavy handles of wood with nails hammered into the end in case a goblin needed scaring, but reed swords were like a knight's weapon.

They made it to the river an hour later, not a goblin in sight. The wind still wasn't blowing, and the absence put both boys into a riotous mood. They hummed as they walked, and then they sang, regardless of endless warnings of drawing attention of the beasts that roamed the Hop-Vasser swamps.

The river water was brown where it pressed close to the swamp banks, but further out it cleared. It was a wide river, and the boys knew it only as the river. It was the only river they had ever seen. Varratim led his brother wide around a patch of rough brambles and briars to a lone willow that stood leaning far out over the water. The willow was curved sharply, growing almost horizontally, cowed by the usual gales from the west.

The boys climbed the tree, and watched the river pass by below, the long fronds of the willow dipping over them, a pocket of shade and cool.

'Papa says we might ought to move to Urforren,' Russich said at last, 'to be safe.'

Varratim snorted.

'Safe from what?' he said. 'Knights are just a story I reckon. They still have the blight in Urforren, and crow-men on every corner! You ain't been, little Russ. I went with Pa once before Ma... four summers back I went. Walls and towers and smoke and noise, Russ. It's not like Hop-Vasser. You can't catch a frog, not in all Urforren!'

Russich frowned. Varratim knew Russich greatly enjoyed catching frogs. They went on to discuss frog-catching techniques at length, pausing only as a white-scaled crocodile lazily breached the waters of the river a stone's throw away, and then rolled back under.

They heard the scream as they headed back through the mire towards Hop-Vasser, and they exchanged wide-eyed stares before they pulled their small cudgels from their belts and crept low, towards their home. The scream had been loud and high, and cut short. The boys approached the houses from the west, walking the game trails past old Symeon's kelp patches. Varratim led, and when the centre of the hamlet came into view he stumbled back and pulled Russich into a bed of rushes.

'Knights!' he hissed, and felt Russich start to shake. There was a voice now, deep and low, saying words he could not quite catch. Peering forward through the rushes the boys saw old Symeon, the Pelleg brothers, the Torins holding their daughter close, and their father. On the ground before them was a woman coated in blood but Varratim couldn't see her face. Russich started to moan and Varratim gripped his brother's shoulder tight to quiet him down.

All the villagers were kneeling in front of a man dressed in black, with a red cloth tabard emblazoned with a golden lightning bolt. There were rings of chain mail gleaming from the folds of black clothing, and he wore heavy metal gauntlets, one of which held a sword bigger than any blade Varratim had seen, even in Urforren. It looked sharp, and wet with some sort of oil, and Varratim felt his lungs burning; he had stopped breathing. The man was sneering, his crooked nose and pale skin twisting as he spoke to the kneeling villagers in a tongue Varratim could barely hear and could understand none of.

Behind the man with the sword, a man with no chain mail, no weapon at all, a slender bald man with dark brown skin and sharp eyes. Behind them, *more knights,* Varratim thought, seeing a dozen armoured soldiers holding blades and bows, men and women, blood-red cloth covering their chests, scarves of red covering their mouths. He blinked and bit his lip and pushed Russich further down into the reeds. Russich squirmed but Varratim pushed him down low.

The man with the huge sword was shouting now, words Varratim didn't know and then he pointed at old Symeon's house and the bald man beside him raised a hand and...

Varratim pissed himself as a line of flame cut from the bald man's hand to Symeon's house, and he moaned softly as the building burst into flame. *Storm-knight,* he thought, and in an instant he was on the ground next to Russich, pressing himself as low as he could go. He could feel the hot piss soaking his trousers and the cold water of the reed bed filling his boots, could feel the sharp reeds cutting at his face and his arms as he forced himself lower.

'I can't see,' Russich whispered, and Varratim just held him tighter, pushed his brother's head down so he would not see what must come next. His own gaze he could not turn away. *Papa,* he thought, over and over. *What should I do?*

Old Symeon lurched to his feet and lunged at the sword-bearer but an arrow seemed to sprout from his chest before he had finished his first step – a gaunt faced archer holding a shortbow already had her second arrow nocked by the time Varratim's gaze picked her out. The sword-bearer called something out, and the knights descended with blade and bow on the unarmed villagers – men, women and children cut down in moments. Varratim cried out as the bald man himself raised a hand at his father, still kneeling, and the edges of his vision blurred to darkness as his father went from man to flaming torch, clothes and skin and flesh itself alight in a monstrous roiling flame of black and red.

Varratim awoke and it was dark, and the wind was pressing through the reeds, and Russich was pressing at Varratim's cheeks with his bare hands, mumbling his name over and over.

'Varra, what do we do?' he said, again and again, and Varratim forced himself to his elbows and then sat up. They were deep in the reed bed, right at the edge of the bite-kelp. Twisted veins of rotvine spread around them, but Russich must have pushed them back somehow and dragged his brother in. A broken bite-kelp frond lay beside them, its teeth and spines smashed.

'Varra,' Russich said, 'Varra, what do we do?'

~

Together they walked back into Hop-Vasser under a roiling sky. Distant lightning danced behind closer clouds, too distant for thunder to reach them. The backlit clouds tumbled and clashed. In Hop-Vasser houses were burned, even their house, and its roof had collapsed down onto the single room below. Varratim pictured his bed, the blue stone his mother had given him, the warmth and safety it had all been.

'Go and look carefully in the houses, get food and water,' he told Russich, but he had to push Russich to make him leave; his brother was staring at the pile of charred bones in the centre of the village. The knights had piled everyone up and burned them, and the pile was still smoking. They hadn't done a good job; Varratim could see hands, a foot, a face. He made himself look away from that, back at his brother.

'Food, Russ,' he said again. 'Food and water and I'll find us somewhere to sleep.'

They spent the night huddled under a blanket Russich pulled from the remains of the Pelleg brothers' house, pressed into a stack of dried kelp that old Symeon had been piling up by his field under a covering sewn from old crocodile skins.

'What are we going to do, Varra?' Russich asked, long after Varratim thought him asleep. Varratim stared out from under their meagre shelter up at the sky above, the churning clouds of the rotstorm a morass of red and black and purple and darkness, lit only by the lightning that streaked across it or behind it in bursts of purple. The rain had started, and with it the wind, and Varratim's face was wet with tears. He wiped it on his sleeve and pulled his brother closer. The rushes whispered as the wind pulled and twisted them and they swayed together.

'I've been to Urforren before,' he said eventually, 'with Pa. We'll go there, and we'll be safe there, Russ. I promise. I know the way. We'll be safe.'

He repeated that thought over and over until sleep took him.

The next day, Varratim woke stiff and cold and hungry and Russ was sobbing. He went to the sack of food they had gathered the night before and pulled out a flat loaf of black bread, tearing it in two.

'Eat this, Russ,' he said, pushing his brother's arm, and Russich wiped his nose on his glove and took the bread. Together they sat on the dry kelp and stared out. The rain had stopped, replaced by a dreary mist of grey with sporadic streaks of red as motes of blight cloud flitted through it on unknowable currents.

'What we doing, Varra?' Russ said, his mouth full of bread. 'Ma and Pa are dead. Everyone's dead. What we doing?'

'Urforren,' Varratim said, gripping his brother's shoulder. 'Me and you.'

'Me and you,' Russ repeated, and then he was crying again.

They left Hop-Vasser on the north trail, Varratim keeping his brother by his side and guiding him behind the broken stone and timber of the houses so they didn't have to look at the bodies. Varratim remembered the route: you had to take the north trail, and after a day there was a great dead oak with a white trunk, the biggest tree in all the marsh. You turned west there and walked another day; you walked until you reached a waterfall on that path, and then there was a crossroads and you went north again. *Simple*. North and west and north again. Varratim went over it in his mind again and again, trying to remember. It had been four summers back. Simple.

They walked, and did not speak. They walked through the rain, pausing only to dodge clouds of acid mist, either running back to safety or pushing themselves down into the dirt and hiding their faces in the mud, only coming up to breathe when they absolutely had to. Their cloaks were burned up in the house, but Varratim cut the crocodile skin Symeon had been using to shield his drying kelp into two big chunks, and the boys wore them like cloaks, one hand always clutching them tight at the throat. Varratim carried a waterskin and a rough sack of what food they'd been able to pull from the ruins of the houses, a few loaves of stale black bread and some dried crocodile meat and venison. The path was barely visible, but he thought he could see it well enough to follow.

They walked and that afternoon the storm picked up and they had to hunker down until it calmed. The winds grew wilder and wilder, and they found a copse of twisted silver trees not far from the path where the soil was dark and no rotvine or bite-kelp grew. They rested there and ate one of the loaves, but after the wind died Varratim grabbed Russ and pulled him to his feet.

'We need to go,' he said. 'We need to make it to the biggest tree by dark.'

'My feet hurt,' Russ said, but Varratim ignored his protests and pushed him out into the drizzle. They walked, and high above there was a low rumble, and then it was hours of lightning. Not much of it came to ground, but the clouds above danced with it as bolts passed from cloud to cloud and back, split and reformed. Night fell and they were still walking and Russich began to whine again about his feet. Varratim grabbed him and shook him.

'Do you think I want to do this?' he said, pressing his face close to his brother's. 'I don't want to do this! We have to do this or the knights will get us. We have to go; we have to keep going. Stop whining or I'll leave you for the crocodiles!'

He pushed Russich down to the mud, and stalked off. He heard the footsteps scrabbling after him, and then it was another hour of walking. The swamp was changing, changing from the reeds and bulrushes and little rivers of Hop-Vasser. Now it was dark earth and peat, thick banks that climbed up and down, little hills. *I remember this,* Varratim said to himself, desperately, *I must remember this.* There were banks of pepper-thorns, twisted bramble with cruel spikes, and stands of bite-kelp that would emerge from shadow and mist, tendrils swinging at whatever moved, mouths always opening and closing.

They did not find the tree that night. The next day light rose and Russich chewed on a lump of venison, and drank the last of their clean water. They had slept pressed together in the lee of a boulder, a stone of slick black rising from the tumbles and hillocks and patches of bog, a layer of red moss covering half of it. Varratim refilled the waterskin from a pool of stagnant brown and drank it through his mask. It tasted thick and salty and his stomach twisted as he drank, but it was better than thirst. He ate a piece of the venison and then they stood to go.

'Where's the path?' Russich asked, and Varratim looked down at his feet. He put a hand against the black stone and felt his breath catch. Varratim looked around, and then he took a few faltering steps away from the stone and looked for the path, for north, for south, for anything. There was only the mist, and above them patches of pale light filtering through the ever-rolling storm.

'This way,' he said, walking forward, and he felt sick in his stomach. Russich walked after him.

They did not find the tree that day. They found nothing for hours, until they had to rest, and nothing again for hours more. Eventually they crossed a small hill and found a goblin, scrawny and grey-skinned, eating an eel. It was huddled by a pool of water a little bigger than most of those they had passed. The eel was limp in its hands. The pool looked clean, and Varratim needed to refill the skins.

'We are friends,' he called out, and the goblin turned its black orb eyes to him and backed away, cowering. He kept one hand on his cudgel. A goblin shouldn't bother him. They were harmless enough, his father always said. A bit wild, sure enough, but poor beasts. Treat them kind, his father had said.

'Stay back a bit, Russ,' he whispered over his shoulder, 'in case it's a bad one.'

'Careful, Varra!' Russ said, and Varratim nodded to himself. Leaving Russich behind, he went to the pool and filled the skin with water. The water was silty and dark, and flecks of rain were dropping across the pool, sending out ripples. A crack of thunder somewhere distant, and the goblin looked up at the sky and opened its mouth, a long tongue falling past rows of serrated teeth.

'Do you know where the big tree is?' Varratim asked, and found himself shaking. The goblin was almost as big as he was. He could see an axe of broken stone on the mossy ground at its feet as it sat on its haunches, naked, chewing on the fish in its hand and staring up at the clouds in turn.

'No,' it said at last, voice thick. 'No tree.'

'Do you know Urforren? Is it near? Please,' he said, glancing back to where Russich was sitting on the dark earth staring at his feet. 'We are lost.'

The goblin stared at him for a long moment and came forward, sniffing through the slits of its nostrils.

'Lost,' it said at last, and then it pointed out across the marsh to its left.

Varratim bowed in thanks the way his father had done to a crow-man in Urforren and backed away, and the goblin made no move towards its axe.

'It's this way,' Varratim told Russich, and he believed it. The mists grew thicker as they walked, and then it was nightfall too soon, and the next day they were walking again. They saw no goblin, none of the stunted deer the Pelleg brothers hunted. They saw nothing but mist and the marsh. It got wetter and the few trees they had seen became a memory. There was rotvine in thick mats, twisted and twining, pepper-thorn brambles strewn in huge banks up the side of hills. They walked around all of those. They kept their masks high, and they kept walking.

'I'm cold. I'm wet,' Russich said. 'Is it far?'

'Dry soon enough, Russ,' Varratim said, and felt the chill in his own chest. His throat felt raw, and whenever he thought of home he had to walk faster so Russich wouldn't see him cry. *I have to be strong.*

Night came again and this time the winds rose and the rain began, and clouds of red began to swirl in the mist around them. The boys settled in a hollow in the earth sheltered by pepper-thorns on three sides.

'Are we lost, Varra?' Russich asked, and Varratim held his little brother close.

'It's close, Russich,' he said, 'just a little further. Tomorrow.'

They held tight as the marsh itself began to rise from the rain, and soon enough their hollow was pooling with water and they were scrabbling for a new place to shelter. After stumbling in the dark for a few minutes, Varratim's hands were shaking from the cold of the rain. They found a hollow in the bank of a peat ledge, where a stream was cutting out the bank and pressed down low. A lightning strike, and thunder.

'Do you see that?' Russich asked, and Varratim followed his brother's gaze out from their shelter. He saw only rain. He stuck his hands into his armpits and huddled closer to Russich.

'Someone is out there,' Russich said, his voice breaking. 'Varra I can see them, someone is out there!'

The lightning flashed again, closer, and the sound rolled over them an instant later. Varratim's eyes adjusted to the glare and he saw a cloud, a cloud of red denser than a blight-node, denser than any mist but less solid than any beast. It stepped forward, thick legs pressing down. The rain did not seem to affect it at all.

'What is it?' he said, and then it was running at them. It was as tall as a house, four thick legs, a round torso and hump on its back before its head, a snout pushing towards them over open jaws. *A bear.* He recognised it from stories of the beasts of the world his father would tell. It was a bear, but all of it sculpted from red mist and impossibly large. He could see no eyes. It was a hundred yards away, then a second later it was standing over them and there was lightning and a roar of thunder and the mist-beast opened its jaws, wide enough to encompass them both, and Russich screamed.

'No!' Varratim yelled, and in his mind there was a burst of light and he saw a pattern over his vision, nodes and webs connecting all things in pale light. Russich, the moss, the water, the insects, the rain, *him*, tangles of pattern that were all connected in a writhing living network. And then the mist in front of him, endlessly dense, a tangle of pattern he could make no sense of. He screamed and swung his cudgel at its face, but then it was biting down and he could see only the red mist and then it was in his eyes, his lungs, and he gripped Russich's hand and saw only blackness.

The pain woke him. It was still dark, but as he opened his eyes he could see the rain had passed. High above, there was only black cloud, and a tearing wind was sending it fast across the sky. The wind pulled at him, and he let out a moan.

Every bone hurt. *Is it here, the bear? Am I dead?* Varratim blinked away tears. He felt *wrong*. He tried to sit up but his legs were too long. He raised his left arm in front of him face and saw his hand, but the fingers were stretched. He tried to make a fist and felt bile rise in his throat. The fingers ached, and there were too many joints. *Too many.* He turned his head to Russich, still holding his hand tight, and let out a scream of horror.

Where Russich had lain was a goblin. Pebbled grey skin and black orb eyes, rows of sharp teeth and a lolling black tongue behind. No ears, and slits for nostrils. Its head was too large for its body. It was holding his hand and with its other hand trying to cover its eyes. It was wearing Russich's clothes. The goblin was sobbing, a dry coughing cry.

Varratim tried to pull his hand back, but the goblin squeezed tight.

'Varra,' it said, its voice rough, 'Varra, help...'

'*Tullen traded his eye not after he had learned the way of the skein-wreck, but before. He traded his eye in an attempt to see that elusive thing – the pattern, the rhythm, the beat that underlies all things. In the skein all is a writhing morass of connection and power and debt and distance – to see the pattern is to know how to alter it; to alter the pattern is to rule the world*' – History of the Skein-Wrecks, Campbell Torbén of Aber-Ouse

Once the houses were aflame and the villagers had fled, Janos destroyed the mill. It was a two-storey building angled precariously over the edge of the red river, a clumsy water wheel spinning slowly turning the millstones inside. His mind hooked into the skein, Janos took heat from the vines and grasses around him, the bugs and odd-shaped mice, the air itself, and drew it together into a pea-sized ember in his palm that he propelled through the air in a long arc. He felt a wave of nausea as the energy passed through him, as he paid his own price, felt his blood cooling.

It was a hot day past the Stormwall. The commandos were securing a perimeter around the village that the rust-folk called Brantonn, and then the plan was to head back to the Stormwall and regroup. Three rust-people lay dead in the vines and weeds in the centre of the rough hamlet, those who had tried to resist. They had yelled in Ferron and brandished scythes and had been cut down with shortbows.

Under Captain Lilith's watchful eye, Benazir had read the decree to the rest of the villagers, her Ferron stilted but passable – *none of Ferron to settle within fifty miles of the Stormwall, on pain of death, by command of the Council of the Undal Protectorate.*

The mote of fire flew through the sky and through the empty frame of the mill window, and within seconds the ground floor was aflame. Janos could see Floré off to the side cutting through a goblin who had rushed at them from the swamp. Always the goblins came when the commandos raided, came with their long knives and rough grey skin, their black orb eyes. Floré stabbed the goblin once it hit the dirt, even though her first blow was sure to have killed it. Floré always made sure.

The rust-folk fled, and Janos felt a heavy wave of fatigue threaten to take him. He should have used less of himself for the flame, should have sought energy elsewhere, but always the skein took as much as he made, and in the adrenaline he had felt he could take it.

From the rear they brought forth the salt sacks and poured them into the bite-kelp pools and the rough well. A call came out from the perimeter – 'Cloud!' – and one the commandos raised their face masks and squinted. When they returned to the Stormwall their eyes would weep for days, would wince with the merest sun. The semi-opaque cloud of red burning mist passed quickly in the brisk wind, and Janos sighed and flexed his hands in his gauntlets. *Two rules past the Stormwall,* he remembered, *never lose your gloves, and never lose your blade.* The thought made him smile; as a skein-mage his blade was his mind. Another hour of clearing the village, and the scouts returned. The rumoured rotbud was gone, carried west into the storm, deeper than they would dare follow. They had lingered too long in the hamlet, and now this summer the rotbud was safe, and a mighty rotsurge would pass across the protectorate spawning goblins and rottrolls and rotvine and chaos in its wake. They returned to Stormcastle XII empty-handed and exhausted, and Commander Starbeck spent the winter in a foul mood.

~

As the winter passed Janos spent his hours practising under the tutelage of Thum-Pho, the bald Primus, centring his mind on the skein. Nostul and he would spend hours meditating under Thum-Pho's direction, or listening to old Hurien's theories on pattern and liminal energy. The skein came to Janos fast, a river of power always there. It drew from him as he used it, and when he pushed he could feel something *pull* back, taking from him as he took from it. Thum-Pho was of Ona stock, but a Fallow Fen lad through and through; he swore like a sailor and drank as much as he could steal. As a skein-mage and a primus, he could steal a lot. He had lost three fingers on his left hand in the rotstorm two summers past and now always wore a black leather glove with those fingers stuffed with wrapped cloth, even on this side of the wall. Janos didn't join him in his drinks, but he borrowed the poetry books Thum-Pho favoured whenever his studies overwhelmed him. By Deadwinter he was reading a handful of poems every night before he slept.

Janos spent his winter in studies of Tullen One-Eye and Ihm-Phogn, of the Sun Masters of Cil-Marie and the shrouded Unnamed Knight of the Tullioch. All his life there was no skein-wreck in the Undal Protectorate, only memories of Hussain the Blue. The Tullioch's Unnamed Knight – had they been a skein-wreck? Or a succession of skein-mages burning themselves to nothing to protect their realm? The rumours persisted, and the Tullioch calmly rebuffed all but the smallest interaction from the outside. Like Old Undalor they had been a nation once, bent and bowed by the Ferron Empire.

Undalor had fallen, and for hundreds of years its simple fiefdoms had been turned to plantations and work camps and mines to feed and fuel the empire. Slaves from across the world had been brought to work under the Ferron, and when the empire faltered, from the fields rose the Undal Protectorate: strength in unity, leadership through servitude, free of chain or judgement.

Janos knew the Tullioch had been broken less thoroughly – those captured were used as slave warriors, but Ferron was sated by the destruction of the grand Tullioch spire. Their clans persisted during the empire, retreating to the far reefs, and when Ferron fell they returned but they did not unite.

Janos frowned at his notebook; the rough map of the world of Morost sketched within it. Cil-Marie across the sea; Ona far beyond; Isken to the east along the Star Coast with the strait kingdoms past it, and to the north-east Orubor forest and then Tessendorm. The Antian below and through it all, their strange underground forts and walls appearing where least expected – Janos could make no sense of their distribution, nor could any of the scholarly works he consulted. Finally, west was the unceasing hell of the rotstorm and the ruin of Ferron.

As hailstorms fell, Janos sought out Voltos Thirdskin, the Antian advisor who shadowed Commander Starbeck. When he had arrived at Stormcastle XII Janos had marvelled and recoiled at the strange squat furry creature, always in tight silk robes with ceramic armour plates, but the Antian wars were two decades past and Undal had sworn to leave the sunken kingdom to their own devices in the armistice of Aber-Ouse.

'Master Thirdskin,' he said, finding the Antian reading in his tower room, door ajar, 'might I bother you?'

Voltos rose and bowed stiffly, pressing one hand to his face to keep his spectacles in place. Janos had always thought Antian dog-like, but here, this close, he thought perhaps a mole was a more apt comparison, except for sharp eyes replacing dull, and nimble fingers replacing digging claws.

'Janos-Mage, you honour me,' he said. 'Please, do join me. I have wine, of course.'

Janos bowed in return and stepped into Voltos's tower room. It was opulently appointed compared to his own quarters or Floré's, a low fire burning and a thick bearskin rug on the stone floor. Bookshelves lined the north wall, and to the east a wide window. To the west was only thick stone.

'I do not mean to be a trouble to you, Master Voltos, I realise—'

Voltos cut him off with a wave of the hand.

'You wish to question me about Antian "Witches",' he said, with something that could have been a smile, and he poured a cup of dark red wine for Janos and gestured for him to sit. Janos sat and drank the wine, red-faced.

'Not only that,' Janos said, 'but, well. Yes.'

Voltos saluted with his cup and carefully placed a marker

in his book, laying it to one side. Janos cocked his head, the skein suddenly forgotten.

'Is that *Sea Collection* from Yggrid the Bloodless?' he asked, and Voltos laughed and squinted an eye at the young skein-mage.

'It is indeed. Are you a fan of Caroban Poetry, Janos-Mage?' he asked, and lapped at his wine. Janos politely averted his eyes.

'I don't rightly know, Master Thirdskin,' he said. 'I've read a smattering of Huna Droll, but aside from that I've not had much chance. I tried to write in the meter of Droll, which Thum-Pho said is usual for their style, but it is hard from such a limited example to draw forth the laws of it all.'

Voltos looked at the Janos for a long time, and Janos felt his cheeks grow hot.

'Do you know why I am here, Janos-Mage?' he said at last, and Janos shrugged and gave a small smile, hoping his ignorance would not offend. Outside the hail battered at the east window, and the wind from the west pushed and screamed.

'I am here,' Voltos said slowly, 'for the armistice. To provide aid and information to our allies, the Undal Protectorate. Those allies include the Stormguard, and the skein-mages. They include you, Janos-Mage. I am here to share information. So, ask me your question, young poet, and I will answer.'

Janos stared out of the window at the raging storm and then at the book of poetry by Voltos's side and then directly into the Antian's eyes.

'How do I become a skein-wreck, Master Thirdskin?' he

said. 'How do I see the pattern below the pattern? How do I take without giving?'

Voltos refilled their glasses and handed Janos the bound paper of *Sea Collection* by Yggrid the Bloodless.

'Thum-Pho-Mage and Janos-Mage,' he said. 'Two fire-slinging skein-mages of the Stormguard Commando, clad in red with the gold bolt; silver daggers at your side and the blades of a garrison of commandos at your back. Clad in leather armour that you might be nimble, heavy gauntlets that you might push past anything in your way.'

Voltos gave his approximation of a smile again, and raised his glass in a toast to Janos. 'The "Witches" follow a different path to your skein-mages, or the skein-wrecks of Cil-Marie. They are perhaps more like the teachings of Mistress Water and the whitestaffs, little that I know of that.'

Janos held the poetry book in his lap and examined the cover as he listened, as the wine lingered on his tongue and the fire danced in the hearth. The name of the publishing house was stamped on the cover: *Red Desert*. After a long moment he realised Voltos had stopped speaking and was staring at him intently.

'I have a question, if you will humour me, Janos-Mage,' he said, and Janos nodded. 'I have spoken to Thum-Pho. I have heard murmurs from others. You show great promise, but there is concern. You know of what I speak.'

Janos felt his cheeks burn and took a sip of wine. Voltos scratched at his whiskers and smoothed down the fur of his muzzle.

'You study Tullen One-Eye. You ask for stories, seek out books, texts, rumour, folklore, legend. You do not hate him,

Janos, the way to the whitestaffs and most of the Stormguard hate him. If you would tell me why, I would tell you of our "Witches", and what I know of the skein-wrecks.'

Janos sat back in his seat and drummed his fingers on the cover of *Sea Collection*, and then nodded.

'My village, Garioch, was burned by goblins, demons, crow-men; a rottroll. It was a night of blood and chaos. The Stormwall is little more than a ditch that far north. The lancers and the forest watch patrol, but this group made it past somehow. We thought… it was thought the village was far enough from the wall, across the high moors, to be safe.'

Janos pictured his home, the stars his father had carved in the wood panel over his bed.

'Tullen One-Eye did terrible things, but while he lived his people were safe. He protected them. The Undalor he destroyed was not the righteous protectorate we live in now. It was corrupt and backward and hellish. I do not forget his crimes, but I do respect his power. It is a power the protectorate needs. We have enemies on many sides, and others who would smile and trade and plunge the knife if ever we were to falter. I want peace, but to assure that we must prepare for war.'

The Antian and the skein-mage sat quiet for a long moment after that, as the fire crackled and hummed, and the wind and hail pushed at the thin glass of the tower window.

'I will tell you what my mother told me, in a way,' Voltos said, removing his glasses and glancing out of the window at tempest beyond. 'It is no chance you are drawn to the poetry; poetry is pattern, Janos-Mage, and the skein is pattern. To be a whitestaff is to observe the pattern, to truly understand it, and anticipate it. To follow it where it may lead. To be a skein-mage is to impose your will upon the pattern, to draw forth the laws of it, yes? A skein-mage can write a poem, but the cost is dear. To be a skein-wreck is to know the pattern so well that your touch is a feather – you can change it without yourself being changed. With poetry, as with the skein: to use it, it will change you. A skein-mage is a poet, Janos, taking rules and structure and forcing them on the world, art as a lens. A skein-wreck is a poem incarnate, free of those constrictions. Yet do you think a poem is unchanged by the context of its reading?'

Janos stared down into his wine.

'It doesn't matter if the poem is changed, what matters is the poetry exists. If I can protect these people, do they not deserve it?'

Voltos finished his wine and set down his glass.

'Do you think Tullen intended it? To protect, to write poetry that would save his people, keep them safe? Or do you believe he began with the intent of the chains, the empire, the horrors? Did the power change him or was he always thus? Are you strong enough to be good, with the capacity to do such ill? Are you brave enough to find out?'

Janos let himself slip into the skein, pushed his mind into that web of intricacies, the connections underneath everything, and pictured in his mind his mother, his father, his village.

'I don't know,' he said, at last, and together they sat in silence.

Night Raid Past the Stormwall

'A daughter of Fallow Fen, a daughter of the mountains, and that boy with the power to kill us all if the mood took him. I prayed to Anshuka for a skein-wreck, and gods forgive me she delivered him unto me. Just another flame-slinger, until he spent the winter with Voltos and the girl and it clicked – and now I push him forward with the daughters of fen and stone at his side to test his power, and I ask him to do the unimaginable: I ask him to prune the shoots.' – Private Diary, Commander Salem Starbeck

Benazir pulled up her scarf, but she could still feel the rotstorm pushing through the thin fabric. The mist felt thick in her lungs. She forced herself not to cough, not yet. She pressed forward, a crouching half-crawl of a run with one hand gripping her shortsword and the other armoured fist gripping at the earth, the mess of rocks and vines and weeds. She felt the thick bodies of rotvines bursting under her weight and tried to focus, to keep moving. A hundred yards ahead she could make out the copse of trees, twisted black branches and gnarled trunks contorted by the winds and ever shifting red mists. When she got fifty yards from the copse she came across Guil, kneeling in the dirt, soaked and weeping. Guil looked up at her, eyes red and vacant. Guil's head was bare and her scarf had fallen away, her sword was gone, and one gauntlet was missing. She reached out to Benazir with her bare hand; the skin was taut and covered in vibrant pustules. Her cropped red hair was plastered against her head, thick with mud and sweat and the rusty water of the marsh.

'Captain,' she began, eyes wild, and Benazir batted her hand away and pulled her to her feet by her tunic. Half-dragging the private, Benazir crossed the last fifty yards of mire and rotvine, squelching through acidic water and feeling the red mist burning at her eyes and every inch of bare skin. She forced herself to focus on her foot placement, her breathing, the grip of her hand on Guil's waist; anything but what she had left behind. Still, as she stumbled forward the image of Lothal the god-wolf's bones kept recurring, jutting from the ground larger than any building, blackened ribs thicker than oak trees She felt cold to her core. She had never really believed, but it was all true.

Finally they reached the copse of trees, and pushing through the branches found a semblance of sanity. Two dozen trees formed a tight-knit circle, and in the centre was bare earth, a sanctuary in the nightmare of the rotstorm. A single burning torch roughly forced into the ground guttered a pale yellow light over the scene: Floré was there tending to the shredded legs of the blacksmith boy Orun, torn open by the jagged blades of goblins the day before. Yonifer and Fingal were nervously tallying rations and water, when at least one should have been on watch. In the centre, Janos sat cross-legged, his face haggard and his hands coated in blood, his gauntlets limp in the dirt by his right foot. His eyes were staring straight ahead, looking at nothing.

'Guil is rotsick,' Benazir said abruptly, and dumped the freckled girl to the ground. Panting she lowered herself to the earth and ripped free her scarf, gulping in the relatively clean air of the copse. Guil lay insensate on the ground, mumbling. They all turned to her save Janos, who continued to stare at nothing, his breathing coming in a steady rhythm utterly unconcerned by the rotsick private or the returning captain.

'Did you find it?' Floré asked, and Benazir turned away.

'Fucking rotsick,' Benazir said, her voice cracking. 'Lost her glove. Her fucking glove! Lost her steel, lost her fucking senses.'

With her own gauntleted hands she felt at the antler hilt of her silver dagger, felt the reassuring shape of it. The fire rune on that blade had burned out the hearts of a dozen goblins in the last day at least, grey bodies leaping from shadow and undergrowth, wielding stones and rubble or nothing at all. They attacked with no sense, no pattern, screaming in barely passable Old Ferron. Benazir's eyes darted around the copse, at gaps between the trees where a figure might pass through.

Floré came forward from tending Orun and went to the collapsed girl on the ground, checking her eyes, her mouth, her fingers. Benazir's presence seemed to bring Floré into focus.

'Yonifer,' Floré said, 'you're meant to be on watch. Get your eyes sharp or I'll make sure whatever goblins catch us keep you alive.'

Yonifer stumbled across the copse, pulling up her mask, and stepped in between two of the trees, facing out. Janos still sat impassive.

'Damage to her hand isn't too bad,' Floré said. 'Nothing will be lost.'

She turned her gaze meaningfully to Fingal, who nodded quickly and came forward to take over the care of the collapsed Guil, who was lapsing in and out of consciousness.

'Are you hurt, Benny?' Floré asked, reaching for her, and Benazir shrugged off her hand. Floré pressed a waterskin into Benazir's hand and went to Janos, rousing him from his trance with a heavy grip on the shoulder. He looked up at her and blinked, and seemed to return to the world. He rolled down his sleeves, covering the stark red sigils etched into his skin, and then smoothed his hair back from his face. He turned to Benazir, to Floré, and then back to Benazir.

'Did you find it?' he asked her, and Benazir pulled off her gauntlets and threw them to the dirt and gave a laugh. She drank a long swig from the waterskin, trying to clear the taste of the mists from her mouth. She leaned forward and ran her hands through her hair, her knees on her elbows, and tried not to rock on her feet, tried to focus her eyes on Floré and Janos and not let herself picture it.

'Did I find it? Fuck. Anshuka's hairy arse I *found* it, Janos. There are three crow-men floating about it chanting some nonsense, a rottroll at least ten feet tall, two dozen goblins, and about twenty fucking rust-folk following along. It's a regular fucking caravan, and one we are in no way prepared for. It's by the bones, Janos, Lothal's fucking *bones*.'

Benazir felt her whole being burn with coursing blood as Janos turned away from her to ask Floré, 'What do you think? Distract the crows while I deal with the meat?'

Before Floré could answer Benazir forced herself to her feet.

'It's not your command, skein-mage,' she said, panting, sweating, 'nor hers. Starbeck gave me this raid, and I say they are too many. We need to retreat. Guil is rotsick. Orun is shredded. Myte and Frolic are dead, and Fingal and Yonifer are fresh meat. We turn back, come for the rotbud another day. They are camped under *Lothal's bones*, did you not hear me? The bones of a god, their god!'

The two of them stared tensely and Janos broke eye contact, looking down instead at his own blood-stained hands. Fingal stared between the three of them, eyes wide, and then focused back on Guil, murmuring low and keeping a hand on her brow. They were four days deep past the Stormwall, four days of burning clouds and rotvines, acidic marshes, goblin scouts testing their defences, hints of mooncalf crocodiles in every ripple of open water. Their water was almost out, their food was down to scraps. Still staring at his hands, Janos set his jaw.

'I can do it, Benny,' he said, and Floré stepped closer to him and began to raise an arm. 'Every day I'm stronger. I can see the pattern now. Three crow-men or three hundred, it doesn't matter. If Floré keeps them off me so they don't block the pattern, I can take them all.'

He looked to Floré for support and Floré lowered her arm and looked to Benazir, then back to Janos, her sword and gauntlets still looped on her belt.

'No,' Benazir said, her voice cracking and trembling, 'no. It is my order, skein-mage, skein-wreck. Janos. You stand down. Captain Artollen is not in charge. I am in charge. Starbeck gave *me* this command, and it is my call. You aren't ready for this. Guil is fucking rotsick, and we need to go now. The rotbud can wait.'

The copse was silent except for Guil's soft moaning as she passed from wakefulness. Orun stared at the scene, grimacing as his legs bled on the black dirt through layers of dirty wrappings, and Fingal focused on Guil, rubbing salve on her burned hand. At the edge of the copse Yonifer stared out into the storm and the falling night, arcane storm clouds of black and purple churning above them with barely contained wrath. The braid of her blonde hair catching the torchlight and shimmering golden. Her eyes were wide when she turned back to glance at them, and Benazir could see how young she was, how scared.

Turning back from Yonifer, Benazir saw Janos and Floré exchange meaningful eye contact and she felt her stomach drop. Floré reached for her belt and pulled on her gauntlets, and then pulled up the red cloth scarf from her neck to cover her face. She rolled her shoulders and loosened her sword in its scabbard and then turned to Benazir.

'He can do it, and it needs to be done,' she said, and Benazir felt herself breathing hard. She pushed herself to her feet and stepped in close to Floré, close enough to whisper.

'Lothal's teeth, Floré, *you will die out there*,' she said, 'It can't be done, sister, and I'm saying *Lothal's teeth* like a curse behind my mother's back, but I just saw them Floré, I saw the teeth and the claws and the skull and all of it. We are too deep. We need to turn back.'

Floré shook her head. Benazir stepped in close and gripped her arm, pressed her head against her friend's.

'Please, Floré,' Benazir said, her voice a whisper, 'I can't go again. I can't. You can't go. You will *die*. The rotbud will spawn a storm, but we can warn the protectorate. It will be okay; we don't need to do this.'

Behind Floré, Janos pulled on his gauntlets, readying himself before he stepped into the swamp of acid and spines, bristles and thorns and spikes and poison and venom and everything in between.

'I can see the pattern,' he said. 'We will be safe. You don't understand, Benny; I'm not a skein-mage, not anymore. I can see it now. Thum-Pho agrees. I'm ready.'

As Floré pulled away from Benazir, Benazir pulled her father's silver dagger from her belt and pressed it into her friend's metal-shrouded hand.

'I'm sorry,' she said, and Floré sighed, her amber eyes bloodshot, her face tight.

'It's been a long summer, sister,' she said. 'Get them back safe. We will follow.'

Then they were gone into the endless twilight purple of the rotstorm, and Benazir was alone except for four privates, one shredded, one rotsick, two green.

Benazir slumped back down to the dirt and bit her lip.

'An hour,' she said, 'and then we head back to the Stormcastle.'

Fingal spent the hour fussing between Guil, who slowly calmed and found a semblance of sense, and Orun, who was starting to look unsteady at the thought of heading out. His legs were torn, jagged slashes into his thighs and shins and calves from blades of stone. Floré and Fingal had between them done as good a job as they could with the bandaging, wrapping bandages tight around thick pads of sphagnum moss pulled up from the black peat. The moss stained the bandages a burned black, but it would keep the infection off until they reached the Stormcastle. Orun pulled his feet towards his chest and winced and started to sob a little until Fingal muttered some low words and clasped him tight for a long moment. Benazir watched the tender moment, unblinking, and pressed her fingers into her legs until the sharpness of the pain brought clarity.

Benazir felt a level of calm returning to her, and forced herself not to think of Floré and Janos dead in the marsh beyond. *Fingal, Guil, Yonifer, Orun.* They were all that mattered. She had to get them back; she had already lost Myte and Frolic on the way out.

Benazir wiped her face on her scarf and forced herself to clean her shortsword with an oilcloth from her belt pouch, and then she stood and stretched her legs around the copse, a hand on Yonifer's shoulder, a nod to Fingal, a quiet smile to Orun. She tried to do what Starbeck would, a moment of calm for each of her troops. She felt a bag of snakes in her stomach, writhing, hissing, but held her face calm.

'Is it far to the next copse?' Myte had said to her as they hiked through the swamp, and as she turned to answer his mouth was pouring blood as a javelin sank into his back. Floré had cut that goblin down whilst Frolic and Fingal sent a volley of arrows into its two companions. That had been two days from the Stormwall, before the rain started in earnest. Myte had died in her arms and she pulled his rank badge from his tunic and slipped it into her belt before letting him slip down into the black water of the swamp.

Private Frolley, Frolic as they'd called her, was killed the next night as they made camp in a copse. Rain was falling thick and fast and Frolic was meant to be on watch, but she was either asleep or a fool, and Benazir had woken to Frolic's screams as a half-dozen goblins swarmed her with knifes of knapped flint and clubs of gnarled wood. The troop had scrambled and Janos reacted fastest, a bolt of white lightning cutting from his hands into the swarm.

Then it had been knife work, and her knife had burned whenever it found flesh. *Idiot,* she thought, pacing the copse, picturing Frolic and her smile, her crooked nose broken and rebroken so many times. Frolic should have kept a better watch. *Or I should have known she couldn't be trusted to keep the watch.*

Benazir paced in circles, thinking of Myte. *I should have kept his sword, his knife,* thinking of the stillness of his eyes as she let him go. Guil reached a hand up to her leg as she walked past.

'Will we be okay, Captain?' she asked. 'It's so far, it's so far to home.'

Benazir dropped to her knees and checked the bandage on Guil's torn hand.

'We'll be fine, Guil,' she said, and gave the private's shoulder a squeeze, wishing Guil and Fingal and all of them hadn't seen her lose her composure with Floré and Janos. She stood and exhaled and felt her hand go to her dagger, but it was gone.

When the hour was up, Benazir had the privates form up and had Fingal cut a staff for Orun. It took him a few minutes to find a branch vaguely straight in the morass of gnarled trees, but in the end Orun had a reasonable crutch. Benazir ran her eyes over the group. Fingal and Yonifer still had their bows and their blades and their gauntlets. Guil was down to a knife and a lone gauntlet so Benazir swapped her own sword for the private's knife. Orun had lost his dagger and bow but kept his shortsword, though he was struggling to balance even with his crutch. Benazir let him keep it; it might serve to keep him calm at least. Orun had strong shoulders and arms from his youth at the forge, and he strained with all his might to balance on the awkward crutch.

By her reckoning they had enough hard biscuits and salt meat for perhaps three days if rationed, or two good meals. They had water for a day more, but charcoal and rags in Orun's pack to filter the rust water of the marsh.

'We need to go home,' she said at last, licking her lips. The privates stared at her with hope in their eyes and Benazir held her face calm even as the wave of panic in her gut threatened to climb further. *Fingal, Guil, Yonifer, Orun, I will get you home.*

'I will get you home,' she said to them, and put steel in her voice. They set off into the swamp and storm, pulling scarves over mouths. Benazir set Fingal to the front as she and Yonifer took turns walking with Orun, a steadying hand, a shoulder to lean on for every rough step. Every step was rough. Guil followed behind clutching Benazir's sword and staring into the storm.

It had taken them four days to cross the swamp, four days of long travel to reach this deep. They walked. Fingal led, never more than a few hundred feet ahead, scouting low and slow through the tangle of moss and peat and root and vine. Probing rotvine reached for them whenever they stopped to rest, or slowed to climb a hillock, but they pressed down with boot and gauntlet and blade and it recoiled away. The sky overhead was purple and black and streaked with lightning, occasional murmurs of thunder. Clouds of acrid red mist passed them by, or they skirted around. One came fast on an errant gust of wind and they crouched low, faces pressed down to moss for long minutes until it was gone, coughs echoing into coughs. Benazir did not think about Floré and Janos; would not. *Fingal, Guil, Yonifer, Orun. Home.*

Hours later they staggered to their rest. They spent the first night in a half-cave carved by a thin river of red water, a hollow in the black peat. They had slept there on the way out, days before, chasing the crow-men and the rumoured rotbud. There had been eight of them then, and to Benazir it felt palatial with only five. She tried to sleep when it was her time, but could not. She kept picturing Frolic's grin, and knew if she slept she would see again the private in her last moments, swarmed by goblins and screaming.

Fingal, Guil, Yonifer, Orun, she repeated to herself. *Home.*

The second day passed in near silence. They broke their fast on hard biscuits as what passed for sunrise struck the rotstorm, the roiling black and purple shifting so slowly to grey and purple, the occasional shaft of sunlight cutting through a brief hole in the storm. They drank a third of what remained of the water. It was little enough. Guil had recovered enough of her faculties to start helping Yonifer and Benazir shepherd Orun through the maze of peat, up streams and over beds of moss. They avoided the reeds, where the bite-kelp waited for any movement. They avoided the thick banks of pepper-thorns, stems of black and thorns of grey curling and tumbling seemingly always in their way.

Fingal tried to cut through one bank of thorns to reach a patch of water behind, a dark pool that looked fresh, and the rest of them caught up as he was cutting back the last few thick stalks. At his feet, amidst the cut pepper-thorn were a few crushed rot-vines that had tried to snare him as he worked, and Benazir took a moment to grind her heels into what remained: better to be safe.

'The Antian lad, Voltos,' Fingal said, hacking away at thick stems, 'he said the water by the vines is fresher. The roots do something.'

Benazir nodded and signalled the troops to settle for a break. Orun huffed as Yonifer lowered him down, and Guil came to sit with Benazir. Together they watched Fingal cut through the last of the vines and step through to the pool. He looked back smiling, and waved, and Benazir half-raised a hand to him and nodded.

'I'm sorry, Captain,' Guil said, 'I'm sorry. I won't lose it again, I swear. Please forgive me.'

Benazir moved her eyes across the torn vines and thorns on the black ground, and then up at the storm above. The wind was tearing through the hills and vales of the rotstorm, but the pepper-thorn seemed to have sapped it of some of its strength.

'It's okay,' she said, quietly, and made herself smile, made herself meet Guil's eyes. The girl smiled back, and then Fingal was calling her name and she stood, picking her footsteps carefully around the pepper-thorns; even in tough boots like hers, if one hit a seam or a weak point she'd be limping for days.

'Fresh water, Captain!' Fingal said, turning from the side of the pool to gesture at her, and then he was screaming. From the dark water, white jaws leapt forward, a mooncalf rotstorm crocodile, and with a single movement Fingal's torso was caught between those jaws, one arm crushed to his side, the other flung widely.

He screamed, and Benazir made to step forward and

then found herself stepping back, falling back into the black earth. The beast had stepped two legs out of the water and was thrashing Fingal from side to side, blunt teeth the size of daggers sinking deep into his stomach and back. His scream fell silent as she scrambled to her feet and she could only hear the dull tearing of his flesh, and she saw one red eye of the crocodile as it thrashed. It was huge; the Slow Marsh to the west had crocodiles, indolent lizards basking in the sun, the terror of the shepherds and their flocks. They were eight foot of muscle and alien temperament, snaring sheep who wandered too close to the deep ponds and endless streams. This was mooncalf, an aberration born of the rotstorm. It's head alone was at least as long as Benazir was tall.

Benazir stood speechless at the sight, holding Guil's dagger, and then Yonifer was there with their final bow and she was screaming, trying to sight a shot as the beast shook her brother.

'Bastard!' Yonifer yelled, sighting down her bow. 'White bastard, mooncalf bastard! Fingal!'

Fingal let out a keening note, a note of pure pain, and the beast stopped shaking and squeezed its jaws. Benazir glanced over Yonifer and saw her quiver was empty; she only had a single arrow left. *How did I miss that?* Fingal moaned and Guil made to step forward with her sword but Benazir held her back, gesturing wildly at the thrashing waters to the left and right of the crocodile. The crocodile looked at them unfazed and it levered its jaws and Fingal screamed.

'Yonifer,' Benazir, said, clutching Guil's dagger with one hand and Guil with the other and scanning the water for movement. 'You need to finish this.'

Yonifer made her shot, and Fingal fell still, the arrow sunk deep in his chest. The crocodile held there a moment longer, and then it slid back into the water. Yonifer stormed back from the pool, pushing past Guil and Benazir, swearing and cursing and tearing into the pepper-thorn vines with her sword. Guil pulled Orun to his feet, and they retreated from the pool, Yonifer hacking at the thorns as she went until she fell to her knees, weeping for her brother.

That night they slept in the open, hunched beneath their cloaks pressed tight next to a slab of black rock that cut up from the peat. Yonifer sobbed into her cloak, and the rest of them sat in their thirst and their silence. Fingal had been carrying the waterskins.

Two more days passed marching, always east, out of the storm. The mists grew thinner but every few hours rain would come, and Orun grew slower by the hour. Guil and Yonifer took turns with him, one of them always with a shoulder at his side, a hand to help, and Benazir took the lead. She killed four goblins those two days, each one with a throw of the dagger. She did not miss a throw. Always they were alone. Two of them had been dressed in animal skins and clutching crude weapons, the others simply wandering the swamps, living off bugs and frogs. They had nothing of use.

On the fourth night from Lothal's bones they stopped in a burned hamlet, a collapsed windmill and a few farmhouses. The timber and thatch were all burned away, but the stone foundation walls of one of the houses remained and they gladly sheltered there from the rain and driving wind. The rotstorm picked up at night, and blooms of purple lightning sparked across the sky, clouds forming intricate fractal whorls as they cut across the heavens.

'Never thought I'd bless the rust-folk,' Guil said, 'but these stones are strong.'

The well had been salted, likely by Stormguard, but they found some standing water in an old bucket and filtered it through Orun's charcoal and cloth. When Guil kept watch and Orun and Yonifer slept, Benazir let herself believe they might make it back to the wall. It was a scarce twenty miles more, twenty miles that were mapped and known and patrolled, twenty miles with game trails and paths. In the dark of the night when the wind was strong enough to cover the sound, she wept into her cloak for Floré.

In the morning Benazir went to wake Orun and then stopped, her hand over his shoulder. He was dead, eyes wide and still, but his body twitched. She pushed back his cloak with the end of her dagger and covered her mouth; rotvine wrapped around him like a cocoon beneath his cloak, his torso, his legs, thick grey and purple strands of it, sporadic leaves budding with sickly yellow flowers now that the vine had fed. She could see where a thousand tiny mouths inside the vine strand had opened, had bit, had *fed. Why didn't you call out?* she thought. *I should have saved you. I'm so sorry.* Guil screamed when she saw Orun but Yonifer simply stared and then looked away. Benazir retreated to the stone wall where she had slept and thought about Floré. Would Floré have done something differently? Checked on Orun in the night, cautioned Fingal from the pool? *If I had headed to death, would Floré have abandoned me, the way I abandoned her?*

Guil tried to press her sword into the rotvine cocooning

Orun's corpse, but each cut to it passed through the vine and found his flesh, and she pulled back. Benazir did not know how long they waited there, but Guil came to her eventually and pressed a hand to her shoulder and then Benazir was on her feet, with orders, with the next thing to do. She couldn't dwell on it, on any of it. If she did, she would never be home.

They walked faster without Orun, in silence save for the cutting wind, and as night fell that final day Benazir saw the lights of Stormcastle XII, the height of stone, the distant sky beyond, fresh and clear. Benazir took the final place in their ragged trio and let herself fall two dozen yards behind to hide her tears from Yonifer and Guil.

Horns on the wall sounded and they stumbled through the gates of Stormcastle XII, starved and burned and cut and wrecked. In the courtyard past the gates, she sat and drank water and waited long minutes for him to come. He emerged from the tower, his cloak black and his eyes cold.

'Dead, sir,' she said in response to Commander Starbeck's stare, 'dead. Three crow-men and a rottroll and a dozen goblins, perhaps two dozen rust-folk. Rotbud is lost to the storm.'

She could feel herself swaying as she spoke, could dimly sense Guil and Yonifer being carried away. Commander Starbeck gestured for someone to catch her and turned to walk away. Benazir spent the night in a vale of tears and isolation in the infirmary.

It was another day after that when the horns sounded and Floré stepped through the storm gate. She dragged Janos behind her on a litter, her scarf and armour lost, her tabard in rags but her gauntlets firmly in place and her eyes sharp.

Janos was blank-eyed and rambling and gaunt, crying and exulting in equal measure about the pattern.

'I can see it!' he said, croaking, staring at the wall. 'Salt beneath, all to salt!'

By the time Commander Starbeck reached Floré, Benazir was in the crowd along with half the garrison. Floré was drinking water from a skin and watching as the skein-mages held their hands over Janos. Thum-Pho hovered his hands over Janos's forehead for a long moment and then turned and yelled out to the crowd, 'Get the whitestaff! Get her here now!'

Starbeck stalked forward, the crowd parting around his tightly muscled frame like long grass around a wolf.

'Report, Captain Artollen,' he said, and Floré dropped the waterskin and pulled herself up and gave a crisp salute. Her chain shirt was gone and she wore only leggings and boots and tunic and gauntlets. Her scarf was gone, her sword blade was broken and the weapon slung over her shoulder with a belt, scabbard long gone. Red welts and burns criss-crossed every inch of flesh. Benazir's blade sat sharp in her belt and her gauntlets were slick with gore. Dried blood adorned her in arcs and spouts of goblin green and crow-men black and human red.

'Captain Benazir found the rotbud,' she said, voice hoarse, 'and retreated with the injured privates. Janos-Wreck and I completed the objective. The rottroll is dead; the goblins are dead; the crow-men are dead; the rust-folk are dead. From them, the rotbud is taken.'

Her voice flattened with the final sentence, and her eyes were wildly wide and staring as if daring anyone to argue with her account. The entire courtyard was silent as Floré reached into a pouch at her belt and pulled forth a twisted crystal the size of a fist, organic in its irregularity and arcane in its colour; a colour nobody beyond the rotstorm would see and one none could truly describe; a colour that felt like lightning at night.

Starbeck narrowed his eyes and looked at Janos and back to Floré, and gave a curt nod.

'Captain Artollen. You bring the Stormguard honour, and with this rotbud you take from our enemies a weapon. The storm this bud would spring could cut across the protectorate. You have shown your worth. You lead in servitude, Bolt-Captain Artollen.'

There were cheers, and there was celebration, and Benazir stepped back and felt hot tears sting her eyes. Her hand went to the empty sheath at her belt and she did not meet Floré's seeking gaze. She turned and left the courtyard, leaving the Skein-Wreck and the Bolt-Captain behind.

~

The sword-knots were given out three days later. For Benazir and Guil and Yonifer a stripe of red silk for a successful mission beyond the Stormwall. Benazir felt her stomach clench and her blood turn to acid as the silk was given to her in the courtyard of Stormcastle XII, could feel her cheeks burn as Commander Starbeck tersely congratulated the three of them for her service. She already had a red silk sword-knot, a dozen of them. All Stormguard commandos did.

Her first mission across the wall, her first true raid with Floré at her side, they had been privates. Trained since childhood for action beyond the Stormwall, finally it was time for a true excursion. A pack of goblins led by a rottroll had been spotted by a patrol south of Stormcastle XI. They were lingering near a patch of half-broken palisade where the earthworks had crumbled in the incessant winter rain. The wall patrol had reported back, and Captain Yute had added Benazir and Floré to his strike team. They wore cadet tabards, no golden bolt and no trim. Yute came to the two of them as they checked each other's gear.

'The lancers have armour that can stop a sword, an axe, a spear,' he had said, running his eyes across their outfits, pausing to tighten straps or check buckles. Benazir remembered it so vividly, the stubble at his jawline, the dead weight behind his stare. Yute had spent a decade at the Stormwall, raiding, pushing back. He had been at the fall of Fallow Fen, not a scared girl like her, a soldier with a blade and a mission.

'They'd drown twenty feet past the wall,' he continued, adjusting Floré's scabbard, and Benazir checked her own scabbard, loosening her sword.

He kept them close as they hiked down the Undal side of the wall, getting closer to where the patrol had spotted the goblins.

'Fewer women in the lancers,' Yute had said, and one of the commandos walking behind them, a hulking man named Tornald, laughed gruffly, leaning on the palisade for breath and looking out at the rotstorm beyond.

'Lucky them,' he had said, and a female commando with a shaved head snorted and gave him a shove. Benazir couldn't remember what happened to that woman. Tornald had been taken by one of the white crocodiles, the next summer. She remembered his teeth outlined in blood; a scream higher than you would have expected.

'A lancer needs strength,' Yute had continued, ever serious, 'but a commando needs resilience and speed. Wear plate armour past the wall, you'll be tangled and drowned in an hour. Wear a helmet, you'll bake in it. You cover your skin, you cover your mouths. Gauntlets on. Blade sharp, eyes sharper. Understand? Women, men, don't matter past the wall. All that matters is if you can take a beating and get back up, a hundred times over.'

Floré and Benazir had both nodded, but once Yute had turned away, Floré had rolled her eyes so hard that Benazir had to bite her tongue.

As Benazir stood in the courtyard and watched Commander Starbeck award Floré, now Bolt-Captain Floré, the sword-knot, she wanted nothing more than to be fighting goblins with her friend, side by side, knee-deep in swamp, swords flashing, trusting each other completely. Floré had come looking for her at least three times since her return from the rotstorm, but Benazir had hidden. She could not face her friend.

That first mission, the eight of them found the rottroll easily, when the sun was high. Ten feet tall, it had been sat gnawing on a rotting catfish, the dozen goblins lying around its feet asleep or squatting in tight groups muttering to one another. Two fought over the scraps and bones at the rottroll's feet. The rottroll itself was a horror, gangly arms on a torso that seemed to have too many bends in it, skin gnarled and spiked, a mane of matted black hair hanging lank over eyes that were orbs of grey, long ears dropping out and away from its head. As it chewed on the meat of the fish she could see its teeth, so like the goblin teeth, serrated and jagged and recurring in row beyond row, deep into its mouth.

Yute had signalled for bows, and from fifty yards eight shafts of yew flew forward. All hit their mark. Benazir exhaled as she let her arrow fly and did not wait to see if it hit – she had nocked another arrow, Floré next to her performing the same action in perfect concert. The troll screamed and threw up an arm, still holding the catfish.

As the second volley hit the troll it was lurching to its feet, screaming and roaring, its voice something between a horse's whicker and a bear's roar. The goblins scattered, reaching for crude wooden spears and clubs and knives of sharpened stone. The third volley sank into the troll as it started to take heavy steps to the line of Stormguard commandos, red tabards resplendent in the sunshine, knee-deep in swamp water, heavy gauntlets wrapped tight around their bows. Eight more arrows, and it fell into the fetid water, black blood spilling from its lips.

'Swords!' Yute had called. The goblins came onward in a rush.

Now, in the courtyard of Stormcastle XII, Starbeck presented Floré with a strip of red silk with a white stripe at its core. The white stripe was known across the protectorate – it was the highest mark of valour.

'This silk,' Starbeck intoned, his eyes never leaving Floré and Janos, 'was cut from the robe of Mistress Water herself; Mistress Water of the first Revolutionary Council; Mistress Water who united the slaves and overthrew Ferron.'

The courtyard was utterly silent, every commando and lancer and cook and steward and squire craning forward from all possible vantage points. Starbeck leaned in to speak into the ears of Floré and Janos, and Benazir felt the familiar hot bile of failure in her throat. After long moments Starbeck drew back and flourished the sword-knot high above his head.

'Mistress Water spent thirty years in the dry hell of a Ferron salt mine before she felt the skein,' he continued, 'and from that moment, never was she dry again. This silk, this silk will never dry!'

Starbeck looped the sword-knot onto Floré's gauntlet. Benazir could see the daze in her friend's eyes, the sheen of sweat. Her armour was immaculate.

As one the assembled crowd drew steel, or brought fists to chests, and intoned their dedication. Hundreds of voices raised in harmony.

'Stormguard, preserve the freedom of all people in the realm. Suffer no tyrant; forge no chain; lead in servitude!'

Cheering and applause broke out, and Benazir slipped away, feeling the gnawing in her stomach, the tingling in her fingers and toes. A lifetime ago on her first raid, sword drawn against a rush of monstrous flesh, Floré had stood shoulder to shoulder with her and when she faltered her friend had grabbed her tight and held her strong. Now she had failed, again, but it was Floré she had failed, and she could accept no strong hand to steady her.

ACT 3

HIDE YOUR EYE

Obeisance to the mountain
Obeisance to the Highmothers
Obeisance to the forest

Prime laws of the Orubor

13

THE HANGED MAN

'*Nessilitor grieved for Berren, it is said, or simply cared little for what the empire did. But when Lothal and Anshuka clashed, it was a war of gods – the skies burned, and the grounds shook. So Nessilitor came to make peace, and met her fate – death at the hands of Ferron's mad skein-wreck. Only Anshuka left that place, and behind her the rotstorm has raged evermore. The slaves revolted, and from blood the protectorate was born; a nation of free people, former slaves from across the world united in one thing – a hatred for Ferron, and a wish to be better.*' – *The Fall of Ferron*, Whitestaff Anctus of Riven

Floré, Tomas, and Heasin made ready to leave for The Hanged Man. Floré went back to their rooms and donned her sword belt and gauntlets along with a travelling cloak, but did not put on her Forest Watch tabard.

'Can we come?' Yselda asked, and Floré gave her a long stare as she adjusted her sword belt. Cuss was sat behind

Yselda, his face pale, one hand absently rubbing at this chest. Cleaned from the grime and dirt of travel, Floré could see Yselda's face clearly – the bags under her eyes, the strained quality of her gaze, the way she leaned forward into their conversation. Floré pictured Benazir in a copse of trees, in a storm, coated in blood. She pictured Benazir a dozen times over with those same eyes, with that same stance, each time in a situation where they were far from home, far from safety. She turned to the shuttered window facing east and closed her eyes and tried to picture her friend.

'Best not, Cadet,' she said at last, and turned back to the pair of them, stretching and flexing her hands to loosen the joints of her gauntlets. Cuss was staring off at a wall now, his gaze distant, the weight on his mind clear. Both looked tired. Floré breathed in and almost asked, almost asked each of them if they were okay, but she knew it wouldn't help to talk. There would be time for that afterward – for now, Marta was still missing, Petron was still missing, Janos was still… *Janos is gone,* she thought. With plated hands she rubbed at her own face and realised she probably looked as tired and on edge as the two cadets before her.

'You remember how to service your blades?' she said, her voice dropping reflexively into the cadence of her old commander, Starbeck. Cold and certain.

'Your bows, your arrows, your boots, your tabard, your swords. Eat, drink, and get your gear squared away. I'll be back, and then it is north until we find answers.'

She dismissed them with a curt nod and went for the door. She paused in the doorway at the sound of Cuss's voice.

'Are they going to be all right, Sergeant?' he said, and she held on to the doorframe. He sounded so young, so lost. She turned her head back and smiled at him, at Yselda – she made herself smile wide, and said what Janos would have said.

'They are all right, Cuss,' she said, smiling at him, 'I promise.'

As she left the room she heard a thump and Yselda's stern tone: 'It's *captain* now!'

It was enough to make her smile for real.

When Floré came downstairs the common room was still bustling but Tomas had managed to catch the ear of the innkeeper, Julius. Floré gave him a small wave and went outside, where she found Heasin standing in the shadow. They stood quietly in the cool evening, appraising each other. Floré had met Tullioch when she had visited Undal City, but did not speak any of their languages, and her knowledge of their clan system dated back to half-remembered lessons of her childhood. Heasin looked back at her frankly, his eyes lingering on her sword, her gauntlets, and her supple leather armour. He let out a long hiss and flexed his neck, eyes blinking horizontally. She turned her gaze to the town and allowed him his assessment.

'Which one of you commands?' he asked at last, and Floré turned back to the hulking Tullioch and smiled.

'Tomas-Mage is Primus of Storm Castle XII, and so he holds the higher rank.'

Heasin clicked his jaws together and reached a hand out to the stone wall of the inn, trailing a claw across the rough stone.

'This is not my question, this *rank*,' he said, and Floré

crinkled her nose and cast a quick glance behind. The door was still closed, Tomas still inside with the innkeeper.

'Tomas commands,' she said at last, and held his gaze. He did not speak further, and after a long moment of silence she stuck the tip of her tongue between her lips and furrowed her brow.

'Storms, you aren't easy are you?' she said, and Heasin moved his mouth in what might be an imitation of a smile.

'Much at stake, Captain. My daughter, the children of the Tullioch. I will go north. I would ally with you in this.'

Floré ran her armoured fingers across her sword hilt and knot, and nodded.

'I've been away some years now on special mission for the Grand Council,' she said. 'So the matter of rank, of command... it is unclear, Heasin, but know this – my daughter and your daughter were both taken. I will follow any command that leads me to them – but any other? A skein-mage is a useful ally, and I'd not lose that lightly, even one as... charming as Tomas. He seems content to follow along in this, for now. I will go north, with you. This I promise.'

Heasin nodded once, flicked out his tongue, but said no more. Floré leaned back against the wall of the inn savouring the cool night air. Looking up, she saw there were thin bands of clouds cutting across the sky – the winds from the south were pushing again, but she felt only the slightest of breezes behind the palisades of Ossen-Tyr. Tomas emerged a moment later, and the opening door cast warm light our across the street cobbles.

'He told me where to go,' Tomas said, 'but we might have some issue. The Hanged Man is a person as well as a place

– local criminal, or something similar. So eyes sharp, and so on.'

Floré gazed down the quiet street and felt a tremor in her right hand. She gripped the handle of her longsword in its scabbard, her mouth set in a grim line.

'Let's get this done,' she said, 'and then north.'

They walked through Ossen-Tyr and Floré turned her head to take in the sight of the town at night. It was largely quiet, but as they entered the west end of the town and the cobbled streets gave way to mud and compacted dirt, they did pass one feasting hall whose customers spilled out into the street beyond, singing and drinking. They were mainly short men, caked in dirt and clay, each one wiry. Floré led them on a wide path around that place – she had known enough seasonal workers on the lumber mills who had done seasons elsewhere to know the reputation of Ossen-Tyr's miners for violence as entertainment, and right now they didn't have time for that. Heasin stayed close to her side and hunkered down, his hood raised, his head turning at every alley and street to take in threats or simply to see more of this place, Floré did not know which.

A few streets later there was a well with a half-broken wall, and Tomas turned left and then they were on a street that was mainly shacks, rough timber walls and shuttered windows, heavy doors or none at all. A few rough sleepers sat in doorways, and Floré licked her lips and flexed her hands. She had seen such things in Undal City before, but always with an air of deference or shame; these men and women openly stared at them, expressions ranging from openly predatory to quietly hostile.

'If this isn't a whitestaff,' she said quietly, 'remind me

to give Yselda and Cuss a lesson in information gathering when we get back.'

Tomas sniffed and raised his head pridefully. He rolled up the sleeves of his robes to the elbow, displaying deep red tattoos, sigils etched bright into his flesh.

'You have been too long in the forest, Artollen,' he said, gesturing at the Stormguard Commando tabard he wore over his robes. 'We have nothing to fear.'

Tomas gestured at a dimly lit building ahead of them. Unlike the dark houses along the street, a brazier was lit outside the front door. This building and those nearby were free from vagrants or beggars. Above the door, a noose hung from a beam ten foot off the ground. Heasin rubbed at his neck.

'This is a… good idea?' he asked, and Floré and Tomas looked at each other.

'Probably not,' Floré said, and together they stepped forward.

Tomas entered first, followed by Floré and Heasin, and the low murmur of conversation stopped as they stepped through the doorway. There were perhaps ten people in the tavern room, and nobody behind the bar. The people were a mixture of men and women, mostly wearing leathers or worn clothing except for a trio of women with flowing dresses who sat at a table by the bar. Tomas glanced around and stepped forward to speak, and as he did Floré assessed the room. There was a back door, but no other exit. The windows were high, small, and barred. The tables were heavy and scratched but the chairs all looked relatively new and flimsy and, seeing that, Floré rolled her shoulders and began to twitch her foot. She felt a burning pain and a clenching in her right arm, a tremor of lightning running down to her fingers and a taste of acid and spit in her mouth. She knew chairs were the first thing broken in a bar fight. There were sword belts on pegs on the far wall, and she was sure that except for the three women in dresses the other seven all had belt knives at least.

'Greetings,' Tomas said. 'I seek Auren the White.'

All of those sitting turned to the table with three women in dresses. One sat between the others, lips rouged, red hair tumbling to a blue dress.

'You are lost,' she said, 'and this is a private party. Leave now.'

Tomas grinned at her and took in the room again.

'I apologise if we are intruding, but we can of course compensate for any bother. Perhaps I could buy you a drink in exchange for the whereabouts of the beggar?'

A low fire was burning in the hearth, and one man stood from his table and slowly walked to it, placing a log in the fire and then picking up an iron poker and idly prodding at it. Nobody else spoke or moved for a long moment, and Tomas's grin faltered, replaced by a cold fury.

'Auren does not need visitors,' the woman in blue said, 'and this is a private club.'

She gave a wave of her hand and six chairs pushed back and Floré let go of her sword handle and closed her gauntlets into fists.

'She said piss off, pretty boy!' called a voice, and from the side of the room a woman with cropped black hair and golden skin hurled a tankard at Tomas. He did not move except for a flex of his fingers, and the tankard stopped in mid-air three feet from his head, the ale inside splashing out and onto his face and the floor. Tomas turned to face the woman who threw the tankard.

'Step carefully,' he said, his eyes narrowing and voice rising. 'Do you know who I am? I am Tomas, Primus of—'

The second tankard hit him in the head from the other direction, and he stumbled. The tankard held in mid-air fell. From the corner of her eye Floré caught a pulse of light from his forearms, his sigil tattoos burning with stored energy as he readied himself to fight. The men and women began to advance warily and Tomas raised his arm, and then Heasin pushed him aside and stepped forward, casting back his hood.

'Enough of this!' he roared, tearing his hood back, and the advancing gang reeled back. The man holding the iron poker raised it high, though he was across the room. Heasin loomed, and puffed his chest and spread his heavily muscled arms. The firelight reflected from the tips of his curved claws.

'My daughter was taken, by lights in the sky. We need whitestaff; you have whitestaff. Bring him to us now!'

As a punctuation point to this declaration, Heasin used one hand to flip a heavy table into three of the advancing toughs, who fell groaning to the ground. The woman in blue laughed a tinkling laugh and looked at Heasin, and then the ale covered Tomas and she took a sip of wine.

'Very well,' she said, holding out a calming hand to her subordinates. 'I admit I'm intrigued. A skein-mage, a warrior, *and* a Tullioch. Just when I thought this was going to be a dull night.'

She finished her drink in a single pull and then stood

gracefully. She held out one hand with two fingers extended and swept it around the room.

'Nothing to worry about, my darlings,' she said. One of the three tangled under the heavy oak table began to protest.

'He broke my bastard hand, the bastard!' he said. 'I'll have his bastard heart!'

The woman tutted and pursed her lips.

'We'll do you right, Ket, but you hush now. I'll handle this.'

Floré shifted her feet into a defensive stance as the man finally pulled himself free of the table and stood clutching his mangled hand, but he made his way to a table and sat down heavily rather than advancing any further. She looked at Tomas, who was rolling his sleeves down and wiping at his ale-soaked hair and face, bemused.

'Now,' the woman in blue said, focused on Heasin, 'you will have to follow me. The mighty Auren the White, Riven-trained master of the skein, is out back in the pigsty.'

~

Cuss sat on an old armchair with his legs folded beneath himself, his boots on the floor, and Yselda lay on the rug in front of the fire staring up at the ceiling. The innkeeper had given them a set of rooms that centred on a small communal space with a fireplace and a few chairs, and the two cadets sat and waited for the rest of their companions to return.

'They're going to send us home,' she said, and Cuss furrowed his brow and nibbled at the loaf of bread he held.

'They can't,' he said, and Yselda half sat up and turned to look at him.

'They will,' she said. 'For certain, Cuss. The sergeant… the *captain* only let me tag along this far because, well, I think she understands why I don't want to be in Hasselberry. Same for you. But if they are headed into the Blue Wolf Mountains, to fight who knows what. They won't want us holding them up. You're no good with a sword, and I'm hardly better.'

She shook her head and lay back down. Cuss continued frowning, and looked at Yselda. He had always liked Yselda, but she was so sharp that he felt himself endlessly a word away from reprimand, and so he paused a long time before replying.

'I need to find Petron,' he said quietly, 'and that isn't up to the captain, or Tomas, or Voltos, or Heasin. If they don't want me with them then fine. I'm a cadet, not enlisted proper yet. I'll… I'll go alone if I must. I'm not going to leave him. I can't. I know I'm not the best with a sword but I swear, Yselda, I'll find him. I can learn. Mum and Jana, they… I *have* to find Petron.'

Yselda reached a hand up from the floor and held his arm, and gave it a squeeze.

'I know, Cuss,' she said. 'I'm with you.'

They sat in stillness for a long time and then Yselda withdrew her hand and they began to talk of other things – the Tullioch and the Antian and how strange they were, Ossen-Tyr and its smell of mud and the clothes of the locals. They did not speak of Hasselberry, or their families.

There was a knock at the door, and Cuss jumped.

'Who is it?' called Yselda, scrambling up from the floor, but there was no answer. After a long moment, another knock came, heavy and loud. Cuss climbed out of his chair and Yselda padded barefoot across the room for her sword. Cuss slipped his hand into the knuckledusters he now always kept in his pocket. Looking back, he could see Yselda was ready, and he pulled open the door.

'Oh Judges,' he said when he saw the face before him, and the Orubor in the doorway stepped into the room. Yselda let out a shriek and Cuss made to swing his fist but the blue elf caught it easily with one hand and pushed him back to the floor, and then... *it bowed?*

'I am not your enemy,' the Orubor said, closing the door behind it. It flicked its hood back and Yselda dropped her sword. Cuss stared up – the pale blue skin of her face was etched with red rune scars, and her eyes were orbs of dark gold with no pupil and no iris visible, framed by long lashes. She was bald, her long ears pointed and curving away from her head, and she was as tall as any human woman Cuss had ever seen, but thinner, willowy. The Orubor was clad in dark leather including long gloves and a scarf around her neck of red silk, all of this beneath a flowing green and grey cloak.

'I am Ashbringer, of the Orubor. I seek Artollen of the Stormguard. Is she here?'

Cuss pulled himself to his feet. He knew Orubor could read minds, he knew they ate human flesh, and would kill on a whim. Nobody entered their forest and lived, and no Orubor ever left.

The Orubor turned its gaze over the two of them and Cuss felt Yselda press close behind him and hold his hand.

'I am an ally,' the Orubor said, and Cuss realised he wasn't breathing and his vision was going black. *Don't eat me!* he thought as strongly as he could, but then he was falling, surely dead.

~

Petron was in the cavern with the altar, chained to the wall. A girl introduced herself as Ana and gave him some water, stale water from an old cracked waterskin. He had watched her laboriously fill it by holding its mouth flush against a trickle of water that ran down the rock wall. He drank it gratefully.

'What happens now?' he found himself asking, and Ana shook her head.

'We wait, and we die,' she said. She had a bob of black hair and a snub nose and Petron tried to smile at her, and then winced in pain. Even the wincing hurt.

'Where are you from, Ana?' he said. 'I'm from Hookstone forest. Do you know Hookstone forest?'

She shrugged and leaned back against the wall, biting her lip. Petron pulled himself up a little and saw the rest of them by the light of the green fungi, and the edge of the glare cast from those horrible runes incised in the black altar stone. A Tullioch, two Antians, and a dozen humans. Petron stared at the Antians and the Tullioch and blinked. *Real Antians and Tullioch, like the stories. Cuss would love to see a Tullioch.*

'There were more, I thought,' he said at last, and she closed her eyes.

'There were more,' she agreed. After a long pause, she held her hand out to him.

'Will you pray with me, Petron?' she asked, and he raised an eyebrow.

'Pray to Anshuka,' she said, insistent. 'The shaman in my town always said we owe everything to Anshuka. Without her we are slaves.'

Ana raised her manacled hands and shook them weakly, and gave a wry grin.

'I think we maybe need to pray more, as Anshuka isn't listening.'

Petron kept his hands by his sides and lay back and gazed at the roof of the cavern and thought of his mother and sister and brother. *Do they live?* He could not bear it.

'How does she hear us? Can she hear us?' he whispered, and the girl Ana curled up on the stone next to him with her head on her arms and looked at him, seemed to trace the cuts on his skin with her gaze. He had woken wearing nothing but a pair of loose trousers, and even then the feel of the cloth on his lacerated skin itched and pained him.

'The skein is under everything,' she said, 'and everything we do can touch it. She can hear us.'

Petron remembered sitting with his family in the Hasselberry shaman temple, listening to Jule and his fire-and-brimstone sermons. He always said they must ask Anshuka for protection, for guidance, for love, and if they did not she would not protect them. Without her protection their souls would be cast to the nameless fire below. He felt himself crying again.

'We don't deserve this,' he said, looking down the row of sleeping children. The youngest were scarcely three or four summers old, being held by those close to them and comforted in low voices. Ana simply shrugged.

'I am going to pray, Petron from Hookstone forest,' she said. 'You can do as you like.'

In the dull glow of the fungi she closed her eyes and prayed, a quiet murmur to Anshuka. Petron closed his own eyes and focused on his pain, but he could hear her quiet chant over his heartbeat, her simple prayer to the god-bear.

'Praise Anshuka, praise to the breaker of chains, praise to the strength in our hearts. Praise Anshuka, the mother bear. All glory to the bear-god, wrath of Ferron, protector of Undal. Praise Anshuka. Mother, watch over us; Mother, give us peace; Mother, help us help ourselves; Mother, tell father I am okay; Mother, please, please take me from here; Mother, I am afraid.'

Ana's voice caught as she prayed, and she sniffed, but she continued repeating her quiet invocation, every time a different question or request or simple confession of feeling or fact. Petron lay still and silent and focused on her words. When she stopped praying the only sounds were the quiet whimpers of the other children, the drip of water, the scuff of bare feet shuffling for comfort on cold stone.

Petron heard Ana start to weep and felt the sadness pooling over him, a sadness that buried his pain and his worry and his fear with an inescapable weight. The tears on his face were running into the cuts that covered his skin, and it burned, but the weight of that sadness was enough to drown it all out. He reached out towards her in the dark of the cave and found her hand. He squeezed her hand and she squeezed back, and he did not speak because he had no words, but eventually she stopped crying, and the weight was less somehow.

Petron slept fitfully. He dreamt of his mother, of his father. He dreamt he was in the water of Loch Hassell with Mother and Father and Cuss and little Jana on a summer day, but then one by one they slipped below the dark water, and the sunlight grew cold, and he woke with a start.

'Cuss,' he said, before he could think, and then he blinked and recoiled from a shape moving next to him.

'No,' Ana was saying, pleading, sobbing. 'No, please. Please.'

In the dim light of the cavern, Petron's eyes widened as he saw the goblins swarming over her, right next to him, inches away. Their skin was pebbled grey, smooth-headed and snarling and muttering around jagged teeth and slavering tongues. Their fingers were long. Ana fell silent as one of the goblins held her face in its hands and turned her this way and that. By the altar Varratim waited, his gaze fixed on the black of the stone.

One of the goblins grabbed roughly at Ana's arm and she shrieked and Petron lunged forward but then he was on his back, a cloaked demon standing on his chest. Her hood was back, showing a shock of red hair. Petron shrieked as her boot opened a thousand cuts on his chest, and the floor of the cavern opened a thousand more on his back.

'Still, boy,' she said, her accent sharp and cold, and then drew a thin runewand of iron with a green gem from her robe and pointed it down at Ana.

'No!' Petron tried to yell, but the breath was gone from his lungs and a bolt of green light shot from the wand and Ana slumped still. A goblin fumbled with a key and unlocked her manacles from the chain holding them to the wall, and three others helped it drag her roughly across the cavern floor.

'Please,' Petron said, but the woman standing on his chest did not look at him, her eyes following Ana as more goblins dragged her up onto the altar under Varratim's supervision. Petron saw sparks of light in his vision and struggled to draw a breath, his hands scrabbling up the demon's boots and grasping at her robes. She glanced back down and reached down to slap his hands away, and then eased her foot from his chest.

'Watch,' she said, leaning down to him, 'quiet. Or boot again.'

Then she was gone, striding away to join the other robed figures filing into the cavern. Petron pulled himself up to the wall and breathed deep, the damp air filling his lungs, clutching at the torn skin on his chest even as his breaths tore open barely healed cuts on his ribs.

The demons chained Ana face down to the altar and gagged her, and then Varratim waved a hand and she was awake. Her face was towards Petron and he tried to lock eyes with her but she was gazing around the room wildly, flexing her neck and yelling behind her gag. Varratim leaned down to her and from his belt drew his awful knife and Petron yelled out, 'No, no, you don't need to do this!'

A goblin scampered across and kicked him, its bare feet digging into his ribs and its black tongue flicking out past the rows of intricate teeth. He cowered from its stare, those impossible black orb eyes, and then it was next to him, turning his face to the altar, one hand in his hair gripping hard and the other at his throat.

Varratim was speaking but Petron couldn't hear over the blood rushing, his own heartbeat, the muttered hisses of the goblin holding him fast. Varratim drew his knife, and Ana's eyes found Petron's.

'Please,' Petron whispered, and Varratim cut free her gag and the goblin at his ear fell silent. The whole cavern fell still. Varratim gestured at the assembled demons and goblins and then turned back to Ana.

'I will allow you a last word as is custom; do not waste it on pleas, I pray.'

Ana began to weep, and Varratim pushed her hair back from her face. Her eyes did not leave Petron's.

'Please,' she said, and Petron screamed as Varratim drove his blade into her back and the runes on the altar pulsed with nauseating light. Petron reached for the skein, but again felt only chaos interspersed with nothing. There was no pattern in this place.

Over and over he screamed inarticulate rage, one word only: *no*. The goblin at his side held him by the hair and the throat but did not squeeze tighter, did not stop his yells. Slowly, the light from the runes on the slick black altar stone faded and Varratim wiped the blood from his dagger on Ana's ragged shirt. Her eyes were still locked on Petron, unmoving. There was a moment of silence, the chained children cowering against the wall, and the goblins and demons staring reverently at Varratim and his knife. Petron strained against the goblin, his hands tearing at the arms holding him. In shuffling rows, the demons and goblins began to file out, and Varratim walked away from Ana's body towards the exit of the cavern. Petron managed to tear the goblin's hand from his throat with a jerk of both his arms.

'I'll kill you!' he yelled into the silence, and Varratim paused, turning back. Goblins were unchaining Ana's still-bleeding corpse from the altar and dragging her from the room, he dark hair cascading across her face. Petron felt his throat swell shut with the grief, felt the cuts on his skin and the muscle below tearing with every breath, felt his every nerve burning. He forced himself to breathe through his nose, hard, and wiped tears from his eyes. He kept his eyes locked on Varratim. The goblin at his shoulder whispered something into his ear, sharp teeth clicking around alien words.

Varratim strode to Petron, and the other prisoners. He leaned forward, and as one they recoiled. The younger children began to sob, and Petron felt his heart was about to burst.

'Not,' Varratim said quietly, 'if I kill you first.'

He strode from the room and the goblin holding Petron threw him down into the dirt and scampered after him, and Varratim stroked its head lovingly. Petron curled up on the cold stone and buried his face in his hands and prayed for Anshuka the god-bear, the mother of Undal, to save him from the demons.

'Praise Anshuka,' he said, quietly, his voice scarcely a whisper, 'praise to the breaker of chains, praise to the strength in our hearts. Praise Anshuka, the mother bear. All glory to the bear-god, wrath of Ferron, protector of Undal. Praise Anshuka.

'Mother, watch over Ana.

'Mother, give us peace.

'Mother, help us help ourselves.

'Mother, I am so afraid.'

He prayed and prayed, and waited for an answer.

14

Fire in the Sky

'I was raised in Tessendorm, where there is no Pantheon. There is Baal above, there is nameless flame below. In between, there are men. The Undal see gods in oversized spirits, and demons in Ferron sorcerers. A demon is a crow-man but an Undal magician is a skein-mage? A Judge is a god, but the spirit of a glen is a bogle? It is nonsense, I say. They ascribe moral authority to animist beasts, and this leads to a brutality of thought. The Undal have no finesse.' – Private diary, Campbell Torbén of Aber-Ouse

The woman in blue led them through the back door to an enclosed courtyard.

'Fifty silver pieces,' she said, and Tomas scoffed at her, still rubbing ale from his face. His dark hair was plastered to his forehead.

'Do you know who I am?' he said incredulously, and behind him Floré rolled her eyes. She tried to gaze past

Tomas and the woman, and could just make out a figure asleep on the straw, clad in white.

'I'm Primus of a Stormcastle, you stupid whore. You and your friends are lucky we don't string you up one by one by your bastard necks for all this nonsense. If we weren't in a rush, I'd have you all hanging by your ears from the city walls by dawn!'

If the woman in blue was impressed, it did not show. She held a lantern she had taken from inside the inn, and turned it to cast light on the sleeping figure.

'The price is fifty silver pieces to consult my tame whitestaff,' she said, smiling, 'Normally he would talk to you for a copper piece out on the street, but I don't like you. Do you know who *I* am?'

When Tomas opened his mouth to answer she held up a finger. Floré could feel Heasin tensing beside her expectantly – he was as tired as she was with this pantomime.

'You are new in town, I appreciate that,' the woman continued. 'But I *am* The Hanged Man. This is my town. Nothing happens here without my consent or knowledge, and *nobody* comes into my private club and starts brawling, regardless of what rank they—'

Floré's right cross caught the woman on the sternum. She had stepped sideways past Tomas and turned her shoulders so the blow had a good body rotation behind it, and the woman didn't see it coming in the gloom of the courtyard. The Hanged Man crumpled to the ground, pulling in weak breaths. Floré reached down and picked up the lantern with one gauntleted hand, and with the other grabbed the woman's thick red hair and pulled her face up into the light.

'I don't care about your parochial bullshit,' she said. 'Understood?'

The woman opened her mouth to speak, her hands clutching at her sternum, but only a wheeze came out. Floré threw her down to the mud and then straightened and stalked to the sleeping figure in the hay. Heasin followed, whilst Tomas stared down at the gasping figure on the ground. The beggar reeked of booze and shit, and as Floré shook him roughly she heard Tomas kicking the woman behind her on the courtyard.

'Tomas,' she called, 'enough.'

He came to join them, slicking back his hair, and Heasin eyed him coldly.

'Can you wake him?' Floré asked the mage, her own rough shaking doing nothing, and Tomas nodded. Closing his eyes briefly, he furrowed his brow slightly and then the beggar gasped and sat upright.

'A whitestaff, all right,' Tomas said. 'I can feel it. Auren, isn't it?'

'Who are you?' asked the beggar, and Floré pulled the blindfold from his face roughly. Behind it, one eye was missing; the socket was surrounded by ragged scars, and the other eye was milky and did not track to her movement, or react to the lantern.

'He is blind after all,' she said. 'I thought that to be a trick.'

In the courtyard behind them the woman in blue was trying to crawl towards the inn, but she could still not draw enough breath to call for help. One hand slipped in the dirt and Floré glanced back at her and scrunched her nose.

'Quickly, Tomas,' Floré said, removing one of her

gauntlets, and the mage squatted down and drew a belt knife. He pulled the blade across the back her wrist and collected a few drops of blood on it and held it out to the blind beggar.

'Listen to me, Auren,' he said, 'we need your help. We are looking for a child. I have the blood of the mother here. You need to do the second circle of finding, and tell us what you see. Understand?'

The beggar blinked his milky eye and sat up straighter.

'A drink,' he said. 'I can't... can't think without a drink.'

Floré pulled her gauntlet back on and stood. 'My daughter,' she said, 'is missing. Do this now, beggar, and I will get you enough drink to drown in. But we do this now. Understood?'

Her voice was ice, and Auren squirmed and nodded. He pulled himself into a cross-legged position in the straw slowly, and taking the blade from Tomas began to whisper. The blood on the blade began to suffuse with blue light.

'Almost,' whispered Tomas, and from the courtyard behind them the woman in blue managed a gurgled half cry. The back door of the inn opened and from it they all poured out – seven thugs, four of whom now held swords and the rest cudgels or short blades, save one who still clutched the iron fire poker. The two women who had been wearing dresses, sat with the woman in blue, held a crossbow each, one in a yellow pleated dress that contrasted with her dark brown skin, the other in green frilly satin that stopped at her knees, blonde hair cascading to her shoulders. She stepped forward and nodded her head and a woman in worn leather moved past and pulled the woman in the blue dress up; she started to carry her back to the inn.

'He is almost done,' whispered Tomas, his eyes darting, and Floré drew her sword and stood in a single movement, drawing it to her shoulder in a high guard position. Beside her Heasin hissed and flexed his claws, and across the courtyard the nine armed criminals stared at them coldly. The lantern by her feet provided the only light in the courtyard, and its flame flickered across blades and focused eyes.

'Guard him then,' Floré said to Tomas, and she ran at the fight.

~

Yselda woke Cuss up with a glass of water to the face. He gulped and blinked and stared around wildly.

'Cuss,' she said, 'it's okay, she's a friend.'

Cuss sat upright and then scrambled backwards on the floor from the Orubor who now sat perched on the edge of an armchair, holding a clay cup of wine. It looked at him with those golden orb eyes and tilted its head.

'I do not eat human flesh,' it said, 'unless necessary. I cannot predict the future or read minds. I track the orbs, as do you.'

Cuss pulled his knees to his chest and turned to Yselda, and she smiled at him.

'Her name is Ash,' Yselda said, trying not to show her own fear at the exotic and near-mythical creature in the room with them. Cuss wiped at the water on his face and gave a quick nod.

'Pleased to meet you,' he mumbled, 'but I think we should wait for the captain.'

Yselda sat down on the edge of the armchair opposite Ash and tugged her sleeves straight.

'I don't know what to call you, Ash – I have never met an Orubor. Is it miss, or ma'am or something else? A... rank or title?'

'It is,' the Orubor said, 'Ash.'

Yselda nodded and looked to Cuss for help but he just sat there wide-eyed.

'How is it you know of Captain Artollen?' she asked, trying to think what the captain herself would do.

'Rumours,' Ash said, 'A Tullioch at the Ollen Mill seeking orbs, Stormguard headed north and quickly. I met her once, years ago. I sought her husband's... advice on a matter. Now she seeks orbs; I seek orbs. Fortuitous, I thought. Is Master Janos with her?'

Cuss pulled himself up from the rug and got into a chair, pulling his sheathed sword onto his lap, and he began picking at a bowl of grapes on the table.

'Mister Janos died,' he said in a low tone, not meeting her eyes, 'when the orbs came. A demon came down and killed him.'

Ash bowed her head and spoke a few words in a lilting tongue Yselda did not recognise.

'If the singer is dead,' she said slowly in Isken, 'it is a loss for us all. His poetry truly was beautiful. I do not think it is so easy to kill a singer such as he. You saw him dead?'

Yselda shifted uncomfortably and tried not to picture Mister Janos, or Shand, or any of the others. She shook her head in concert with Cuss.

'Then I will hold to hope and fate,' Ash said, and her face tightened into something approximating a smile. She stared down into her cup of wine and they sat silent for a long moment. Yselda could not look away from the Orubor's eyes and skin, her bald head, her jagged teeth.

'I did not think Orubor left the forest,' Yselda said, forcing clumsy words past a nervous tongue.

Ash nodded. 'Only me,' she said, 'and my line before me. We hunt the Deathless one at the command of Anshuka. She showed him clemency, but he does not abide by it.'

'What do you mean?' asked Cuss, and Yselda watched as the Orubor brought a hand to her face and covered one eye with it.

'Deathless,' she hissed, 'Tullen One-Eye: the man who broke the Tullioch Shardspire; the man who broke Old Undalor; the man who chained its people and people from across the world to grow his empire; the consort of Empress Seraphina, daughter of kindly Ferron. The man who rode Lothal the wolf into battle and cut down endless lives.'

'Tullen One-Eye is dead,' Yselda whispered, and outside there was a gust that rattled a window shutter and she saw Cuss shiver. The Orubor lowered her hand and sank back in her chair, sipping her wine through thin lips. Yselda saw the hint of serrated teeth beyond.

'Anshuka killed Lothal, and Nessilitor fell by Tullen One-Eye's hand, and Tullen was defeated in turn. Anshuka cursed Ferron and called the rotstorm that the empire might never rise again. She spoke her true voice to Tullen and bade him watch forever the plight of his people, but never intercede. And so he is bound by her energy, her pattern. He lives, endless, but cannot intervene. Three hundred years he has wandered, always aware of what he once was, what his people once were, forced to see the world move on without them. She bade him repent, but he will not.'

Cuss stared solemnly at the Orubor and ate another grape, chewing it loudly, and Yselda breathed out through her nose.

'So why do you hunt him if he can't intervene?' Cuss asked, and Ash smiled with a mouth full of jagged teeth and breathed a heavy sigh.

'Anshuka bade it,' she said, 'before she fell asleep. The elders say she commanded my ancestor to ensure Tullen faces judgement – but she did not say how. So we ask him if he will face judgement, and then we do our utmost to kill him. Ever I ask. I have hunted him many years. I find him, I ask him. He refuses. I attack him, but he will not die. It is a puzzle – how to kill the deathless man? Perhaps it is a test, a reminder to him so he does not simply move onward. Ever an Orubor will find him, and remind him to face his past. Perhaps one day he will ask forgiveness, and death will take him.'

Yselda saw Cuss open his mouth and could imagine the next ten minutes of him listing his ideas, so she coughed and cleared her throat.

'So why do you seek the orbs of fire?' she said. 'Can you help us? Cuss's brother Petron, and Captain Artollen's daughter Marta, they've been taken.'

Ash shifted at this news and turned her gaze on Cuss.

'Something is afoot here,' she said, 'and it stinks of Ferron. These orbs, this is not the empire. It is older than that. The Orubor take no threats lightly. I will help you if I can. The orbs go north but… I have a theory. Their goal is not north. I have spoken to farmers of the Slow Marsh, Tullioch of the reef, Antian of the broken tunnel: all tell the same tale of orbs of light, stolen children. Not the Orubor. Why not? The orbs veer far from our lands, they circle and dance but never do they cross our border. Yet every night when they retreat to the north, they pass closer to our lands and they hesitate. There is only one thing they could want in the end, these orbs, only one true target of any worth in this world: Anshuka.'

Her hand came to linger on the long bow that she had brought into the room, a silver wood that reflected the firelight warmly, and Yselda felt a rush of awe. An actual Orubor longbow: her mother had told her tales of Orubor shooting when she was child, a second arrow in the air before the first had found its mark.

The door slammed open and Voltos burst in, panting and clutching at his knees. The Orubor was suddenly holding a knife, an antler hilt with a rune-inscribed silver blade. Yselda's hand went to the knife Floré had given her.

'We're in trouble!' Voltos said. 'A lot of trouble!'

He regained his breath and looked up and saw the Orubor in the armchair, teeth bared and golden eyes gleaming, blue skin dark in the candlelight. He widened his eyes and his hand went straight to his obsidian dagger as he took in the lay of the room. Seeing Yselda and Cuss sat calmly he did not draw his blade, but kept his hand on the grip. He frowned at the Orubor and then nodded his head in a minimal bow.

'Really rather a lot of trouble...'

~

Floré sprinted forward across the courtyard and heard two clicks but both crossbow bolts went wild. She knew a crossbow bolt could kill her in a heartbeat from that distance, but neither of these women had the stances of marksmen and she relied on that. She dashed forward in a series of busts, long strides and quick sidesteps, and with a flourish of the blade she fell upon the right flank of the group.

Two of them came to meet her with swords. The first she parried once, twice, and the second was on her and she pushed aside a glancing blow. Stepping inward, she caught the left-hand man's sword hand in her free hand and squeezed, feeling fingers crack under her fist. With her other arm she held her longsword out and parried the right-hand swordsman's probing strokes. She batted his blade aside with a heavy swing and then released the left-hand man and shoulder-charged the right, her blade tucked close to her stomach. It cut into his guts as her shoulder rammed into his chest, and he fell backward. Ducking low Floré spun, sweeping her blade out, and scored a hit on the left-hand man's leg. His own scything blow cut through the air over her head and he crumpled to the ground as her sword bit deep.

With a glance she saw Heasin, and a feral grin spread across her face. On the left-hand side of the fight the Tullioch had shed his cloak. One woman lay dead at his feet, neck snapped, and another was crawling in the mud away from him. There was a ball of fire as Tomas threw a bolus of flame at the hands of the crossbow wielder in the yellow dress, who shrieked as her weapon went up in flames. She had just reloaded, and as she dropped it the weapon went off, the bolt sticking with a quivering jolt into the side of the outhouse.

Floré finished her wounded opponent with a quick rally of blows, battering past his defences as he tried to stand and sinking her sword into his chest, and then she turned. Three cudgel-wielding criminals stood before her, along with a woman in a green dress aiming a crossbow. She took a step back and dropped her sword, and then grabbed a wheelbarrow from the mud of the courtyard and charged them. The force of her charge knocked two of the cudgel wielders to the ground, and a wet scream cut the air as Heasin ripped the throat from another bandit with his claws; the scream came from that woman's comrade, a man now coated in the arterial spray of claret red that had moments before pulsed through his accomplice. He turned and tried to flee over the courtyard wall, hands scrabbling at smooth stone.

Floré held the wheelbarrow in front of her, and the woman with the crossbow dared a shot. The arrow stuck deep into the wood of the barrow. Floré tossed the barrow aside and stalked forward. The two she had knocked down were getting back to their feet, and the other circled to her left.

'Tomas,' she called. 'Silver pays gold!'

She kept heading forward and heard Tomas swear under his breath behind her. Heasin was dancing with a flaxen-haired woman, who was keeping him at bay with a series of defensive sword slashes. He nimbly moved his feet to keep always a stride away, his long arms snatching in at her whenever her guard failed. The woman in the yellow dress had fallen to the ground and was weeping, staring at her burned and ruined hands.

'Call it!' Tomas shouted, and Floré broke into a short charge at her three opponents.

'Left!' she shouted back, just as she reached the three cudgel wielders. The first blow she dodged, and then she grabbed one swinging cudgel with her gauntleted hands and ripped it from its owner. Tossing it behind her, she turned and laid in with heavy jabs and crosses to the two on her right. The one on her left, still holding a heavy wood cudgel studded with iron rivets, lifted it behind her head and swung forward viciously.

A silver coin flew from Tomas's hand across the courtyard, whistling as it cut through the air, and hit the cudgel wielder behind Floré in the side of the head. Her skull exploded into red mist as the coin exited the other side of her head, coating the crossbow-wielding woman in the green dress with blood and brain and fragments of skull as she tried to pull a short knife from her dress.

Floré caught a swinging attack with the outside of her left gauntlet, deflecting it away, and then she had stepped inside her attacker's guard and hit him with a tight uppercut. She felt his jaw snap under her plated fist, and he fell back with a strangled cry. She threw her left elbow back, catching the arm of the woman trying to crowd her from the side. They grappled and she began to headbutt, over and over, driving her forehead into the nose and face of the woman.

'This isn't right,' a voice said weakly, cutting through the mess of grunts and the scrape of boot on stone.

As she dropped the unconscious and bleeding woman from her grasp, Floré picked up a cudgel. The woman in the green dress was being violently sick, her face and hands coated in vomit and the skull fragments of her comrade whose head Tomas had exploded.

'This isn't right; I've done it wrong,' the voice said, and Floré brought the cudgel down hard on the woman's temple.

She crumpled.

'You said she was far, but she is near, but still far,' the voice continued, and Floré went to the woman with the burned hands and hit her with the cudgel until she stopped moving.

The courtyard fell still.

Floré ripped a scarf from a dead man and wiped blood from her face and glanced about. Their attackers were dead or unconscious or writhing on the ground, hurt. Heasin was wiping blood from his claws and face with a cloak from a fallen foe; his side of the fight was a mess of blood mixing with mud, grievous slashing wounds on every foe. The woman in the blue dress was gone, whisked inside by one of her team in the fracas.

'Floré,' Tomas said, and she turned to the mage and the whitestaff. Auren sat in his straw and mud and filth, but his matted and dank hair lifted from his head as if pushed by an invisible breeze and his posture was alert and upright. Floré picked up her sword from the mud and crossed the courtyard.

'What did you see?' she asked, and the whitestaff turned his milky eye towards her.

'You said far away, but she is close,' he said. 'Very close. Closer every moment.'

'What does that mean?' Floré demanded, and her heart beat a staccato rhythm. The combat had barely stirred her but now she felt her chest squeeze tight.

The blind man began to weep.

'I see it now,' he said, 'I do, I see it. Silver and fire. Crow-men. *Demons*. Silver and fire, my master said, to truly kill a demon. Do you have silver? Do you have fire?'

Tomas shook the man and slapped him.

'Tell us!' he roared, and Auren collapsed back into the hay.

'They are already here,' he said, and immediately above them the sky blazed with white fire as a hundred feet up an orb suddenly shone with incredible intensity. Floré felt a wave of pressure pushing at her ears, felt the world go strangely muted and nearly silent. She stood with Tomas and Heasin and together they stared as a dark spot emerged in the centre of the orb and from the blazing sphere a figure began to descend.

Floré gripped her sword and set her stance, and then felt her mouth fall open as a stream of fire at least a hundred feet long shot from the orb and into thatched roof of The Hanged Man before them. The roof was instantly ablaze and the stream of fire ceased. A jet of purple light shot from another facet of the orb, and the courtyard wall next to them blasted backward as if hit by a falling tree.

Heasin stepped to one of her shoulders and Tomas to the other as a circle of light focused on the ground fifteen feet in front of them and the figure grew clear. It was a man, holding a bundle? No, holding a...

Floré felt every nerve in her sharpen as she saw Marta. A man clad in black with a knife at his belt, hooded, brown gloves and boots, tall, his joints ungainly and his limbs too long, held Marta. Her daughter was crying, weeping, and her hair had been cut short roughly. She was dressed in black fabric and had tired bags under her eyes, shadows. Floré heard Tomas swear under his breath and she knew he was thinking the same as her.

'Judge's shit,' he said, his voice barely audible through the strange silence that seemed to accompany the orb, '*Demon. Crow-man.*'

Floré dropped her sword. It would only inconvenience a crow-man anyway. She reached into the pouch at her waist and calmly pulled out four silver coins. With practised dexterity the coins clicked into slots on her gauntlets, two on each hand over the knuckles. Those raised ridges of steel that looked decorative perfectly held the coins in place, leaving the leading edge protruding over her knuckles when she gripped her hands into fists. She drew the silver dagger she had taken from Captain Tyr's cottage and spat into the mud.

'Silver pays in gold,' she said, and beside her Tomas flexed his fingers and began to mutter to himself as Heasin hissed and thrashed his tail.

'I am Heasin!' he roared. 'Where is Hassin of House Shardkin? Tell me, beast!'

The figure touched down, feet gently stopping on the mud of the courtyard of The Hanged Man.

'I've been up there some time,' he said, glancing about at the dead men and women on the floor, 'watching you do what Undal always do. I am Varratim.'

Varratim gave a small bow and Floré bounced on the balls of her feet. He was fifteen feet away. Mara was held by one arm, looking at her mother but too afraid to speak. Floré locked eyes with her daughter, saw her hair chopped short, dressed in odd black clothes. Eyes red from crying, too afraid to cry out. Floré felt something inside her break, and suddenly she was shivering with fear. Above them the orb of fire shot out another purple beam, and then another stream of flame, out past The Hanged Man.

'Oh Judges,' Tomas said, tugging at her sleeve. 'There are more of them!'

Floré did not take her gaze from Varratim, but she heard the screams and the destruction from across the city.

'Let her go,' she said, and Varratim drew a wand from the back of his belt, a green gem on the end of a squat iron bar. Heasin growled.

'Hassin of House Shardkin! Where is she?' he yelled, and Varratim glanced at him.

'Who? Oh. Dead, I think. I'm sorry.'

Heasin howled and leapt forward but Varratim sent a bolt of green light from the strange wand in his hand and the Tullioch collapsed into a heap, unconscious or dead. Floré felt every muscle in her tense. She had fought crow-men before, had killed crow-men before, but never when they held her daughter. She had never seen a weapon like the one held in the demon's hand. Before she made it three feet Marta could be dead. Tomas next to her shifted uneasily.

'We seek answers, Varratim,' he called out, and the hooded man nodded.

'Good,' he replied. 'That is a good thing to seek.'

'Let her go,' Floré said again, and could feel tears in her eyes. She could not look away from Marta. *Mama,* she saw her daughter mouth silently, and felt her eye twitch and her fists clench.

'No,' said Varratim. 'Not yet – but maybe if you behave. I would like you to come with me.'

He waved a hand, and the light concentrated around him, and Heasin, and Tomas, and Floré. Heasin's limp body began to rise from the ground, floating up towards the orb and its blazing light and terrible silence.

'I can get him,' Tomas muttered, and Floré bit her lip.

'Too dangerous,' she said, and he grabbed her arm. Ahead of them Varratim was slowly beginning to rise, only a foot off the ground. Marta had begun to wail.

'We have a job to do, Artollen,' Tomas hissed, 'and it is bigger than one girl. Whoever this is he needs to be stopped. Distract, and I make the move. Now!'

Tomas pushed her forward, and with tears running down her face Floré turned and punched him, a single punch to the temple. The mage fell to the ground limp just as her feet began to rise, lifted in the column of light towards the orb of fire.

'Too dangerous,' she said, again, to herself, and felt tears running down her cheeks at the sheer helplessness of it all as his unconscious body lifted with her. She rose to the orb, the field of silence enveloping her, and as she did she saw the other five orbs over Ossen-Tyr; she saw the flame, saw beams of fire and beams of purple light cutting the town to shreds. Soldiers on horseback and on foot could do nothing, and arrows that struck true against the orbs' blazing exteriors fell back to the ground, broken.

She heard the wails and the cries, and then only silence and pale light and a dark iris before her. With a final glance down she saw Auren stand tall and walk into the courtyard, and she saw the beam of fire take him; he was a shadow in burning flame but then she was in the light and she saw nothing but white.

15

The Mountains of the Blue Wolf

'It is hard to say, but much was lost when Ferron fell. Much was lost before. Long before Tullen One-Eye and the empress, before the plantations and mines and wars and conquest, Ferron himself founded a kingdom. Only mixed reports remain of that gilded time, where technology and magic melded to bring peace and plenty. The fall of Ferron is not the rotstorm, but the corruption of Empress Seraphina and Tullen One-Eye. From exuberance to decadence; from innovation and kindness to greed and fear.' – The Fall of Ferron, Whitestaff Anctus of Riven

Cuss didn't know what to say. He had spent the brief moments since the orbs arrived cowering, huddled at the side of the window. When the feeling of pressure and muted stillness fell over the inn he wanted to curl on the ground, to close his eyes and cover his ears and wish it all away, but instead he had gone to the window, gripping the sill and peering through the small dirty panes of glass. Now he heard Yselda argue with Voltos, but Voltos held firm with his plan – as soon as he saw the first orb, he said he was leaving the city.

'After I spoke to my people I checked in with the Antian advisor of the City Watch. Messages came in by bird this afternoon. The reports say the harbour at First Light is overrun by crow-men, and the Stormwall potentially breached in a dozen places north of Fallow Fen. Lancer regiments are gathering at Aber-Ouse to the north and in Undal City. I need to get back to the wall. If Tomas and Floré are alive, tell them to follow. We've wasted too much time on these orbs.'

Cuss sniffed and wiped his hands. 'You said you'd help find Marta, and Petron,' he said accusingly, and Voltos rubbed at his muzzle and threw up his hands.

'I tried!' he said. 'But they are either dead or beyond our reach, Cuss. I'm sorry. I'm leaving. I'm needed at the wall.'

Ash stood by the window through all of this, staring at the destruction raining down.

'We should leave also, Cuss and Yselda,' she said calmly, and Cuss lost his temper at that.

'I'm not leaving without the captain,' he yelled, 'and even then *I'll* be leaving to go north to find Petron, not to the bloody Stormwall!'

Yselda came and hugged him close and he felt the cuts on his chest tearing slightly.

'Goodbye,' Voltos called, gathering his belongings, and Ash lazily grabbed him and pulled him to the window.

'Look, Antian,' she said, 'the second orb. A Tullioch and two humans?'

Voltos gripped the windowsill and peered into the maelstrom of fire and light beyond.

'Damnation!' he yelled, and Ash pulled him close.

'Anshuka is in danger,' she said, 'you must tell your protectorate. Orubor are few. Do you understand?'

Voltos wrenched his arm from her and then he grabbed his pack and ran from the room without looking back at Yselda and Cuss.

'What is it?' Cuss asked, and Ash gestured them forward. Through the window, out across the walled garden of the inn he could see the roofs of houses, pillars of smoke. An orb hovered maybe two streets away, wantonly dispensing beams of fire and purple light, and beyond that Ash gestured at a second orb. Yselda gripped Cuss tight. Figures were being carried in shafts of light towards it, levitating upward.

'I don't understand,' he said, staring at the orb. 'You don't think that's...'

'I'm sorry,' Ash said. 'I don't think there is another Tullioch in town. It appears the captain and the Tullioch have been taken. The mage will be with them, or dead.'

Ash stood and began filling a small leather satchel with food from the table: a loaf of bread, apples and pears, a wedge of cheese. She sniffed at each item and muttered to herself quietly in a language full of rolling vowels that Cuss had never heard the like of.

'What do we do?' Yselda asked, and Cuss stayed at the window watching.

'We go,' Ash said, throwing Cuss his boots. They hit his arm and fell to the floor. He couldn't tear his gaze from the figures, but then they reached the burning light of the orb above and he could see them no more.

'For now, out of the town,' she said. 'We can discuss further when we are safe away from these orbs. I return now to Orubor – you may journey with me. I am not done pursuing this.'

Yselda and Cuss made eye contact and then came together and gripped hands.

'I need to keep looking for Petron,' Cuss said, 'and the captain needs us. She might be alive as well.'

There was a scream from outside the inn, perhaps only thirty yards away. Ash turned to them both and stooped to eye level with the two cadets. Up close, Cuss found her orb eyes even more disconcerting, and he could see the sharpness of her teeth.

'My people are your best option,' she said, 'and if this is Tullen or another, then their plot will involve Anshuka. It is Ferron, of that I am sure. Orubor must be warned.'

Cuss grabbed his boots and sat on the floor, pulling them on. Yselda wrung her hands and stared at the orbs.

'The captain said to stay,' she muttered, blinking rapidly and turning around the room as if the answer lay somewhere just out of sight.

'Yselda!' Cuss said. 'We need a better plan but right now I don't have one.'

She nodded slowly and began to gather her things, but Cuss saw her hesitate at the window and one of her hands was always at the dagger at her belt.

'We can't leave the captain,' she said as they gathered at the door. Cuss put his hands on her shoulders and looked her in the eye and tried to think what Petron would say. Petron always knew what to say. He was younger, but he spoke so much, always speaking as Cuss was always silent and looking.

'The captain needs us to survive,' he said, 'so we can save Marta, and Petron. That's what matters most.'

They slipped into the street as the orbs left, flying north-east. The innkeeper was nowhere to be seen, though the common room was full of figures huddled under tables in the dark. The candles had been snuffed out, the hearth fire doused, and Cuss saw a dozen pairs of eyes track them as they sped through common room and out into the street. Watching the orbs cut through the sky away into darkness, Cuss felt a weight leave him as the pressure in his ears returned to normal. The faint nausea that had been churning in his guts faded in the cool of the street, and he gripped his knuckleduster tight. The weight of it was reassuring.

Along the next avenue they saw their first patrol, grey tabards running past with pails of water. It became a clear pattern; Stormguard roved the town, putting out fires and helping the wounded. Ash led the two of them down side streets, and soon they were at the south gate. A handful of Stormguard City Watch conferred with a dozen lancers, half of whom were mounted on horseback. The others held a combination of longbows, halberds, and one held a huge crossbow, leaning it on her hip.

'They will not like to see me tonight, I think,' Ash said, and Cuss couldn't help but agree. In the starlight and reflected flame the Orubor looked even more strange than before, her golden eyes seeming to absorb all light. She pulled her hood low and her cloth scarf high.

They slowly worked their way back into town to the river. Ash led the way, and Cuss and Yselda followed doggedly. There, the scene was much more chaotic. The river gate and portcullis were unguarded and aflame, and the smaller gates on either side of the river had been broken down, the walls around them smashed to lumps of rock.

'Be casual,' Ash said, and they followed her as she walked quickly to the gaping holes in the city wall. Within moments they were out of the gate and soon after into clear country. They walked a long hour in the darkness, scrambling into the bushes whenever a racing horse came by, carrying its rider to the desolation of Ossen-Tyr. The city was visible from miles around as it sat at the top of the hills, those hills that were so full of intricate mines and bountiful ore. The plumes of smoke and fire spiralled ever upward, and the three of them walked through the night. Cuss found himself looking back often, and the smoke columns only grew as the night progressed.

'Anshuka is in danger,' Ash repeated as dawn began to edge its way over the distant horizon. They had stopped in a copse of beech trees three dozen yards off the trade road and Cuss and Yselda were sharing an apple and some bread.

'Anshuka is in danger,' she said again, 'and I believe that whoever is behind this, they will come to Orubor. Orubor will be ready, if we are in time. If you want to fight back, that is the way. I had hoped for Artollen, but two of her children will suffice. Will you join me?'

Cuss and Yselda exchanged looks, and then Yselda nodded. Cuss worried at his fingernails as they walked east, and kept glancing to the north.

I'm sorry, Petron, he thought, *but I don't know what else to do.*

~

After her visit to the infirmary, in the courtyard Benazir found a moment to dip her hands in a bucket of cold water and wash the sweat and dried blood from her face. She rubbed her face dry with a cloth handed to her by the squire Whent, as the grim-faced Captain Jerrek updated her on the status of her garrison.

'The archers are getting low on arrows,' he began, gesturing at the ramparts and the figures stood by their braziers, staring west into the storm. His face was slick with sweat but he was breathing steadily. With night upon them to the east the sky was dark but to the west the edge of the rotstorm spat spark and arcane flurries of light, green and purple coruscations cutting through black and red cloud. Benazir glanced around the courtyard, the dead Stormguard, her men and women, the dead goblins, the dead crow-men, the dead rust-folk in their leather and fur and scales. The rust-folk had gained the wall with the dawn and it had been a day of fighting to clear them out, to push back the army that had appeared at her gates and her wall with no warning. Benazir slipped her gauntlets on and cinched them tight, and her right hand went to her sword hilt.

'Whent,' she called, 'take six cadets and go to the training yard. Yute kept some emergency stores beyond my orders, back of the weapons room behind the halberds. Get them up to the walls, and get back to me with a count of how many bows we still have up there.'

The boy ran off, and Benazir waved for the captain to continue. Yute was dead, old Yute, seasoned and salted and with his blade blooded in a hundred hundred fights, the man who had taken Benazir and Floré on their first raid past the wall. He lay dead on the rampart, killed by a rust-folk woman with a sickle in each hand and a song on her lips. The woman was dead on the wall, too, cut down by a Stormguard lancer resplendent in blue. It was a haze. Benazir started walking in the direction of the gates. She needed to see the gates, the walls. She needed to see again the cleared ground beyond the ramparts, past the border. She gestured at Captain Jerrek to accompany her and the two of them stepped through the central courtyard around bodies and over shit and blood, bowels loosened in death adding to the stink of goblin blood.

'Mulligan's lancers took heavy losses in that last sally out, perhaps a third gone,' he continued, 'but they took down the rottrolls so the ram won't be an issue anymore. Iris-Mage and Nostul-Mage are both recovering now I think but they did good work breaking the rust-folk formations. The Lady Kelvin... she is gone. Crow-men stopped her magic; goblins tore her apart. Sergeant Yonifer's squad managed to take another three crow-men down but lost half their team, and there are still at least a dozen out there. Captain Guil fell to a rottroll; I'm sorry.'

Benazir paused at that, at the image of Guil, freckle-faced and smiling and earnest Guil who she had known ten years or more, since Benazir was a young corporal and Guil only a cadet. Guil in her bed the night before and the hundreds before that, a hand on her cheek. She licked her lips and pushed it down, the sickness she felt and the grief that would rob her of her senses. She pushed it all down and away with a promise to feel the guilt later, but *not yet*.

Together they checked in at the gates, but the situation was unchanged. The great wooden gates opened to a kill chamber, and then a second set of gates. Those outer gates were broken and twisted by the crude brutality of the rottrolls, Benazir knew, but the inner gates were yet undamaged. Nostul, one of her skein-mages, was overseeing the defence, and the lancers and commandos with him were dutifully following the barked orders of the diminutive mage, his red hair and pale skin reflecting light from the braziers. Benazir nodded to him but moved on. She needed Tomas, the Primus. Tomas always had an answer.

She needed Voltos here, his insight, his critical eye hunting always for the weakness in any plan, the reality of the situation. Both were gone. Janos and Floré were gone to their retirement, Tomas and Voltos gone to seek them, Starbeck was gone to Undal City three years now to bring sense to the Grand Council. Guil was gone. Yute was gone. The Lady Kelvin, all of eighteen summers old and the sweetheart of the garrison, was ripped apart by goblins: *gone*. Benazir bit her cheek and glanced at stern Jerrek, Jerrek from Stormcastle VI with his inscrutable, dour face. She did not know him well, but he was here and he would have to do.

They climbed the ramparts and when they reached the top Benazir pointedly did not look over the wall, instead pausing briefly with each archer, sometimes with a quiet word of encouragement, sometimes a nod, sometimes simply a hand on a shoulder.

'Commander,' they murmured, or exclaimed, or whispered. Their eyes were shadowed and the rampart was littered with dead goblins and rust-folk and Stormguard alike. Each archer carried a longsword and side-knife, and their knives and tabards were black with blood.

'Captain Jerrek,' she said, loud enough for the archers to hear. 'Get food and water for these men, a measure of rum each, and more lancers to guard their backs. They do Anshuka's work today. Have the rampart cleared of the dead, sand put down. Cut away any of these hooks and ropes still hanging. I'll not have any climb made easier by sloth on our end.'

The archers responded with muttered thanks or tired salutes, and Jerrek bowed his head briefly and went to do her bidding. Benazir turned, red cape flowing behind her, and leaned on the rampart staring out. Her hands, cosseted in steel and leather, closed into fists on the slick stone of the rampart as she tried to take in the horror below.

The fighting was done, for now. From the base of the wall, for three hundred feet the Stormguard cleared back the reed and kelp and vine each summer, cut down any tree hardy enough to stake a claim. Three hundred feet to the swamp, the bog thickets of rushes, copses of trees, lingering red mists and tussocks of dark grass growing from black earth. Those first three hundred yards were rough ground, black peat cut through by streams.

The dead covered the terrain, a tableau of gore that made Benazir's stomach flutter. Dirt and blood and darkness, and as the night was falling she could scarcely make out the battlefield below. She found her eyes searching for Guil's red hair and bit her lip until she felt the flesh tear, felt blood on her tongue. She had spent the day rooting out rust-folk who had crossed the wall, leaving the ramparts to the archers, with instructions to Mulligan and Guil to sally out where necessary, for Nostul to hold the gates. When the rottrolls brought their ram, she had been at the gate. When the goblins swarmed up the trade road from the south, she had led the defenders in a brutal melee; the south of the Stormcastle was ringed in stone of course, but the village that had sprouted from its southern wall had no such defence. Hours of fighting in between cottages, leaping into fenced gardens, cutting down goblin after goblin in sty and field and orchard all. When the last of the villagers were safe inside the Stormcastle she had instructed the gates closed, and then there was something else, an order to be given, always another order to be given, to the infirmary, the cadets.

Now she was staring at the death beyond the gates and knew she should have been right there, at the wall, all along. She could see rottrolls and rust-folk cut down, dead horses and blue tabards of Mulligan's lancers. Of course the horses were dead. *Had he really tried to ride horses past the Stormwall? Could a captain be such a fool?*

'Bring me Captain Mulligan!' she yelled, and Whent jumped and began to run off. She had not noticed him arrive. Alone for a moment, she felt her stomach turning to acid and the familiar fear that was always there, bubbling beneath. She stared up from the carnage at the sky, the rolling cloud of red and black above. She stared up, unblinking, and tried to find calm, tried to become the balanced blade. Lightning arced through the clouds in a purple fractal dance, and her eye twitched.

~

Floré woke up still in her armour. The last thing she remembered was the light of the orb. She blinked rapidly and tried to assess herself. She was still armoured, still had her boots on. Wrists and legs were free to move. It was dark. She slowly pushed herself up, and then it was light. Shielding her eyes from the glare she crouched back as they adjusted. She was in a room with bare stone walls and a stone ceiling. Uniform patches of the ceiling were glowing softly with a yellow light. The floor of the room seemed to be stone also, seamless, and she could see no door. There was a ewer of water and a small steel basin next to it, along with a cloth.

'Hello?'

Nobody answered. She went and paced the walls and felt and looked for seams but found none, the same in the floors and ceiling. Finally, she returned to the steel dish and the ewer of water, and reasoned that since they could apparently send her to sleep without much effort, poison seemed unlikely. She drank, a little at first and then great gulps, and the water was crisp and clear, and then she used the rag to clean her face. She caught her reflection in the bottom of the steel dish; she looked tired, haunted.

With the rag and what little remained of the water she made a vague effort at cleaning her gauntlets, and noticed they had taken her silver dagger and money pouch and the silver coins she had slotted into the gauntlet knuckles – and yet had left her the gauntlets themselves.

A voice came through the wall and she recognised it as Varratim.

'A Stormguard commando and her gauntlets – never come between them!' he said, and Floré slipped her hands back into the comfort of leather and metal and pulled the straps tight.

'What is it you want, demon?' she asked in a flat voice, and in response an opening appeared in one of the walls, a hole circling out from a single patch of wall until it was the height of a man, the stone folding back on itself like a liquid. Varratim stood there, hooded, and two crow-men behind him, a woman and a man both clad in black. Each held iron rods about a foot long, tipped with faceted green crystals. They pointed them at her in the manner of readied weapons. Both were wrinkled and aged, sagging skin on their faces with mottled complexions and stooped postures.

'I want to talk, Captain Artollen,' he said, 'about your husband.'

Floré spat on the floor and Varratim looked down at the gobbet of phlegm.

'We understand about the gauntlets of course, as only one from the rotstorm would,' he continued. 'You understand, Captain, as you spent so many years in the rotstorm killing my people. Shepherding your reluctant Skein-wreck Janos, the Salt-Man, the Stormguard's disappointing hero. *Never remove your gloves.*'

As he spoke he peeled back his own gloves to show his fingers, overlong and curved. The back of one hand bore a bright scar. Floré sniffed and smirked.

'Crow-man got stuck by a pepper-thorn? That's a new one to me. I thought you demons were meant to be Ferron's legacy, not raw recruits.'

Varratim smiled thinly, pulled the glove back on and

lowered his hood. Floré saw his eyes then, pale irises and inside pupils that were not natural—they gyrated and danced, unfocused, split and reformed, spun and folded in on themselves.

'We all start somewhere,' Varratim said. 'I saw Urforren, you know. After. A circle of salt a mile wide, burning even now. How many hundreds dead? I walked the market there, the schools, the houses of healing. Your husband was a monster, but luckily he lacked the conviction to be a competent monster for too long.'

Floré yawned and blinked slowly. 'Am I meant to be getting something from this back and forth, demon? You literally have stolen children from their beds. I'll not debate morality with you.'

Varratim stepped into the room and glanced around. 'Do you have something better to be doing? How many of the rust-folk have you put to the blade – man, woman and child?' he asked, and Floré clenched her fists. The two crow-men at the door were still tracking her movement with those strange iron rods or wands and she had no idea where Marta was. She had no silver, and she had no fire. She had to force herself into a role: the brutal bolt-captain, not the anxious mother. If she showed weakness, she did not know how this would end.

'Can we skip any extensive monologues,' she said, 'and you just tell me your plan and what you want to know about Janos? I am tired.'

Varratim laughed, and with a gesture from the floor two protrusions grew up from the dark stone floor and formed into chairs. They sat and stared at each other, not breaking eye contact. Eventually he nodded.

'You have shown you will disobey your commands for your daughter's safety. This is good and right – no loyalty should take precedence over that of a mother to a child. My plan is simple and I am happy to enlighten you: I will kill Anshuka, with the blade of Tullen One-Eye.'

Floré did not react, but felt a tremor in her right fingers, her right arm, a deep pain, a vibration running up the bones of her arm. The first pulse of pain in the depths of her skull made her eye twitch, but she squeezed her fists tight and forced her face into a mask.

'This blade is honed by the destruction of pattern,' he continued, gesturing to a knife of obsidian tucked in his belt. The handle was twisted white bone, and a thick green gem sat at the pommel.

'All life and all things are a pattern, but the pattern of an untrained skein-user is the choicest whetting stone. Hence the children. I sacrifice them here, in the Blue Wolf Mountains where Ferron kept his experiments and toys, and I hone the blade that Tullen used to kill Nessilitor. It is so very sharp now, so charged with pattern and power. I believe it will kill a god. I do have one reserve, however.'

Floré waved her left hand to indicate he should continue, and she clenched her right fist and her jaw. He couldn't be serious, she thought, surely nobody could believe they could kill a god. She thought this, and then pictured orbs of light the size of carriages flying through the town. She pictured the rotstorm, ball lightning and acid rain and tornadoes of purple mist that would *change* you, about bones the size of cathedral buttresses standing stark from mounds of peat. She had seen a dead god, after all. She thought about the bravest woman she knew, turned craven, about friends weeping gloveless in the acid mire as the winds tore skin from muscle and muscle from bone. Men, women and children fleeing back into that storm as the Stormguard shot arrows after them. *Rust-folk*. She focused on keeping her face still.

'With Anshuka's death,' he continued, 'her work will be undone. The blight will end, the rotstorm will lift. The goblin will become human, again.'

He paused a long moment then, staring intently at her face as if assessing her reaction.

'What do you mean?' Floré said slowly.

'When a Judge dies, their work is undone,' Varratim began, but Floré shook her head.

'I know the idea. Berren died and his crops failed. Nessilitor died and her art faded. I've heard the stories. No, "*the goblin will become human*". What do you mean? Explain.'

She could feel her face growing hot. She could remember killing so many goblins. Every year, from wet-lightning strikes they rose and she would hunt them through Hookstone forest. At the Stormwall she had killed hundreds, either hunting them through the swamps or facing them in pitched battle. At Fallow Fen she had led scores of commandos in brutal sorties, slaughtering their way to the town's emancipation. At Urforren she had told Janos to *do it,* to turn the town and its rust-folk, its demons, its thousands of goblins to salt and fire. Varratim frowned at her and swallowed audibly.

'Russ!' he called, and from outside the chamber a goblin entered. Floré recoiled instinctively from its black orb eyes, the serrated teeth, the coarse grey skin. A wet black tongue dangled from its mouth. The goblin went to Varratim and stood by his side like a loyal dog, and Varratim placed hand on its head. She had never seen a goblin wearing robes before, only naked or fresh pelts and animal skins, mud and excrement, blood and filth of every type. This goblin was clean, dressed in simple black cloth.

'Anshuka punished us with the rotstorm and the blight,' he said, 'with destruction and humiliation; she tore down our great cities and ravaged our armies; she ate our scholars and trampled their houses of learning; and most perversely, she poisoned the very land itself. Why do you think the rust-folk always push at the Stormwall, always closer to the border? The rotstorm is not natural. It is not... good for development. You, you and your people have only ever been to the periphery. If you spend too long in the deep rotstorm, Anshuka will find you. Her dreaming form will hunt you down. For those rare, those few who can touch the skein you will awake a crow-man – that's what you call it, correct? A *demon*. You touch the skein within the chaos, and learn the nature of that chaos, but it is a hard lesson. Most of those so touched go mad, or simply die.'

He ran his hand over the goblin's head and drew it close.

'If you spend too long in the deep rotstorm as a child she will find you, and if you cannot touch the skein, you die, or... there are changes. A new pattern is enforced, the will of your great mother. My brother Russich was younger than I was when we were driven into the rotstorm by the shining knights of the Stormguard. When they burned our village to the ground, killed our father. He could not touch the skein. I could, though I did not know it then. We went seeking sanctuary, but it was too deep, the storm, and Russich...

he is not the same now, are you, Russich? Neither of us are the same.'

The goblin looked up at Varratim with shining wet eyes, and Floré took a step back.

'You are claiming the goblins as... children of the rust-folk?' she asked, and felt the room start to spin, forced herself to breathe. Varratim hugged his brother close and leaned forward a little.

'Children of the rust-folk. Every goblin, every rottroll, every wyrm even. A child. How many of the Stormguard know this truth, Bolt-Captain? Do you think your council know? I believe they do. Even if they do not, well. You hardly hold your blades when we appear human. Would this change anything?'

Floré stared at the goblin holding on to the leg of the crow-man, and forced herself to keep breathing. She felt sick. *The goblins are children. How many of them have I killed?* She pictured the great wyrm at Fallow Fen, a fifty-foot beast of scales and horn and nightmare that Janos had killed. *A child?* Janos stroked Russich's head, and the goblin closed its eyes and pressed close to him.

'I want to know any secrets you know of what it means to be a skein-wreck, Artollen. If you tell me, I won't use your daughter to hone my knife, and you can walk away when this is over. This I promise you. There are things I would know, but I dare not waste more time. Even the Stormguard can be competent, given enough time.'

'Marta cannot touch the skein. She is too young,' Floré said, her voice faint. 'She won't hone your knife.'

Varratim just shook his head. 'Now, Bolt-Captain,' he said. 'We both know better than that.'

16

The Bear & Her Daughter

'Benazir does not understand why I chose the gauntlet over the balanced blade. Benazir will sit on the Grand Council one day, of this I have no doubt – but when the hard job needs doing as in Urforren and Fallow Fen, you don't need a politician, or delicacy. You need a soldier who will work until the job is done. Artollen will put on her gauntlets and she will keep us safe, if she must kill Lothal's ghost itself.' – *Private Diary*, Commander Salem Starbeck

Petron was praying when the new prisoners woke up. His wounds itched and he found prayer a distraction, forcing himself to meditate on the power of the great bear and all she represented. The prisoners had been carried in unconscious: a slim man with dark hair and clothing and a Stormguard Commando tabard, and a huge Tullioch with deep green scales and a black spine ridge. When the Tullioch came in, they had all looked to the single Tullioch prisoner. She did not speak Isken, and she ignored their questions and mimes. Most of the time she stared at the altar or her own hands, but now she stared at the unconscious Tullioch. The goblins chained them up and two aged crow-men checked the manacles before leaving.

There were only six prisoners left: the Tullioch, one Antian, Petron, and three children. The youngest children had been left, and Petron thought Varratim perhaps hoped not to have to use them, but truly he did not know. He tried to comfort them but they were shackled far down the wall, and his wounds pained him grievously; they itched dreadfully now, and those he could see were red and swollen and leaked pus constantly. The man with the dark hair slowly opened his eyes. One side of his face was swollen and split, the eye almost occluded by the bruised flesh. He touched fingers to it gingerly.

'Where are we?' he said, and pulled himself into a crouch. The chains would not allow him to stand.

'The sacrifice cavern,' Petron found himself saying, and the man squinted at him. The only lights were the ever-present fungi and the sickly runes, but luckily the runes were half hidden by the altar at this angle.

The man spat, and blood came out. He pushed at the Tullioch, who did not stir.

'You Petron?' he asked, and then waggled his jaw and probed at a tooth with a dirty finger.

'Yes!' Petron yelled. 'Yes, yes, that's me. How do you know who I am?'

The strain of speaking so loudly and pushing against his manacles opened a hundred tiny cuts on his body and he shrank back in pain.

'Been looking for you,' the man said. 'I'm Tomas.

Skein-mage from the wall. Been helping Floré find her wayward kids, and now here I am. The cavalry is here.'

He shook his chains and then sighed.

'The sergeant is all right? Is… is… do you know… do you know who else is…'

Petron couldn't continue the question. He began to weep, and when he managed to wipe his eyes and raise his head Tomas was staring at him.

'They didn't go easy on you, did they,' he said, and Petron shook his head, sniffing.

'Your brother Cuss is alive. Yselda Hollow too – you know her? Them, me, this hunk of lizard have been trying to track you. That demon bastard has Artollen's daughter.'

Tomas grimaced and tested at his shackles. 'Right,' he said, 'enough of this.'

Tomas closed his eyes and furrowed his brow, and Petron almost laughed.

'You can't,' he said. 'The crow-men – it's all chaos or nothing. No pattern.'

'All right,' said Tomas, sitting back against the wall, 'all right. Trickier. Tell me then. Tell me everything.'

Petron spoke for long minutes, about Varratim, the skein, his search for a skein-wreck, his god-killing dagger, and Tomas's face grew grave and pale.

'Much to think about,' he mumbled, staring at the unconscious Tullioch, and then they sat in silence. Petron knew he was still tied and captured, doomed to die alone and in pain, but he smiled broadly. *Cuss was alive!*

~

Cuss started complaining when they turned straight south, and Yselda tried to shush him.

'She is an Orubor, Cuss,' she said. 'She knows what she is doing a million *million* more times than we do. We have to trust her.'

'South,' Cuss said, 'isn't *north*.'

He sulked all morning. They stopped for a break by a clear brook in the foothills of Ossen-Tyr, and from there could see Tollen's folly, a long-abandoned fort of one of the old Undalor chieftains. Tullen One-Eye had turned it to solid stone, it was said. Nobody was sure, now, but the tower of the castle was all that was left, accreted with rough stone that filled every room seamlessly.

'Where are we going, Ash?' Yselda asked as Ash refiled their waterskins in the brook. 'I know the answer is Orubor, but how are we going to Orubor by heading south?'

Ash peered about the glade, and then actually smiled. The smile showed her serrated teeth, but also wrinkles that formed on her pale blue skin over the red tattoos.

'Soon,' she said in response to Yselda's question, but would say no more on it. They sat by the brook for an hour, eating and resting.

'What are the red tattoos?' Cuss asked her after a long silence, and Yselda spat out a mouthful of water. Ash eyed him, and then removed her cloak and rolled up her sleeves. Her wrists and hands were coated in the red sigils, just like her face. They were ever so slightly raised from her skin.

'Not tattoos,' she said, offering a wrist for him to touch, 'though human skein-mages have been known to use those. These are scars.'

Cuss recoiled for a moment but then slowly reached his hand out, and when Ash put her arm further forward he traced his finger along a pattern.

'What do they mean? Mister Janos had them.'

Ash smiled at them. 'The skein is pattern,' she said. 'All is pattern. Life is a pattern, and so is death. Skein-mages and crow-men, your Janos, they seek to alter the pattern. When they do so, they must create it. If you already have the pattern made… it is not so hard.'

She rolled down her sleeves and began to pack up their gear.

'It is just a representation,' she said, 'not the pattern itself. You train your mind to associate that rune, that tattoo, that scar, with a moment. It is a pattern that calls to another pattern, deeper and more complex than the first. This way, you reach your pattern quickly.'

She shouldered her bow and stared up at the skies. North of them, purple and black clouds were gathering over the smoke and ash that rose from Ossen-Tyr.

'I don't like the look of that,' Yselda said, and she remembered the rotsurge in Hookstone. *Does the storm follow the orbs?*

'Are you a skein-mage?' Cuss asked Ash, and she looked at him and smiled.

'No, Cuss,' she said. 'I am an Orubor. Now – for some real magic! There is pattern in many things.'

Turning to the glade alongside the brook, she sang forth in a clear voice, high and true. Cuss could not predict the melody, or understand the words, but there was a refrain that returned and returned. After a long minute of singing, from the woods a deer stepped forth. Its coat was suffused with amber light, and its eyes were faceted diamonds.

'A bogle,' Yselda whispered. She had only seen one bogle before, at night in Hookstone forest. Shand had taken her out onto the loch, and a huge eel had surfaced beside them. *The old man of the loch.* The eel had turned over and over, its long jaw snapping slowly under the water. Its eyes were black pits and its teeth shone with green light, and its mottled yellow body had sparkled under the starlight. Shand had given her a fish, and told her to throw it in. Yselda had been terrified, but he had put his hand on hers and smiled at her on the still waters of Loch Hassel.

'It never hurts to give thanks to the local gods,' he had said in his soft low voice. 'Anshuka be praised, you never know who might be hungry.'

She had slipped the fish into the water, and the huge eel had taken it and curled around itself in a complex endless loop before disappearing back to the depths.

In the glade with her friend Cuss behind her and the strange Orubor beside her, Yselda let go of the handle of her shortsword, and she smiled at the memory of Shand, the cold air of Loch Hassel at night. The deer stepped closer. Its amber coat cast a glow across the nearby grass, and its diamond eyes seemed fixed on the three of them. It licked its lips. Ash spoke to it in her high clear voice, incomprehensible strings of what sounded like lilting poetry, and Yselda felt Cuss's hand slip into hers and squeeze tight.

Ash's cadence rose and the deer stepped forward and then walked a slow circle, before bobbing its head once and then it jumped once, twice, and was away into the woods.

Ash sniffed and scratched her nose.

'Bogle is such a terrible word,' she said, 'for such a beautiful thing. Come! We haven't much time.'

Where the deer had circled in the grass a faint trace of orange light remained, and inside it the grass looked different – coarser, longer. Holding one of their hands each Ash led them forward and into the circle and Yselda felt her hair stand on end as if before a lightning storm.

'What do Orubor call bogles?' she said quietly, and around them the circle began to glow brighter. Ash looked down at her with her orb eyes and smiled, showing all her sharp teeth.

'Gods, little one. We call them gods.'

There was a flash of light, and then the glade by the brook in the Ossen-Tyr foothills was empty.

~

Varratim came, and Tomas stared but was silent. Petron watched Tomas watching Varratim. He did not come alone or with his usual few attendants, but with a dozen crow-men and at least twenty goblins behind them. When they were aligned in front of the altar, Varratim drew his obsidian blade and raised his hands.

'You pay prices, my brothers and sisters,' he said, 'such terrible prices. Each flight takes its toll, and steals years. The gifts we have found, these wondrous weapons, these orbs of light, exact their toll. I am sorry. One day this may not be so, but for now it is the price we pay. We avenge Ferron, and we free our people from the chain of the bear-bitch Anshuka, curse her name to every hell!'

The crow-men cheered raggedly and the goblins joined in, though Petron was unsure if they could understand. Tomas was watching thoughtfully.

'A final sacrifice and the blade is honed. I can feel this. I took this blade from the hands of fallen Tullen One-Eye, once our greatest hero. This is the blade that *killed* Nessilitor the lover. This is the blade that can kill Anshuka. With this blade, Ferron is freed to rise again.'

Varratim pointed a hand at the chained prisoners and the goblins rushed over. They started at the Tullioch youth with her mottled green chest and her colourful head crest, and she shied back and hissed at them. The goblins reared back and reached for one of the human children, the littlest one, instead. Petron had never heard her speak. A tumble of brown curls, matted with dirt and grime fell around her face. Petron felt his chest heave. She could only be four years old. She was about the same age as his little sister Jana. Petron swallowed and felt the tears in the skin at his throat, the endless cuts pulling at each other. He pictured Cuss, and a boat at night. *What would Cuss do?* He looked at Tomas but the skein-mage sat back, resigned.

'*Do something!*' he hissed at Tomas, but the man shrugged and held up his manacled hands, and averted his gaze. The goblins began to unshackle the girl and she wailed.

'No,' Petron shouted, 'no. Take me instead. Willingly. Varratim. Varratim! Take me. Leave her. Let her be. If you need one more, let it be me.'

The crow-men parted and the goblins paused, looking to Varratim. He looked at Petron and nodded. Petron felt tears running down his cheeks and he turned to Tomas.

'Idiot boy,' Tomas said. 'What in the hells are you doing?'

'If you live,' he said in a rush, 'tell Cuss I love him, tell the sergeant I did my best, tell…'

Tomas stared at him silently his mouth downturned, and then the goblins had Petron. A dozen of them, pulling at his shackles. They bundled him to the altar and he did not resist. Every touch on his skin woke a hundred cuts, and in a moment he was face down on the stone altar. The rune by his face burned white, and he could feel the others around him, not as heat or light, but as *presences*. Varratim tightened the bonds himself and then leaned down.

'I like you, Petron,' he said, 'which makes this harder – but that is as must be. You are a lesson to me, in your sacrifice. Understand this. I heed the lesson, in that even an Undal may be ennobled by their action. You save a child, and this is a good thing, Petron. Do you have any final words?'

Petron stared past the crow-men and the goblins and saw Tomas with his swollen eye watching him. He turned his gaze up to Varratim and breathed in, and out, and reached for the skein but there was only chaos, and burning towers of unfathomable skein in these runes that sent his head reeling.

'Petron?' Varratim prompted, and Petron felt himself shiver.

'Praise Anshuka,' he said, 'praise to the breaker of chains, praise to the strength in our hearts. Praise Anshuka, the mother bear. All glory to the bear-god, wrath of Ferron, protector of Undal. Praise Anshuka. Mother, protect us. Mother, help us help ourselves.'

Petron began the litany again, louder, and he felt the knife drive into his back and then he felt the skein – *it was back* – and he saw the pattern, and he saw a nexus and a tangle and then it began to fade. It all began to fade.

~

Varratim came to Floré again and this time it was not so simple.

'I leave tonight,' he said, 'for Orubor to kill the god-bear.'

A crow-man stood beside him held out a rod of iron tipped with a faceted green gem, and faster than she could dodge a beam of green light cut across the room and hit her in the stomach. She toppled, paralysed and limp but awake and aware. She tried to blink, tried to move her fingertips, but to no avail. Goblins came, six of them, and stripped her bare and the aged crow-men – demons, men and women both – carried her down long corridors of stone to a room with dark stone walls and tied her to a metal bench. Varratim bade them all leave, and then produced a metal rod with a blue gemstone at its end. Squinting at it in the dimness of the room, Floré could see the gem was inscribed with intricate runes. Varratim pointed it at her stomach and there was a cone of light. A layer of thin scratches appeared, like cat scratches.

'I did this, and worse, to Petron for over a day,' he said, his voice strained, 'and finally I had to threaten to do it to Marta, before he broke and told me about Janos, about you. The skein-wreck and the bolt-captain, two war criminals playing house in the forest whilst Ferron is turned to acid and hell.'

He pressed the gem to her leg. A flash of light, and then

deeper this time, cuts through skin, into fat and muscle. She felt a trickle of blood.

'I'm starting to realise,' he said, 'that there is no point in this conversation. You don't know anything about being a skein-wreck. How could you, a dullard like you? There might be some secret in his blood, but you... you are just sword. Not even a sword. A pair of fists and nothing else. Do you understand me? Can you speak, yet?'

Floré began to laugh at that, and realised she could blink. She tried to flex her fingers and felt a little movement, though she was now securely bound to the table.

'I understand you, crow-man,' she said, and her tongue felt thick. 'I understand my lad Petron at thirteen summers had you beaten. You are a child. The Stormguard will find you, and they will kill you. There is always another pair of fists.'

Light, pain. Her leg again. She could see he was breathing heavily; his pale skin was mottled red.

'I killed him,' he said. Floré stared at the ceiling.

'Artollen, Floré, Stormguard Commando,' she said. 'Bolt-Captain of Stormcastle XII. Special skills: close combat. Knowledge of the skein: none.'

She started laughing again and felt tears in her eyes. A flash of light, pain again. The other leg.

'You kidnapped me to learn how to be a skein-wreck?' she asked, wincing as she laughed. 'Are you serious, Varratim? Judge's eyes, I'm the heavy hand. Janos spent a lifetime of study to become a skein-wreck. I asked him once – want to know the secret?'

Varratim pressed forward and held the green gem to her face, pressing it into her cheek sharply.

'I killed Petron,' he said. 'Didn't you hear me? I killed your boy and now my blade is honed and your mother bear is as good as dead. I found Tullen One-Eye and took his history lessons, and took his knife. I crossed the Stormwall. I found Ferron's orbs, uncovered their secrets. I found the runewands, weapons of kings and gods.'

Floré stared at him, at the frustration etched in his face, and tears for Petron flowed down her cheeks. The wand flashed and she felt a rune cut into her cheeks, felt her tears trickle into the flow of hot blood.

'He told me it was poetry,' she said, smiling though it hurt to speak, 'as simple as poetry. And that is all I knew, or cared to ask.'

Varratim punched her then, his fist closed around the rod, once, twice, three, four, five times in the face. She laughed as he did it, felt her nose break and a tooth crack. She spat blood at him. He stepped back and wiped his face on his sleeve, breathed deeply, and she locked her gaze with his.

'I'm taking your daughter,' he said, 'and I'm going to kill the god-bear. And then I'm going to come back and I'll kill you with the same knife I used to kill Petron, and Anshuka both. That is what I'm going to do. I don't need to be a skein-wreck – I am Varratim of the Endless Storm.'

He turned and stalked from the room and Floré strained with everything in her against the bonds. Sinew and muscle and tendon and bone straining, every part of her pulling and pushing against the bonds.

'I'll kill you, Varratim. I'LL KILL YOU, YOU HEAR ME, YOU BASTARD!'

She yelled until she collapsed back from lack of air and blinked blood from her eyes.

'Varratim of the Endless Storm,' she said. 'Stupid fucking name.'

Alone in the dark, Floré continued to strain against her bonds.

~

When the light faded, they had appeared deep in a pine forest. Immediately Cuss felt relieved at having the press of trees around him. He felt dizzy.

'Was that magic?' he asked, and Ash shushed him gently. She pulled her bow from her back and strung it, leaning on the silver wood and bending it to get the bowstring in place, and from her quiver she pulled a silver-tipped arrow. Yselda looked green in the face.

'How many miles did we just travel?' she asked, and Cuss's eyes widened. Ash looked at them both and shook her head.

'None,' she said, 'and now we are here. Listen close, both of you. This is not Hookstone forest, with timber wolves and logging roads. This is the Orubor, the bed of the god. The wolves here will not bother us, nor the bears, and there are no men. No goblin has ever been here, no rotsurge has ever passed overhead. If I were not here, you would be in immense danger.'

Cuss scrunched up his nose and ran a hand through his hair, which was knotted and stank of ash and smoke from the Ossen-Tyr attack.

'What do you mean?' he asked, and Ash glanced around the forest again. Cuss and Yselda followed her gaze. It felt like the very oldest parts of Hookstone, where no loggers had ever been and the pines twisted upwards many dozens of feet. The forest floor was dark, even in the dim morning light.

'We have to move fast,' Ash said. 'Whilst we are here, I am Ashbringer, not Ash. If any patrols find us, I am bringing you to the council at the tree. Understand? Do not run your mouths or ask questions. Few of them will have seen humans other than those pilgrims they've killed. We brook no visitors to our forest, no outsiders – it is one of our most stringent laws. I take you here now because time is short and the need is great, but you must not leave my side. So we walk, and you stay close and you stay quiet.'

Walking without talking was a lot harder, Cuss found. His feet hurt after an hour – they had already spent the whole morning walking, after all. He and Yselda exchanged some smiles but without talking there was nothing to do but think, and he did not like it. He found himself thinking of his mother and sister and brother, of their cottage aflame. He tried to think of Jana and Petron and mother eating dinner together around the hearth fire, but the image wouldn't stick. The fire would grow and then he would see them, again, as he had the morning after the attack.

'How do you kill a crow-man, Ashbringer?' he asked, whispering loudly to get her attention. She fell back into step with them and glanced about.

'A good question,' she said, 'with a sure answer. Fire and silver, Cuss.'

Yselda drew her antler hilted dagger and showed them both the blade.

'Captain Artollen gave me this,' she said. 'Will this work?

She said it catches fire if it cuts something. Is that true?'

Ashbringer handed her bow to Cuss and he felt his arms droop with the weight of it. Nocked in the string was an arrow of white wood with a head of silver. Ashbringer examined the knife and handed it back.

'A good blade,' she said. 'Perhaps from Old Ferron itself – or maybe from the runesmiths in Cil-Marie. The humans there are grasping the art, for better or worse. Keep it close, and trust it.'

She took her bow back from Cuss and made to start off but he half-raised a hand.

'What is it, Cuss?' she said, and he looked at the ground.

'I have no silver,' he said, 'and no fire.'

He showed her his sword blade perfunctorily and then his knuckleduster.

'The captain gave you that, didn't she,' Ash said, and Cuss nodded.

'Hold on tight to that for now. All being well you will have no need to fight demons this day.'

They walked, and walked, and walked, the pine needles soft under their boots, and Cuss could not tell the difference between one patch of forest and the next. He could see no pattern, no paths, only endless trees arrayed as they liked, but Ash seemed to know where she was going. Yselda glanced at him every now and then and he gripped his knuckleduster. The night before when the orbs came he had cried, had cowered numb whilst the rest made plans, acted. He had to be stronger if he was going to save Petron.

Finally the trees began to thin, and they stepped into

a clearing. Ashbringer smiled and walked ahead, turning back to them.

'Bow before your god,' she said, and Cuss did not understand – beyond the clearing was only a rocky hill, a huge strange tumble of...

He fell to his knees and bowed his head, and felt Yselda next to him. He found himself saying over and over again, *praise Anshuka*. He could not remember the proper words to any of the shaman prayers. Next to him Yselda was crying. After long moments he looked up, and Ashbringer was smiling. There was a small building he had not even noticed, a simple shelter of stone with a rock altar. Behind it, his gaze went back again – Anshuka, a bear as big as a mountain, asleep. The rock did not move. Was she breathing? The rocks were piled as high as a hill, as high as the overseer's fort in Ossen-Tyr twice over. *Was that... a leg?* Was he near a leg of the god-bear? The shape of the bear was there, imprinted in his mind, and he could see moss and lichen, patches of grass and dirt and even a small curling bed of deep green ferns on one shelf. A great bear of stone, as large as a mountain. The hairs on the back of his neck rose and he felt a shiver run down his spine. *The Judges are real.*

Yselda came and hugged him, and he hugged her back and then Ashbringer came to them.

'Is she asleep?' he whispered, and Yselda giggled.

'No need to whisper, Cuss,' Ashbringer said. 'She is asleep, and has been for three hundred years. You are the first outsiders to see her in many decades. We will go to her head, and hope my people are there and prepared. Are you ready?'

Cuss looked at Yselda, and together they stared up at Anshuka, the late afternoon light playing across the rocks and shrubs and trees, the hint of a shape.

'I'm ready,' he said, and the followed the path towards the head of the god-bear.

17

Blazefish on the Reef

'Of the Orubor, make note their opaque eyes and serrated teeth. They move through the forest as lightly as deer. We do not know their diet, we do not know their customs, their language, their history. During the reign of Ferron, the forest was unmapped and marked as inaccessible, with rumours of wild savages. Anshuka rests there now, protected by those most diligent guardians. None have truly encountered them and lived, and so we have only rumour and hearsay. Of their namesake forest – what can you say of a forest with a god at its heart? Anshuka wishes privacy, and so we obey.' – Pantheon of the Protectorate, Campbell Torbén of Aber-Ouse

Tomas felt Heasin wake up, finally.

'They killed Petron,' he said to the groggy Tullioch, 'captured me, you and Floré. Guy's got a knife that can kill a Judge, he claims, and he is off to take his orbs and do it.'

Heasin hissed and pulled himself to a half-sitting position, and then there was a voice, a sibilant call from across the cave. The young Tullioch with the orange crest and green mottled chest was calling across, and Tomas breathed out deeply through his nose and touched his left eye – it was swollen completely shut. The Tullioch spoke for a long moment in their nonsense language and Tomas listened, grimacing, and then there was a silence, and Heasin was utterly still.

'Is that your daughter?' Tomas asked, and there was no response.

'Hey,' he said, 'hey is that your daughter? Heasin? Hello?'

'No,' Heasin said, '… my daughter is dead.'

Tomas raised his hand half an inch to comfort the Tullioch, but pulled back and scrunched his nose.

'I'm sorry, Heasin,' he said, and the Tullioch ignored him and then began to hiss long and slow. The hiss grew into a low growl and then a roar and every muscle on the Tullioch's body strained as Heasin pushed himself against the wall. The manacles were cutting at his wrists and legs but he strained, and strained, and roared, and at the wall the bolt that held his shackles tight began to creak and bend. In between the roars he yelled in his native tongue and Tomas could make out the word *Hassin*, over and over again.

The bolt flew from the wall, and Heasin tumbled free. He was still shackled at hands and legs, but no longer attached to the wall.

'Judge's arse, Heasin!' Tomas shouted. 'Free me as well!'

Heasin ignored him and shuffled to the door, just as a crow-man entered, presumably to check on the noise. The crow-man began to raise a wand of iron tipped with a red gem at the hulking Tullioch but Heasin leapt forward and bore her to the ground, ripping out her throat with his teeth. He patted her clothing and pulled out a long heavy key, and unlocked his shackles. He was halfway through the door when Tomas realised he was just going to leave to hunt more crow-men.

'Heasin!' he yelled. 'Key!'

The Tullioch turned and threw the key at Tomas, who snatched it out of the air, and then Heasin was gone. Tomas unlocked himself and looked back at the children. He threw the keys to the Tullioch youth, and then he scooped up the fallen crow-man's wand. He ran his hands along the polished metal, inspecting it, and felt for the skein – it was still muddled. Tomas had spent enough years at the wall to recognise the muddling effect of a large number of crow-men gathered. Before Urforren, there had been enough crow-men that any mission past the wall might end in disaster, skein-mages neutered as the very presence of the demons made accessing the skein in any useful way impossible.

He hadn't felt the disruption this strongly since Urforren, and he had never seen anything like this wand before, but even through the chaos in the skein he could feel a pattern in it, similar to those he carried in the tattoos on his arms but... so much more refined, and complex. He reached within the skein for the gem and concentrated until the pattern revealed itself and then a grin split his face. *Fire*. He looked down at the crow-man with the ripped-out throat, and could see in her eyes that she was still alive.

'More than a ripped throat to stop you, eh?' he said, and pointed the wand at her head and focused.

The stream of flame that spat out from the end of the wand kept coming – he could feel it draining his energy as a skein-spell would, but not nearly to the same degree, and requiring almost nothing of his training and focus. He moved the wand until the crow-man's whole body was aflame, and then smiled and ran after Heasin.

Tomas caught Heasin two corridors over, bleeding from a deep cut on his shoulder that was in the shape of a rune, standing over three dead goblins and a dead crow-man. The Tullioch was covered in gore. Tomas scooped up a wand that lay by the crow-man, this one with a blue gem, and tucked it into his belt, and then pushed a gout of flame into the torso of the crow-man on the floor. Heasin had disembowelled what seemed to be an old man, with the ungainly overlong limbs of the crow-men, the deathly pallor. Even as Tomas began to reach for the flame in the wand, the crow-man was pushing his own spooling guts back at his stomach.

'No trial for rust-folk,' Tomas said, and kicked the man hard in the face before pointing the fire wand again. Tomas nodded as the wand spewed flame over the crow-man, feeling again the subtle intricacies of this pattern. Already he could see how even encountering this pattern altered his understanding of flame, of the pattern he thought he knew so well. *This is a wonder,* he thought, and gave a grin.

'The captain,' the Tullioch said, and ran a few steps down the corridor away from the flaming demon and began to sniff, deep lungsful of air through his nose, scenting at the air and flicking his tongue. He turned his head and began to run. They found Floré in a room a few corridors over, chained naked to a metal bed, bleeding from a half-dozen deep rune cuts, her face beaten to a pulp, one cheek deeply sliced and freely bleeding.

'Chains,' she said, her voice thick with blood, and as Tomas traced the path of the chains to a thick shackle beneath the metal bed. Reaching below the bed he unlatched the shackle and the coils of chain fell to the stone floor. Heasin caught a running goblin in the corridor outside and tore it in half, roaring as a great gout of green blood sprayed across the corridor. Floré grabbed her gear quickly, not bothering with anything but shirt, trousers, dagger, and her gauntlets. As she dressed Tomas inspected the room, and found a small leather pouch. From inside he drew out a handful of silver coins and passed four to Floré who clicked them into her gauntlets. He pocketed the rest.

'He killed Petron,' Tomas told her, yelling over the sound of screaming in the corridor, and Floré nodded grimly. In the corridor outside Heasin was killing a crow-man by slowly eviscerating his chest using his claws, roaring in its face as he did. Tomas sent a stream of fire over the Tullioch's shoulders, aiming to keep a gang of approaching goblins occupied, and then redirected it to the fallen crow-man when Heasin dropped him.

'Time to go,' Floré said, and Heasin led the way as they ran from the carnage. As they moved more and more goblins filled in the corridors behind them, chittering and yelling, and the trio ran onwards for long moments, Tomas keeping the goblins behind them at bay with long gouts of flame. Suddenly Tomas felt a pressure in his ear and the world took on a muted quality.

'They're leaving,' Floré said. 'We need to be on one of those ships, now!'

They ran, following Heasin, and after a few more turns of corridor they reached the main hangar. Seven discs of dark stone, each sixty foot across and supported on tripods of spindly metal legs, filled the cavern. Each disc had a round seam of what looked like dark glass around their centre, and some had ramps below, which rested on the floor of the cavern. At the entrance to the wide cavern, an eighth disc hovered fifty feet of the ground, and then suddenly blazed with light and flew from the cavern mouth. The next five ships behind it all rose in unison and began to move as well, and one by one illuminated to become orbs of white fire, and then they shot from the cavern mouth.

There were only two left, and only one with its ramp down. Floré sprinted, with Heasin hot on her heels and Tomas not far behind, but he slowed his run for a moment to try to take in all he could of the room, his mouth wide in astonishment. *This isn't Ferron Empire technology,* he thought, *this is Old Ferron, pre-empire. Lost knowledge.* The three of them careened up the ramp and into a low ovoid space perhaps ten foot high, two metal barred cages on a slick stone floor, and at the edge of the space four simple metal chairs attached to the seam of black glass or crystal or whatever it was, raised five feet from the floor. Two were attached to what looked to be giant versions of the wand he clutched in his hand, the other two to strange helmets.

Floré ripped one crow-man from his seat and threw him towards Tomas, who burned the man to cinders with his wand, feeling the energy leaving him as he made the flames. He swayed groggily. Heasin made short work of two goblins that were conferring by one of the chairs next to the giant wands, and Floré had the last crow-man in a death grip, holding him with one hand as the other punched over and over into his face, the silver on her knuckles melting and burning the flesh beneath. Finally she threw him to the floor, still breathing.

'How,' she said, 'does this thing fly?'

~

At Stormcastle XII Benazir stared out at the sea of death beyond the wall, knuckles paling beneath her gauntlets as she gripped the wall and tried to stay calm. So much death. One of the archers, a fat-faced man from Brek, came and stood next to her and joined her in her survey.

'A fine mess,' he said, 'and more to come.'

Benazir followed his pointing hand to the swampland beyond the death, and squinted.

'I see nothing,' she said, her voice quiet and flat, and out in the rotstorm there was a thick belch of thunder, a pulse of yellow light high up in the roiling cloud. The wind began to blow faster, and the archer sighed and reached for his bow, restringing it and drawing an arrow. He leaned close to her in the gap of the rampart and peered with her as if unsure he had seen anything when he had spoken before.

'You were at Fallow Fen when we drove them out, aye Commander?'

'Aye,' she responded, her voice struggling against the wind, 'I was there when they came, and there when we pushed them back.'

The archer turned to face her and then they both looked back down at the courtyard where cadets were piling the dead. Nostul was yelling at a lancer, but the wind took the words before they could reach them.

'Were you at Urforren?' he asked, and she simply nodded.

'Heard the Salt-Man did for the whole town,' he said,

and she could hear the weariness in his voice. 'Way I heard is you and that bruiser Artollen, two of you were cutting down beasties and crow-men left and right and they were all coming for him after Fallow Fen. That true?'

Benazir gazed back to the swampland. Bands of thick mist swirled over the water pools, between the bulrushes, and she could see no movement. *Could she?*

'A thousand of us retook Fallow Fen,' she said at last, 'though he did the work of a thousand more. They fell back to Urforren. Urforren is a town, you know? Palisades, crow-men, rottrolls, more rust-folk than you could count, more goblins than makes any sense. Thousands of them. A whole town, geared for war. We went for a siege, had our battle lines up, but when they realised he was there, after Fallow Fen they threw it all at us.'

The archer swore and nocked an arrow, and yelled down the line.

'Movement, at the line! Hold your shots!'

Benazir saw it coming, then. A wyrm. As the archers ran to their positions, she stared at it. The archer was gone to his post, but she kept talking, talking to the dead, to the storm.

'Floré and I, we were better then. She was bolt-captain, I was captain, he was the mighty skein-mage, Hussain the Blue reborn: the Salt-Man. She had forgiven me, though she wore my father's dagger on her belt. I would not take it back. She had forgiven my cowardice.'

Benazir's words were stilted and drowned out by the wind. The archers were all yelling now for a mage, yelling for more bows, yelling over and over: 'A wyrm, a wyrm!'

Benazir stared at the wyrm as it languidly floated across

the battlefield below, its legless body a few feet from the ground. It was fifty feet long, a body of rippling armoured scales that writhed and twisted as it moved, a tapered tail ridged with horn, a head as large as a bull. It had rows of jet-black eyes running down each side of its body, in a chaotic stripe down the top of its body, and its mouth was a horror, a beak split in three, chitinous mandibles opening and closing, the interior wet and lined with row after row of ragged teeth.

Benazir found her sword in her hand, and then the wyrm was screaming, a gurgling wail that cut through the wind. She descended the stairs.

'Floré was amazing,' she said, to the corpse of a lancer on the stairs. 'She kept him safe; she saved me a dozen times that day alone. In the end though, they were so many and so determined, and so she told him to do it.'

Nostul ran at her and said something but Benazir just pointed at the sally port, and a commando dutifully pulled it open.

Nostul grabbed her and shook her by the shoulders, and Jerrek was there and was yelling, but they fell silent when she stared at them.

'At Urforren they were too many, too brutal,' she said. 'They fought for their home even as we fight for ours. I stood by the Salt-Man as he called on the skein and turned them to salt, their town to salt, the very ground to salt. A mile, from where he stood, an entire town, a salt that burned to the touch, ever burning. Ten thousand rust-folk, rottrolls, wyrms, crow-men, goblins: gone. Elders, children, babes-in-arms: gone.'

Gone, they are all gone, she thought, *but I am still here.*

'Janos-Wreck is not here,' Nostul said, his voice close to breaking. 'Commander, it is a *wyrm*. Our arrows will not pierce its scales, our magic will not burn it. What would you have us do? Can we hold it long enough to bring up the ballistae, to crack the armour?'

Benazir unclasped her cloak and rolled her shoulders. She passed her sword to Whent, who had found her as he always did. She made herself smile at him and nod her thanks. From her boot she pulled a dagger, its blade silver and runed. The handle was simple wood. She weighed it in her armoured hand as beyond the wall the wyrm screamed again, and on the rampart archers cursed and loosed arrow after arrow.

'Commander Starbeck told me the difference between the gauntlet and the balanced blade,' she said, and she smiled as Nostul and Jerrek and Whent winced at another wail from beyond the wall.

'The gauntlet protects, and inflicts punishment. It is a brutal tool. It does what is necessary and it does what is hard. The balanced blade finds the weakness, finds a way where force alone would not. It is guile, and base trickery. It is subterfuge and cunning. It is calm in the face of any foe, calm enough to calculate, calm enough to *know* what to do.'

She turned to walk through the gate but Jerrek held her back.

'Commander, please!' he said. 'What weakness does it have? We need more men, more mages, siege weapons. We need time.'

Benazir calmly removed his hand from her shoulder and shook her head.

'You just need to know where to cut,' she said, and then she stepped past the Stormwall. 'Jerrek, the castle is yours until I return.'

The wyrm was circling, a hundred feet from the wall. Benazir walked to it, slowly, savouring the feel of the dagger in her hand. It was not her father's dagger, but she was glad that Floré had that. Floré had the dagger, and would keep Janos safe, so he could return and save them from whatever was coming. Riders had already arrived to say the fighting was spread beyond simply Stormcastle XII. Every Stormcastle in fifty miles had been attacked. Lights in the sky burning patrols to ash, whitestaffs fled or taken, a wave of woe from hell pushing out.

The wyrm saw her, and it began its slow procession towards her, and Benazir felt herself shaking.

'I'm not a coward, Floré,' she had said, before they went to Fallow Fen and Urforren. They had not spoken that way in years, Benazir having retreated into the formality of their roles, having cut clear their friendship. Floré raged but Benazir would only turn away. Janos pleaded for her to just talk, but she would speak only of the work, the wall, the storm.

'I know, sister,' Floré had said, so quietly, and they had embraced and for a while it had been as it was. Fallow Fen, Urforren, a wonderful campaign, and they had spoken, truly spoken, and laughed despite it all, but then they had left. *Gone.* Her parents, her family, Guil, Janos, Yute, *gone, gone.* Floré, *gone.*

Benazir stepped calmly to the wyrm and it opened its mouth wide, circling a final time, iridescent scales shimmering in reflected lightning from the rotstorm beyond.

Benazir turned back to the wall and held her dagger to her temple in a simple salute and turned to face the beast. She had seen a wyrm before, when they took back Fallow Fen. Ballistae barely scratched its scales, arrows did nothing. Janos had cut the wyrm in two with a furrowed brow.

It came for her, its mouth open wide, and she clenched her fist.

'I'm not trying to punch you in the face,' she whispered, and the ghost of a smile pulled at her lips. 'I'm trying to punch you in the back of the head *through* your face.'

The wyrm lunged forward with sudden speed and Benazir ran and leapt forward to meet it, arms outstretched, and as the jaws and endless teeth closed around her she felt the blade of her silver rune knife bite into the soft flesh of its mouth, and the heat and fire began.

~

Heasin clambered into what the heavily injured crow-man identified as the captain's chair, holding his new captive aloft with one clawed hand around her throat.

'I will kill you slowly if you betray us,' he whispered, and the woman nodded.

'It will take from you,' she said in broken Isken. 'To fly it, there is always a price. Years and years it will take.'

Heasin ignored her and sat down, and began his questions. Floré glanced at Tomas, who was swaying on his feet, staring at the wand in his hand. Heasin slipped the strange metal helm over the back of his head with one hand, and it seemed to alter its shape to fit his skull.

'Tomas,' she called out, 'sit down before you fall down.'

Tomas was reaching for a chair and Floré was making

to tie herself into another and then suddenly they were up. With a lurch and a thrum of power they lifted and from the crystal strip around the centre of the disc Floré could see they were rising. There was a crash and she fell from the chair and sprawled onto the stone floor of the disc. Tomas was across from her, clutching to the bars of one of the metal cages.

'The cavern roof,' Heasin called, and Tomas swore as he got himself back to his feet. The disc felt ungainly to Floré, until Heasin did something and then they were casting a glow on the cavern floor. For a moment they held steady and calm, and then the light flickered and they crashed down again. There was groaning crack and Floré turned behind her to see the entrance ramp they had climbed broken on the hangar floor, along with one of the metal legs that had been supporting the disc. *Berren's blood, how much can it weigh, if it's stone?*

Through the new hole in the floor she could see a glow flicker again and then hold steady, the constant silver glow that had shone over her those nights ago in Hookstone forest. Her hand went out to the wall of the disc and it was truly stone, dark and solid. She shook her head and clambered back up into the chair, bringing her level with the seam of crystal or glass that ran around the edge of the disc. A harness of rope was wound around the chair, and she saw clear enough where she needed to knot herself in.

'Again,' Heasin called, and the orb rose, wobbling and gyrating. Floré could see the cavern and the sky beyond through the haze of glass encircling the disc; the glow from the orb or something tied to it had reduced the dark haze, until the glass was almost perfectly clear. The wall of the cavern was moving up and down, swaying from side to side... She saw a dozen goblins clamouring around the final stone disc that sat motionless on the cavern floor. The goblins were pointing and yelling at Floré's disc, her orb. She vomited on the floor next to her chair.

'Heasin,' she called, 'steady!'

'I don't like this,' Tomas moaned, still down on the floor of the orb, and Floré grimaced in agreement. Gingerly, the orb moved forward, and began to level out, and suddenly they passed the lip of the cavern and were into clear sky beyond, moving out into the dusk. The orb continued to rise, and on the floor of the centre of the stone disc Tomas crouched by one of the two metal cages. Floré caught her breath, and suddenly they lurched forward, pitching upward and they were rapidly climbing. Above her she saw only cloud and sky but then she glanced out of the hole in the floor where the ramp had been and she could see the mountains of the Blue Wolf below, and a town, and a river like a map drawn out below them. The bodies of the two goblins and the dead crow-men slipped across the smooth dark stone floor of the orb, and with his foot Tomas nudged them one by one out of the hole to spiral and spin down towards the forest.

'Not safe,' she heard him say. She could hear nothing from outside, no pushing wind. *The field of silence must be shielding us.* The orb levelled out its pitch but continued to rise and she heard Heasin breathing heavily as they flew higher and higher. Floré let out a slow exhalation. She could see no other orbs. Suddenly they were with the clouds, not trapped in mist, but rising through a *cloud*. The chair she sat in was attached to one of the wands, a rod of metal the thickness of her arm starting at the chair and ending in a huge purple crystal larger than her fist. It reminded her of a rotbud, but less organic. This gem was faceted, worked. Floré didn't think about the blood seeping through her trousers and shirt, the cuts on her feet, her pounding head, the way her cheek tore and screamed when she opened her mouth.

'Heasin,' she called, 'get us above. I need to see. We must find them, or it's all for naught.'

The Tullioch grunted back and she inspected her chair and the strange wand before her. The chair moved when she touched a small stick on one side, slipping around the ring of the disc. The rod was mounted on some sort of suspension, the end of it pointing out of the clear crystal strip. There was what looked like a handle, with a soft patch on it.

Floré squeezed the soft patch and beam of purple light shot out from the gem through the crystal strip and across the sky and she heard Heasin cry out. On the handle, a red light appeared, fading slowly to orange, to yellow, and then to nothing. She tried again, pointing the rod down at a lower angle, and it fired again. Heasin gave another yell of pain, and she looked at the crow-man with the ruined face who was slumped against the wall, one of Heasin's fists still wrapped around her throat.

'It takes from the captain,' she said, 'the one who flies. It takes so much.'

She tried firing whilst the light was red and yellow, and it didn't work.

'I have a giant magic wand,' she said to herself, and Tomas sighed dramatically, finally on his feet and unsteadily walking away from the hole in the floor. Floré could see nothing but clouds below them. Looking around her in the sunset she spotted a sea of black-and-grey cloud stretching out. To the west, the sun was falling past the horizon, casting a shimmering light over the tops of the clouds. Floré peered out, searching. *Marta.*

'It's not all about size,' Tomas called up from the floor of the craft, and went to go to the other chair with a wand attached, but only made it two steps before he looked out the window and then was on the ground, clutching his stomach.

'Judges save me,' he said, and Floré heard no more from him. She made her chair move so it brought her around the disc to Heasin and his captive crow-man. The aged woman was struggling weakly.

'I think I understand it,' Heasin said, and Floré gave him a curt nod. His fist closed, and the woman was dropped to the ground, throat open.

'Fire and silver,' Tomas called out from the floor, and Floré looked back to him.

'I don't care if she dies now, or later, but I don't want you filling this place with flame. You have silver. Get in a chair, and get rid of her.'

Floré had seen crow-men rise from the grave, from endless wounds, dismemberment, disembowelment, even decapitation. Only fire and silver would truly put them down. She thought of Urforren, the burning salt. None had risen from that.

'Take us south. Get us close,' she told Heasin, 'but the lead ship has Marta on it. I can't risk her.'

Heasin hissed and nodded, and the craft shot forward with even greater speed as they headed south, towards Orubor and Anshuka. Down below, Tomas pitched the crow-man out of the hole in the floor, laughing. Her body spiralled down and disappeared into the cloud.

'Do you think she'll heal from that, Artollen?' he said, and Floré simply pointed to the chairs. Tomas went and sat in the chair with the red-tipped wand, stroking it and closing his eyes.

Long minutes passed, and then suddenly in front of them in the dusk she could see the small cloud of glowing orbs. The other orbs were lower than they, and she could make out four, flying in a diamond pattern, headed straight south.

'Where are the other two?' she asked, and Heasin pointed a claw west. Floré moved her chair around the orb until she faced west, and saw at the edge of her vision two orbs of light cutting west. *Towards the Stormwall,* she thought, *towards the rotstorm.* She shuddered.

'We have to assume Varratim is headed for Anshuka,' she said at last. 'We go south.'

Tomas responded by letting off a huge stream of flame from the wand attached to his chair, a spume of white fire leaping out behind them. Heasin howled in pain.

'I like this!' Tomas yelled, and Heasin hissed.

'Captain, Primus' Heasin said, 'when you use the wand – it takes from me. I give willingly, but I do not know how much. The orb, it takes so much. Please. Be wise.'

Floré moved to his side and together they sat in silence for a long moment, watching the orbs ahead of them. She reached a hand across and laid it gently on his arm.

'Do you see them?' she asked, and Heasin nodded, and the orb began moving fast and downward, towards the diamond of lights cutting above the clouds.

'Like blazefish on the reef,' he said, and then they were

upon them like a raptor in the flock. Heasin came in fast and high, and Floré completely missed her shot. She aimed the beam of purple light at the rearmost orb, but instead it cut well behind the craft in front of them. The Tullioch was not worried about missing shots, however. He rammed with abandon the ship to the left of the diamond formation, and even through the silent field surrounding their orb, Floré heard the grinding smash of stone on stone, and a cracking of crystal. Their own strip of crystal was undamaged but Floré saw a crack spreading from the hole in the floor of their ship where the ramp had once been. *How much can this disc take?* She thought, and gritted her teeth.

The orb they had rammed began to lose speed immediately, crashing downward, and Heasin pulled them high again. Tomas let loose a wave of flame but it came nowhere near another orb, and Floré held her shot. The orb they had rammed slipped below the clouds and disappeared. Of the three ahead, the lead orb leapt forward with a burst of speed and the other two circled back and up, turning on their attacker. Floré took a shot at the nearest, but the beam of purple went wide, and then Heasin was diving to avoid the return fire of the enemy discs, light and flame chasing them. He pushed the orb down at a brutal angle, and Floré heard Tomas scream as they were both almost ripped from their chairs. Grey, all around; Heasin had taken them back down into the cloud. Floré turned her wand so it faced behind the orb, and saw the clouds behind and above them backlit by white light as their pursuers drew closer. One held a steady line, and she focused and fired her wand and was rewarded by an explosion of purple light and then one of the pursuing orbs fading away and back.

As Tomas sent another sheet of flame back, Heasin pulled up suddenly and they stopped still, hovering. Below them, in the cloud Floré saw one orb behind by hundreds and hundreds of yards, moving towards them slowly but shakily. Another was cutting below them with rapid movements, searching for them through the cloud.

'Wait,' Heasin said, and Tomas and Floré pulled their chairs close and pointed their wands down into the bank of cloud. The orb below flitted back and forth, searching for them. Glancing south, Floré saw the lead orb off in the far distance, almost at the edge of sight. *Marta.*

'Kill!' the Tullioch yelled, and Floré fired her wand, a beam of purple light cutting down into the cloud as Tomas sent a cone of white fire to join it. There was an explosion of purple light and Floré grinned, but then a beam of purple light was returning up at her and she screamed as their orb rocked and veered left too late, the crystal strip cracking from an explosive impact of energy. The noise of it shook her teeth and Floré was slammed against the rope harness holding her into the chair.

'South!' she screamed, and Heasin complied, their orb tearing to the south an inch above the cloud top, sending up spirals of cloud in their wake. Floré coughed and felt the taste of blood in her mouth, felt the pain in her legs, her face, and saw the two orbs behind them rise from the cloud to follow. One had a dark patch in its sheen of white light at its crest, but the other looked undamaged, though it seemed to wobble and oscillate as it flew. Floré swung herself around to Heasin.

'We can't let them catch us,' she said, worried.

Heasin hissed. 'Humans hunt on the plains, on the

grasses – the flat,' he said, coughing. 'Tullioch hunt in the wind reefs. We hunt from above, below, never where you see. I will lose them.'

As he spoke, a beam of purple light missed them by a dozen yards and he suddenly jerked his controls, spinning them wildly.

'I will lose them!' he said again. He sounded pained. They had been flying long minutes from the cavern at impossible speeds, and the Tullioch looked grey and ill. His scales were dry and his eyes were hooded.

'Heasin,' she said, and he batted away her question with a claw. An explosion of sound rocked them and the orb shook as another bolt of purple light struck the back of it. Floré swore and swung her wand back to the rear of the disc and shot out her own jet of force, and this one connected. There was a flowering explosion of purple-and-white light and the already damaged orb's glow stuttered and then went out, and as a stone it fell from the sky straight down. Tomas let out a whoop. Looking over her shoulder she could see they were gaining on the lead orb, and behind them was only the oscillating orb that was struggling to keep pace and had fired no bolts of light for long moments.

From below them, suddenly there was a cone of fire as an orb rose from the clouds. *The one I hit earlier,* Floré realised. The flame covered the base of their orb and she could feel heat rising, and then it was pouring through the hole in the floor and she was screaming in fear and rage. As one she and Tomas turned their own wands on the craft below, and with an explosion of fire and light the orb below spun away, veering from their onslaught. Heasin yelled out with rage and pain.

'Anshuka,' Heasin called out to her, 'and your daughter. If they can kill your Judge, they could kill mine. They took my daughter, Artollen. You stop them.'

Before she could speak Heasin pulled them into a steep climb, and then a dive, and she saw it all laid out before her. The cloud was clearing. There was Varratim's orb, ahead, over forest, and two more orbs behind them, both listing badly and torn and damaged and cracked, their glow patchy and...

Forest.

Looking ahead, Floré saw the clouds end and then forest – thick tall pine, taller than Hookstone, wilder – and then ahead of that a mountain of rock and earth, a huge shape that pushed up from the forest floor. A bear of stone the size of a mountain, sleeping. Ahead of them, the lead orb. *Marta.*

'Anshuka,' she whispered to the rocks below. 'Anshuka, be praised.'

The orb in front of them Varratim's orb, *Marta's orb,* suddenly shot back a beam of purple light. The bolt struck their orb with an explosion of noise and light right where Heasin sat, the sound of cracking crystal, the tear of shearing stone. Then they were going down, down, and Heasin roared at the controls but still they were lower and lower, spiralling wildly, and they were level with Anshuka and the other craft around and above were slowing.

'*No!*' Floré screamed, the rope harness cutting into her shoulders, the blood in her head pounding as they spun. *No I'm so close, I'm so close. It can't end like this.* She snarled and tried to fire her wand at something, anything, but it didn't respond. *Janos, I must save Marta. Janos, I have to...*

Floré shut her eyes and clenched her fists and tried to breathe, and then all was darkness as they hit the treeline. Heasin hissed as their orb splintered through a stand of tall pines, but then they were spinning again and bouncing and there was a rending of rock and crystal, and Floré's eyes snapped open and she saw clear sky above, branches, green and brown a blur all around her. She yelled and Tomas screamed, and all was chaos.

18

In the Shadow of the God-Bear

'He fears his own powers, scared of the pain he brings, because he does not understand the reason. And so I say this: send him away. Give him a guardian. Let him start a life, so that he might see what we seek to protect. Then, when he understands, we can bring him back when we truly need him.' – Address to the Grand Council regarding Skein-wreck Janos, Commander Salem Starbeck

Yselda drank bitter tea from a cup of twisted tree bark as dusk fell over Orubor forest. She tried to stay calm. They sat around a small fire at the treeline. From the treeline, there was a meadow of wild flowers a few hundred yards across, and at the end of that the head of Anshuka, the god-bear. It was clearly a bear's head, so clearly, a huge head bigger than a house, curled up on a massive stone paw below. She turned away from it again, to the old Orubor by the fire for whom Ash was pouring more tea. She had no red scars, and her hair was long and white instead of shaven clean, waves of it cascading down over thin shoulders and a simple dress of wool. Behind her, conferring in quiet voices, six tall Orubor stood checking arrows and blades and pointing back at Anshuka, around the clearing. The old Orubor turned her golden eyes to the north, where dark clouds were gathered in the distance.

'They are coming, Ashbringer,' the old Orubor woman said, and Ash nodded.

'Are we ready?' Ash asked, and the woman shook her head.

'The patrols are too far, the border guardians too far again. The council is scattered to their homes. Had you brought this news a day ago, we would have an army. For now, it is you and it is I, and the honour guard. And these two Baal.'

Yselda drank her tea and grimaced. *How could they be so calm?* A demon was coming, demons come to kill Anshuka, and it was only her and Cuss and Ash and six Orubor. Ashbringer and the Orubor certainly looked impressive enough, but Yselda would have given anything for a legion of lancers at that point. *What good would six bows do against orbs of light that could shoot fire and beams of destruction?* She shook her head and tried to steady her breathing, tried to stay calm. The forest around them was quiet.

Yselda put her tea down and looked to Cuss, who was staring between Anshuka, the Orubor warriors, and the sky for long moments each. They had not spoken about Petron, or the captain. Cuss had been quiet all afternoon as they walked through the holy forest. When they reached the clearing and Ashbringer had brought them forward, those six Orubor she called the honour guard had emerged from the meadow and forest and stalked towards them, around them, hands on bows and blade. Yselda had not been afraid. She had simply stared at Anshuka, the mass of her, the breaker of chains. She had wept. Cuss had stood and stared, silent, and then the honour guard were embracing Ashbringer and the old Orubor was stepping gently through the meadow and gesturing at a circle of stones, a fire laid and ready.

'I never saw a god before,' Cuss said at last, and then he went and sat by the fire and ate the bread the old Orubor woman had given them. Yselda and Cuss sat and waited and drank tea as the honour guard spoke in hushed tones in their language, so much like a song.

'You do Orubor duty tonight,' the old Orubor said, smiling down to them with jagged teeth, and then she went back to staring into the fire.

'Can't you ask a bogle to get help?' Yselda asked, and Ashbringer shook her head.

'Not enough time, child,' she said. 'The Ferron could be here in a moment, and there are no little gods here to help her. They give her space. We will have to suffice.'

'We have the honour guard though, right? They must be the best of the best!' Cuss said, and Ashbringer looked back at the six Orubor, her mouth thin.

'The honour guard... it is a bad translation. When you are young, when it is time to join the border patrol, or to move to another village and pursue your craft or your art, you take a spell here, in the calmest place, the safest place. You spend a turn of the moon here, in reflection, and when you leave you are Orubor, not a child. Does this make sense?'

Yselda looked over the six Orubor and saw that they were tall and lithe like Ash, but bore no red scars. Their cloaks and bows were new, the leather on their quivers and belts unworn by time or use.

'These are... children?' she asked, and Ashbringer tilted her head.

'Are you a child, Yselda Hollow?'

Yselda did not know how to respond to that.

'They are young,' Ash continued. 'But they are Orubor. They will fight with honour.'

They sat in silence for a long moment, only the sparking of the fire and the sound of branches moving delicately in the breeze.

'Can't we wake her up?' Cuss asked, and Ashbringer laughed.

'She has slept three hundred years, Cuss. Slept through storm and war, plague and famine. She does not want to wake, to be in this world. All of her thought is bent on the rotstorm, on the punishment of Ferron. She dreams it, and so it rages. Should she wake, how long until the storm faltered? What lies beyond it? Ferron must not rise again. This is known. I would not risk waking her, even if I could.'

She refilled Cuss's cup with tea and gestured at the mountainous form of Anshuka with the teapot.

'You are welcome to try, of course. I do not know how to wake a god, but perhaps you do.'

Cuss dropped his cup and cried out, pointing, and Yselda turned to follow his gaze. There, to the north, like fireflies, over the banks of dark cloud four lights were flying swift.

Four is too many, Yselda thought, and gripped her knife.

'Come,' said Ashbringer. 'Come. We go to Anshuka now. Mother, go careful.'

The old woman sipped at her tea. 'I might stay to watch,' she said, and Ashbringer sighed and walked away through the meadow, gesturing at the six honour guards to follow her. The grasses and flowers stirred as they passed, a scent of life filling Yselda's nostrils. They walked forward, to the very fore of the great bear Anshuka, and Ashbringer and the Orubor bowed deep in obeisance.

'We shall watch over you, Mother,' she said, and began pressing her arrows into the dirt and grass, point down, so she could quickly grab them. Yselda strung her shortbow and did the same. She had fifteen arrows. The other Orubor spread out, Ashbringer calling to them softly. They spread in a long curving line in front of Anshuka with Ashbringer and Yselda at their centre, pressing arrows to the dirt, two of them kneeling. Two of the Orubor had no longbows, but drew swords of narrow burnished steel, swinging them in loose circles. Ashbringer called out and those two loped some twenty yards back into the meadow, where a solitary stone of slick black rock pushed up a few feet through the wild flowers. They crouched there, gazing up at the sky.

'What do I do?' Cuss said quietly. Yselda had forgotten him, her eyes on the sky and the approaching orbs. They were larger now, nearly at the edge of the clouds. A fifth orb was catching up to them. *Five*, she thought, *is definitely too many.* Yselda remembered wolves stepping out of the forest in the Claw Winter, the frozen loch. *How many had there been that night?* Too many to count. She felt the fear in her rise, that familiar friend, and clenched one fist around her bow, one on the hilt of the knife the captain had given her.

Are you a child, Yselda Hollow? said Ashbringer's voice in her head, and she stared up at the orbs again.

'I am not a child,' she said to herself quietly, and set her jaw.

'What do I do?' Cuss said again, and Ashbringer broke from ordering the honour guard and turned to him and looked at him with her inscrutable eyes. Cuss was standing a few paces behind her and Ashbringer, staring up at Anshuka behind them and clutching a loaf of the bread the old Orubor had given them.

Ashbringer stared at him.

'You may hide, or you may fight. That is all any of us can do, in the end.' Cuss took a bite from the loaf in his hands and shoved the rest of it into a pouch on his belt. Yselda watched as from his pockets he drew the dark iron knuckledusters given to him by the captain, slipping them over his left hand, and with his right he drew the shortsword issued to cadets of the Stormguard Forest Watch. Swallowing his bread he bowed his head to Anshuka and turned back to them.

'I'll fight then,' he said, and Ashbringer smiled. Yselda gave his shoulder a grab and nodded to him as Ashbringer called across to the two sword-wielding Orubor crouched at the ready behind the black stone out in the meadow, ahead of the line of archers. They turned back and waved to her, and gestured for Cuss to join them.

'My brothers and sisters will watch over you, Cuss,' Ashbringer said. 'Stay your blade until they act, and follow them in their action. Anshuka protect you.'

Cuss ran to the stone and crouched, solid and rounded where the Orubor were tall and slim next to him, his sword so much smaller than their slender blades. Yselda felt her heart beating faster. She gazed up again at the approaching lights, and found her grimace turning to a smile. She laughed, and pointed high.

The orbs were fighting each other! It was a mess of confusion. The lead orb carried ever forward, towards the edge of the clouds, but behind it the sky was rent with gouts of flame and beams of purple light. The four orbs now behind it spiralled down into the black clouds, their concentrated light spreading through the cloud from within, diffuse beams of purple force and white flame painting the sky. They watched, all of them, Orubor and human, eyes trained on the silent storm in the sky. After long moments in the cloud and above, the lead orb crossed the stormfront and flew clear over the forest, straight towards them. Behind, three orbs remained, rising from the cloud, one of them pursuing the lead orb, and two behind it attacking it with force and fire, one wobbling on its axis and the other with its light dimmed and uneven.

'The captain,' Yselda murmured, *it must be* and then she let out a shout.

'No!' she yelled, and together they watched as the lead orb, so much closer now, fired back into the attacker with its own purple beam of magic, and the attacking orb was hit, and going down, falling, spiralling. They were incredibly close now, and Yselda screamed in horror as the trailing craft plummeted into the trees a few hundred yards away with a terrifying crash. She could see a few towering pines falling, and fire and smoke rising from where the wreckage must be.

Cuss made it half a step forward, but one of the Orubor caught his arm and pulled him close.

'The captain would want us to get the job done,' Yselda called, and Cuss turned back to her and nodded, face grim. *Was Petron with them, on the orb?* She couldn't bear to think of it.

Across the meadow, the three orbs touched down on the grass, and with them came a pressure, a muting. The first orb slowly descended, as did the second, but the third landed with a visible impact, and the glow suffusing it stuttered and then faded. A disc of dark stone banded with hazy crystal was revealed, two legs of metal supporting it, the end of the disc tipped down and driven into the earth. The stone on the top disc above the band of crystal was scorched black and cracked deep. Yselda swore but could barely hear it. There was no more rustling of wind in the trees or birdsong, only the pressure the sound of her breath, and the moment. A ramp lowered from each of the three orbs. The ramps on the last orb jutted out at an odd angle and ending a few feet over the ground.

Goblins came forth, dozens from each orb. All of them were robed in black, the light of the orbs behind them turning them to horrible shades. She could make out their open mouths screaming, a scream he could not hear. They began to run towards Anshuka and her defenders. Each wielded a wicked curved knife, and their mouths were open showing row after row of sharp teeth. Yselda drew back her bow and exhaled.

~

Cuss felt an arrow whip past his ear and followed its path as it struck a goblin in the chest. He licked his lips and rubbed with one hand the cuts on his chest, still healing and itching, his eyes flitting from the dim orb to the two glowing in front of it, that calm white light. The mob of shadows running from the orbs towards him, towards Anshuka. He pictured his house, his mother and his sister. He felt blood in his cheeks and his lungs pulling deep. He felt angry. He made to stand but the Orubor to his left held his arm, shook his head. An open hand flat: *wait*.

Petron, Cuss thought, and let out a groan of anger and frustration. He couldn't hear it. There was only the pressure the orbs brought. The Orubor next to him were standing now, retreating a few steps, blades high, and Cuss looked at them and saw even through their utterly alien features that they were afraid. *Petron,* he thought again, and then turned back to the wave of goblins. They were too close. It was only a hundred and fifty yards across the meadow from the orbs to Yselda and Ashbringer and the Orubor. They were firing as fast as they could, the arrows thick in the air, but they would be overwhelmed in seconds if the goblins made it amongst them. Cuss saw Yselda's face, the concentration and fear as she fired arrow after arrow, Anshuka behind her sleeping. Cuss realised what he needed to do, and breathed out twice. *Yselda and the captain will find you, Petron,* he thought, *or Ash. I have to fight.*

Cuss leapt forward. With a yell he couldn't hear he barrelled towards the goblin charge. In his left hand his knuckleduster that Sergeant Floré had given him, and in his right he gripped his shortsword. They were many, dozens and dozens and armed with their wicked-sharp blades, but he had four times their mass at least and when he finally hit the front row of them he sent them tumbling.

With every stride another blade cut at him but he ignored it, ignored the searing pain in his legs, his back, his stomach, his arms, and kept pressing, and could see goblins dropping as Ashbringer and Yselda and the Orubor sent arrow after arrow at his attackers. He swung his fist in mad arcs, his sword battering around like a club. He picked up into a run, his legs never stopping, looping around the pack of goblins with his long strides and then charging in at them. One swung at him and he managed to get his own sword in the way, and then he grabbed the goblin by its arm and hurled it into a trio yelling and slavering and running from the other side. He ran, slicing, and then a goblin was leaping at him and his sword was on the wrong side of his body, his other hand already around the throat of another goblin. It lunged towards his heart but a slender blade intercepted its leap and it crumpled to the meadow. The two sword-wielding Orubor stood with him, yelling loud but silent in the pressure from the orbs. Cuss let out a laugh and threw the goblin he held to one side and turned to the rest of the mob.

He ran, he fought. The two Orubor followed slower, methodical, slicing down at the goblins he managed to knock to the floor or lunging forward to cut down any who sought his flanks. They were cut and bloodied as he, but still standing. He felt his lungs burning and a deep acid pain in his gut, a warmth down his legs, but the goblins were dying in droves to the arrows of Ashbringer and Yselda and the Orubor. One of the sword-wielding Orubor, the male, suddenly collapsed, a curved knife cutting into his neck from behind. The other went to him, her sword culling everything around her, but she was stationary. Cuss yelled a warning but she could not hear, and he could only watch as four goblins swarmed her, two of them cutting down at her ankles until she collapsed.

Cuss staggered back, drawing his sword free of his latest kill. There were only a dozen goblins or so left standing but no more arrows flew. He glanced over his shoulder and saw Ashbringer was yelling, but he couldn't hear her. She drew her sword and gestured for him to come to her, and Cuss ran. *Petron,* he thought, and he ran towards Anshuka, feeling the goblins hot on his heels, and then one was on his back stabbing wildly and he felt the blade bite deep through his cloak. He threw the monster from his back and staggered forward, and then there was another one somehow ahead of him. He rolled on the balls of his feet and jabbed and crossed and ducked and weaved, doggedly. *Where is my sword? When did I lose it?* His knuckleduster caught the goblin in the face and it fell back screaming, writhing on the ground. *My sword is gone. Where is my sword?* Cuss stepped forward and grabbed the fallen goblin's head and wrenched at it, and then Ashbringer was there.

Ashbringer came into the last dozen goblins pursuing him as a whirlwind, four Orubor behind her wielding short blades, dirks and knives nearly as long as his shortsword. Cuss stumbled towards Yselda and Anshuka, and Yselda ran to him. She pulled arrows from dead goblins as she went, filling her quiver.

'Cuss!' she called, and he realised he could hear, could hear her. He could hear blood rushing in his ears. He went to put a hand on her shoulder but fell to his knees before he could reach her. She dragged him a few paces to the black rock in the meadow, propping him up, her eyes searching his. Cuss looked to the orbs.

'You have to save Petron,' he said, but Yselda wasn't listening. She was looking where he was.

In front of the first orb, Ashbringer had just brought down a goblin with its own dagger, and she drew from her belt a shortsword that glittered. *Was it a broken longsword?* Cuss shivered, and felt strangely cold. Ashbringer grew still and drew her broken blade into an elegant guard pose, and around her the remaining goblins screamed curses and leapt at her. Her four Orubor companions were charging forward to support her and Cuss felt his head spinning as he tried to follow their fluid movements. Ashbringer blocked one attack by shearing the goblin's hand clean through, and at the same time kicked out, catching another in the face with her boot. Following through on that momentum she stepped through on that leg and brought the other in a low sweep, knocking a rushing goblin down, and as she did so her blade cut deep into the chest of another. Pulling it clear in a spray of blood, she brought the broken sword back around and down once, twice, thrice. Each stab stilled a goblin that had been knocked to the ground. Another of the Orubor threw her knife, and then was scrabbling amongst the dead, throwing knife after knife at the few remaining goblins.

The goblins died, and after wrenching her blade through the throat of the final goblin, Ashbringer pulled herself upright. Cuss saw the four Orubor spread out behind her. Ashbringer flicked blood from the tip of her blade and advanced towards the orb, delicately stepping around the corpses of the goblins.

'Did we win?' Cuss said, scarcely believing it, and then threw his hand up to cover his eyes. From the second orb, its light glowing weaker than the first, with patches of dark stone showing below, a beam of purple light cut through the air. When Cuss had blinked away the stars in his eyes, he saw two of the Orubor were just *gone*. Where they had been was a trough of scored earth, a scar across the meadow.

Ashbringer dropped to a crouch and pointed at the remaining two Orubor, who were already running. They sprinted right, past the first orb, heading up the dark ramp and into the orb itself. Ashbringer ran short steps back to examine the gouge rent through the meadow and then turned again to the first orb, stepping towards it.

'No,' Cuss said, his eyes on the scarred meadow, but he couldn't think of anything else to say. Yselda stood and drew an arrow. From the orb to the right a gout of black flame poured down the ramp, and then one of the Orubor staggered out, his face charred, as the light covering the stone and crystal disc faded. Cuss felt the pressure at the edge of his senses lessen, and he pushed himself to his knees. Nothing further came from the second orb but smoke.

'We have to fight, Yselda,' he said, but then he was coughing, and his hand came away from his mouth red with blood.

Down the ramp from the first orb, from the burning white light, two figures appeared. One of them was a grey-skinned goblin robed in black holding a child over its shoulder, the other a hooded man. Cuss saw the cloak, the limbs too long, the body too tall. *Did you take my brother?* He managed to get to one knee, and gripped Yselda's arm.

'He took Petron,' he said, his voice wet. Yselda looked down at him and he saw the fear in her eyes.

'We have to *fight*!'

Yselda pulled him to his feet and they started to press forward across the meadow. Far in front, Ashbringer drew back her sword and charged towards the ramp. The hooded figure rolled down the end of the ramp and came up bearing two wands of metal ending in faceted blue gems, and from them beams of light cut through the air. Ashbringer rolled away from the first, but the second caught her in the leg and she hissed as blood poured from a deep wound. Dragging her wounded leg, she closed distance with the figure but just as she went to strike the wands caught her, both at once in the chest. Ashbringer's chest blossomed in blood as deep runes were cut into her flesh and she fell back, collapsing in the flower meadow.

'Marta,' Cuss said, for he had seen the child on the goblin's shoulder and it was... it was her. It was Marta. They were still more than fifty feet from the orb, and he could still just about hear his own voice. He couldn't see Petron. Yselda next to him drew an arrow and fired it at the hooded man, but he waved a hand and it fell from the air. She shot another, and another, and then the man was a dozen yards from them with a wand pointed forward. Yselda dropped her bow and pulled her sword. She drew the sword into a high guard, and a flutter of fabric caught Cuss's eye. A scrap of grey cloth, tied around the handle of her sword.

Cuss went next to her and raised his fists, his sword

long gone, and together they faced the hooded man. He stopped a few steps from them and cocked his head at them, seeming to gaze over each. The light from his orb cast him as a perfect shadow, and Cuss could not see his face.

'Marta,' Cuss said, his voice thick with blood, 'and Petron. In the name of the Forest Watch. Give us Marta and Petron, or we'll cut you down.'

Yselda stepped forward and brandished her sword but the man waved a hand and it flew from her grip, the blade sinking into the soft earth of the flower meadow a dozen yards away.

'I'm not afraid of you,' she said, and Cuss swayed where he stood, tried to find the energy to fight, to help her. *Crowman,* he thought, *demon. Fire and silver.* His reached a hand to his belt pouch and felt his fingers tighten around the silver mark Nash had given him at the Ollen Wheel, larger and heavier than the few copper coins he had. He pulled it out behind his back and tightened his fist around it. Next to him, Yselda drew her silver dagger, leaping forward with a scream.

'Sleep, child,' the man said, and a beam of green light hit Yselda and she fell to the grass beside Cuss, the dagger tumbling from her hands. The man lowered an iron wand back to his side, and stared at Cuss.

'Judge spit on you,' said Cuss, feeling the hot blood from a dozen wounds pouring over him. 'I hope Anshuka bites your head off, demon!'

The figure leaned forward and nodded, seeming to inspect him. Cuss tried to stand and fell back, his breathing coming in staccato bursts, his limbs refusing to answer him. Behind the demon, the final goblin had come close. It had

Marta slung over its shoulder and stood a scant six feet away. Marta seemed to be asleep, or unconscious.

'By order of the Forest Watch, let her go!' Cuss managed, but his voice began to fade and the edges of his vision were turning dark. He tried to take a step forward but staggered down to one knee. He hurt in so many places, in so many ways.

'Let her go,' he said, and he held the silver coin in front of him. 'I'll burn you with silver, demon. You have to let them go. Marta and Petron.'

'The brother,' the figure said at last, and turning to the goblin, added: 'Well. I see. Brothers *are* important.'

The figure lowered its hood and knelt, close to Cuss. His face was plain, normal even, and then Cuss saw his eyes. Even in the falling darkness he saw the man's pupils split and dance and reform and spin. He felt sick.

'You let my brother go,' he said, and swung a fist at the demon. The crow-man barely had to lean back to avoid it. Cuss felt the silver coin slip from his fingers, scrabbled for it in the dirt.

'Please,' he said, falling still, 'you can take me instead. Just let him go. Please.'

The figure stood and frowned and stepped back, running a hand over the head of the goblin next to him.

'I am sorry, child,' he said, voice quiet. 'I truly am sorry. Perhaps one day you will understand the why of it, but I know it will never make it right. Know this: your brother died well, saving others. He thought of you often, and he was brave.'

Cuss lunged forward and grabbed at the demon with everything he had, gripped and swung but then strong hands were holding his arms, forcing them back, pushing him back down to his knees.

'You are right to be angry,' the demon said. 'It is a righteous thing.'

He pushed Cuss down into the dirt and Cuss stared back up at him.

'I am Varratim,' the man said, 'and this is my brother Russich. We are of Ferron; of the rust-folk.'

He gestured to the goblin holding Marta, and Cuss screwed up his face.

'When all of this is over, learn of our people. You will understand one day, perhaps, why this sacrifice had to be made.'

The green light from the wand hit Cuss, and he saw no more.

~

Floré came into consciousness coughing and burning. She had fallen from her seat, which was now gone, and the bones in her right ankle felt hot and wrong, throbbing with pain and sending lances of agony spiralling up her leg with any movement. The orb was half cracked, a pine tree having bludgeoned through its dark stone shell. The upper half of the orb was just gone, the lower disc now rimmed with shards of dark crystal. She spotted Heasin, hanging from his chair, eyes open but body utterly still, and she closed her eyes for a moment and swallowed and then tried to force herself to move. She felt sick, felt so tired. *Marta,* she thought, picturing the orb ahead of them cutting through the night and down, down towards Anshuka. *What will he do with Marta?* She lay still for a long moment, her breath coming in short gasps. She had said she would bring Marta back. *I'm sorry Janos…*

'Floré,' a voice called, and she snapped her eyes open. She forced herself to her knees, her right arm quivering with old pain, her legs and face throbbing with the fresh cuts from Varratim's wand. Her ankle was full of hot coals. She stayed on her knees for a long moment and then roared with pain and rage, punching the stone of the floor. *No. I'm not dead yet.*

Floré pulled herself up and staggered through pine boughs and broken slabs of thin dark stone. Every step was agony and she let it fuel her. Pulling aside a bough thick with green pine needles, she found Tomas.

'You all right?' she asked, and he shook his head. He was pale and bloodied, shaking and crushed between a pine bough as thick as her torso and the stone hull of the orb. His free arm clawed at the branch pinning him but it was utterly immobile. His eyes were wild as he gasped and a sob left him as Floré tried to move the bough. It was too heavy with her injured ankle; she only managed to raise it a scant inch before having to drop it back as her right leg crumpled. Tomas grunted with pain as the bough fell back onto him.

'I have to go,' she said, pulling herself back to her feet. 'I'm sorry. You want a blade?'

Tomas stared at her, panting, confused, and Floré turned and limped away.

'Wait!' he called, but she did not slow. *I have to go.* She clambered through the orb, wincing and clenching her jaw with every step. Around them the forest burned, and the flames began to blaze through the boughs of pine that filled the broken stone disc. Floré felt the tremors in her right hand start and pinpricks of fire behind her eyes, the old wound, now of all times. She let it come.

'You can't leave me!' Tomas said, his voice ragged as she stepped from the ruined orb to the forest floor. 'How can you leave me? You bitch! Damn you, Artollen, get back here! You can't leave me!'

Floré left him.

As she walked, Tomas's cries grew quiet, and Floré found herself in a mess of wreckage: her chair, a broken cage, the giant wand with the purple crystal. She looked around, and saw through the trees on her left a glow, the pure white glow of one of Ferron's orbs.

When Floré limped from the treeline, she realised she was already too late. Varratim had won. A hundred yards away to her right the crow-man stood in the long grass beside Anshuka's head, dagger in hand raised high above him. She swayed in the breeze and gazed for a heartbeat at the Judge Anshuka, protector and saviour of Undal, slayer of Lothal the wolf. Doom of Ferron.

'Hey!' she yelled. 'Crow-man!'

Varratim looked at her, and seeing what was in her hands he frowned. Dragging behind her and angled over her shoulder, Floré carried the purple wand from the demon orb. She squeezed her hand and a beam of purple light four foot across shot out. It went well wide of Varratim, slamming into the bulk of the rock of Anshuka behind him, and Floré shuddered at the thought of the slumbering god awakening. She fell to her knees as a wave of nausea took her, and she felt a chill running through her very blood. Part of her realised this was the wand taking its toll, and she realised the agony Heasin must have felt with every moment of flight.

'We aren't *done* yet!' she yelled, and Varratim lowered his knife a fraction. Floré could see the knife was pulsing with strange energy, black and purple light that had coalesced around the black stone of the blade. Varratim's eyes were wild. Across the meadow to her left, one glowing orb remained, two others only dim stone. One of those was tipped into the ground. Around them and in front of her, the bodies of dozens upon dozens of goblins lay in a field of arrows and blood between flowers and long grass.

'Your choice, Artollen,' he called. 'The bear or the girl!'

And he pointed down to the meadow just below him, and sure enough there was Marta, Cuss and Yselda unconscious in the grass next to her. Marta's head was held back and a knife held to her throat by a goblin with a slavering black tongue. Floré saw Marta, her hair cropped, her face streaked with tears, and she saw that Marta saw her. Marta opened her mouth but Floré could not hear what she said over the thrumming blood that coursed through her.

Floré clenched her right fist in her gauntlet, squeezed until she felt the bite of steel through leather on her flesh, and quenched her tears before they had a chance to spill. She looked back at Varratim, his gangly form looming over the sleeping Anshuka, and she pictured Janos standing with a sprig of lilac in his fingers, a smile on his lips a poem in his heart. Floré coughed and pushed herself back to her feet. She pulled at the awkward weight of the runewand, hefting it to her shoulder and slipping her gauntleted fist into the firing mechanism.

'You fire that at me, my brother kills the girl!' Varratim called and Floré felt the tremor in her hand begin to still. After all of it, what could she do? Kill Varratim, damn Marta, and most likely Cuss and Yselda. She could try to shoot the goblin, but likely kill Marta anyway. She could drop the wand, and try to get Marta away to safety somehow. She could sit down, and wait for death.

Floré looked up at the form of Anshuka asleep before her, the rock and stone that covered the slumbering bear. Varratim's dagger looked so pathetically small in comparison, but now that he held it in this place she could see the power in it, the way the world seemed to shift towards it. She looked at Anshuka and thought of the years in the rotstorm with Janos, the years in Hasselberry. Before that, the words: *Stormguard, preserve the freedom of all people in the realm. Suffer no tyrant; forge no chain; lead in servitude.*

'Janos,' she whispered, looking at Marta. 'I'm sorry.'

She squeezed the trigger and the wand fired, and she was running. In the instant she fired she saw Varratim blasted against the rock of Anshuka's spine, broken, aghast. She was sprinting then, on the ankle that burned and screamed, running and screaming towards the goblin that had its knife raised and it was plunging down towards her daughter.

And then it wasn't.

The goblin stopped still, as if frozen, and Marta pulled herself away from its grasp and ran to her mother. In the flower meadow in the shadow of the god-bear, Floré fell to her knees and they embraced.

'Hey,' Floré said, 'hey hey hey hello, little poppet. Hello. Oh, Marta.'

They embraced for a long time, and Floré forced herself to her feet, still clasping Marta.

'Mummy, where are we going?' Marta sniffed, and Floré gave her a kiss on the head.

'Mummy needs to deal with that goblin,' she said, and though each step brought her agony, forward she went, forcing herself to move, not to stop and think about what had almost happened. She pulled Marta close to her chest, wrapped her arms tight around her. The goblin was still as a statue, the landed orb of Varratim reflected in its black eyes.

'No, Mummy,' Marta said, but Floré kept walking.

'Mummy!' Marta cried, and Floré stopped.

'I have to do this,' she said, 'and then you'll be safe.'

Marta shook her head and looked at the goblin.

'I can feel the shapes again, Mummy,' Marta said, 'when the bad man fell. I can feel the shapes. I'll do it.'

Floré swallowed and then felt her mouth open and her heart break as the goblin paled, and its stillness went from a held breath to a painting, and its skin and its clothes and its knife turned to salt. A breeze pressed through the flower meadow, and the salt blew away in spumes and spirals. Floré held her daughter close. She knew it was salt. Janos always said salt had a pattern to it; it called to him. Urforren was a mile-wide circle of ever-burning salt, a city turned to ruin, and Janos had spent the rest of his life writing poems in the forest, ashamed and afraid and aghast at what he had done. Salt had a pattern.

'Papa said not to touch the shapes,' Marta said, sniffing, and Floré kissed her head.

She started to go to Cuss and Yselda, unconscious in the grass, when a firm hand caught her elbow and a wizened

Orubor was there, flowing white hair framing a delicate face. Floré squinted at the opaque eyes and serrated teeth, so similar and yet so different from the dozens of dead goblins that lay around them in the grass of the meadow.

'I'll deal with the sleepers and the girl,' the Orubor said, reaching for Marta. 'They'll be all right. Anshuka keeps good company, tonight.'

Marta cuddled in closer and Floré recoiled, and the Orubor tilted her head and turned to Anshuka.

'Fire and silver, child of Baal. The threat remains, until it does not.'

Floré pressed a squirming Marta into the Orubor's hands, and from the grass next to Yselda's unconscious form she picked up Benazir's silver-bladed rune dagger. Yselda was unconscious but looked unhurt, but Cuss was torn and bloodied from endless wounds. She knelt by him and put a hand to his chest, felt it rise and fall faintly. He opened his eyes and looked at her, mouth grim.

'Petron is dead,' he said, his voice a broken thing and she lowered her forehead and pressed it to his, gripping him tight as he sobbed.

'I know, son. I know.'

He pressed one hand to hers, and passed her a silver coin. Floré looked down at her gauntlets and saw that the coins from the Blue Wolf Mountain were gone, perhaps lost in the crash. She snapped the coin into the ridge on her right gauntlet, the broken chain symbol facing out.

Floré stood and the old Orubor, still holding Marta by the hand, knelt at Cuss's side and began to murmur soft words. The lad shivered and his eyes closed. With a calming kiss to her daughter, Floré limped towards her god.

She found Varratim crawling in the grass, dragging himself by one arm towards Anshuka, clutching his knife. His left leg was broken and his face was a mess of broken veins, bruises, deep cuts. She could see teeth through his cheek. When her shadow fell across him, he turned and began to raise the blade but then she was on her knees on the ground and her fist grabbed his.

Floré squeezed, feeling his delicate fingers crack under her own as she pressed them against the handle of his knife, and then she twisted her hand and he dropped the blade. She felt stillness in him, and before he could work whatever skein-magic he planned her other hand slammed into his chest, then his throat, batting away his weak attempts to defend himself. The silver coin slotted in her gauntlet burned whenever it touched flesh, and he shrieked.

He coughed black blood and stared at her with those wild unfathomable eyes, eyes broken by unknowable magic, the pupils splitting and dancing, coalescing and cascading in endless directions. They split and split until he had a dozen pupils in each eye, until the whites of his eyes were nothing but a lattice behind orbs of black. His own orb of light sat in the meadow, and the fires of her crashed orb and the light of his intact orb both played in those pupils. He whispered through cracked teeth, words rough over a cut tongue.

'No trial for rust-folk,' he said, and Floré hit him again and again and again, her left hand dragging him up and pressing him against Anshuka, her right hand clutching Benny's dagger but still punching. The silver coin still slotted in her gauntlet burned his flesh like acid, raising huge welts.

'I can tell you—' he began to say, between hits, begging through a ruined mouth, and then she drove the silver rune knife into his chest and twisted it. He screamed as the silver tore into him, and then the rune on the blade flared and his torso began to char and burn from the inside. Floré leaned in close, feeling the heat from the flames, feeling him thrash.

'No trial for rust-folk,' she said, and pushed. As he went limp she dropped his still-burning body to the ground. From the wild flowers and grass she scooped up the obsidian blade, and she tucked both daggers into her belt next to Captain Tyr's old silver blade. She limped back, back to Marta.

The old Orubor was tending the wounds of Cuss and Yselda, and had dragged another two Orubor who bled from heavy wounds across to join them.

'There is tea by the fire,' she said when Floré reached them, gesturing out across the meadow, and Floré was too tired to even think of the absurdity of it. She dropped her gauntlets into the wild flowers, and dropped Benny's knife, and Varratim's knife, and Tyr's knife, and then she reached for Marta's hand. Together they crossed the meadow to the fire and she held Marta, and they sat and watched the stars.

EPILOGUES:
LEAD IN SERVITUDE

TAKE YOUR FLIGHT

'Ferron himself passed this task to you, Tullen. He raised the Judges up, and our people with them. Their fate and ours is entwined. The loss of Berren, the gardens, the crop, this will undo us. I need your strength now, my dearest friend. As we debate in council, the savages of Undalor nip at our borders. Take Lothal, and drive them back, and bring us fresh fields to till. The children of Ferron need feeding. Nothing else matters.' – Private *letter*, Empress Seraphina of the Gilded Spire

Tullen One-Eye warmed his hands over the dying fire, huddling close to the last of the heat and light. Next to him, a wolf the size a horse lay sleeping. The wolf's fur was black with streaks of silver that glowed pearlescent in the moonlight. Tullen drank from his waterskin and gazed at the embers with his good eye, the light of the fire pressed close by the tall pines of Hookstone forest. Above, the sky was clear, black cut with purple and a thousand thousand stars. Through the trees, the sound of the waterfall at Black Dog Rock whispered, and he let himself focus on the whisper of the water over stone for a long moment. Tullen raised his eyepatch and scratched at the empty socket beneath, then resettled the worn leather thong and glanced at the forest.

'You can come out now, Ashbringer,' he called out, and then reached down and placed a thick branch onto the smouldering embers of his fire, sending a few desultory sparks spiralling up to the night sky.

An Orubor clad in leather and cloaked in shadow stepped from the forest edge and the wolf opened one green eye, languidly closing it again after taking her measure. The pale blue skin of her face was etched with red rune scars, and her eyes were orbs of dark gold; no pupil and no iris were visible. He could see the edges of thick cloth wrappings beneath her armour, and stiffness in her stride.

'Greetings,' Tullen said, and Ashbringer bowed. She pulled back her hood and swept her cloak back as she took a seat on the ground by the fire, and Tullen saw the antler handle of her sword, the antler of a stag long dead. He pulled his pipe from his robe and began to fiddle with it. Finally he lit it with a touch of his fingertip. He inhaled deep and blew formless clouds that spiralled and dissipated up towards the stars, and the three of them sat in silence for a long time. The branch on the fire slowly caught and soon they were bathed in flickering light, and Tullen took in the Orubor's torn cloak and muddied boots. She looked tense.

'How fare you then? It has been long months since you tried this last. You look worn.'

The Orubor removed her gloves and rubbed at her face with one hand and then smiled at Tullen, showing her serrated teeth.

'I am well, Deathless,' she said, slowly, her thick tongue working hard to add edge to the words, 'Your boy was stopped, and Anshuka slumbers in peace. You failed.'

Tullen sighed and raised a hand. Across the fire by his bedroll, his satchel opened, and a bottle emerged and gently floated across to him. He pulled the cork and took a long drink, and then handed it across the fire to the Orubor, Ashbringer. She gently took the bottle, and sniffed at it before taking a sip.

'Nothing to do with me,' he said, sniffing. 'Three hundred years, I've been watching. You think my plan would be as clumsy as all of that? Once the bear's shackles are off me I'll have no need for orbs.'

They both sat in silence and Ashbringer took a long draw from the bottle.

'You never believe I would poison you, do you, Ashbringer?' Tullen asked, and Ashbringer smiled again and passed him back the bottle.

'No, Deathless. I do not believe you would poison me. You have your rules, warped as they are.'

Tullen nodded and ran his thumb and forefinger across his moustache, smoothing it away from his lips. He had the face and body of a man in his prime; he was a few inches over six feet tall and well-muscled, but when he moved and spoke she could see the mannerisms and gaze of the aged. Ashbringer retrieved a leather pouch from her belt and weighed it in her hand.

'Deathless, my mission is that of my line, as Anshuka

bade before her slumber. I am bound to ask you – will you change your course? Will you submit to judgement?'

Tullen closed his eyes when she began to speak, and sat in silence long after she finished.

'No, Ashbringer,' he said, finally. 'No, you cannot judge me, or change my course. I had hoped we might talk more, before this. Can we not spend an hour? You have travelled far. You do not understand, of course, but nobody does, and you at least know something of the truth of it all.'

He gestured at the wolf, whose eyes were open now. It rose, and began to pace the forest clearing where Tullen had made his camp. The clearing was smattered with knee-high ferns that curled around each other, stems that had turned brown and red as autumn rolled through the forest. The wolf was easily twenty hands high, as tall as a work horse at the shoulder, muscled and lean. The Orubor bowed her head and brought her hands together in obeisance when it neared her. The wolf sniffed at her and its tongue lolled out, hepatic teeth the size of fingers glinting in the firelight.

'Lothal is with me, and as such I am just,' Tullen said, and the great wolf howled. It was deep and resonant and lasted long enough for Tullen to draw two puffs from his pipe.

The Orubor stood and drew her sword, pouring diamond dust from her pouch along the silver blade. The blade was etched in runes, hundreds of tiny runes from tip to hilt, etched in light and power, and as the diamond dust fell it was drawn to the runes and they began to shine intensely with blue light.

'Lothal is no longer the arbiter of justice, or honour, if ever he was,' she said, standing and raising her sword into position at arm's length, and Tullen stood to face her, still smoking his pipe. The wolf stood to the side of the fire, tense and poised, claws like daggers digging into the wet earth of Hookstone forest.

The Orubor swung at Tullen, and he made no move to dodge. The runes on the silver blade flared as it cut through the air towards his neck, and then with a scream of metal the blade was broken, Ashbringer was on the ground, the wolf was howling, and Tullen stood smoking his pipe.

The Orubor sat up, clutching at her sword arm. Lothal bounded away, into the forest.

'I really thought that rune combination with the extra infusion would work, Deathless.'

Tullen snorted and pulled her to her feet and Ashbringer gathered the broken pieces of her sword and they sat again by the fire. She held out a hand and Tullen waved and the brandy went to her, and she took a long draw from the bottle.

'Was it ever as this, Deathless? With my forebears? Will it ever be this?'

Tullen laughed.

'No, Ashbringer. You are... honourable. A child, but honourable. Your grandfather tried to bury me alive; your mother poisoned a dozen men in an attempt to send me to a dreamless sleep. Your great-grandfather who started this fool quest even tried to hurt Lothal, once. Anshuka's will binds me to this world, and yet in her name you hunt me. It is idiocy.'

The Orubor glanced into the tangle of pines where the wolf was watching, surely.

'The little god is not Lothal, Deathless. We have discussed this. Anshuka destroyed Lothal the Just. This beast is a shade, a reflection. It is nothing but a shadow.'

Tullen blew out a lungful of smoke and shook his head.

'Shadows are cast, Ashbringer. Lothal the Just is not dead, and so my mission is unchanged, and you cannot judge me. Shadows are cast; the shadow cannot be without the light, and so the light persists. I just need to find it. Berren and Nessilitor, Lothal and Anshuka. Four forces balanced Ferron, and Ferron balanced the world. Without us, you are children playing in the dirt. As far as Ona and Caroban and the Last Ocean, for all of Morost, we were progress. We were light and hope, and we will be again.'

With a stick, he idly drew a circle in the dirt and bisected it twice, ending each line with one of the runes of the Judges: ᚷᚤᚠᛏ, *feather, claw, flower, and eye.* He smiled down at his work.

The assassin removed her cloak and wrapped her sword fragments in a bundle, then stood and bowed stiffly.

'I forget your hubris sometimes, Deathless. Slaver. The man who broke the Tullioch Shardspire, the man who broke Undal and bowed Tessendorm. Rivers of blood flow from you, mage, dead beyond count. You killed Nessilitor the Lover. Anshuka give me strength, I will find a way to kill you. Three hundred years you have watched the ruin of your people, and after such an age of passivity I sometimes forget your character. Justice is dead, but vengeance lives.'

Tullen waved a lazy hand at her and she shook her head and walked to the edge of the clearing, turning for a final remark.

'Power is not wisdom, and age is not wisdom,' she said. 'When we next meet you will die, Tullen One-Eye.'

Tullen puffed on his pipe but it was burned dry. The assassin faded into the forest and the wolf returned and lay at his side. Tullen ran a hand through the wolf's thick fur and muttered to himself, staring at the crude rune-compass scratched in the dirt.

'Anshuka the bear; Berren most fair; Lothal the Just; Nessilitor the Lover. Strength and art and justice and love; community and solitude and violence and compassion,' he muttered, staring into the fire.

'Art is dead; justice is dead; love is dead. Only strength remains, if they are right. The boy Varratim failed us, but what of you, my little cub? Are you not hope that Ferron may rise again?'

Tullen One-Eye sat by the sleeping wolf in the silence of Hookstone forest and considered his next move.

'Any whitestaff could theoretically throw fire like a common skein-mage. The essence of our order is to lead in servitude; we must not seek power. We must use the skein to grow and to teach, never to harm. So we keep our patterns from the skein-mages who would forge a new empire. We will not repeat the hubris of Ferron.'
– *The Way of Riven*, Mistress Water

The Orubor moved through the forest as a breeze, leaving only the faintest impression as they passed. Occasional rays of moonlight cut through the pine canopy, diffuse silver dappling the floor of the forest and playing over shaven heads, shortbows, furs and leather. There were five of them, four moving in a diamond a dozen feet across with the fifth in the centre. Autumn had come to Orubor forest, and the ground was spotted with thickets of brown curling ferns, the forest floor hidden beneath a layer of old pine needles.

The Orubor did not speak, and in the centre of the diamond the leader of the party kept one hand on his dagger hilt and the other on a leather pouch hanging around his neck. His eyes were orbs of black, his face contorted into a permanent scowl. All wore the grey-green cloaks of the Orubor Scouts over their flexible hide armour, and all moved barefoot. They moved with the silent co-ordination of years of shared experience, like a pack of wolves always aware of each other, compensating for their counterparts as they navigated tree and rock, hill and dell. They moved quickly, and soon reached the river Boros that cut from its source in the north of the forest down south and east, until it passed through the forest edge at the Falls of Dust.

When in spate the river could not be crossed here in the depths of the forest, but after the long hot summer the water was only shin-deep and it splashed and tumbled as it passed over and around boulders, fringed by drooping grass and reeds. The boulders and rocks were slick with moss where the water reached, but their tops were coated in dust and dead and dying lichens. The river sang and whispered as it ran over stone and under drooping willows, a song the Orubor knew well.

The first Orubor crossed the river, hopping from rock to rock as the others kept a weather eye up and down the opposite banks. The youngest had his bow already half drawn, his head turning in snaps up and down the river, his face pushing forward as his gaze tried to discern movement on the opposite bank. The Highmothers had decided the knife of the would-be assassin must be taken to the weapon smiths of Elm, but even within the ultimate safety of Orubor forest the mere presence of the blade added a weight of unease to the groups' minds.

The second Orubor crossed easily, and then their leader stepped forward and began to hop across the rocks. The Boros ran swift beneath his leaping feet, and he remembered crossing it before as a child with his brothers in midwinter, when the water had been locked below a layer of ice and snow. He was almost halfway across the river when he smiled at the memory and raised his arms out to either side as he had as a child for balance.

The missile came fast; it was roughly the size of a fist, a piece of jagged stone whose edges were not smoothed by the endless calm rushing water, but broken and sharp. It flew from the riverbank and hit the Orubor leader in the back of the head; all he knew of it was the hint of a rush of air, and before he could begin to turn it had passed through his skull and out through his face, a cloud of blood exploding after it. He fell forward and landed upstream of the next stepping stone, the current pressing him tight against it, rivulets of red diluting into the flow of clear water.

The two Orubor still on the east bank of the river yelled in wordless dismay and fell into crouches, bows levelled, looking around for their assailant. From the far bank a querulous voice called out, 'Eski-du? Eski?' and on the east bank one of them whistled back, two sharp short tones.

The bough that came down on them moved faster than falling. It was a wide pine bough, as thick as a man's thigh, and it came down hard and quicker than they could dodge, even if they had seen it. It had made no sound of breaking. One of them coughed blood, a branch from the bough having pierced his shoulder and through to his lungs, and the other did not move at all, his torso twisted and crumpled, blood pooling out from his mouth and eyes.

'Eski-du?' a voice called from across the river on the west bank, and then silence. After long moments, a low whistle, and then silence again. The Orubor coughing blood on the east bank weakly raised her arms to the bough pinning her to the dirt, but after a moment of scrabbling hands she fell still. The weight was too much. She tried to purse her mouth to whistle, and instead coughed, and coughed again, and then went limp.

Long moments passed, punctuated by low whistles from across the river, and then there was nothing but the sound of the night breeze in the trees and the rushing of the river. Long moments passed, the river pushing onward in its flow. Finally in a burst of noise and motion from the west bank one of the remaining Orubor sprang forward, moving low, heading towards her leader whose corpse still bobbed against one of the fording stones. There were half a dozen rocks between the west bank of the river and the body, and the Orubor scrabbled and leapt, one, two, three—

The stone took her in the knee, a small pebble cutting through the night air as a blur. The crack of the scout's kneecap breaking was followed by a scream, and a splash, as she fell into the river. Pushing her head free of the water with her arms she stayed low, moaning, trying to drag herself back to the west bank. The river was low enough she could almost stagger through it, pulling at rocks, one useless leg dragging behind her. She splashed wildly, weapon lost, the water dragging at her cloak.

'Fa,' she yelled. 'Fa, Iblin!'

From the shadows of the east bank, Tomas stepped forward and smiled. He was wearing a dull brown traveller's cloak over simple leather armour and riding boots. His dark hair was cropped short and his beard had grown out, almost covering the ragged burn scar on his right cheek and forehead, pushing back into his hairline. The top of his right ear was a mangle of flesh. He stepped forward and hopped to the first rock, and then drew a dagger from his belt.

With a small flick of his hand it was thrown, and then with a pulse of skein-energy it was pushed much faster. It struck the Orubor in the back and she slumped into the water face down, the current beginning to drag her away. The dagger removed itself from her back and floated slowly back to Tomas, who took the hilt and frowned for a moment. He closed his eyes to ensure that the final Orubor was not looping back – *yes, fleeing north to raise the alarm*; he could feel them in the skein. *No matter*.

Carefully, he crossed the remaining few stones until he was at the Orubor leader's body. Reaching down he grabbed the leather pouch at their neck, and with his knife cut the leather thong that bound it to the corpse and stood. The moonlight pressed down on the river Boros and he turned so that the package would be fully illuminated. Gingerly he opened the pouch, and stared at the prize within. The obsidian blade of Varratim. The blade Tullen One-Eye used to kill Nessilitor the Lover. The blade Varratim would have used to kill Anshuka. A blade empowered and honed with the pattern of countless skein-sensitive children by some arcane rite far beyond his comprehension, or the comprehension of perhaps anyone living.

The moonlight caught on the black blade, and Tomas grabbed the twisted bone handle and raised the dagger to eye level. The green stone in its pommel glinted oddly, casting powerful reflections of light at strange angles that seemed impossible.

Tomas stared at the blade and let himself fall into the skein, and what he saw there was magnificent; it was not a blade, not some crude weapon. The pattern in the obsidian crystal was a nexus in the skein, a focus that seemed designed to draw energy towards it. Holding it and looking at it in the skein he could feel that pattern, feel himself as well, the tangle of lines and chaos and pattern that made up his very being. He could feel them both so close, connecting.

Tomas stood for a long time in the middle of the river Boros, the dead Orubor patrol his only company. As dawn rose to the east, finally, he let out a contented sigh and a smile touched his lips. Tomas opened his eyes, and within the brilliant blue irises the pupils danced, gyrated and split and merged, shrunk and grew, spun, ever moving.

THE END OF BOOK ONE

Acknowledgements

Thank you for reading this book. It means the world to me.

Thank you to my mum for always having a houseful of books, and my dad for making sure those books had swords and dragons in them. You have both been ceaselessly supportive and I am endlessly grateful. Thank you to Abigail, who is a font of idioms, horse-knowledge, and encouragement. Without her this book would not exist. Thank you to my alpha and beta readers Erick Loomis, Richard Thomson, Adam Beech, Anthony Walsh, and Simon Moriarty. Thank you especially to Simone Haysom and Anna Jean Hughes who provided extensive earnest feedback I could only have hoped for. Thanks to Tom Hunter and Sam Morgan, whose early enthusiasm drove me to complete my first scrappy draft. Thanks to Sean Preston, Nikk Woolf, Jonny Virgo, and the Brick Lane writing group and Open Pen crowd. Thank you Molly Flatt for her encouragement and enthusiasm, and to Imogen Pelham for her sage advice and counsel. Thank you to Oliver Cheetham for his encouragement and vision.

Thanks to Helena Newton for copyediting, and to the Ad Astra and Head of Zeus marketing, design, and production teams – all involved!

Finally, thanks to Holly Domney for taking a chance, and for her endless enthusiasm.